Praise for *Etern*

"*Eternal Shadow* reads like a Michael Crichton sci-fi thriller, as there is lots of tension building with the events in the book, but what I find just as fun is that the work and science is also done with the cast and those involved around the world... Eternal Shadow is a compelling read that balances the science well with the action."

—*San Francisco Book Review*
(4.5/5 stars)

"Fans of the hard science fiction of Andy Weir (The Martian) and Isaac Asimov—of epic tales and strong female lead characters—will have their eyes glued to the pages of *Eternal Shadow*... an edge-of-your-seat near future space odyssey."

—*IndieReader*
(4.9/5 stars)

"*Eternal Shadow* is a tense science fiction story that paints a thoughtful, intelligent portrait of humanity's first contact with extraterrestrial life."

—*Foreward Reviews*
(4/5 stars)

"In his series opener, Williams offers a wealth of well-informed, highly technical, and scientific details that will captivate fans of hard sci-fi... When apocalyptic disaster looms, humanity turns to science and technology in this well-crafted tale."

—*Kirkus*

"Overall, Williams' *Eternal Shadow* is a pleasing debut, well-paced and crafted. He manages to fully flesh out the characters (human, alien, and AI) while building to a satisfying ending which leaves open many tantalizing avenues for future books to explore."

—*Manhattan Book Review*
(4/5 stars)

ETERNAL
SHADOW

FALL OF GODS

TREVOR B. WILLIAMS

First Edition: November 2019

Book cover and typesetting by Anamaria Stefan

ISBN 978-1-7331118-3-6 (Trade Paperback)
ISBN 978-1-7331118-8-1 (Trade Paperback - B&N)
ISBN 978-1-7331118-1-2 (Hardcover)
ISBN 978-1-7331118-0-5 (ebook - Kindle)
ISBN 978-1-7331118-2-9 (ebook - EPUB)
LCCN 2019910027, 2019907155

www.trevorwrites.com

*Dedicated to my loving wife—my unending
source of inspiration—and to my daughter who
I hope will explore the stars*

PART ONE

DISCOVERY

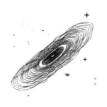

1.0

A soft but piercing tone cut through the white noise of the humming computers.

"What the hell!" Samantha Monroe, a research scientist, winced as the tone blended with the 90s music streaming from her MP3 player. She yanked the earbuds out of her ears, her eyes wide. She'd worked at the Search for Extraterrestrial Intelligence Institute for six years, but she hadn't heard that particular 400Hz triangle wave tone in years. Not until now.

She pushed away from her desk and craned her head around the wall of her cubicle so she had a clear line of sight to the back corner. The Very Large Monitor Database, a suite of computers hooked up to four 40-inch monitors that had live data continually fed from the Allen Telescope Array, was the source of the tone. The lower-left monitor was lit up with a red-outlined alert window with "SIGNAL DETECTED" flashing in the center.

Almost falling out of her seat, she ran to the VLM. Without taking her eyes off the alert window, her mind ran through the possibilities as *Groove Is In The Heart* started to play. Sliding the earbuds back into her ears, she took a deep breath as she sat in front of the four monitors. They displayed spectrographic data that should've been impossible.

Okay, okay, okay, is this real? This can't be real, but is it?

"Time to confirm," she said out loud as the tone fell silent upon her clearing the alert. *Time to see from what area of space the detected signal originated.*

As the main riff of the song played, Sam's mind and energy honed on this signal, her fingers typing while scanning local wide-band and narrow-band frequencies. Her first goal was to rule out any Earth-born signals that could've bounced off a satellite and hit the radio dishes at ATA.

"Holy shit," she whispered as the data in front of her confirmed the space-born nature of the signal. Twice. Three times.

No. This can't be real.

Sam chewed on her lip, scrutinizing the formulas on the monitor in front of her that broke down the narrow-band frequency into several distinct sections. She looked for common errors in the software that could've triggered the alert, then looked for modulations in the signal that would indicate a spinning pulsar or a late-type star generating the signal.

The analysis software worked as intended—no stars or pulsars existed in the direction that the signal emanated from.

This just can't.

She glanced at the desk phone to the left of the keyboard. *No way I'm calling anyone,* she thought. *Have to confirm everything.* She knew better than to cry wolf when there were false-positives in the past. Calling in the entire brigade would result in her being in hot water if it turned out to be anything other than extraterrestrial in origin—something that seemed more and more likely.

She sucked in a large breath of air as she leaned closer to the monitor which displayed the source of the signal: Pluto. Pluto! At least, all indicators said that approximately seven hours ago the downgraded planet was the source of a possible extraterrestrial beacon.

She typed several commands to process the fresh data even further, triangulating the approximate location on or near Pluto that the frequency originated. After mashing the ENTER key, the displayed dataset made her blink rapidly with a slackened mouth, as if the data was a mirage and blinking would correct it. The signal originated fifteen thousand kilometers over the surface of Pluto and not beyond the planet. With every false-positive in the past, the signals originated from other stars. Detecting one just 7.5 billion kilometers away from Earth was a first. She had to make sure every decibel, every frequency, every number that had to be carried over another number—that everything was correct. And she checked again. And again.

As *Groove Is In The Heart* came to a close, Sam glanced at the date and time in the corner of the monitor. The signal was broadcasting itself for at least seven hours, the amount of time needed for it to reach Earth from Pluto. Everything pointed to this not being a fluke.

"Holy shit," she proclaimed again, her right leg rapidly bobbing under the desk. "I need to call Jennifer. Get more people here now."

She reached for the desk phone and dialed Jennifer Epstein's cell, one of the Senior Research Scientists at SETI and Sam's superior. She rarely called her outside of regular work hours unless it was an emergency or critically important—this signal classified as both. Her heart pounded as she kept staring at the spread of information on the four monitors. The sound of Jennifer's phone ringing from the desk phone speaker was loud, but not enough to drown out the thoughts running through her head.

This is real.

○ ◎ ○

Covered by an open magazine that contained articles on current world events, a smartphone began playing the first six seconds of *Beethoven's 5th Symphony,* a ringtone selected for all stored SETI contacts. The sound from the phone's speakers were loud enough to cause Jennifer to shift under her cotton bedding. It took three rings before Jennifer flung her hand over to the phone, knocking the magazine and her reading glasses onto the floor from the nightstand.

As she mentally ran through the short list of people that had her cell number, Jennifer, now resting on her side, brought the now-muted phone at eye level. Though everything was blurry and some of her shoulder-length black hair further obscured her vision, the name on the phone's screen was unmistakable.

Jennifer exhaled as she slid her thumb across the screen, answering the call while she pressed the speaker button, amplifying the excited voice of Sam. "Dr. Epstein! Get here quick!"

"What happened, Sam?" Jennifer queried, her mind still hazy from the abrupt wake-up call.

"I was just, you know, doing my usual graveyard shift, running some algorithms through the latest batch of spectral modulations from Allen—data mining and all that—"

"Please, cut to the chase," Jennifer interrupted, her head now firmly planted back in her pillow and eyes closed.

"Signal detected, doc. Signal detected!"

Ah, this again. Jennifer had participated in dozens of events like this, all of which ended with false positives or were new astronomical discoveries that happened to emanate radio waves. One more such event, though exciting, shouldn't get her protégé so frantic.

"Have you run the frequency through normal detection procedures?" Jennifer continued to make herself comfortable in her warm bed, not reacting too much to this news.

"I've triple-checked everything. This is real and coming from Pluto!"

"What?" Jennifer pushed herself into a sitting position against the back of her bed. Her brow raised slightly at the mention of Pluto—a signal coming from one of Earth's own planetary neighbors was a twist.

"We need to bring in the rest of the team pronto, doc," Sam said. "Gordan, Nic, the whole team! Alert the director, too."

Jennifer leaned over the side of her bed to scoop her glasses off the carpeted floor. She opened the drawer to her nightstand and grabbed the thin, black slab that was her SETI-provided smartphone. Unlike her personal phone, this had secured access to SETI's servers which included an app designed to push the same alerts the VRM received. After the screen turned on, she tapped her password.

"Dr. Epstein? Doctor?" Sam impatiently waited for a response as Jennifer swiped down on her phone screen to see the signal notification that was pushed to her phone at 4:39am. It included the signal origin coordinates and its frequency: *Right Asc: 18h 52m 57.7s Decl: -20° 14' 37.1" ; Freq: 5106.82MHz.*

The numbers all came into focus as she slid her glasses on. She cocked her head as she scratched the side of her jaw. The frequency presented was far higher than anything they've detected in space before outside of pulsars—except this originated from Pluto.

"Why would there be a signal from Pluto?" Jennifer asked herself rather than to Sam.

"That's what I can't wait to find out," Sam said. "Shall I call in the rest?"

Jennifer shook her head, despite Sam not being able to see the gesture. *Stay composed.* "Once I review the data, we'll decide if having the team on-site at six in the morning will be better than at nine," Jennifer said. She dropped the smart phone onto her bed while she slung her legs onto the floor and started toward her closet. She eyeballed a button-down shirt and pants that she could quickly throw on for her twenty-minute drive to the office. "However, I'll be there immediately."

Despite it being a weekday, the drive along Route 237 West was uneventful and fast. Jennifer knew the highways around her home well, though she was never a fan of waking up early enough to beat rush-hour traffic. Her work phone, loosely nestled in the cup holder in front of the unused CD player, dinged with text messages from Sam. She picked up her phone and scanned the first message before she placed the phone back down: "Still can't believe it. Nicolas is on the way."

Of course Nic's on the way, Jennifer thought—he's one of the most obsessed support scientists on her team. Even the slightest variance in a star's brightness would send him into a researcher frenzy to understand everything there was to know about that star. Where his bursts of energy came from, she might never know, but his contributions to the team couldn't be denied.

As she left behind the suburban blocks of Milpitas and looked at the water-starved fields just beyond the Los Esteros Energy Center, thoughts of both the past and future filled her mind.

Though she'd been working at SETI for over twenty years, every "signal found" message always found a way to send chills down her spine.

If this is really happening, everything will change, Jennifer thought to herself as the dried fields gave way to vast corporate parks and the large set of runways that sat behind the NASA Ames Research Center. Her personal phone vibrated atop her work phone. The predicted text message from Grace, her mother, arrived on schedule: a verse from the Bible that she likely felt was appropriate for the week.

Hopefully, Jennifer thought as she looked at the message from her mother while hearing her work phone chime once more. *Hopefully this signal could bring the change we all need.*

1.1

Nic's hybrid, a dark blue sedan from 2009 that'd spent way more time in direct sunlight than the paint could handle, was already in the parking lot. Bringing her car to a halt next to his, Jennifer went through the motions of turning the car off with one hand while smoothing down her shirt with the other, aiming to keep composure. Nevertheless, her heart raced faster than usual as she took long strides to the front of SETI.

At minimum, she allowed herself a brisk pace from her car to her team's corner of the building where Vern—her pet name for the Very Large Monitor Database system—churned through data. She passed through the automatic doors as her ID badge reeled itself back against her waist after being swiped. As she got closer, an odd warbling sound filled the air. A sound that emanated from where she worked. When Jennifer swiped her card and entered the office, Nic's voice was just over the pitched warbling sound that pulsed every second from the VLM speakers.

"The amplitude of this section is incredible!" Nic said as he adjusted his glasses.

Jennifer started her way toward Nic and Sam, both of which sat in front of Vern. They were both fixated on the monitors in front of them.

"What is going on..." Jennifer began, but trailed off when she saw the very focused, strong spike of the signal on the bottom monitors. On one screen was a live feed of the warbling pulse, each second turning the center of the frequency medium into a jagged spike just past the five-gigahertz level. The screen Nic and Sam were looking over had parts of the signal broken out into static screenshots for analysis.

Above them were the remaining two monitors. The right displayed a graphical representation of Earth along with the sea of satellites that orbit it in the form of red, green and blue dots, while the left had a scrolling text-based feed of the signal's location and frequency, with the initial capture of it pinned at the top.

Just seeing and hearing this warbling blast of audio made her skin tingle as blood rushed through her in response.

Sam had one leg extended away from the VLM, as if she wanted to run over to her own computer, but was glued to the screen in front of her. "Doc, I've been running this through every spectrum analyzer and pulse reader we have."

"Have you checked all civilian and military sources?" Jennifer asked as she ran to her computer a few desks down on the same wall as Vern, dropping herself into her chair.

"Yes, ma'am," Sam affirmed as she continued swiping through frequency analyzer programs. "So far, AWAC reported back negative. Nic, what's the status on spacecraft activity, NORAD sats?"

"No unusual activity in our neck of the woods," Nic pulled up another window that flashed in the task bar. "Got confirmation on ATA status."

Nic turned toward Jennifer, his eyes beaming through his glasses. "All forty-two dishes reporting green operations, and all are picking up the signal."

As Jennifer's computer awoke from sleep mode, she glanced at her smartphone, which still had the original signal notification on display. "Is there any possibility that our software or hardware is malfunctioning?" she said aloud to nobody in particular, but knew she would get a response.

"Looking into that now," Nic stepped back from the main VLM console and pulled out his sticker-covered laptop to start diagnostics.

"Doc, I have confirmation on sidereal motion for the signal," Sam stated, her excitement palpable as she kept her focus on the monitors in front of her. "Interferometric positioning still places the signal origin fifteen thousand kilometers over Pluto."

"But that doesn't make sense," Jennifer darted her eyes toward Sam as she brought up astronomical mapping displays on her screen.

"Can you confirm when we first received the signal, and confirm again right ascension eighteen hours, fifty-two minutes, fifty-seven-point-seven seconds; declination minus twenty degrees, fourteen minutes?"

"I'll run the numbers again, Doc," Sam said.

Nic's laptop snapped shut as he started for the server room. "So far diagnostics are coming in clean. Gonna directly access the servers."

Jennifer looked at Nic with urgent concern. "Do you think someone could be spoofing this?"

"It wouldn't be the first time," Nic said as he swiped his card on the security panel, causing the lock on the heavy door to open with a click. "But we now have dozens of safeguards and detection criteria in place that would make such a hack significantly more challenging today. In the past, yes, we had several false-positives thanks to backdoor attacks, but I'm certain this is not one of those events."

Just as the doors to the server room closed, the office door swung open, the wall groaning as the door arched to the fullest extent on its hinges. Jennifer turned to see Gordan Ivanovic, another research scientist who worked alongside Jennifer, marching toward his desk. Like Jennifer and Nic before him, he paused when he saw the signal data on the VLM.

"Holy Christ," he said as he ran his fingers through his gray hair. "Where are we with signal confirmation?"

"You're missing the action, Gordan," Sam quipped. "I can use your help analyzing the signal pattern. Did you see the ascension and declination positions?"

"Yes, and I still don't believe it," Gordan regained his composure and threw his messenger bag into his cubicle before walking over to Jennifer. "What are your thoughts, Jennifer?"

"Well, Nic is checking the servers for possible online tampering while Sam could use you over at Vern," Jennifer said while pointing at one of the spectrum breakout charts on her screen. She allowed herself a quick chuckle. "It would be nice, though, if it weren't another false reading!"

"Agreed," said Gordan as he lightly patted Jennifer on the shoulder before walking to his desk. "Perhaps we can get Kabir on the line to run a check for us."

"Yes, go for it," Jennifer said. Kabir Reddy worked out of Pune, India, home of the Giant Metrewave Radio Telescope which was operated by the Tata Institute. Though Tata drove the goals for the radio telescopes—most of which didn't align with SETI's objectives—Kabir, being one of the few people staffed at the GMRT, used his position to redirect some of the dishes to aid in SETI research. Jennifer didn't even hesitate with Gordan's suggestion. It made perfect sense: Pluto rose right about now over India, and Kabir was manning one of the few radio telescope arrays for thousands of miles.

She heard the server room doors unlock, which prompted her to rotate her chair toward the door as Nic exited. "Give me some good news."

"No unauthorized activity or login attempts over the last four weeks." Nic noticed Jennifer's raised eyebrow in response. "I just wanted to be thorough. But yes, the only thing my audits found was a three gigabyte download of music, which I traced back to Sam's laptop."

Sam turned toward Nic and Jennifer, both of which looked over at her. "Hey, if you want this girl to code, she needs her weekly dose of number one, two, and three hits from the greatest decade for the ears!"

"Oh, not that conversation again," Gordan rolled his eyes, something that Sam could sense despite not seeing him. They've had way too many debates about which decade in the twentieth century produced the most culturally significant musical works.

"Don't worry, I think we may have the greatest song singing from Vern's mouth right now," Sam added as she brought her right ear to one of the speakers, letting the warbling sound flow into her body.

"Hold that thought—just got Kabir," Gordan leaned toward his computer monitor, a habit of his, despite the webcam being mounted above his head. Jennifer, Nic and Sam all dropped what they were doing and crowded around Gordan as Kabir's face and office filled the screen. "Hello my friend!"

"Good morning to you, too," Kabir greeted Gordan with a smile. "Why do I have the pleasure of speaking with you on such short notice?"

"I just sent you an email with a signal I'd like you to turn your dishes toward."

Kabir shifted in his seat as he reached behind his head to scratch an itch. "Oh, you know our telescope is currently in use right now for studying relativistic electron emissions—"

"I know, you guys are slammed," Gordan politely interrupted, "But this is something you will want to listen to. We just need confirmation from another site before we consider going public."

"Not a problem, Gordan," Kabir nodded. "I'll realign dishes six through twelve now and see what we have..."

Kabir rolled away from his desk and turned his back to his webcam as he pulled out a keyboard drawer from the servers behind him.

"Come on," Sam whispered, her leg trembling as she and the rest of them waited for Kabir's feedback. After a few minutes, the warbling pulse passed through a sound system near Kabir.

He returned to the camera after he ambled off-screen to the unseen speakers on his end. "What is this?" Kabir asked with a confused look on his face.

Gordan looked up at Jennifer, who looked over at an exhilarated Sam. He shot Kamir a broad grin. "Possibly the greatest discovery in the history of mankind."

"Holy shit!" Sam jumped and grabbed her hair, disheveling the bun that kept it together.

"Keep on tracking the signal, Kabir," Jennifer leaned closer to the webcam. "Log everything that you can. Jump into chat with Gordan and keep him apprised of any findings—you'll be in the loop."

"I, too, hope this is what you all are thinking," Kabir stretched an arm off-screen, an increase in the signal's volume following his motion.

"Finger's crossed, my friend," Gordan nodded and disconnected the video feed.

While Sam rushed back to Vern to scan the latest batch of received data, Nic rested against one of the nearby cubicle walls, his legs shaking from this overseas signal confirmation. For the first time, a signal of unknown origin was being easily picked up by another radio array, and from across the world, no less.

Jennifer patted Gordan on the shoulder and started into a slow pace, her mind recalling SETI protocol. "Kabir was a great start, but we need more confirmations. Gordan and Nic, start pinging every station around the world and get everyone tuned in—we want to track this signal twenty-four-seven. And double-check with our boys at the Jansky Array in New Mexico—it's possible they recorded the signal like we did."

"I'll tally up stations in East Asia that should have full visibility to Pluto," Nic began as he ran for his desk. He collided into one cubicle corner on the way, which sent some loose papers and a poster of the solar system onto the floor. He didn't feel the jolt, though. He was way too excited to care.

"Sam, put on your music and try to learn more about the signal—maybe we can figure out what exactly is being transmitted."

"Yes, captain!" Sam beamed while she saluted Jennifer. "Expect results faster than—"

The warbling sound stopped pulsing through their speakers. Sam froze in her tracks, her hands in front of her as if she balanced herself on a gymnastics bar. Nic and Gordan both stood up from their desks. Jennifer turned toward the VLM, her face almost crestfallen.

"No," she said as she pointed to Sam. "Sam, talk to me."

"Uhhhhh..." Sam rushed over to the main console for Vern, now with a somewhat different mission in mind. She looked over the various livestream analysis windows that graphically displayed the signal—they all flatlined, with only the common background noise of space making the lines move. "Give me a moment."

"Nic, are you sure we haven't been compromised?" Jennifer asked. Back at her desk, she brought up a screen capture of the signal and looked over its range, wavelength and other metrics to see if there was any possibility that this was a fluke or an unidentified natural phenomenon.

Nic glanced at Jennifer before he scooped his laptop from his desk and ran for the server room. "I haven't been wrong about this sort of thing before, but I'll double-check the logs again."

The speakers remained silent, the remaining sounds being Sam typing away vigorously on the keyboard with a seeming intention on making the keys clack. Gordan sighed as he slumped into his chair and rested his head on its back, his hair draping over. Jennifer stopped trying to will the signal back into existence and just listened as normalcy tried its best to settle over the office. Sam soon stopped typing as well, letting the hum of the many computers in the room become the dominant sound.

Sam ran her fingers through her brunette hair as she released it from the disheveled bun and looked over toward Jennifer. "Doc... what's the next step?"

Jennifer ran her finger over her smartphone that was on her desk, bringing up the time. It's been ten minutes since the signal dropped like a rock into the abyss. Though the signal ceased, she knew their computers and Vern had collected everything on it. The data wasn't going anywhere—they just had to parse it, break it into as many components as possible and see what it meant. Even if the signal never came back, there were so many questions already, especially if it turned out it was genuine. She looked at Sam before scanning the mostly empty office.

"We need more people."

1.2

The quartet that listened to the signal live now played the sound back from recordings for the benefit of the rest of the staff that streamed in after they contacted every scientist that worked in the region. That was almost six hours ago. As the afternoon sun bled through the half-opened window blinds, lots of commotion filled the office as other research scientists pored over the captured data. Gordan sat at his desk with two research assistants flanking him as he debated with Kabir regarding the potential source of the signal. Nic and two others sat next to Sam as they geeked out over the strength of the signal, not letting go of the possibility of its extraterrestrial origins. Sam, however, held a bitter smile following her brief call with the Lick Observatory, whose telescope pointed toward the Andromeda galaxy, the complete opposite direction from where Pluto was in the sky.

Jennifer, meanwhile, stood alongside Vern, its monitors displaying the signal frozen in time with various modulation details, along with a small window dedicated to information on Pluto. And standing across from her was Brian Ethans, the Director of SETI. He was a tall, but stocky individual who commonly wore navy blue slacks and a light-colored button-down shirt—usually blue or white and with a necktie. Today, he bucked the expected trend by foregoing the tie, the top button left undone, but then again, nothing about this day was ordinary. And seemingly as a nod to Sam's inappropriate jokes, the fluorescent lighting amplified that he had a smooth, hairless head. He looked at Jennifer through his thin-rimmed glasses with a fair amount of skepticism, his arms crossed, since the signal stopped broadcasting.

Brian spoke. "Look, this data is rather unusual and even

reminiscent of the famous 'WOW! Signal', but so far all I see reminds me of the astronomers in the 1970s—they spent months trying to wrap their hands and heads around it before realizing the trail ran cold."

The astronomer, Jerry Ehman, was well-known amongst those at SETI. He worked at Big Ear Telescope that made the discovery of the now-famous signal in 1977 that was surnamed from his one-word description of it: "Wow!" It lasted seventy-two seconds, but never repeated itself after that fateful night despite several consecutive months of active searching and listening.

It made sense why Brian would compare it to this event, but Jennifer still clenched her jaw at his seemingly jumping to conclusions. She summoned all her will to not raise her voice, her feelings of annoyance kept at bay. "I know where you are coming from, but our signal not only repeated itself every second for over two hours, but it was also picked up by other observatories."

Brian didn't immediately respond—he was listening for a change.

"Give us a week to analyze what we have. At the very least, we'll have discovered a new kind of star, pulsar..."

"Or maybe little green men?" Brian asked, with nary a hint of sarcasm in sight.

"I'll keep you posted, Brian," Jennifer ended their conversation before she got wrapped into another debate about false flags and protocol. She feigned a smile before she walked over to Gordon's desk. Brian stood in place for a moment before turning away and headed for his corner office.

Despite the surrounding activity, Jennifer tuned it out as she ran through everything that happened so far on this very unusual day. Everything pointed to the signal, which was not only picked up by at least two radio telescopes across the world from each other but, for a short time, repeated itself. *Ethan may have a point, but this is much bigger than the WOW Signal,* she thought.

"Give me an update, Gordan," she asked as she closed the gap between their desks. The other two research scientists buried their heads in their laptops, one having an online chat with another peer in the UK, while the other stared at live frequency spectrum data.

"Kabir got permission to redirect all observation capabilities on his end to the signal," Gordan began with what almost looked like a smile on his usually stoic face. "In addition, we got confirmation from eight additional radio telescopes that picked up the signal."

"Eight..." Jennifer repeated that number to herself. "Eight... keep it up—there has to be more confirmations. Any word from Arecibo or SALT?"

The Arecibo Observatory, in Puerto Rico, and the Southern African Large Telescope, in South Africa, were the two largest observatories in the world—if there were any locations that would have received the signal, it would've been them.

"We are getting telemetry from Arecibo now," Gordan confirmed, nodding as he pulled up browser windows on his monitor. "No word from SALT just yet, though I'm sure the Arecibo of the East will come through—"

"They always do," Gordan and Jennifer said at the same time, Gordan with some disdain and Jennifer with friendly mockery.

"What is it about SALT that you don't like?" Jennifer asked.

"You know I'm not a fan of Khulu Global or their foundation," Gordan said, placing his webcam microphone on mute as he continued. "Even if their founder proved that he wasn't associated with blood diamond trades, the corporation is responsible for a lot of trauma in this world."

She knew this argument well enough due to the occasional debates that Gordan spearheaded whenever Khulu Global came up. Despite the many pots that the multinational corporation had its hands in, they still birthed one of the most well-funded foundations in the world, the Unity Foundation. Thanks to one of the core missions of Unity being a focus on advancing the sciences and supporting the kind of work the SETI program lives and breathes, the foundation's received a lot of admiration and esteem in the scientific community. Some people however, like Gordan, still viewed the organization as one that profits on the suffering of others, even if they aren't directly causing that suffering.

"Nevertheless, SALT is an invaluable resource, along with any telescope and observatory," Jennifer said, refocusing the discussion.

"Indeed," Gordan conceded. "I'll wave you down when I have more updates, including from SALT..." He trailed off as he noticed

Kabir miming knocking on his monitor, trying to get his attention. Jennifer rounded the corner to have a better view of Gordan's monitor. She brought a hand to her lips when she saw the live feed of the signal pulsing—a feed that originated from India. The alien sound sent a flush of adrenaline through her body.

She wasn't the only one—almost all the surrounding conversations ended in gasps as Gordan turned up the volume on his desktop speakers. He, too, looked to be breathing harder at the return of the alien sound.

"When did the signal restart?" Gordan asked.

"A few seconds ago," Kabir said, now seated at his desk, though he rolled just off-screen as he spoke to someone else in Hindi. Despite it being almost two in the morning, Kabir's surroundings were buzzing with activity.

"Are you sure?" Jennifer asked as she squeezed in front of another assistant to get a closer look at the screen. She had to get confirmation.

"I haven't been more sure about anything," Kabir said. "The signal frequency is exactly the same, down to the thousandth hertz."

"From Pluto?" she asked.

"Coming," Kabir instant messaged, the clacking of the keys audible through the speakers. The commotion on Kabir's side seemed to have quieted for a moment as the people there congregated around select monitors. Jennifer glanced behind her and found Sam and Nic behind her. Most of the activity at SETI ground to a halt soon after Jennifer's unintended announcement about the signal's return spread.

"Location, Kabir!"

Kabir's face grimaced as he muttered, "This can't be right." Then in Hindi, "Rupak, this can't be right—double-check the equipment again!"

"What is it?" Gordan asked, shifting in his chair as if it became uncomfortable.

"Gordan," Kabir said in English, "The signal is coming from Neptune."

Jennifer looked at Gordan, then at Kabir, arms crossed. "Wait, wait... Can you repeat that?"

"He said Neptune," Sam murmured.

"Neptune," Kabir said before being interrupted by another researcher that gave him a sheet of paper. He spoke in as clear an English as he could while he scanned the paper in front of him with narrowed eyes. "Yes—right ascension twenty-two hours, thirty-seven minutes, twenty-point-six-seven seconds; declination minus nine degrees, twenty-eight minutes. We are confirmed."

Nic grabbed a notepad and vigorously wrote astronomical equations. "That's nearly 30AU from Pluto," he said in amazement.

Jennifer slid Gordan aside as, while kneeling, opened SETI's stellar observatory software to view the exact location of the coordinates shared.

"I could've done that, you know," Gordan said, though Jennifer was too focused on what appeared on-screen to acknowledge him. As the numerous statistics listed themselves to the left of the focal point, Jennifer raised her eyebrows as she reviewed the stats from GMRT—all the data looked undeniably accurate.

"This is just off to the side of Neptune, look at this," Jennifer pointed to a spot near the orbit of Proteus, one of Neptune's larger moons. "About one-hundred-and-ten-thousand kilometers away from the planet."

"There's more," Kabir said. He focused not on Gordan and Jennifer, but what he pulled up on-screen. Some men came into view, walking just behind Kabir—one of them leaned forward and pointed at what he was about to share. "We're tracking the signal's location live, and it appears to be moving."

○ ◎ ○

The conference room that sat at the front of the building contained six heavy rectangular tables that combined to make one big table. Floor to ceiling windows spanned the length of the room that faced the office, though most of the blinds hung at random heights, resulting in not providing much in the way of privacy. A large circular speaker phone sat slightly off-center, its cables meeting a batch of additional computer and power cables and cords that were wrapped together on the floor. Above the table was a projector, mounted on the ceiling with a thick steel rod, that cost more than everything else in the room combined. The fans whirring as they flushed the heat from the active unit, it displayed on a wall-length projector screen the planet Neptune, signal statistics, and a single, fat, red dot that represented the signal's current location in relation to Neptune and some of its larger moons.

Around the table was Jennifer's team with each person, save for her, with their laptops and some papers. Jennifer sat two chairs away from Brian at the long end of the table, facing the screen.

"We need to go public with this," Nic said, his level of excitement palpable.

"Before we do anything with the media, we have to have our facts straight," Brian raised his hand to calm everyone down, with limited success. "Believe it or not, there are protocols in place to ensure we don't disseminate any false information."

He looked over to Jennifer. "You've already started the process of confirming signal data with other SETI programs. Where are we on that front?"

Jennifer observed everyone at the table, each person waiting for her to fan the flames ignited by this otherworldly ping. Except for Sam, who was deeply focused on her laptop. "We have four radio telescopes between India and Russia tracking the signal. It was confirmed that the signal is definitely originating less than one hundred thousand kilometers from Neptune and not from a star beyond our solar system."

"What happened to the signal from Pluto?" Brian asked.

There was a pause before Jennifer responded. "We don't know. It seemed to have just stopped."

"And started again, but now at Neptune," Gordan said as he gestured to the screen.

"This has to be broadcasting from an alien ship," Sam said as she continued typing.

"Okay, we don't have to dive into hypotheticals, Sam," Brian said.

Sam smiled as she finished typing, lifting one hand off the keyboard with dramatic flair while she used her other hand to turn her laptop around to face the team.

"Check this out: We received the signal for the first time from Pluto around 4:45am today, and barely an hour passes before the signal disappeared. Then, a little over eight hours later, we—as in Earth—are hit with the signal again. But now it's at Neptune."

"Brevity, Sam," Jennifer said, knowing Sam could easily consume the rest of the day diving into the numbers she's shared.

"Oh, sure. So. We have an alien craft—"

"We don't know that," Brian jumped in, but Sam continued.

"—that traversed over 4.5 billion kilometers in just over 4.6 hours!"

"Do you know what you're saying?" Brian said sharply. "Even if this were a ship, you're saying it traveled at, what, ninety percent the speed of light?"

"Yes, that's exactly what I'm saying!" Sam nudged her laptop further in Brian's direction. "All the numbers check out."

"If we assume you're correct in that this is a space craft, why didn't we pick up the signal while it moved?" Brian asked. "And if it were a ship, why didn't we pick up the signal much, much earlier than today?"

Sam's shoulders slumped, looking slightly deflated from Brian's prodding. "Fair points. That will be something to dig deeper into..."

"If the ship were traveling ninety percent the speed of light, any radio frequencies it would broadcast would be heavily red-shifted to the point of the frequency being non-existent," Jennifer said. "Especially if it were moving toward us, even if indirectly."

Brian sighed. "Okay, but that doesn't explain the signal's sudden appearance."

"You are right," Jennifer agreed, "The origin of it is an unknown right now. With what's in front of us, there's still a lot we can do."

Nic raised his hand, waving it in the air, much like an eager college student confident in the answer they were about to give to a question. "We have a database full of radio data. We could take what we currently know about the signal and compare it with what's been collected over the course of SETI's history. See if there are any potential matches."

"Sounds like a good place to start," Jennifer said. "Maybe even go back to the days of the 'WOW' signal to see if there are any hints that were missed."

"We can also get some observatories that are already pointing toward that patch of space to share images of Neptune and Pluto," Gordan suggested.

"That's what I was trying to do earlier," Sam said. "Lick Observatory would likely take twenty minutes to realign, but I bet you my media player we'll find a handful in the Far East ready to report in!"

Jennifer nodded at Sam, then looked to Brian. "I'm for this idea— if this is an alien craft, we'll likely be able to see it. The radio frequencies are live once again, so any observatory facing Neptune should be able to pick up its physical presence."

Brian eyed Jennifer, then Gordan, then Jennifer again. "Do it. Gordan, I think one of our contacts in India could help us."

"I just had Kabir on the horn," Gordan said. "I'll call him back now."

"Good. Meanwhile, any useful information about the signal itself?"

"Nothing as yet," Sam said. "Though the recorded frequency is consistent, our software didn't seem to pick up anything anomalous."

"Give it time," Jennifer added. "Keep recording whatever comes in."

Brian pressed a button under the signal, separating the densely packed frequency peaks into four additional segments. He used the mouse cursor to circle one of them. "It's possible there's more embedded in the signal than meets the eye. This section may suggest that imagery could be encoded."

"Another signal buried in the core signal?" asked Gordan.

"Perhaps," Brian said as he passed a free hand along his hairless head.

"I'll bring up CASA and see what we got," Nic said. CASA was one program, used by organizations that ran radio astronomical telescopes, that required a lot of hardware horsepower and required a desktop computer as part of its minimum requirements. A handful of the computers at SETI had computers with CASA installed, having the dozen terabytes of hard drive space and more than enough memory needed for maximum performance.

Brian, with the look of satisfaction on his face, stood up from his seat. "Okay, it sounds like we have the next few immediate, if not large, goals to tackle."

"It's a good start, I agree," said Jennifer. "Now let's get back to work. Hopefully we can avoid any more conferences like this while in the midst of this historic event." When she stood up, everyone else collected their laptops and papers from the table. She noticed that Sam stayed in her seat, though she kept her laptop open, her eyes focused on it in contemplation.

Jennifer walked over to Sam's side of the table and sat in one of the nearby swivel chairs. "What's on your mind?"

"You know what's one thing that doesn't make sense?" Sam began as she drew a circle with her finger around the signal on her screen. "Why is this object moving—at increasing speed—towards Neptune?"

∘ ◎ ∘

The Girawali Observatory in Pune, India was Gordan's first choice for opening a line of communication. If their infrastructure allowed, he could establish a live feed into what their telescope could see. The location was ideal for two reasons: It was just an hour away from the Giant Meterwave Radio Telescope—Kabir's domain—and Kabir knew the two scientists that worked the graveyard shift.

Jennifer was still in the conference room when Sam jumped out of her seat at the sight of Gordan waving them down to join him. As Jennifer walked to his desk, with Sam following behind, she heard the banter he had with Kabir. His animated face was in a video window on Gordan's second monitor. On Gordan's primary, larger monitor was an email marked as high priority which had a file attached. The body read: Please review the initial images. We will try to establish a live connection between us and SETI. भगवान हमारी आत्माओं पर दया कर सकते हैं

"I don't normally get Hindi in my emails, especially not translated by the sender," Gordan said to Kabir. A new window appeared over the email when he double-clicked the attached ZIP file, listing five separate image files, ready for extraction and viewing.

Kabir scratched the back of his head as he read the email and translated the Hindi. "It says 'May God have mercy on our souls.'"

Just as he opened one of the images, Jennifer spoke. "Did you get anything use...ful..." she brought her hand to her lips, cutting her trailing question off.

"What... the fuck," Sam said.

The image opened had Neptune in the center of an all-black background with Triton, its most prominent moon, in the upper-left side. However, to the left of Neptune was a white streak that looked like a fuzzy stemless champaign glass on its side. And Neptune, a blue-white orb in most pictures of it taken from ground level on Earth, looked faintly elongated on the side facing the object in the image. The planet stretched into a wide cone that met with the object.

Some whispers from scientists behind Jennifer were audible, but she ignored them. The signal pulsed in her mind ever louder as she focused increasingly on this object almost nestled within Neptune's upper atmosphere. Silence gradually filled the office as word of the image spread. It hung in the air, unwanted, as those with immediate access to the files ran through possible scenarios in their minds on what they could do with this information.

Gordan opened the other files in sequential order, allowing Jennifer and him to see a broken timelapse going from the present to a little over an hour ago. As he cycled through the pictures, a chunky animation of the object depicted it backing away from Neptune and then, in the final image, not be present at all.

"Is this the signal source?" Gordan asked, breaking the silence.

"It has to be," Sam said. "But what is going on with Neptune in the latest picture?"

Jennifer closed her eyes and snapped out of the daze she was in, the signal no longer substituting her hearing for what was around her. With her eyes closed, however, her mind merged the five images into a fluid animation of what should have been impossible. An object appeared and was destroying the eighth planet in the solar system.

"More like, what is this thing doing to Neptune?" she said as her eyes opened.

They looked at each other just as Brian approached. He stopped himself at the foot of Gordan's desk at the sight of the Neptune snapshots. He opened his mouth, as if to say something, but stopped himself, unsure of what to say—a rare moment for him.

Gordan stopped clicking through the images and looked to Jennifer, uncertainty in his eyes. "What do we do?"

Jennifer stood up and looked at those around her. There was something very close to Neptune, and that something was irrecoverably altering the planet just by its presence. Something like this was far bigger than simply picking up an extraterrestrial signal. Her eyes met Brian who, with tightened lips, gave a slight nod, knowing what she would say. More important, he would agree. His affirmation of not just her positions around the events of the last couple of hours gave her a swell of authority she hadn't held in years.

"Get every observatory, space telescope, and radio telescope on that object. We must connect with NASA, too—if NASA isn't already aware of this, they will be in the next few minutes." She got up and started for her desk, but continued speaking with gusto. She wasn't looking at anyone in particular, but others took notice and paid close attention. "Get on internal chat and coordinate calls and email sends so nobody doubles up on communication—pick an observatory and share that decision with everyone. The directors will target the big guys: NASA, the Russian Space Agency, the European Space Agency." Jennifer counted the agencies on one hand as she came to a halt by her desk, looking over the office that just a few moments ago froze with fear because of images of the object by Neptune. People now funneled back to their desks, some in groups, as they picked up phones and logging into the SETI internal chat platform.

Jennifer, guided by the drive to get more people in front of this, turned to Brian. He just reached the door to his office. She almost ran over to join him. "Brian, let's get NASA on the line."

◦ ◎ ◦

Sam stayed beside Gordan, who still held his gaze on the images he continued cycling through. She leaned in and looked at Kabir. "Hey Kabir, can you get the folks at Girawali to pull snapshots of Pluto as well? The signal originated there," she paused and thought about what she would say next. "Given what we're seeing with Neptune, I wonder if Pluto will give us an idea on what to expect."

Kabir unmuted himself, interrupting a conversation he had with a colleague. "Yes Sam, I'll contact them immediately. We're still trying to make sense of these images, too."

"What do you expect to see with Pluto?" Gordan sounded deadpan, but it hinted at knowing the possible answers that waited for them.

"I don't know, but I want to be wrong," Sam said, her tone taking on that of someone that expected a death in the family.

It didn't take long for Kabir to forward an email with another file attachment, though this time it was just a single image. The email body read: We double-and triple-checked everything. Telescope fully operational. No glitches or bugs. RA: 18h 53m 1.89s DEC: -20° 14' 28.9"

Gordan opened the email and double-clicked the image, which filled his monitor once more. Sam gasped while Gordan's face sank into his hands.

The image was completely black.

1.3

A soft breeze caressed the rolling terrain that surrounded the Southern African Astronomical Observatory, which sat atop the tallest collection of hills. The glow of the last quarter moon brought out the occasional howls of local jackals and hyenas, most of which learned to stay away from the research facility. SAAO was one of the most esteemed astronomical facilities on the planet, with the largest single-aperture spherical telescope in the world, nicknamed "Cheetah's Eye." It sat between two hills, with thick support beams sitting on even thicker concrete foundations for all the spots that weren't carved into the hillsides. Small telescopes comprised the older parts of the facility, aimed at various parts of the sky. Some of them worked in tandem while others coordinated with observatories in other parts of the world.

On the highest hill sat the Southern African Large Telescope—or SALT, as the media and the general population called it—a tall cylindrical building with a movable geodesic dome at the top. The array of mirrors within the dome stared into the night sky, fixated on the large swath of space that contained the outer planets of the solar system. Among the fifteen telescopes, SALT was the largest. Though it was just one of several telescopes, most of those that talked about SAAO frequently referred to SALT instead—it rolled off the tongue better than any other acronyms.

Just to the west of all the telescopes and Cheetah's Eye were the batch of boxy administrative buildings and a visitor's center which had a planetarium attached to it in the rear. It was the only building in the bunch that had a circular shape. However, it was one of two buildings with a domed roof.

The second building was the SAAO Administration Center. It had a tinted all-glass geodesic roof, the focal point for all the data collected across the observatories and Cheetah's Eye. It was here, on the top floor of the five-storied building, where Muzikayise Khulu, CEO of Khulu Global, called his home away from home.

Muzikayise—known by the world at large and by most of his peers as Muzie—stood by the window that spanned the length of his bedroom and arched, triangle by triangle, high above him. Muzikayise was, by all accounts, a dominating figure. In a corporate gala with thousands of donors and stakeholders, he would be heads taller than everyone around him. Combined with his height were his wide shoulders and athletic physique, qualities that were highlighted when he wore one of his trademark dark blue plaid suits during interviews. He maintained a short goatee and light mustache which were below a wide nose and deep-brown eyes that seemed to always have an interrogative look to them. The moonlight and the stars faintly glistened upon his smooth, hairless head.

He wasn't supposed to be overlooking the rows of telescopes in the distance. A sixteen billion dollar contract with Delta Air Lines sat unsigned on his desk back in Cape Town. The high priority message he received on his secure Blackberry phone, however, changed his plans. To the shock of the airline world, he canceled the meeting where many expected to witness the usurping of Airbus as one of the core providers of narrow- and wide-body aircraft for Delta. *That signature will have to wait,* he thought earlier as he got into his personal helicopter on the roof of Khulu Business Center.

The message would be considered unbelievable to most, but the images he also received from one of SALT's sister telescopes in Japan sent a chill down his spine. The feeling reminded him of the decision he made decades ago to reinvest his family's fortune without their support.

Muzikayise heard the minute sounds to his bedroom door opening, looking over his shoulder in response. Ami Kone, his personal assistant, walked over to his large, L-shaped desk. Her form-fitting business attire which accentuated her dark skin was a stark contrast to his off-white linen pants and matching button-down shirt.

She slid a series of full-color images in a manila folder to the head of the desk. It contained various astronomical and radiological statistics that complemented the pictures. The images comprised Neptune being altered by the object along with images of the same object behind Pluto. "Here's everything you've asked for, Muzie."

"That includes the latest findings from Gekko Observatory?" He asked, looking back out the window with his arms crossed.

"Yes, sir—looks like you have your triple-confirmation."

"Thank you," he said with a matter-of-fact tone. Three different telescopes in three parts of the world confirming the same thing: the impossible. He released the tension he felt in his shoulders. "Any response from the Delta CEO?"

"He was surprised at your sudden disappearance, but he agreed to postpone the contract signing until next week."

"He'll live." Muzikayise took the few steps between the windows and his desk and took a seat, bringing his fingers over the images as he did so. A lot of the scientific notations and stats he didn't fully understand, but he didn't have to. The object partially shrouded in Neptunian atmosphere and Pluto missing was all he needed to have his mind run through a variety of Earthbound scenarios.

Ami, still standing at the foot of his desk, leaned forward to take a glance at the images, the slight motion of which caught Muzikayise's attention. Despite the buttoned suit jacket Ami wore, there was a hint of cleavage for his eyes to fall on. His expression unchanged, he leaned back in his heavy, walnut desk chair and looked at her, his hands crossed over his stomach. "Do you know what we are looking at?"

"I know what *you* were just looking at."

A sultry one, she is. He chose to not respond to her quip. "This could be the greatest threat in the history of all civilization."

Muzikayise stood up and paced, but with immense focus, ignoring Ami and talking to himself. "Throughout history, there have always been individuals—philosophers, musicians, politicians—that debated about the requirements needed to bring humanity together in solidarity. A reason for everyone, regardless of political affiliation, religious doctrine, race, economic background, to band together in a singular cause." The Radcliffe Telescope opened and aligned with the remaining active telescopes, the hum of its movements passed through the wall-and-ceiling windows, filling the room. It was finally back on-line. He looked up towards the stars that filled the sky, too numerous to count. "Humanity has shown itself to be incredibly resilient, especially when threatened. A possible existential threat like this can bring untold benefits to the world if we can resolve the problem."

Ami walked around to the front of the desk and propped herself against it. "You mean if Khulu Global can resolve the problem."

Muzikayise chuckled. He turned toward Ami, his stolid expression replaced with some levity. "Precisely."

Ami smiled back at him though it didn't hide the concern he felt emanating from her. "What's on your mind?"

She pushed off the desk and moved closer to Muzikayise. "Well, wouldn't it make sense for you to want to work with as many organizations and governments as possible? Anything that could threaten humanity would require, I imagine, a lot of resources and manpower."

He grunted in agreement. "We don't know enough about this... object... to make any lasting decisions," he said as he turned his gaze back to the outdoors. "However, I want to start monitoring all communications between all observatories, radio telescopes, and astronomical organizations that receive funding from the Unity Foundation."

"I'll have our boys in Mountain View get on that at once," Ami said. She slid her smartphone out of her back pocket, punched in her password, and started tapping and swiping in his now growing list of tasks.

"Now, two planets being destroyed won't be missed by any government with a half-decent space program. That said, it seems that America's SETI program was the first to acknowledge the signal and are currently the de facto leader in global coordination around the signal and this object."

"I can request a conference call with their director so you can speak with them about cooperation."

"Good," Muzikayise said. "Put me in touch with the US government as well since they will almost certainly intervene in SETI's operations once news of this UFO reaches the president."

"Of course."

"Kindly inform them that Khulu Global is more than willing to loan our west coast launch pads to their greater cause."

Ami darted her eyes at Muzikayise. "For a price."

"Now, now, we don't need to bring up money at a time like this," he said as he turned toward Ami. "I'm sure there'll be plenty of time to discuss blank checks once they understand the magnitude of what's happening out there."

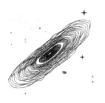

1.4

The parking lot that ran around two sides of the SETI Institute was vacant on most days by 7pm. Many researchers spent as much time traveling for their work as they would at a desk as they fulfilled the goals they've set for their assigned projects. Today, however, more than half of the lot was littered with vehicles. As word of the signal—and the object the size of Neptune—spread, anyone that lived within two hundred miles dropped what they were doing and made the trip to Mountain View to help the growing number of scientists that were deciphering the signal and the data it contained.

Amid the bustle of scientists moving and bumping into each other was a line of people that started near the front door of the office and along two of the walls. At the front of the line was a table which offered various ordered foods: mostly pizza and Chinese, and a lot of soda and coffee. Nobody wanted to leave—some were in a continued state of excitement and awe at the situation, while others didn't want to miss any new developments that may occur. Across the board, though, was a strong undercurrent of uncertainty and fear.

Despite her decades of experience, even Jennifer wasn't immune to the feelings that some of her colleagues expressed in murmurs to each other, hoping nobody heard their quiet conversations. She kept those feelings as far below the surface as she could manage though she understood where they were coming from. It's not every day that an alien object appears in your solar system and destroys two of your planetary neighbors.

Vern had, on its top two monitors, a livestream of the object as the front half of it blended with Neptune's multi-layered atmosphere. Despite Jennifer making the rounds to ensure other radio telescopes and observatories were refocusing their equipment to detect, track, and watch the object, she always kept an eye on the screens. And to a lesser extent, Sam; she all but relocated her belongings to the desk in front of Vern, staking a claim to continue her signal spectrum analysis work. She also hadn't peeled herself away from Vern for over three hours. Again, Jennifer couldn't blame her.

As Jennifer walked closer to Vern and Sam—part of her umpteenth lap around the office—Sam spun her desk chair around. She saw Jennifer despite the crowd that formed a half-ring around Vern, watching the monitors. "It almost looks like it is consuming the planet," Sam said as she pulled one earbud out of her ear and used her arms to make a small path for Jennifer so she could join her at her makeshift desk.

"It appears that way," Jennifer said, disbelieving, as Sam got up to meet almost eye-to-eye with her.

"I think there's some merit to the possibility," Sam countered as she pointed at an open window on the bottom-left monitor. "Look at the planetary atmospheric data coming in from SALT and its sister observatories. The high-res images of the deep-cloud spiraling away from Neptune, while the high-altitude clouds wrap themselves around this object. In addition, there are significant temperature increases throughout the planet, combined with a massive spike in electrical activity as this object completely throws off the magnetosphere. But most importantly, all the new wind patterns suggest that the planet's atmosphere, as a whole, is not just moving toward the object, but *into* the object."

Jennifer looked skeptical. "But that doesn't make any sense. Why would a sentient species build a ship that would destroy a planet in this manner? It seems... so inefficient."

Sam couldn't help but smile at that. "Yeah, there are so many other ways an interstellar civilization could leverage a gas giant, depending on their technological abilities. They could harvest the rings for water and helium-3 compounds, use the strong winds in the atmospheric bands to generate a near-unlimited source of power, siphon elements from the inner atmosphere or even the mantle for manufacturing—"

"Yes, yes, I get all of that. Knowing this, why destroy a planet outright if it's not meant to be a sign of aggression?"

Sam shrugged. "Maybe the ship has a way of harvesting all the elements that comprise a planet?"

"Unfortunately, I think trying to figure out the kind of logic behind the origins of an object like this should be tabled for another day," Jennifer said with a sigh. There were way too many questions that she, Sam, and numerous others at SETI wanted to figure out about the object itself. *Once we have full access to Hubble and the many NASA-owned satellites, we can explore this even further,* she thought.

"What we can do," Jennifer continued, "is decipher this radio signal."

"Ahh, well that's one area that Nic and I have made lots of progress," Sam said as she walked towards his desk, indicating to Jennifer to join her. Nic had his head buried in a sea of papers covered in hand-written mathematical equations, many of which had large ovals around the answers. Sam gripped the side of his cubicle wall and hopped. "Nic, tell the Doc what you shared with me a couple of minutes ago!"

Nic almost fell out of his chair in surprise. "Sam, geez! How about less jump scares and more proper greetings?"

"I think you'd be less edgy if you haven't been consuming nothing but coffee all day." Sam pointed at the line of empty styrofoam cups in one corner of his desk.

His breathing slowed as he realized Jennifer was with her. "Yes, I'll be sure to grab some of that cold pizza soon."

"What do you have for me?" Jennifer asked Nic.

He adjusted his glasses and picked up one of the more recent sheets of math-filled paper. "A couple of things, in fact! First, the signal seems to be as strong as it is because it isn't pointed directly at Earth. In fact, it's broadcasting omni-directionally from the source. Second, despite the strength and high frequency of the signal, whatever is stored within it is pretty simplistic."

"Have you determined if there is an embedded message or data?" Jennifer asked.

Nic stopped himself from giving a response and instead turned to his computer.

"If I take my equations and apply them to our harmonics analysis program... I get this." After a short period of him punching his numbers into the computer, the "Results" panel displayed an image that had two concentric circles on opposite ends of the tall image. The top circle and its concentric circles were thick at the start, but became thinner as they reached the center of the image. The bottom circle was whole, but the concentric circles it made were gray except for a small section above the circle which was solid black, and spread out as it met the thinning concentric circles that started from the top, giving the visual of a narrow cone.

"Concentric circles," Jennifer said as she examined the image.

"Yes, two sets of them," Nic pointed to the top of the image. "One has circles emanating from the top, and the other circle seems to be making a cone-like structure."

"What do you think it is?" Jennifer asked as Nic submitted the image for printing. About as fast as he sent the command, the large office printer warmed up the ink in preparation for ten printouts.

"Could be a structure of some kind," Nic suggested. "Maybe a stylistic representation of the tower the signal is originating on the object."

"I dunno," said Gordan, who joined them after scooping the ten copies of the image from the printer. "But then why have two sets of concentric circles?"

"Maybe they prefer the use of circles as the backdrop for generating imagery," Nic said, outlining the circles on the image with his finger.

Jennifer had other, more Earthly theories. "Perhaps this image was generated simply based on your equations? Maybe this isn't how it's supposed to look."

"No way, doctor," Nic said to Jennifer, affronted. "I crunched the numbers twice from scratch already and passed them through analysis —my numbers are correct."

"Nobody is accusing anyone of wrongdoing," Gordan jumped in as he saw Nic's crestfallen face. "We're all in this together. That said, it couldn't hurt to get a few other people to crosscheck your numbers, just to be sure."

"You know, maybe we're thinking about this image the wrong way," Sam said after she stared intensely at the printed image.

"Care to share your two cents?" Gordan gestured to the space that was open in the hallway.

"I'm always on a podium to share my thoughts—I thought you knew that already," Sam quipped with a smile. "I think we're giving this picture more credit than its due. Think about it: If you were a highly advanced alien civilization and wanted to make first contact, how would you do it? If they wanted to make deliberate contact, they would likely focus a radio transmission directly toward Earth. Maybe use snapshots of old Olympic footage or some random sitcom they snagged from our broadcasting to the stars over the decades. Maybe they would've had enough time to decipher our language and actually translate their language into ours."

Sam paused for a moment, letting those around her mull her words. Jennifer knew she was on to something and didn't want to break her train of thought, though that was highly unlikely given her expression.

Nic, however, also understood and wanted to piggy-back on where she was going with this. "But if the signal is omnidirectional, that means they never intended for the signal to be just for us."

"Exactly!" Sam snapped her fingers. "Maybe this signal is less of a 'Hello, Earthlings,' and more of a general beacon. They aren't here for us, but they are letting any sentient civilization in their vicinity know that *they* are here."

"Where does this embedded image come in?" Gordan asked, his face almost allowing itself to say "I'm impressed".

"Well, if I only cared about broadcasting my presence, I would do away with 'little details' like primers and simple mathematical constructs."

Jennifer injected herself into the conversation. "But establishing a foundation for language, even if mathematical, would pave the way for additional forms of dialogue. You cannot discount the importance of primers in a first contact situation even if the extraterrestrial was just broadcasting themselves."

Sam glanced at the ceiling as she massaged her chin in thought. A smile spread across her face as she turned to Jennifer. "Okay... Better: They have the means to share details like a mathematical primer, but they want to know that someone else is aware of their presence before attempting to even start talking about one plus one. Therefore..." Sam took her printout to her desk and grabbed a marker. Uncapping it, she pressed it against the image and filled in the conical circles from the bottom up, followed by crafting an arrow pointing upwards toward the top circle. She then wrote "Earth" next to the bottom circle and "Object" next to the top circle. "... They want us to send a signal back to them."

Jennifer looked at her copy of the image in her hand. The circles radiating outward from two opposite points, with the top appearing to reflect an omnidirectional broadcast. The design of having the circle with the conical emphasis at the bottom and not the top looked more like a response as opposed to the passive nature of Earth's historical broadcasting into the void. Sam's words resonated in her mind, and as they did, what she described made more and more sense.

"Whoa, hold on now," Gordan raised a hand in protest. "I'm as much for learning more about this thing's intentions as the next person here, but sending a response is something we just cannot do, at least not yet."

"I must agree," said Brian, whose ears perked up at the mere mention of the idea of us contacting them. He marched from his office to the group, almost pushing others out of his way. Their discussion was loud enough to let him eavesdrop, but he had to step in when he realized where the conversation was going. And he knew Sam could make quite the impression on those around her when she was as enthusiastic as she was right now. "I know I've said this already, but we have protocols to follow, even for the situation where those making contact with us want us to respond."

Jennifer darted her eyes at Brian, which narrowed. She tired of him much faster than normal, but she didn't always sit alongside him on back-to-back conference calls. Even without that it had been an exciting, if not tense, day and everyone was running on fumes. "Nobody is saying we have to respond, nor is that the only interpretation of the image." She noticed beads of sweat that rolled off his head. *Someone get him a goddamned towel.*

"Did you see the image that was embedded in the signal?" Nic asked Brian.

"Of course I did," Brian responded. "And I think it's worth getting a few more eyes on this before we draw any rash conclusions."

"Which is something we would be doing anyway, as part of working with NASA," Jennifer said. She hoped that her cutting into Brian's position on the matter—and acknowledging it—would satisfy his need for control over this event that would, without question, grow beyond SETI's grasp.

Sam pursed her mouth into a smirk. "I'm sorry, Dr. Ethans, I didn't know you were providing constructive dialogue to our conversation." *And there it is.*

Some people snickered at her comment though Brian didn't acknowledge them. "I am here to ensure we all are successful in SETI's mission—the last thing we need are people who operate solely on their gut and ignores policy!"

Gordan stepped in-between Sam and Brian. "Okay, guys, okay. I think we all need some fresh air. We're all on the same team."

The sudden silence in the office allowed Brian's ringing desk phone to be very audible. He looked over to Jennifer after pressing his hand over his head, some beaded sweat landing on the floor. "That's likely the Central Bureau for Astronomical Telegrams. Jennifer, keep her in line."

A flash of light on Vern's top video monitors grabbed everyone's attention. Then a second flash of light. The ringing phone being ignored, everyone walked back over to Vern to witness the aftermath of two Neptunian moons impacting the object. At the same time, Neptune glowed a vicious red as its atmosphere stretched grossly around the object.

"What just happened?" Brian asked as he pointed to the screen that focused on where the bright flashes of light occurred.

"If I didn't know any better, I'd say some of Neptune's moons just slammed into the object," Gordan said.

"This ship just took two direct impacts from planetary satellites? And is still in one piece?" Brian sounded incredulous.

"Proteus and Galatea, from the looks of it," Nic said as he pushed his glasses against his head and sniffed. He ran quick estimates surrounding the potential explosive force released by their impacts.

"That last big flash must've been Proteus, the second largest moon. Based on the moon size and potential angle it came in, that impact likely had an explosive force of about 2.32 trillion megatons. Can we get rollback data on Proteus, Sam?"

She already pulled up the last available metrics which was an hour old. "Already ahead of you, Nic! And wow, has nobody been looking at these numbers?"

Nic stared at the revised orbital characteristics of Proteus, dumbfounded. "Incredible... it had an orbital—well, impact—speed of over twenty-two kilometers a second. Galatea at twelve kilometers a second. Both of those moons at impact, individually, made the Chicxulub impactor look like a small pebble in the ocean by comparison." He released an involuntary laugh; the continuous observation of the power of these impacts—and the clear lack of effect they had on the object—were both fascinating and terrifying.

"Those were nothing," Sam said as she sat back in her seat and brought up the latest batch of numbers aggregated from SALT and Cheetah's Eye. "Triton's orbital path adjusted by more than seventy degrees, is less than thirty thousand kilometers from the object... and picked up a shit-ton of momentum, too." She turned to those behind her. "Impact with the object in two hours fourteen minutes."

1.5

The warm light of several sodium-vapor bulbs illuminated the SETI parking lot, their yellow glow bouncing off the handful of cars that remained after most of the scientists left well after sunset. Not by choice, given the circumstances. Brian and Jennifer didn't want everyone to leave, but a "larger than skeleton" crew was to stay behind, monitor the object, and maintain active communications with all other participating observatories. And there were over twenty that were not only communicating with SETI but between each other as well, checking and cross-checking the data their dishes and telescopes had heard and seen. Despite the gross disparity in fiber connectivity between the many locations, a combination of video chats, email correspondence, instant messaging and phone calls ensured that whatever new information—mathematical or visual—was shared and analyzed.

Through all of this, the dozens of professors, astronomers, and scientists that took the lead at their respective observatories recognized Sam and Jennifer's role in being the discoverers of the signal—and by extension the object. Because of this, everything was being coordinated through the SETI Institute, making the two of them the de facto leaders. This wasn't lost on Brian, who wasn't one for sidelining what he considered not official policy. He viewed the discovery as a finding made by SETI, the organization—but he knew the outcry that could emerge from pushing the "discoverer" out of the way for the sake of organizational efficiency, so he kept himself quiet.

The two discoverers remained, their cars still parked in front, across from Nic's car which now had a ticket stuffed under its windshield wiper for parking across two parking spots much earlier.

In front of Vern lay Sam, and in front of her was not just her laptop but a stack of empty cups that once held coffee. Not that all the coffee in the world would overcome her biology and the need for rest, however. It had been almost twenty-four hours since she had even a proper nap, let alone actual sleep. Despite all she did to keep herself focused on the monitors, her eyes drifting over a single batch of fresh data from Arecibo Observatory was enough to slump into her folded arms on the desk in front of her in exhaustion. "Just one more download...," she muttered as she closed her eyes.

Jennifer could hear Sam's muffled snore from the conference room which elicited a smile from her. Though there were still seven people in the office to burn the midnight oil—six more than usual—she relied more on Sam's intuition and focus when dealing with large volumes of raw data. She blinked and looked at the time in the corner of her laptop screen. Almost one in the morning. A deep breath escaped her as she reviewed all the collected data on the object which a handful of half-drunken astronomers from the Green Bank Observatory in Virginia dubbed 'The Creature'.

"Are you serious?" Jennifer asked Gus Polyak, Senior Astronomer at Green Bank, during an ongoing video call.

"Think about it for a moment," Gus began, his face beet red from the two glasses of wine he downed in response to the multiple confirmations of an extraterrestrial signal. "The object not only destroyed Pluto, but didn't leave a trace of the planet or its moons. It then proceeds to consume Neptune and most of its mass. And if—"

He brought his hand over his mouth as his cheeks puffed out, a guttural sound suppressed, and his eyes clenched shut. A few seconds passed before he composed himself. "Apologies, it's been a while since I've imbibed."

"It's okay," Jennifer smiled as she suppressed laughter. "Please go on with your reasoning."

That he did, an almost-empty glass of wine still in his hand. "Evidence suggests that this object has some form of telescopic opening in its front. Did you look at images 43-a through 43-d? The earliest image depicted the object with a solid, dome-like front. At least it looked like a dome. The next image? There's an opening and the dome is gone!

One moment there's a dome, the next it's gone. Therefore, it opened up shortly after arriving a few hundred thousand kilometers from Neptune—like a mouth!"

A deliberate pause filled the air between the two of them before Jennifer leaned back into her chair. "I think we need a bit more evidence before we anthropomorphize this object."

"But you believe what I'm saying?"

"No, not in the slightest." Thoughts of her hardline parents dashed through her mind after saying that. *No, I won't be like them.* "But I cannot rule out the possibility. Plus, I don't think giving it a name so ominous as 'The Creature' would play well with the public when we cross that bridge."

"Well..." Gus began before slapping his hand over his mouth and slipping out of his chair and off-screen, onto the floor.

"I think that's my cue to drop off for now," Jennifer said to a spinning chair on her monitor. "Watch out for that alcohol content next time, Gus! We'll pick things up in the morning."

o ꙅ ᑯ

The data that came in regarding the object became more accurate once the remnants of Neptune were no longer visible. However, having Neptune initially adjacent to it made the running of some numbers viable. Jennifer still couldn't believe the values they were all working with just in terms of scale alone. The object was approximately seventy-seven thousand kilometers long from front to back when the frontal dome was closed—sixty-four percent longer than Neptune's diameter and six times larger than Earth. So far there wasn't a consensus on the mass of the object, but they had the velocities of the moons that collided with it and the new orbital escape velocities of the remaining moons that relied on Neptune for their distant orbits. Based on those values, the object had a mass the equivalence of fifteen to twenty Earths, bringing it on par with the mass of the gas giants in the solar system. Finally, based on the time it took for the object to close the gap from its initial position to entering Neptune's atmosphere, the object was moving at about 8.3 kilometers per second.

Beyond those metrics it was all speculation and there was a lot to speculate about. The biggest two questions: how should they handle the deciphered message? What exactly is the object?

She looked at the clock again before she heard an alert coming from Vern. An advisory window—the object started to realign itself—greeted Jennifer as she rounded the corner from the conference room and toward the computer station. Though Sam was snoring away, she wasn't on top of the keyboard, so Jennifer pulled the keyboard and mouse away to access the alert and get more details.

Oh, there were two alerts back-to-back, she thought as she discovered a second alert behind the first—this one related to gamma ray bursts. Two gamma-ray observatories that agreed to sync their data collection efforts with SETI detected a large gamma ray burst that originated from the object.

"Nareen, can you confirm the updated position of the object?"

"Absolutely," Nareen responded from her desk with a light Scottish-American accent, pulling up the same alerts that Vern displayed and dug into them. Nareen Sconce was one of the Senior Astrobiologists who'd been running herself ragged since the object appeared where Neptune used to be. She was known for having quarterly hair color changes—it was currently a fiery red that rested just above her shoulders, ending in curls. Even her manicured eyebrows got a similar treatment. "It appears our UFO shifted point-seven-six seconds—it's changing course. It also lit up its surrounding space with over 700keV gamma rays."

Jennifer turned toward Nareen, her eyes widened with surprise. "I'm sorry, did you say what I think you said?"

"Yes, ma'am—712keV gamma rays, to be precise."

"Do you know what that means?"

"I don't want to make assumptions, ma'am, but that may be a pretty solid candidate for the utilization of antimatter as a form of propulsion."

Sam fluttered awake at the activity next to her by Vern. "Did I just hear someone throw out the word 'antimatter' just now?"

"Oh good, you're back from your power nap." Jennifer pointed Sam to the monitor in front of her, rows of data readings from Nareen waiting for a double-confirmation. "Let's make sure these numbers are accurate before I decide to have a heart attack."

It didn't take long for Sam to jerk back from the desk at the sight of the gamma ray burst. "This is..."

"Yes, I know," Jennifer said, thinking about the sheer amount of energy required to emit such powerful gamma ray bursts, let alone what kind of technology was needed to harness such energy to begin with.

"I have new coordinates for the object... still shifting... still shifting," Sam was already in her zone. "It's slowing its rate of adjustment... approaching a full fifty-three degree change in heading."

Nareen knitted her brows at her monitor, which had, among the many windows open, a video feed of the object. It looked odd, as if the object was reflected in a spherical mirror. "Guys, something weird is happening."

Both Jennifer and Sam looked at the live feed of the object—still blurry despite multiple observatory sources being spliced together by Vern to increase the resolution. However, the object wasn't the champagne glass shape they've gotten used to—it curved slowly around and into itself. In all the years Jennifer's spent analyzing various spacial anomalies, she's seen nothing like this.

What they were witnessing hit Sam like a ton of bricks. "It's not changing shape... it's light distortion, though it looks like it's in a bubble of some sort." She looked over to Nareen, who was standing in front of her desk a few seats down, then at Jennifer. "I think the object might be speeding up. I mean *really* speeding up."

"How fast must an object move in order to distort itself like that?" Nareen asked. The object now seemed to be compressed into an oval shape before it moved outside of their view.

"It's gone," said Jennifer, her mind rapidly processing what she just witnessed. They'd run simulations of what light distortion could look like—the work usually based around observing black holes—but seeing it occur live was about as heart-stopping as everything else that they'd all witnessed over the last twenty-four hours.

"I don't know," Sam said to Nareen, but still focused on the monitors. "But this does add value to the possibility that this object traveled between Pluto and Neptune at ninety percent the speed of light."

"Where is it going?" Jennifer motioned to Sam. "Talk to me."

"Okay, working out the numbers now," Sam said, her fingers blurred across the keyboard as she ran the numbers against the position of nearby stars. There weren't too many stars in the same plane as the object, based on its movement before it moved off-screen. She asked herself aloud, "If this was moving towards Pluto—us—at sub-light speeds, we should have detected it years ago, especially considering how big it is."

Jennifer thought about that for a moment. "Maybe. Something that large moving in our direction would've been heavily blueshifted —not just a blueshift on the light spectrum, but a gravitational blueshift, too. All of that we should've picked up—at minimum, NASA's satellites would've seen this coming years ago."

"Exactly!" Sam stopped typing and turned to Jennifer. "So why can we track it now?" A pause as Sam brought a finger to her lips as if to silence herself. "What if this ship travels at superluminal speeds between stars—or maybe use wormhole technology for instantaneous jumps between stars?"

Jennifer would've cut Sam off at this point, but given everything they've witnessed already she let Sam continue. Unlike previous conversations that leaned toward the fantastical, she gave Sam her full attention.

With Jennifer's unspoken approval, Sam continued. "If this was the case, then the ship using sub-light traveling would indicate one thing: It's traveling locally. Fifty-three degree change in heading from its previous course that brought it literally through Neptune. And before that, it arrived at Pluto." She loaded satellite tracking software and entered the origin spatial coordinates of the object, its speed and heading starting from Neptune, and plotted out possible destinations. The software generated results just seconds after she submitted her data for analysis. A new window popped up with a map of the outer planets of the solar system. Each of the gas giants were symbolized as solid circles connected to thin rings representing their orbits around the sun.

A small, red dot that pulsed a red circle appeared on top of Neptune. It had several curved gray lines burst out of it which reminded Sam of several Hohmann transfer orbit proposals. In most cases, astronomical coordinates and delta-v budgets were provided at various points on the lines—represented as a small, clickable gray circle which hid verbose details. Sam grunted at the displayed data—all the numbers provided assumed that this was for a man-made satellite like Voyager or New Horizon.

"Let's update the thruster velocity to be the object's," Sam said. She swapped the default values with the object's speed which, when translated to kilometers per hour, went beyond the field size on the screen. Only zeros were visible once Sam finished her entry. Without hesitation, she submitted the new satellite velocity. Jennifer and Nareen, now behind Sam, watched as all the previous vectors deleted themselves, but replaced with an alert window that wanted to confirm the velocity entered by Sam. She laughed at the warning and bypassed it which allowed the software to continue plotting the data to its final, updated result. In place of the series of curved lines coming out of Neptune was a single straight line with a single gray circle for a delta-v adjustment. It was accompanied by a triangular warning icon. At the line's destination was another warning icon that had "FAILURE—COLLISION" in bold next to it.

The line terminated at Uranus.

Sam sunk her fingers into her disheveled bun and pulled it out in frustration, letting her hair fall just beyond the back of her chair as her head flung back. "You gotta be fucking kidding me!"

"Sam, really?" Jennifer chided her. Some habits from her much younger, conservative family upbringing seemed to always find the most inopportune time to come out.

"Are you not freaking out about this right now?" Sam threw her hands toward the monitor with the extrapolated trajectory of the object. The estimated journey time clocked at two hours forty-eight minutes.

Jennifer sighed as she slumped deeper into her chair before she sat back up and rubbed her eyes.

"Sorry about that—old habits die hard, especially when you're tired. You already double-checked your numbers?"

"I always do," Sam said with a frown. "However, I did email them to Kabir for verification since he's most likely fully refreshed by now." One of the perks for having connections in timezones far removed from your own: There will always be someone wide awake and ready to corroborate work. "I imagine he and his team are in the process of confirming and then getting sick from the implications."

Despite the burst of energy from Sam, a long yawn escaped from her which, like a chain reaction, made Jennifer and Nareen yawn afterwards. Jennifer found her eyes heavy and her vision just becoming hazy around the edges. Her whole body was sending signals of its own for a few hours now, signals that she resigned herself towards.

"I can't believe I'm going to say this, but we have to get some actual sleep," Jennifer said as she stretched her arms into the air.

Nareen agreed. "You guys won't miss anything—I'm not going anywhere. I'll make sure Nic wakes up shortly so he can take the lead on monitoring the object."

Sam was about to raise a finger in defiance, but her heavy eyelids betrayed her. Jennifer knew that regardless of the event—even as one as large as first contact—you can't review, parse, and derive results from all the new data that would inevitably come from the object's arrival at Uranus when you're a slow blink away from collapsing into an involuntary slumber on your desk.

"Thank you, Nareen. Take care of anything that Vern spits out until the morning crew comes in. Keep active communications with Kabir and get his confirmation on Sam's trajectory numbers for the object." Jennifer thought through her next words for Nareen—words she knew Brian would appreciate. "Lastly, I wouldn't be surprised if the press gets wind of what's happening as early as tomorrow. There is no way anyone on Earth can cover up two planets missing, possibly three if Sam's prediction comes to pass. If anyone that isn't from astronomical or government circles call you or anyone here..." She didn't want to give the order, but she knew how people could react to the truth. "... Redirect them to Brian's voicemail."

Jennifer scooped her army green jacket from the back of her chair.

"We'll reconvene first thing in the morning. Sam, I've seen you drive when you're exhausted, so I'll take you home."

"I just woke up, doc—I can get more work done." She talked through one large yawn, her body slouched low enough in her chair to press her head against the back of it, treating it like a head rest.

Jennifer tapped Sam on shoulder, which elicited a groan from Sam. "You're as awake as a black dwarf star. Let's go."

○ ◎ ○

It was a straight shot to Milpitas, and Sam didn't live too far away from Jennifer. Once the car started towards the highway, Sam's body slid into a comfortable position in the front passenger seat. Between her head nestled into the headrest and her rhythmic snores showed just how easy it was for her to fall asleep. Jennifer wanted to sleep, too, and was looking forward to throwing herself onto her bed after taking a quick shower. At the same time, there was so much going on. Many expected that the first sign of extraterrestrial intelligence would've been in the form of a signal similar to what SETI had, in fact, detected this time yesterday. What the signal would signify would be anyone's guess, though the more popular positions astronomers took revolved around one core idea: That any signal received would be from a civilization that didn't mean any harm to us. And why would they want to harm us? Anyone with the technology for transmitting a coherent message from dozens, if not hundreds, of light years away directly to Earth knew about our existence as a species. They would know how harmless we would be to any species that was capable of sending the very signal we would receive.

The signal they received contained what appeared to be a simple message. In most scenarios, this would be cause for celebration. However, the signal originated from an object—a ship, a "creature"—that was not only in our local space but was responsible for wiping out Pluto and Neptune. And now Uranus looked to be in its sights, too!

Jennifer took a deep breath as she let her thoughts run through the course of the day, and what the very near future looked like for her, Sam, and SETI. A snort from Sam broke Jennifer's focus on the many questions whirring through her mind, most without answers, and some that only had unfavorable possibilities. She looked over at Sam, whose head tilted toward the window, eyes closed, her hands loosely gripping her brown, patch-covered messenger bag. They worked together at SETI for a little over five years. Sam was transferred to Jennifer's team in the last year after her previous boss left SETI for a computer engineering gig at NASA. Despite the ten-year age difference, she enjoyed watching Sam grow and develop. She had a foul mouth, which normally wouldn't be an issue, but Sam's uninhibited nature when it came to speaking her mind was the only reason Jennifer could think of as to why Brian hadn't promoted her by now. Then again, Brian wasn't as flexible as she if she wore his shoes. Given the fact that Sam was now associated with the signal and the object, it was now inevitable. She would likely receive a position—at SETI or elsewhere—that would provide her the flexibility and responsibility she should have today.

In a way, Jennifer saw a bit of herself in Sam, which was why she liked being around her. A youth that was a decade younger and still had the fire that burned bright—a nice counter to Jennifer's temperament. They played off each other's skills, knowledge, and mannerisms, all of which struck a surprising balance. This expressed itself in their office banter and how they, as a team, got their work done. She even considered them to be friends, though outside of the rare extracurricular job-hosted event, they hadn't hung out. In fact, they hadn't spent much time together in a way that could result in a lasting relationship beyond SETI.

These thoughts, for a time, replaced all the uncertainty that resulted from the signal's discovery and everything related to that. A smile spread across Jennifer's face as she brought her car to a stop in front of a single-story house. It was partially lit by the street light on the sidewalk. The home mirrored that of those around it. A single, small attached garage was integrated into the home, with a hipped asphalt shingle roof that had small plumbing vents and a steel chimney pointing to the sky. Two wide windows and a narrow door filled most of the front wall of the house.

Once Jennifer parked the car, she looked over to Sam and nudged her in the shoulder which only solicited a groan from Sam. "Hey, time for you to get some proper Z's," Jennifer said as she poked Sam again on the shoulder.

Sam made a few grunts before she opened her eyes and slid upright. "I don't know if I'm gonna get anything more than a power nap or two. Too much to think about."

"I agree," said Jennifer as she unlocked all the doors. "All the more reason why we both need rest. Now get out so I can get home and sleep, too."

As Sam opened the door and slid her legs over to the sidewalk, she paused and glanced back at Jennifer. When her eyes met Jennifer's they suddenly dropped to her lap. "Would you like to come in? Maybe share a quick coffee over talks of ET?"

Jennifer blinked as she noticed Sam's slight smile on the corner of her face. Averting her eyes, she looked ahead as her hands tightened around the steering wheel. "I'll see you in the morning."

Sam scooted off the seat and stumbled onto the sidewalk as if she hadn't used her legs in years. "Good night, doc."

"Good night," Jennifer said as she sat back and watched Sam walk to the front door of her home, her grip relaxing.

Before Sam shuffled through her bag for her keys, she looked back toward Jennifer's car and waved. "Don't forget to pick me up, or my next Uber is on you!"

By the time Sam opened the front door and walked into her house, Jennifer drove out of her parking spot and back onto the boulevard. Her final destination: an unkempt bed with a really comfortable mattress topper.

1.6

Sleep came easily when Jennifer got home. Staying asleep proved to be a bigger challenge as thoughts of the object permeated her dreams and twisted them into her worst fears.

From the front of her house, Jennifer found herself watching a bright white dot in the daylight opposite the sun. The surrounding commotion grew as the distant speck did: neighbors rushed to load cars and pickup trucks with their belongings, children wept in terror, arguments breaking out after vehicles collided. Overhead, news helicopters hovered as avenues clogged with paralyzing traffic. This was all background noise for Jennifer, transfixed by a dot grown larger than the sun.

A groan emanated from the object, a low-pitched growl that made concrete vibrate, windows shudder, and fellow suburbanites screech in pain. Jennifer felt her muscles involuntarily loosen as if the alien sound was encouraging her to slump to the ground and give up. A chorus of cries rose as neighbors succumbed to the urge, and nobody, save for Jennifer, remained standing. From the center of the now-massive object, an orifice irised open, exposing its eternal black interior to the Earth. The sky-encompassing brightness that set the object apart in the heavens was replaced with total darkness, a black circular counterpoint in space.

An unnatural wind began to blow around Jennifer as she faced the object, legs planted firmly and arms outstretched, tears rolling down her face. A gust of ozone-scented air lifted her from the ground. The dark circle filled the eastern sky, and news helicopters, distant planes, and clouds sloughed into the void. A crescendoing roar seized Jennifer's attention, and she realized with horror it was the sound of the Earth itself opening beyond the horizon. As the still-growing object finally eclipsed the sun, the only light left was cast by a wall of fire. It stretched across the horizon to hail its new master, an inferno paving the way into the maw of the beast. As the flames swept up and consumed Jennifer, the Earth passed into the object, its blue-green sheen of life extinguished forevermore.

∘ ◎ ∘

Jennifer jerked awake with a deep gasp of air, her arms pushing herself up to a sitting position. A thin layer of sweat covered her entire body, the beads pooling into larger droplets that rolled down her head, arms, and chest once she sat up. Her breathing was rapid as her chest heaved in and out. It took a minute before she released her grip on the bed and her breathing settled. She slid her bare legs over the side of the bed and picked up her SETI smartphone from the nightstand, its notification light blinking. When the screen turned on, a list of major alerts presented themselves: the signal coordinates now placed the object about a hundred thousand miles from Uranus, just as Sam predicted; two alerts concerned the object breaching the atmosphere of Uranus; and a single email alert contained subject lines and links to over a dozen emails, most with image attachments from Gordan.

She noticed that her right foot was bouncing on its own after scanning the alerts. Resting a hand on her thigh, she brought the jitters to a stop and took another deep breath with her eyes closed. A lot was riding on her shoulders. She knew enough about world politics to know it was only a matter of time before someone from the government would step into their scientific arena and apply political agendas and goals.

An expected step, but something she was not looking forward to experiencing.

By the time she was dressed, Jennifer glanced increasingly at her smartphone, but didn't have missed calls or additional notifications. She at least expected to hear something from Sam, who she imagined would've been all over these automated messages from SETI and the block of emails. Jennifer checked the time on the phone as she grabbed her keys and headed to the front of the house. When she opened the front door, she noticed a man leaning against a spotless black sedan parked in front of her home. The car was notable because every other car on the block had a visible coat of grime. Wearing black shoes, dark blue jeans, and a white button-down shirt, he could've passed for any of the techies that lived and worked in the area. He waved as he pushed himself off his car, approaching Jennifer. She stayed in the frame of her door, her hands not leaving the keys which were still in the doorknob. His eyes did not have the enthusiasm or brashness of a techie, however —he was all business, with little emotion to read on his face.

"Davis Reeves, FBI," he said as he pulled his ID and badge from his pants pocket.

Jennifer said nothing as Reeves closed the gap between them and presented his ID up close.

"You can verify the agent number if you want, but there are some people in Washington that want to talk with you. We're here to pick you up."

"We?" She asked as she leaned over to get another look at the car. Two more people were there, one of which got out from the front passenger side and joined her partner. Her toned legs exposed below a business skirt enforced her athletic build—likely a former track runner in her younger days.

"You don't have to be so stoic to everyone we meet, Dave. I'm Angela Willis, pleased to meet you." Angela said with a smile as she came up to Jennifer.

"What is this about?" Jennifer finally asked as she scanned Willis's identification and badge.

We don't know, to be honest," Willis said, "But you and your colleague, Samantha Monroe, will be convening at SFO for a direct flight to DC, leaving as soon as you arrive. I've been told that your hotel accommodations were arranged."

Jennifer's heart, once again, began to race as her eyes darted between the two FBI agents. "And what's in DC? I have a lot going on here as does Sam."

Willis shrugged. "I imagine the work you two perform is related to the meeting that's on the books."

○ ◯ ○

She wasn't given much time to pack. The agents assured her that "little things" like clothing and toiletries would be waiting for her at the hotel, much to Jennifer's surprise. She didn't know what to expect once the Obama administration and NASA learned of the object. Knowing what she didn't know, she still took a few extra minutes to fill a messenger bag with all the electronics and personal essentials she wanted by her side.

The drive to San Francisco International Airport was fast, though to Jennifer it was nothing when compared to how fast the FBI agents got her through airport security. They bypassed it altogether thanks to a private terminal they used leading to a business jet that was already primed for takeoff. Its engines were roaring, ready to taxi onto the runway once its passengers boarded. The airplane was designed for ferrying VIPs, the inside configured for comfort and security. International dignitaries, heads of state, the president. And now SETI researchers.

Jennifer passed who she imagined could've been a Secret Service agent that greeted her. The man wore a suit that looked relaxed enough to conceal a firearm and had a transparent earpiece. As she advanced further into the plane she started to overhear a conversation. A familiar voice, which relaxed some of Jennifer's tense muscles.

"Do we already have the Keck and Mauna Kea Observatories redirecting to Uranus?" Sam could be heard almost yelling at her phone. When Jennifer turned the corner after boarding the plane, she saw Sam and her impromptu workstation at a fold-out table meant for two people. She sat facing away from the pilot's cabin, her laptop and phone planted in front of her, its power cord running over the side and under the table. Beyond Sam was the rest of the plane which was divided into two sections. The front half looked more like a very narrow office and conference room than a traditional passenger jet, while the back half had plush seating which reclined into sleeping positions. The lighting throughout was soft, yet bright enough to conduct all manners of work. Despite the jet engines being a couple of feet from the windows, their sound was almost inaudible.

"That's great, Gordan! I wish the object chose a better planet to devour," Sam said as Jennifer walked past and took a seat across from her, to which Sam took Jennifer's balled hand into hers and shook it with a grin before letting go. "Hey, Doc's here, so we'll call back in five. Keep the data flowing! Bye." Sam tapped the side of her Bluetooth earpiece, ending the call.

"It sounds like we're getting telemetry on the object's new position," Jennifer said to Sam as she looked for a place to place her own laptop.

"Once Kabir and company backed my findings, they just had to wait for the object to come to a stop—at least in galactic terms," Sam laughed.

Jennifer's lips curled into a slight grimace. "At least one of us is finding some humor in this situation."

"When there are entire planets being destroyed in our own backyard, how else would you want to respond?" Sam responded, a smile still on her face as her eyes fell on Jennifer's before falling to her monitor.

Jennifer's shoulders slumped—she couldn't argue with that. "So what's the news on Uranus?"

Sam looked at her laptop, but brought her eyes back to Jennifer. "Not good. The object arrived at Uranus approximately two-and-a-half hours after we saw it leave... what was Neptune. The signal arrived from Uranus, along with visual confirmation, at 4:06am Pacific Time. We have snapshots of Miranda, one of the larger moons, which made an impact with the object within an hour of its arrival. It seems the object arrived in the middle of its orbital path."

"Okay Doctor Epstein, Doctor Monroe—please secure your belongings and grab one of the back seats for takeoff," Willis said as the passenger door closed with a shump behind her, blocking out all sound from the outside. The Secret Service agent and the remaining FBI agents walked toward the back of the plane for their seats as the plane taxied toward the runway.

"Are you telling me I just spent all this time getting myself comfortable only to dump everything back in my bag?" Sam said, arms crossed.

"Ma'am, you can leave your laptop and monitor in the compartment under the table—they won't move around during takeoff there."

Sam released a loud huff before she acquiesced to Willis's request. Jennifer, too, clenched her jaw as she shuffled her laptop back in her bag, not even getting a chance to use it. With Sam's electronics secured, minus the phone which she kept in her hand, they relocated themselves to two adjacent seats, both very generous in size and comfort. Sam dropped into the window seat, letting her head press against the plush leather headrest. Her eyes closed as she moaned. "God, these seats are insane."

Jennifer felt her body sink into her seat as well. "Yeah, they certainly beat everything we have in the office, or at home for that matter."

"Good morning, by the way," Sam said as she rolled her head toward Jennifer, still pressing it against the headrest.

Sam's brown eyes flashed, eager for her response. She seemed extra attentive, as if the last twenty-four hours had cemented a new familiarity between them. Jennifer wasn't sure if it was because they'd found themselves working far closer since the discovery of the signal. Maybe it was their entire situation—how alien it was to receive so much attention, even from the government and maybe the president himself—that made her find solace with Sam. Knowing that Sam was going through the same experiences as her, maybe asking the same questions behind those eyes and that widening smile, brought a surprising amount of relief amid the uncertainty.

In the face of the unknown, the familiar come together.

"Hi, Sam," Jennifer responded.

Sam lifted her phone in front of her.

"When should we call Gordan and team back?"

"Are you sure one of these guys won't snatch it away?" Jennifer motioned towards Reeves and Willis who sat two rows behind them.

"Nah, I was told we can use our devices from end-to-end—seamless connectivity."

Jennifer blinked a few times as she looked down at her own phone, whose signal was still strong. "Huh, I guess that makes sense—government plane and all." She flicked open her email app and pulled up the email with the batch of image attachments of the object and Uranus. "We'll have a video conference once we're in the air."

Jennifer brought her hand to her mouth at the sight of the images, some of them in the infrared light spectrum to make the Uranian rings stand out against the backdrop of space. One image, in infrared, depicted the object fifty thousand miles from Uranus, but close enough to have thrown its ring system in complete disarray, the narrow bands being both warped around the object and bent like a sine wave. It was clear that parts of the ring system—and some of the moons—would break away from the object and Uranus and head into deep space. Another image was a close-up of the rear section of the object where Miranda collided. A large, blurry crater that had to be over a thousand kilometers in diameter was visible, yet the object didn't appear affected. As she examined one image after another, the peace and quiet of the jet interior were eclipsed by the sounds she heard in her dreams. The low-pitched growl that increased in intensity as her vision narrowed onto this stemless champagne glass that was destroying—consuming —Uranus. The rolling growl overlapped with the sound of the signal, the pulse that almost sounded like a slow, beating heart...

"Doc? Jennifer?" Sam took hold of Jennifer's arm, which snapped her out of her daze.

Jennifer blinked a few times, her breathing slowed and normalized, and the sounds of the engine filling the background noise once again. A slow smile crept over Sam's face as she relaxed. The pressure of the jet taking off and arching toward the sky pushed them into their seats. "Where were you just now?"

Jennifer looked at her phone again and swiped the image away before turning off the screen. "Just thinking about Uranus..." Her voice lowered as she turned her head toward Sam, her face downcast. "By the time we land in DC, it won't *be* anymore."

∘ ◎ ∘

One long conference, a decent lunch, and several hours later, Jennifer and Sam found themselves at Reagan National Airport around four o'clock in the afternoon, EST. It wasn't long after landing before their government entourage transported them to the Watergate Hotel. Jennifer was surprised to not only be given very fancy accommodations but also several sets of clothes laid out on her bed, in her size. When she walked over to the bed and picked up one of the blouses, she looked over her shoulder and around the room, seeing if there were any cameras present. *How did they know my size—and what I liked?* She thought.

Less than an hour later, she and Sam shared a large, mahogany table in the White House with John Holdren, Director of the Office of Science and Technology and Science Advisor to the President; Susan Rice, National Security Advisor; General Martin Dempsey, Chairman of the Joint Chiefs of Staff; Chuck Hagel, Secretary of Defense; and Allan Wheeler, Director of NASA. Jennifer knew Holdren, Wheeler, and Rice, at least by name, but just by their postures and sheer presence, she knew that Rice, Dempsey, and Hagel were looking for answers. Everyone had a dossier surrounding the object, dubbed "The Ship" on the front page of the dossier which contained everything collected about it over the last twenty-four hours.

Rice started the group conversation after clearing her throat and standing from her seat. "It's a pleasure to have the two of you here this afternoon," she gestured to Jennifer and Sam. "The purpose of today is to lay everything on the table on what you know about The Ship. Know that prior to today, everyone here already had a meeting which included Brian Ethans, the Director of SETI. Though he answered several important questions, he was the one that recommended that you two handle the technical inquiries presented in the dossier, especially since Doctor Monroe organized most of this data.

"There are many questions from the president. Before I pass them to you, I think it would be prudent to allow you to speak first—and start from the very beginning. The dossier covers extensive technical details on what SETI and the many observatories around the world have discovered—I just want the summary."

Jennifer looked over at Sam, and then to the group at the table. Both Dempsey and Hagel had the perfect poker faces, their eyes focused on Jennifer and what she would share. Hagel kept a hand on his dossier which he flipped open. Wheeler made the slightest nod at Jennifer, his face serious but understanding. With her chin up and eyes focused on everyone in front and to the side of her, she spent the next five minutes walking through the events that started the previous morning and led to the events that occurred in space. The discovery of an artificial signal of extraterrestrial origin within our own solar system. Getting visuals of an object in local space that was several times larger than Earth that was also extraterrestrial. The message found within the signal.

The destruction of Pluto, Neptune, and Uranus.

A moment of uncomfortable silence filled the conference room when Jennifer finished her review.

Dempsey was the first to speak. "You know, even after trying to explain this to the President, I still have a hard time interpreting this Ship's actions as anything but a clear sign of aggression."

Hagel stopped his scrolling through his dossier when he arrived to full-page images of The Ship and sighed as he rubbed his temple. "To be frank, this data was verified not only by our own people but confirmed by our networks abroad," he said. He glanced at Jennifer, but focused his attention to Dempsey and Rice.

Dempsey brought his hand away from his forehead and nodded to Rice. "I recommend that we militarize this operation immediately and bring all information about The Ship under wraps— "

"Wait, hold on!" Sam blurted as she leaned forward in her seat, her finger nails digging into the polished table surface. "SETI is a nonprofit organization and we've been working with other private organizations and universities around the world for years."

"And given the nature of this situation, it would've been best to have never reached out to so many organizations," Dempsey said as his aged eyes narrowed.

"Without the help of the international scientific community, we would not have learned as much as we have about The Ship, sir," Holdren jumped in.

"What my colleague, Dr. Monroe, was saying was that we were—and continue to—operate in the interests of scientific discovery and understanding the unknown," Jennifer said. "Bringing the military into this will only do more harm than good." Sam relaxed her posture after Jennifer spoke though she still looked like she was ready for a fight.

"Do you think we should freely divulge knowledge of an alien ship that has the capacity to destroy entire planets to the public, Dr. Epstein?" Dempsey asked.

"With all due respect, General, but how would you propose we cover up entire planets missing?" Jennifer countered, her voice still holding an even tone, though she felt internal pressure to break her demeanor.

Hagel held up a hand. "This is why you are here, doctor. Between his previous meeting with Ethans and the details in this dossier, the President has already decided to not cover this up. He concluded that the... disappearance... of two planets and a planetoid is too large to not disclose to the public." He looked to Dempsey, who shook his head at Obama's decision.

"The majority do not have the means to observe these planets, but the press would have a field day if constant bells kept going off from astronomers around the world crying wolf," Wheeler said, his distinct Midwestern accent unmistakable. "And we do have a very large wolf on our property."

"There have already been reports of some astronomy blogs and small-time news sites reporting on both the signal and the disappearance of planets," Rice said, pointing to a group of pages at the back of the dossier that were appended. "However, I think given the unbelievable nature of the circumstances, mainstream organizations have ignored such submissions or buried them as crank news. Once the president brings it up, the gloves will come off."

"Given the distances we're talking about, would it not be possible to put a cap on such discussions from reaching the public at large?" Dempsey suggested. He brought his hands together and formed a steeple shape with his index fingers.

"I'm sorry, but how would that be pulled off?" asked Sam, her trademark wit making an inappropriate showing. "Do we shut down all observatories, ban the sale of telescopes to the public, and put those that have telescopes already into prison?"

"Monroe, no need for sarcasm here," Rice said with a sharp, authoritative tone.

"I apologize," Sam lowered her eyes as her cheeks reddened, though she took a deep breath to reign in the pigment changes.

Rice nodded towards Sam, then looked over at everyone else. "It is okay, but just remember that we're all on the same side here. What we discuss here will ultimately play a large role in what the president will present to the public—let's not forget that."

Not deterred by Sam's outburst, Dempsey continued, his voice level but stronger. "How do you expect the people of the United States to react to the fact that—just to restate what Dr. Epstein already shared—an alien ship that is many times larger than Earth simply appeared beyond the orbit of Pluto and proceeded to destroy it? And then using methods of propulsion we've never seen before, advanced on Neptune and then Uranus—two gas giants—and proceeded to destroy them as well? How do you expect the average Joe to respond to those facts, stated as such?"

Sam's face reddened even more as she gripped the leather-padded arms of her chair.

"Now, I'm not saying that we prevent astronomers and space hobbyists from doing what they want, but we have to consider that given how far away all of this took place, we cannot place a cover-up off the table. Having the president validate what is currently being seen as fringe news will have unforeseen consequences," Dempsey concluded.

"Duly noted," Rice said. "Unfortunately, what sort of consequences will there be if the US government doesn't acknowledge this? And what happens if another country—say, Russia or China—has their leadership break this news before the United States?"

She leaned forward as she rested her elbows on the table, her fingers clasped together. She looked at everyone with unwavering eyes that came from her decades in the political arena. "No, we must be first at making this public knowledge. Regarding that overall message which will be delivered to the public, it must be both clear-as-day but also not so direct that it would scare the daylights out of those listening."

Holdren adjusted his reading glasses before he spoke up as he re-directed the discussion. He turned to the page that outlined the time-frames for the object's movements through the solar system, along with a predicted path to Saturn. "Speaking of the message, having a good idea as to what The Ship will do next is paramount. Are these numbers accurate, regarding The Ship's path so far?"

"Ah, that's correct," Sam responded as she ran her finger down the list of printed data in the dossier. "As you can see, this Ship has shown the capacity to move at speeds scientists have, at best, just hypothe-sized. At least it didn't break c—that would almost certainly force us to toss out most of our understanding of physics and special relativity. Well, not break c as far as we know."

"You mean c, as in Einstein's speed of light?" Hagel asked, to which Sam nodded with a straight face. "It sounds like you believe it already broke the light barrier."

Sam relaxed. "And here I thought you guys did nothing more than skim my notes!"

Hagel almost cracked a smile in response. "Even if I don't fully understand it all, I read everything."

"'As far as we know'?" Holdren asked Sam, his graying eyebrows raised at her alluding to the possibility that the light barrier was broken.

"Well, I think it's possible that the object—The Ship—arrived in our solar system using some sort of superluminal method of travel." Sam observed Dempsey, Hagel, and Rice, and considered her audience before continuing. "Faster-than-light. It may have arrived here using exotic technology that prevented us from detecting it years ago."

"The speculation on how it got here is well and good," Wheeler began, "but I believe we should focus on the here-and-now. The Ship is here, it destroyed two planets and a planetoid, and is currently idle where Uranus used to be."

Wheeler turned to the pages where Sam provided detailed predictions on where it could go next, based on the patterns it already expressed. "You're suggesting here that if its present actions stay consistent, it may start for Saturn in approximately one hour? That's a bit of a stretch, don't you think?"

Jennifer knew what was coming next. She maintained her composure, sitting upright while smoothing her shirt under the table. Her eyes darted between Dempsey and Rice, seeing the growing lines next to their narrowed eyes and clenched hands in front of their faces, betraying the incredulity they undoubtedly had. She stopped herself from digging her fingers into her legs as Sam moved to the more damning part of their report. The portion of the report that everyone had to be thinking about. It was impossible to avoid.

"Despite the concerted efforts of over thirty observatories and telescopes around the world, we still have limited information regarding The Ship's motives," Sam said with a slight shrug.

"The way I see it, there are three possible outcomes," Jennifer said. "One, The Ship proceeds to Saturn—then Jupiter, then Mars... and then Earth. At the speed that it travels between planets, we could be looking at our destruction in roughly two days."

Wheeler shuffled his legs under the table while Dempsey leaned toward Hagel and said something in his ear, which was inaudible to Jennifer. She took a deep breath through her nose and continued. "Two, The Ship leaves our solar system—the best possible outcome for us. Or three, it does something that we cannot predict."

"Regarding your first option," Hagel began, "Is there anything we can do to deter or stop this Ship from approaching Earth?"

Silence, once again. Wheeler answered after he took off his glasses. "I'm sorry, sir, but there is nothing we can do in terms of a physical deterrent. Nothing at all. Even if you took all fifteen thousand nuclear missiles from around the world and found a way to deliver all of them, at once, to The Ship for a direct hit the explosion would, at best, just create a radioactive crater on its surface."

"We've witnessed entire moons collide with The Ship," Jennifer said. "Some of these impacts released more energy than anything we could ever produce—and yet The Ship stayed its course as if it were an ant biting your arm. I must second Wheeler's position here."

Hagel stared at Jennifer, his lips tightened, but didn't follow up. Even Dempsey looked weary, his shoulders slumped down and his eyes toward Hagel. It's not every day you confess that all the might and weight of the world's remaining superpower means nothing.

"What about the message you guys deciphered?" Holdren flipped to the single image discovered within the signal and turned his dossier around for the rest to see.

"Yes, this was a bit of a conundrum for us when our colleague, Nic, filtered this out from the rest of the signal's noise," Sam said. "If you ask me, I believe this may be a pictorial version of the request 'If you can hear this, please contact me.'"

Holdren to Sam: "Please, elaborate."

"Look at the top circle, the one with the solid black concentric circles. This has to represent The Ship as it matches what we've already confirmed about the signal: That it is broadcasting from The Ship in all directions. The signal is not focused on Earth, but we are still receiving it. Now, the bottom circle has gray concentric circles, a portion of which forms a bold, black cone that spreads outward to the top circle."

Sam let her words resonate in the air. She had everyone's attention, so she continued. "We at SETI propose that this message is a call for anyone that receives it to respond. The bottom circle represents us—Earth—and the cone reflects our ability to direct a focused response to The Ship."

"But why the use of circles to deliver this sort of message?" Wheeler asked with crossed arms, but was curious for her answer.

"Maybe whoever is on The Ship figured that any civilization advanced enough to pick their signal up would understand the concept of radar and radio communications, which is what their simple image looks to depict."

Hagel grimaced, speaking more forcefully than before. "I honestly do not believe attempting to communicate with these aliens is in any way a good idea."

"Agreed," Dempsey nodded. "Considering that three planets were destroyed, responding to their hail would be giving us away, letting them know we are here—come on over."

"We don't know what the intentions are behind the message," Jennifer said. "But we cannot make any decisions regarding a response until we know more about who or what we are dealing with."

"What if responding to the message lets them know that we are here, so they leave us alone as a result?" Sam asked, wanting to not lose any form of communication as an option.

"I think all we have right now are unknown unknowns regarding this message," Wheeler said. "For now, I think we can sideline that aspect of our discussion until we know, provided that Dr. Epstein's first scenario doesn't play out."

Dempsey and Hagel glanced at each other, then at Rice. She maintained her tight gaze toward Jennifer and Sam. Jennifer's nerves gave out, her eyes seeking the comfort of her lap. She gripped her leg and darted her eyes back at Rice.

"Listen," Rice said to Jennifer and Sam, and indirectly to Wheeler and Holdren. Her eyes scanned across all four of them. "The president will be giving the order to provide SETI and NASA whatever is needed to learn everything we can about The Ship, and the aliens that may be on it. For now, SETI will retain its nonprofit status, but we will let you know if that has to change in the future."

Sam's eyes widened at Rice's words. Jennifer looked more reserved, but still felt her stomach flutter.

Wheeler beamed a grin as he picked up where Rice left off. "It wasn't mentioned upfront, but know that NASA's resources are also fully available."

"Can we get Hubble pointed at The Ship?" Sam asked without hesitation.

"We'll talk more afterwards, but we'll be pointing everything at The Ship," Wheeler said, his smile unbroken.

Sam's hand darted for her side pants pocket and fished out her phone. Jennifer knew the protocols regarding cell phone use during what they were told was a sensitive meeting prior to entering the conference room. The only reason Sam would deviate from the rules would be—

"Hey doc, The Ship's moving," Sam said, though she was looking at her phone, swiping away the notifications and bringing up their SETI app to view the finer details. "Another gamma ray burst detected... bigger than the last one."

Wheeler's smile straightened into thin, pressed lips as he leaned towards Sam to get a look at what was on her phone. Jennifer's had her phone set to silent mode, but when she pulled it from her small bag she saw the same two notifications waiting for her. Ship movement data and a very large gamma ray burst originating from the ship flashed onto her screen.

"The burst was 1,203keV gamma rays," Sam's mouth dropped as she looked up at Jennifer.

"Coming from an artificial source, impossible," said Holdren, louder than intended. He walked over to Jennifer, gesturing for her phone. She tilted it so the both of them could see what was being recorded from SETI.

Jennifer's screen was replaced with the SETI logo as Gordan called her. Holdren's focus was broken as she answered the phone and began pacing back and forth. "Gordan, give me more."

"One of the gamma-ray observatories we're working with had their sensors maxed out from that last burst. It appears the object is now emitting a continuous stream of gamma rays, but at a much lower electron volt levels." Jennifer could hear a fair amount of commotion in the background when Gordan stopped speaking.

"What about its movement?"

"Checking... it's adjusted its heading by twenty degrees so far. Based on current angular velocity it's not done yet."

Jennifer placed a hand over her phone and turned to Wheeler, working to keep her hands from shaking. "Can you get Hubble on The Ship now? Now, please?"

He hesitated for a moment, but then nodded and walked to one corner of the conference room as he pulled out his phone.

While watching Wheeler huddle for his call, Jennifer listened to Gordan as he updated her on The Ship's changing heading and speed. "Still holding at about 5km/s, with a heading of sixty degrees and still changing. Seventy. Slowing down... Vern predicts that the object will rest with an eighty-two degree heading change."

"What is going on?" Hagel asked aloud, sensing the sudden shift in mood from everyone around him while Jennifer and Wheeler were on the phone, both talking with great urgency. Sam was back in her seat scribbling equations in her dossier, her phone propped up next to her feeding live data from Vern.

Holdren rubbed the coarse, gray-white hair on his face and chin as he leaned over to Hagel, his voice filled with concern. "I think we'll be learning very soon if Dr. Monroe's predictions are about to come true."

"Sam, are you getting these numbers?" Jennifer asked as she pointed to Sam.

"Ahead of you, doc," Sam said, her pen rolling over her dossier, working towards possible destinations. She didn't have the luxury of having satellite mapping software on her phone, but she could derive some rough approximations they could work with until they returned home. She hesitated when she reached the final equal sign, knowing exactly what her answer was. Though her writing hand quivered, she took a breath to calm her nerves and wrote in her answer, circling it in a single stroke. Biting her lips as the weight of her pen grew in her hand, she glanced at Jennifer. "Can someone double-check my numbers?"

Wheeler and Jennifer rushed over to Sam, flanking her on each side. Wheeler's finger drifted over her scribbles as he reviewed her work, his head tilting from side to side as he ran the numbers in his head. "So far, so good," he said. "Do you usually crank out mathematical equations like this on a daily basis?"

"I'll take that as flattery," Sam said, though she responded with involuntary fidgeting of her pen. Rice plodded over to them, arms crossed.

"The gamma ray emissions from the object aren't stopping," Gordan said to Jennifer.

"New behavior," Jennifer responded as she, along with Wheeler, ran down the lines Sam created before she reached the final line with the circled answer.

"You got it," Gordan said. "By now, it would have at least wrapped itself in that light-warping bubble that we saw before."

"So if it's not looking to go as fast as it did before... it's staying here. But where will it go..." Jennifer looked at the end of Sam's formulas and pieced all of it together. After forming a mental image of the solar system on a plane, she saw where Sam concluded. Her heart sank into the pit of her stomach.

"Is The Ship... preparing to head for Earth?" Wheeler wrinkled his brow as he started on the numbers again, hoping Sam was wrong.

"Correction, Dr. Wheeler," Jennifer said as she took a step back from Sam. "It's already heading for Earth."

1.7

TRANSCRIPT: PRESIDENT OBAMA'S EMERGENCY PRESS CONFERENCE

Obama: "Good morning, everybody.

"I have news to share with you and the world today—something that I never imagined I would share in my lifetime. Today, I will be talking about the efforts of our scientists at the SETI Institute, the Search for Extraterrestrial Intelligence, which is based in Mountain View, California.

"The SETI Institute, a non-profit research organization, focuses on learning more about the universe, specifically around the origins and nature of life. Using the latest advancements in radio and optical telescope technology, they are able to observe the cosmos with incredible detail and listen for any unusual radio waves that may emanate from nearby sun-like stars. Now the folks at SETI pick up radio signals all the time, just about all of it filtered out for a variety of reasons. It could be the sounds from any of the radio broadcasting stations on Earth, or it could merely be cosmic noise—background static that represent remnants of the very beginnings of our universe.

"There have been several moments in our history where SETI picked up what was thought to be radio signals of extraterrestrial nature. One of the most cited examples of this is the famous 'WOW! Signal', which was initially received by Ohio State University's Big Ear Radio Telescope in 1977. This signal represents, to this day, the closest we've ever come to a narrowband radio frequency from an extraterrestrial source, but since it never repeated itself, we may never know if the 'WOW! Signal' was truly extraterrestrial in origin.

"However, on Friday, June 20th, 2014, around 4:45 in the morning Pacific Time, Doctor Samantha Monroe was the first person on Earth to confirm a new signal of extraterrestrial origin. This not only met all the benchmarks for an alien radio transmission, but one that consistently and predictably repeated itself. Doctor Jennifer Epstein, the senior research scientist that leads Samantha's team at SETI, led the process of getting additional signal confirmation from various universities and radio observatories from our allies around the world. All that SETI contacted confirmed the signal's existence over the course of that day.

"What was a source of confusion and concern for them was the origin of the signal. Normally, the process of ET radio detection assumes that the signal would originate from a nearby or faraway star. In this case, the signal originated approximately nine thousand miles over the surface of Pluto, or about 4.5 billion miles from Earth.

"Please, sit down. There will be time for questions though I imagine some of your questions will be answered by the time I'm finished.

"So, the signal was detected by Pluto. However, ten hours after the initial discovery, the signal moved rapidly from Pluto to Neptune, the outer-most gas giant in our solar system. It was during this time that SETI, in collaboration with the Girawali Observatory in Pune, India, obtained the first-ever images of an interstellar spacecraft of undeniable extraterrestrial origin.

"I say 'undeniable' for two reasons.

"First, this spacecraft is larger than anything we've ever built, by several hundred orders of magnitude. Lengthwise, the spacecraft is about 48,000 miles long from front to back. To put this in another perspective, it is longer than five Earth's lined up in a row. It is also about 17,400 miles wide from top to bottom—a little more than two Earth's tall. It is safe to say that this is an object that is impossible for us, as a civilization, to construct today.

"Second, the speed at which it traversed the astronomically substantial gap between Pluto and Neptune has confounded scientists around the world. It's been suggested that the spacecraft may utilize antimatter as fuel, a material that has been referenced in many popular forms of science fiction but does have a basis in modern theoretical science.

"So what does this mean for us, for humanity? That brings me to what just occurred when this spacecraft approached Pluto and Neptune—and as of two days ago, planet Uranus. There is no easy way to say this, so I'll be straightforward with you: All three planets were destroyed. Now, we do not know if this was a malicious act or merely the consequence of the craft being in close proximity to those planets. There are no assumptions being made as we are not in a place to know what a truly alien species would be thinking.

"That is where the signal that we've been receiving from the spacecraft comes into play. I, along with SETI and NASA, are in active communications with China, Russia, India, South Africa, the members of the European Union, and our many other allies regarding the message that was found within the signal and whether we should respond. Again, no assumptions are being made regarding the nature of the message or whether it is being sent with good intentions, but that is why these critically important talks are taking place.

"And what about the spacecraft as of today? Evidence suggests that despite the spacecraft being capable of traveling close to the speed of light, we have confirmed it is now heading for Jupiter or the inner solar system at speeds significantly slower than what we've witnessed when it moved from Pluto to Neptune, and then from Neptune to Uranus. Because of this turn of events, it is difficult to determine exactly where it may be going, but no matter where it's headed it will be many years before it reaches its next destination.

"Fortunately the scientific community, with the support of their respective governments, has banded together to monitor the spacecraft and to learn as much as we can so we can plan for the future. Every telescope at mankind's disposal, from the Hubble Space Telescope and Puerto Rico's Arecibo Observatory to South Africa's 'Cheetah's Eye', are in the process of being redirected toward the spacecraft.

"There is uncertainty surrounding the nature of this spacecraft and those that are piloting it, what their intentions are, what the message is that they are sending—what all of this means. However, know that I am not quitting my day job over this news—I will be working hard, ensuring that the United States and its allies continue to move forward. Know that with your continued support, cooperation, and understanding, our great nation will rise to the challenge that was thrust upon it. Our nation, our people, and our world will prevail.

"With that, I'll open the floor to some questions..."

o ◎ o

JULY 7, 2014

Watching orbital launches never seemed to get old for Muzikay-ise. He stood inside the Khulu Launch Control Center in Edwards, California, where the fifteenth test launch of *New Leopard*, a reusable two-or-three-stage rocket, lifted off. Muzikayise watched, with hands clasped behind his back and his chin high, as the rocket kept ahead of the smoke trail it left behind as it crept into the clear blue sky. He couldn't attend every launch, and his schedule kept him away from the deserts and grassy plains where his business-owned launch pads and control centers resided. This launch was an important one, however, both for the future of Khulu Global and for him. Once *New Leopard* returned to the same launch pad it departed from—and completed five additional runs to eliminate any bugs—the plan was to promote the *New Leopard* and its proprietary "KE-4" staged-combustion rocket engine for active space missions.

As *New Leopard* became a smaller and smaller needle in the sky, the bright flames and smoke trail obscuring it from view, Muzikayise walked up to Karl Moreno, Flight Director for KLCC, and patted him on the shoulder. "Once again, I think congratulations are in order," he said.

Karl stood near the front of the control room, a microphone and earpiece wrapped around one ear. They were at the lowest tier, with four more tiers of tables behind them, each row four feet higher than the last, making the space feel like a miniaturized performance hall.

Large trios of monitors sat in front of each person while five wall-sized screens was on the wall opposite the four long rows of desks. The center-right screen tracked *New Leopard's* ascent while the center screen provided an unobstructed view of the two launch pads that were a mile away thanks to some well-placed cameras. He took a moment before he registered the pats after which he turned around and gave Muzikayise a firm handshake. "Everything is green across the board, Muzie. All systems are go."

"Good," Muzikayise said. "And we're aiming for high-altitude, high-velocity reentry today?"

"That's right," Karl confirmed. "Going for a ninety-one kilometer ascent, a little more than a third of the way to the ISS."

"Excellent." Muzikayise shook Karl's hand again before he eyed everyone in the control room, giving each person a second or two of acknowledgment before walking up the long steps to the glass-walled offices that overlooked the control room. As he approached one of the offices, the door opened from the inside thanks to Ami.

On the other end of the office was NASA Director Allan Wheeler, who had his suede shoe-covered feet propped on the desk. He looked over to Muzikayise and flashed a large grin.

"Your assistant informs me that you run a tight ship when it comes to your little space program, but I must admit I am impressed by what she's showcased," Allan said as he dropped his feet to the carpeted floor and faced Muzikayise.

"You would have seen our working environment sooner if you hadn't turned down my previous invitations," Muzikayise took the other guest chair and sat himself opposite from Allan. They both leaned toward each other and shook hands.

"You know as well as I do that I couldn't make any commitments for what would amount to a personal tour of your launch facilities, given my busy schedule." Allan leaned back into his chair and rubbed his chin. "That said, it's a pleasure to witness the results of the seed money from NASA: Those lovely KE-4 boosters not to mention the CRS contracts."

"And a pleasure it is to have you here," Muzikayise said as he propped a foot over his thigh and rested his arms on the armrests. He looked out the office window and toward the wall screens. "I hope you're satisfied with the view."

Allan glanced at Ami who kept her position by the door, her hands folded together over her phone. She caught his eyes before he looked back at Muzikayise. "It's good to see an investment come to fruition."

Muzikayise turned back to Allan. "Which is why I'm glad we are finally having a face-to-face discussion." He paused. "Of course, you wouldn't come all the way out to the Mojave Desert just to watch renewable rocket test flights. You've known about these tests for months now."

Allan allowed himself to chuckle. "I guess my presence instead of the usual representative is a bit of a giveaway, huh? Well, let's cut right to the chase." He sat upright, his jovial expression replaced with one that was all business. Muzikayise wanted to lean in, but refrained from doing so—no need to give away interest, not just yet.

"You know what's going on up there." Allan pointed toward the ceiling and Muzikayise nodded in response. "NASA, along with the

ESA and the Russian Space Agency, have been in constant talks ever since President Obama went public two weeks ago with news regarding the Leviathan."

"The Leviathan," Muzikayise said to himself, under his breath, subconsciously rolling his eyes. This was the name the masses clung to after a well-known theologian went on four major broadcast networks and likened the spaceship to the mythological creature of the same name. In Christian mythology, this creature consumed all those that were damned at the Last Judgement in the Book of Revelations. It was meant as an allusion to the powerful nature of the starship and its mysterious, alien nature, but a few interviews and several out-of-context quotes later the name stuck.

Allan caught the Muzikayise' subvocalization. "I don't know if I would've agreed to even giving this ship a name, but that's TV for you. I'm just here to ask you two questions."

"Please continue," Muzikayise said with open hands.

"Since we know it will take at least ten years for the Leviathan to reach Earth, that gives us a decent window to try and learn as much as we can about it. The first step towards obtaining this knowledge is to get a better understanding of what exactly the Leviathan is. To be blunt, your rocket technology is some of the best in the world, and we need only the best to be on our side. Therefore, I want a renewable rocket ready for live use in the next six months, the amount of time I've given my boys at NASA to complete the James Webb Space Telescope. Our partners in the Flagship Program already agreed to this accelerated timetable, so all that's left is obtaining the latest in rocketry to get it in space and a second stage vehicle to place our telescope in its home 1.5 million kilometers from Earth." Allan pointed toward the wall screen that now had a graphical cross-section of *New Leopard* on-screen with various lines streaming from the rocket to diagnostic summary windows, all with green indicators. "Can you deliver me your rocket in six months?"

Muzikayise blinked, the only outward indicator he allowed himself to express on an otherwise deadpan face. He hadn't expected such an aggressive timeline. "Though I appreciate such a request from my business, the potential costs for moving up all my timetables, constructing more test rockets for simultaneous runs, and just the staffing— "

"Muzie, if you can commit, you'll see an early renewal of your CRS contracts, along with a new contract for crewed spaceflight services."

Muzikayise's eyes darted toward Ami, who was already documenting everything on her phone. "Ami, arrange a meeting with the flight control remote staff and the directors of Khulu LC and Overberg LC. Book for tomorrow, and clear everyone else's calendars—this is top priority."

"Yes, sir," Ami said.

"I'll take that as a yes," Allan grinned. "So my second question. More of a request, really. I need you to pair up with Ad Astra Rocket Company and, with additional partnerships with other space agencies, get a working prototype of a VASIMR engine off the ground and into space for further testing."

Muzikayise felt like he had done a mental double-take on that second request. VASIMR, or Variable Specific Impulse Magnetoplasma Rocket, was an even more advanced spacecraft propulsion system that converted a neutral gas, such as the common—and cheap—argon, to a superheated plasma. Thanks to the use of electromagnets, that superheated plasma would propel a VASIMR up to fifty kilometers a second. He looked at the floor and coughed before he raised his head back up to Allan's eyes. "Exactly how far along are you and your friends at Ad Astra with VASIMR? If I recall correctly, the level of funding and interest have both been trending downward for that decades-long venture."

"Not as far as some scientific circles would have liked," Allan sighed. "But again, things have changed, and the political capital for seeing a successful VASIMR engine constructed and operational is now there. We need to get to the Leviathan fast—VASIMR engines will make that possible. Talks between NASA and the other major space agencies around the world are already underway to make VASIMR development a cooperative venture."

"Ah, so the other agencies will have involvement in this particular project as well?"

"Correct—ESA and Roscosmos have already done preliminary research into the technology, though most of it's been shelved in favor of incrementing existing technology. Of course, that has now changed."

Muzikayise was interested in this conversation already, but now he sat upright, with one arm propped up on the armrest as he rubbed his chin. He had a simple question of his own. "Timeline?"

There was little hesitation from Allan. "We want a working prototype in three years, with the goal of being able to send robotic missions to the Leviathan in five."

Muzikayise kept his poker face going strong, but was looking for holes in Allan's projections. "You must intend to bring other contractors into the fold, along with these agencies, to hit that deadline. Even if I were to redirect all company efforts to this one project—something I couldn't do without causing irreparable harm to other important client relationships—Khulu Global doesn't have enough of a physical manufacturing base. Not without significant restructuring costs."

"Indeed, you're right, Muzie. I'll be meeting with Northrop Grumman, Lockheed, and Boeing over the next twenty-four hours to orchestrate the largest corporate partnership in history, for the most important spaceflight project since the Apollo Program. They all work for the US government and NASA in one way or another, but the combined infrastructure of these juggernauts, alongside your substantial holdings, will ensure we meet our goals on-time."

How idealistic, Muzikayise thought. Even with the potential threat of the Leviathan, he didn't expect to see the kind of strategic partnership that Allan espoused, especially where the VASIMR engine was concerned. It wasn't impossible but there would be lots of hurdles and even more lawyers to contend with. If the engine was a complete success, the provider of said engine—and the many related components built into the ship that would use it—would be in an ideal position to generate large profits as the more traditional propulsion systems saw their decline.

"I look forward to seeing the kind of business contracts that are drawn up to make all of that work," said Muzikayise.

"Having at least one of the four future partners on-board now will make that process much easier, I assure you."

Muzikayise got up from his chair and approached the office window that overlooked his flight control team. Most of the officers kept their attention to their monitors while Karl slowly walked down each row while he talked into his earpiece. All valuable resources, both here at the Edward center and Overberg in South Africa, and the remote staff that supported both locations. All valuable resources that would log lots of overtime hours in the very near future.

"Muzie, this is the most important project you'll ever be a part of," Allan now stood, but remained by his chair.

"I've heard that sentence before."

"There haven't been projects before this one where the future of mankind was at stake."

"Strong words, Allan. Will you be presenting these proposals like this to everyone?"

"Only if they hesitate to back the cause, Muzikayise."

Muzikayise turned to Allan, arms folded. After a couple of seconds of tense silence, Allan relaxed his posture and groaned.

"Okay, enough with these bullshit games," Allan grimaced. "To be frank, Khulu, Boeing, the whole gang—you all have to be on-board. There are very few multi-national companies that meet the qualifications to conduct work at this scale in the time that we, NASA and the United States, need to see them completed. It will cost all of you a lot across the board—I am aware of that. Thanks to the president, I can make sure you're properly compensated."

"What about overseas contractors that are working with the Europeans and Russians?"

"You'll be briefed on their involvement as part of the formal contract you'll receive, but I can assure you that *we* will be leading the project."

Muzikayise's stolid face cracked the slightest smile as he closed the gap between him and Allan. He shook Allan's hand as he looked into his eyes, searching for an unspoken caveat, but found none. "This isn't a guarantee—that's what contracts are for—but you can expect the cooperation and participation of Khulu Global and the Unity Foundation in this very ambitious endeavor."

"Hmm. Not exactly a yes, but I'll take it," Allan said with a smile. "Expect to hear from your rep before the end of tomorrow with details on both the CRS contracts and the strategic partnership surrounding the VASIMR engine project."

"As soon as I've signed on the dotted line on these contracts, we'll move forward."

"I know we will," said Allan. He scooped his suit jacket off the back of his chair and slid it on. "You know what to expect when it comes to contracts like these, so I trust you'll sign off quickly."

"Ami will make sure it's on my desk," said Muzikayise. "Speaking of which: Ami, please escort our guest to his car."

"Absolutely," Ami said as she opened the office door and stepped out.

Allan followed Ami to the office door, but stopped short of exiting the office and turned back to Muzikayise. "I think it is worth mentioning that all the money in the world isn't going to matter if our world doesn't exist anymore."

"Excuse me?" barked Muzikayise with raised eyebrows.

"We'll talk soon," said Allan as he took the doorknob and pulled the office door shut behind him.

○ ◎ ○

JULY 14, 2014

"The Armstrong Program," the name given to both the contract and the newly formed NASA program, found its way to Muzikayise's executive desk in his 45th-floor San Francisco office a week after his meeting with Allan. The program's mission was to learn as much about the Leviathan as possible in the attempt to answer "The Leviathan Question:" What can be done to divert its course and prevent Earth's destruction? The 300-page bundle of paragraph blocks, engineering schematics, and company logos was surprisingly concise for a government-driven program. Also surprising, even for Muzikayise, was the haste in which the "Big Four" collaborated, argued, and agreed over the finer details surrounding the program.

Northrop Grumman, Lockheed Martin, Boeing Defense, and Khulu Global—a strategic alliance that Muzikayise would have once found inconceivable—but as the saying went, adversity makes for strange bedfellows.

Though Muzikayise preferred to conduct most of his important meetings from Cape Town that didn't mean he would cut back on making Khulu's US headquarters a comfortable space to work. He had the off-white walls kept bare, save for one that ran between the doorway and his desk. Several newspapers and magazines in natural wood-toned frames hung along it. Each frame contained a snapshot into a critical moment in the origins and growth of Khulu Global into the global enterprise it was; the most recent was TIME Magazine's 2007 "Person of the Year" issue which had Muzikayise on the cover. The ceiling had inset light fixtures shaped like crescent moons, complimented with soft lighting that followed the baseboard around the room. Much like his space at SALT, he kept his office lights just strong enough to read materials without straining the eyes at night. On this night, it wasn't just the contract that kept his attention.

Spread on the large desk were also some newspapers—The San Francisco Chronicle, Wall Street Journal, and The New York Times. They all presented variants of the news that had dominated the global news cycle, the headlines hard to ignore: 'ALL THREE PLANETS WERE DESTROYED'; DOW PLUNGES ANOTHER 500 POINTS; US—EU SANCTIONS AGAINST RUSSIA LIFTED FOLLOWING UNPRECEDENTED SCIENTIFIC COOPERATION BETWEEN MAJOR POWERS. Muzikayise already parsed and interpreted their contents before he dove into the contract, his mind fresh with current event context to overlay.

In the middle of his spacious office was Ami, who sat in a plush sofa reading a newspaper of her own. Her legs were propped up on the glass coffee table.

"I must say, when the government wants to get something done, very little can stand in their way," Muzikayise said out loud as he worked his way through the contract pages.

"It helps that Obama removed every possible wall that would normally control how much could be spent on a project,"

Ami agreed, her focus still on her paper. "It's not going to last, though."

Muzikayise lowered the contract, peeking over the top at Ami. "You don't believe the United States and her allies will keep their pocketbooks open until there is a definitive solution regarding the Leviathan?"

"I don't believe in anything," Ami folded her newspaper and placed it next to her on the sofa. She looked at Muzikayise with a frown.

"No, of course you don't," Muzikayise said with a smirk hidden behind his contract. He knew more than enough about Ami to know when and how he could push her buttons.

She ignored his attempt at eliciting a reaction. "You know I'm right."

"I know that I am right, which means that you are also right," he said, his voice filling the office. "It's a truly rare moment in history when several major governments will spend as much as—" He stopped himself to flip to the middle of the contract which broke down all the financial figures. "—fifty billion dollars, tax-free, on a single corporation. And that's just for the first year! Khulu Global and the Unity Foundation will pull in more money with the stroke of a pen than the last couple of fiscal years combined."

The contract, its many clauses, the obligations outlined, and the financial and legal compensations were nothing short of extraordinary. Even more so was the transparency which was why the final version was drawn so fast. It also helped that everyone involved got very little sleep once discussions began between all parties.

Khulu Global was given complete ownership of the development and deployment of renewal rocketry, with *New Leopard* as the primary vehicle earmarked for production and enough funding for future iterations. Lockheed Martin would work with Boeing, with some guidance from NASA and Roscosmos, on expanding the International Space Station. They would construct new habitation modules, propulsion modules, and the *Nautilus-X,* the first centrifuge module that would simulate a percentage of Earth gravity in an artificial space environment. Finally, Northrop Grumman, already contracted for completing the James Webb Space Telescope, now had to complete that project in six months—with a bonus financial incentive thrown in for an end-of-year completion and orbital insertion of the Hubble replacement.

The Armstrong Program ensured that the Big Four would provide assistance if the situation arose, which included collaboration between subcontractors—anything to keep the project moving forward and fast. At the same time, full access to NASA's Cape Canaveral and Vandenberg launch sites were granted. Despite the access, all scheduled use of the launch pads would still have to be coordinated with NASA.

The most interesting section in the contract revolved around the VASIMR plans. There would be three phases:

Phase One, which focused on the Unity Foundation concerned driving research into increasing the total engine output from the reported 200kW that Ad Astra achieved years ago to two megawatts—more than enough energy needed to propel space probes and possibly rover missions to the Leviathan. Ad Astra, NASA, and Roscosmos would conduct research on finding solutions to the waste heat problem, a major roadblock in VASIMR viability.

Phase Two would have Khulu Global, with assistance from Ad Astra, construct a working VASIMR prototype by 2017 which would launch into space, orbit the moon, and return into geosynchronous orbit around Earth.

Phase Three focused on the production of the world's first VASIMR satellite space probe, armed with a rover to dispatch onto the Leviathan's surface. This work would commence immediately after Phase Two concluded.

Everyone was getting large pieces of the pie at the table. As far as the results of what would have normally been a painful, drawn-out process, Muzikayise couldn't be more satisfied.

"What's interesting about this contract is what it does not contain," Muzikayise said, putting the contract down after his eyes scanned the final page which had signatures of the Big Four CEO's and Presidents. "Nowhere does it say that the US will get back into constructing ships and components for their space program."

Ami ambled over to Muzikayise's desk, sat across from him, and leaned forward. "Are you surprised that they aren't resurrecting the shuttle program?" she asked with a soft voice.

"With all the money they are willing to spend, I kind of am," he said with a chuckle. "But they know we can get the job done faster and more efficiently. We aren't hobbled by decades of conflicting protocols and policies, nor are we afraid of change."

Ami rolled her eyes. "As long as that change is accompanied by profits, of course."

"Well... we are a business, after all. Besides, that is where the Unity Foundation comes into play. Do you think all the nonprofits and schools we're funding care about profits? Absolutely not—they are advocating for their respective causes, researching the next big scientific breakthroughs, and preparing our young for the future."

"I think you're leaving out the fact that most of what Unity funds has resulted in Khulu Global turning profits—albeit in unconventional ways, but profits nonetheless."

"Unconventional?"

"Come on, Muzie. It's not too hard to see the connections between, say, the tens of millions you've invested into Cape Town's tech infrastructure—'for the greater good of the people'—and the consistent revenue earned from the cable and high-speed Internet service provider you own for the region."

Muzikayise nodded, making no attempt to deny her statement. "The people pay almost nothing for near-gigabit speeds—it's the businesses that support what I've weaved throughout my city. I make a little while the people benefit the most. Who knows where Cape Town and its surrounding suburbs would be without my help." His eyes narrowed. "I see many governments around the world failing at taking care of their own people. Even the United States, the bastion of western civilization, still has people starving on the streets and creating makeshift shelters under elevated highways. I shouldn't have to step into the affairs of some governments and make them look bad at their job by providing critical services and supporting education." He sat up from his relaxed posture, projecting his chest outward, his eyes glowing. "Cape Town is but an example of what can happen when an altruistic corporation like mine steps in. The Armstrong Program will not only see its goals fulfilled, but my presence on the world stage will advance in ways I'm sure Allan Wheeler and his cronies can't possibly foresee."

Ami leaned into her chair as she slightly parted her legs before she crossed them and flashed an almost seductive smile. "You plan on pocketing some of those billions for purposes other than the Armstrong Program, aren't you?"

Muzikayise smiled back as he kicked his legs to the top of the desk and leaned back, his hands behind his head. "Let's just say that the US government knows how to spend lots of money inefficiently. I'm just making sure I can redirect some of those funds to better use." He pointed to a series of lines in the financial breakdown section of the contract and tossed it to her, the document landing in her lap. "To answer your question: absolutely."

1.8

As the morning sun rested in the deep-blue sky over Hat Creek, long shadows fell across the forty-two antennas that comprised the Allen Telescope Array. The antennas—twenty-foot diameter dishes with a sub-reflector mounted just below the center of each dish that were seven feet in diameter—were controlled from a single, unassuming building. It had a gable roof, the weathered green asphalt shingles just bright enough to stand out from the nearby trees and shrubbery that surrounded the facility.

Hat Creek was selected for the array because of how far it was from all significant sources of radio interference, which also meant it was far from any substantial population of people. The seclusion also made it significantly more difficult for the press, UFO fanatics, and terrorists from disrupting the important work Jennifer's team was conducting. Or so Jennifer was told by the driver of their SUV. She didn't bother asking for his name as he had no useful answers to her questions. Most of the four-hour drive from Sacramento International Airport was in a comfortable silence. Even Sam stopped trying to dig for details after the second hour of uninterrupted driving along the interstate. Compared to her first experience with FBI agents, whoever this was did not care much for socialization.

After Obama's press conference, it didn't take long for those fanatics and curiosity seekers to make it almost impossible to get any serious research done in SETI's Mountain View office. With Brian's approval, Jennifer and her team were relocated to the ATA, the source of all the data being fed to Vern.

That didn't dampen Jennifer's mood, though, and she relaxed as the ATA antennas appeared between rolling hills and trees. She looked over at Sam, who looked away from Jennifer, her eyes drifting from one nondescript tree to another outside of their vehicle, shoulders slouched. The volume from her earbuds were just high enough to faintly hear the thump of drum and bass. As the SUV approached the main building, Jennifer noticed a large clearing with construction equipment and large steel shipping containers going out for over a mile. Three tractor-scrapers were in the distance, scooping the grassy land into them, leaving exposed, muddy dirt in their wake. Further behind them were motor graders that flattened and leveled the ground even more to prepare for laying asphalt. Dozens of surveyors strolled through the area as well.

It took a few seconds for Jennifer to realize what was happening. "Are they preparing to expand the Allen Array?" she asked the nameless driver, pointing at the clearing.

"Yes, ma'am," he said. "The latest government directive, from what I understand."

It only took aliens coming to us for the money, she thought as a frown crossed her lips. There were grand plans for the ATA though due to a lack of funding only the first forty-two antennas were constructed. Now it appeared that the full three-hundred-fifty-antenna plan—the largest goal for the ATA installation—would become a reality. In addition, a host of additional dishes and potential facilities were being laid out well beyond the original boundaries of the ATA. Once the work was completed, the ATA would be the most powerful radio telescope in the western hemisphere, even rivaling Arecibo and SALT for the number one spot for radio astronomy. However, though the original expansion plans revolved around other long-term missions, it was obvious that everything would focus on the Leviathan.

The Leviathan, Jennifer thought, a light chuckle escaping her. The one time our civilization encounters ET, and it's the biblical names— characters and monsters of myth and legend—that were ascribed to it first.

Sam rolled her head toward Jennifer, the volume from the earbuds lowered. "What is it?"

"Oh, just thinking about Leviathan, that's all."

"Yeah, who isn't at this point?" Sam looked back out the side window as the SUV came to a stop in front of the main ATA building.

"Alright, we're here," the nameless one said from the front, his tone as flat as the surrounding land. It didn't take long to unload what little they had—the relocation team that was assigned to them, led by Gabi Lebeau, had most of their possessions relocated to their new, shared home less than a mile away from ATA.

Jennifer and Sam stood side by side, each with a roller travel bag which contained their most immediate possessions.

"Isn't this serene?" Jennifer said after she took a deep breath and opened her eyes.

"I dunno," Sam said. She looked around at the stumpy bushes which peppered the terrain that surrounded them. "I liked living in an area that was five minutes away from food and the occasional drink."

"I'm sure Gabi can arrange to have a bar's worth of alcohol shipped to our kitchen if you asked," Jennifer said. "Besides, what's not to like about Hat Creek? Look at the views!" She swept her arm across the horizon, emphasizing Mount Shasta, whose snow-covered peak jutted well above everything else in the distance.

"I suppose you can't get that in Mountain View," Sam conceded with a shrug.

"You won't get the mob crushing against the SETI perimeter, either," a female voice said from behind the two of them. Jennifer and Sam turned to see Gabi as she exited the ATA building.

"I didn't think they would have flown you out here," Jennifer said as she took Gabi's extended hand in hers. Gabi Lebeau, Relocation Director from the FBI, had a modest look for herself, with glasses that sat on her sharp nose, brunette hair tied back into a ponytail, and a business suit. In as many ways as one could manage, she made herself up to look as approachable as possible. She maintained a sunny disposition whenever she talked to people, but Jennifer sensed there was something more about Gabi that made her feel uncomfortable.

"Are they having you bunk with your co-workers, too?"

Sam asked with crossed arms.

"It was the best I could do on short notice," Gabi responded with a smile. "It's not every day the government buys an entire house to live—"

"Wait, you bought the house we'll be in?" Sam asked, disbelieving.

"Oh, yes, just like how we bought out that farm you see over there," Gabi said, her smile almost beaming as she gestured toward the construction.

"I guess that means you're also responsible for the manned security gate we drove through to get here," Jennifer said. "That kind of security was never there for this private establishment before."

Gabi's smile waned at Jennifer's words, becoming more serious. "ATA is still privately owned, but we insisted on the extra security as part of the funding for the expansion project." Looking to change the subject, she dived into her jacket pocket and removed two sets of car keys on two key rings, her faux smile restored. "This is for the two of you. You can find your cars in the parking lot just behind the office. Your key rings also have individual keys to your house on Bidwell Road. On the living room table you'll find IDs that you'll need for getting through security."

"I was wondering what kind of vehicle we'd get while here," Sam said as she took her keys.

Jennifer took her keys soon after. "Thanks," she said.

"Great! The two of you have my number—if you need anything, please don't hesitate to call," Gabi said, walking backwards toward the parking lot.

"Even if we want to order dinner?" Sam asked half joking.

"Especially if you want to order dinner," Gabi laughed and waved. "See you soon, ladies!"

As Gabi rounded the corner to the parking lot, Jennifer and Sam walked into the ATA work center. One side of the small foyer, from floor to ceiling, had boxes of new workstations, monitors, and stray computer parts. Jennifer passed through the double-door to the core of the building—an open-floor office space that she expected to look about the same as it did eight years ago. Nic greeted her after he popped up from under one of the cleared desks. "Hey, Doctor Epstein!"

"Morning, Nic," she said with a slight wave. She looked around at the desks in the office, most of which had stacks of paper and collections of empty ceramic mugs and cups. New spectrum analyzers sat across three cleared desks, their cables draped over other desks and equipment so they could reach the beamformer rack. She scratched her head as she surveyed the space—it looked as if everyone dropped what they were doing and vacated the premises. "What were the previous people doing here? It's a complete mess."

"They probably were as excited about the discovery of extraterrestrial life as the team at Green Bank," Nic responded as he cleared his throat.

Jennifer smiled back as thoughts of her call with a drunken Gus from that observatory over a month ago. "Yeah, it was quite a rush, before realizing what was happening at the source of the signal."

"It's still a rush, as far as I'm concerned," chimed Sam as she rolled her suitcase to the back door of the office. She then pulled her jacket off and flung it over a nearby chair. "Nic, where is everyone else?"

"I guess you skipped over that part of our relocation details," Gordan said as he entered the office space from the server room. "By the way, try convincing your wife about the reasons why leaving your home of over ten years for a house that's surrounded by farmland. That was a fun conversation." His face pinched into a grimace.

"At least you got the largest property out of all of us," Nic said.

"It was the least they could do to accommodate my family," Gordan said, after which he acknowledged Jennifer and Sam with a nod. "Glad to have you guys here."

"Likewise," Jennifer nodded with a sympathetic smile. "I'm glad you still agreed to come, despite the sacrifice your family made."

Gordan's lip almost curved into a smile before he suppressed it. "I'm happy with the decision, and my wife understands, even if she's still slightly irate about it." He turned to Nic, wiping away beads of sweat from his forehead with his shirt sleeve. "So it looks like the LAN connections are all nominal, though I look forward to seeing what you can do for that space in terms of temperature. Only half the racks are active, but it feels like a sauna in there."

"Yeah, they're expecting a major upgrade in ventilation," said Nic, gesturing to a few unopened boxes near the server room doorway. He already memorized all the new equipment sitting in the foyer: high-end multi-monitor workstations and hardware for adaptive beamforming, radio frequency interference mitigation, and imaging systems. There was enough equipment to allow more than double the number of people at ATA—he suspected more scientists would arrive soon. "In the meantime, we have some lovely portable rack cooling units ready for deployment!"

"I digress," Gordan shook his head and faced Sam, turning away from Nic. "Sam, we're the new crew for this facility, at least until the feds deem it safe for us to return to our office in Mountain View." He grimaced at that fact regarding the government's role in their relocation. Jennifer sighed in equal resignation. Despite the incredible level of flexibility they've had thanks to the influx of funds, the very people that granted those funds had already poked their fingers into a variety of administrative duties. A lot of this extra attention and forced procedures placed on them—all for the sake of security—had more than rankled everyone in one way or another.

Regardless of government intentions, Jennifer was still proud to manage the ATA. It felt odd to be at the facility with no graduate students from various colleges around the country and the SETI Institute, but given her role she knew that would change.

She leaned against a steel cabinet and cleared her throat, which got everyone's attention.

"Well," she began as she unbuttoned her shirt sleeves and rolled them up. "For the time being, it's just the four of us. We have a lot of work to do. I know this wasn't the most ideal situation, moving out here, but there's still so much for us to learn about the object—the Leviathan." She motioned toward a desk that had, among some older radio frequency printouts, a disconnected desktop computer that looked like it wasn't turned on in over a decade. Jennifer knew Gabi wanted her and Sam to head for their new home before doing anything else, but the desire to get her hands dirty was strong.

She lifted the dusty computer and brought it to the floor before looking back up at everyone else. "Let's go!"

∘ ◎ ∘

Sam was about ready to pass out after a full day of mostly hard labor and little Leviathan tracking, but at least by the time she left the office, everything was ready to go for tomorrow and the many weeks to come. With the new equipment now online and connected with SETI in Mountain View, they could communicate and disseminate information from their observatory without interruptions, package drops, or latency issues. It would only be a matter of days before their dedicated fiber gigabit connection was established, opening the doors for more seamless connections between them and observatories and agencies in other parts of the world. There was still so much to do, but as Jennifer told everyone as their first day at their new premises came to a close at her command: "One step at a time."

With the sun about to relegate the sky to the stars and a waning crescent moon, she understood why Jennifer preferred being out here to Mountain View. Other than her footsteps on the ground, the only other sounds around her were the crickets and the occasional gust of wind. Thanks to FAA regulations there were no flight paths over them for dozens of miles in all directions, and the nearest major roadway was over two miles away.

She left her car parked next to Jennifer's, which was at the end of a road that terminated next to one of the antennas. A bottle of champagne and two wine flutes that she found in their home were her only guests to this night time celebration. She already removed the wrapping from the neck of the bottle. Her gait almost went into a skip as she approached Jennifer, who sat on a redwood tree trunk that was sliced in half and laid flat side down. It was at the artificial boundary that separated the line of antennas of the ATA and nature, with dozens of small shrubs and succulents planted to act as that line of demarcation.

She knew Jennifer would be out here—she told her as much before their workday came to a tiresome close. As she got closer, she noticed her longing gaze into the sky as more stars faded into existence with each passing minute. Before she could silence her approach,

Jennifer turned towards Sam. Despite the growing darkness, it appeared as though Jennifer was lost in thought.

"Am I interrupting?" Sam asked as she approached Jennifer and the foot of the tree trunk.

"Oh, not at all, Sam," Jennifer said.

"Mind if I join you?" Sam asked, followed by presenting the glasses in her hand. "I brought a little something for us."

Jennifer responded with a smile and patted a spot next to her, to which Sam gladly accepted. Once Sam situated herself next to Jennifer, she gave one flute to her and removed the cork from the bottle with a satisfying pop.

"Here's to the Allen Telescope Array—" She filled one glass to the brim. "—to the SETI Institute changing the world—" The second glass was topped off. "—and to us."

"To us?" Jennifer asked.

"Of course!" Sam responded with her glass raised. "To the two women that made the largest discovery in human history. We never really had a formal celebration or even a toast—I wanted to remedy that tonight."

Jennifer looked into Sam's eyes, which made Sam's heart unexpectedly skip a beat, before she raised her glass. "To us." The two brought their glasses together in a toast with a gentle clink. Sam took a long sip though stopped when Jennifer made a closed-lipped moan to her surprise.

"It's been a while since I've had a drink," said Jennifer. "I've forgotten how delicious some can be."

"I'm glad I could be the one to break your streak, Jen," said Sam, choosing to be informal.

"Mmmmm-hmmmm," Jennifer agreed as she took another sip from her glass. She looked toward the sky once more. Sam scooted a little closer to Jennifer as she joined her staring upward. That was when she noticed that Jennifer looked in the same direction as all the surrounding antennas—toward the Leviathan.

"You know, if the Leviathan receives any more major surface impacts, we may be able to actually see it with the naked eye in a few years," Sam threw out into the open.

"In about ten years, it will be visible at night, no matter what happens to it," Jennifer said as she dropped her head toward her champagne glass with a sigh. She took another sip.

Several thoughts raced through Sam's mind as she tried to come up with a response that didn't sound pessimistic or kill the mood. "We'll find a solution to that great question," she said. "We have loads of unexamined data to decipher, and with the governments of the world practically falling over themselves to boost their space programs, I believe we'll have an answer before our time is up."

"I hope so..." Jennifer trailed off as she fished her cell phone from a side pocket, the screen lit with two unread text messages.

Sam saw the phone and leaned in. "Another message from your mom?"

"No," Jennifer said as she dropped her shoulders. "These were from earlier this week—I haven't read them."

Sam bit her lip as she scooted closer once more, her fingers almost touching Jennifer's on the bark. "You know, in all the years we've worked together, you've never told me the deal between you and your folks."

"There's never been a reason to share such personal details with you," Jennifer said with a monotone voice as she looked at her phone once more.

Sam gave a soft smile though there was a hint of hesitation in her voice. "Well, there's no time like the present, especially since Earth now has a countdown timer lingering over it." She saw Jennifer's doubt. *Was she actually willing to open up?* "Come on, it'll just be between us, the stars above, and the antennas."

Jennifer's eyes shifted between her phone and Sam, then relaxed. She took another sip of her champagne as she passed her phone to Sam. "Check it out."

"Ohh, top-secret access," Sam joked as she swiped across the phone screen, which made an audible click as the icons appeared. After opening the messaging software, the most recent unopened message appeared. It was a quote from the Bible: *No one can serve two masters, for either he will hate the one and love the other, or he will be devoted to the one and despise the other. You cannot serve God and money.*

"How appropriate," Sam said. She swiped through the list of text messages, all from Jennifer's mother.

"I receive messages like that weekly—sometimes daily—depending on the time of year."

"But you don't care for them?" Sam asked as she gave the phone back to Jennifer.

There was a brief pause before Jennifer responded, her eyes first lingering on her phone before looking back at Sam. "What kind of relationship do you have with your parents, where religion's concerned?"

"Oh, well pretty good I suppose. They don't understand my reasons for breaking away from their beliefs, which caused a large commotion a decade ago, but we've since reconciled. I don't see them often, but yeah... we're all close. Thanksgiving isn't awkward anymore so that's a plus."

Jennifer chuckled, but the shared experience made her face crestfallen. "If only all parents were as accommodating."

Sam wanted to say something, but kept quiet for the moment. Jennifer continued.

"See, Dennis and Grace—my father and mother—are devout members of Catholicism. My father, in particular, was stern in our home regarding worship and didn't like how much time I wanted to spend studying the sciences instead of the Bible. This became a defining aspect of my relationship with him and, by extension, my mother who sat mostly on the sidelines when I was being punished by Dennis for all manners of illogical reasons. The age of the Earth, the theory of evolution, discussions of other religions—all of it was practically heresy for him. So when I received a full scholarship from Binghamton for college, Dennis was livid. He threatened to kick me out of the house if I accepted. He already pulled some strings to get me a full rider for King's College, you see, so this was pretty much the final straw for him."

Jennifer sucked in a mouthful of air, her face flush. Though Sam couldn't see the color of her face change in the encroaching darkness, it was apparent to her that Jennifer was getting worked up. "I recall that you did go to Binghamton University..."

"That's right," Jennifer said. "Summer of 1987 was the last time

I lived with my parents. Once I left for Binghamton, I never looked back. Dennis stayed true to his word and basically tossed whatever I didn't bring to upstate New York into the trash."

Sam looked into her lap, her mind and heart still racing, and then reached over with her left hand and wrapped it around Jennifer's right. The warmth from Jennifer's soft hand was welcoming. Jennifer looked at Sam, but didn't pull away.

"I'm sorry," Sam said, not able to think of any other response. "It really stinks that your da—father treated you like an outcast. Still treats you like an outcast."

"It's okay, Sam. I've had years to process my experiences with them. At this point, I feel like I've made peace with this reality."

"What about Grace?"

More deep breaths from Jennifer. This was a subject she rarely discussed with others and it showed. "I won't say she's a prisoner in her own home... but she and Dennis are in a prison of their own design. She's as devout as him, but I'd like to think that if she had the chance, the two of us would work together in trying to turn things around with our family. The weekly text messages are her odd way of communicating with me—her way of showing that ties are not completely severed between us."

"Have you tried reaching out?"

"At first, yes. Many attempts were made during and after college and grad school. A brick wall, Dennis is, and his unwavering faith steel rebar meshed within that brick. It's been a long time since I've tried any sort of communication with them."

"Have you tried recently?" Sam asked.

Jennifer gripped Sam's hand tighter at that, but didn't respond.

"Maybe with the Leviathan making its grand debut, perhaps thoughts on reconnecting with their estranged daughter is coming to the surface. Existential dread can be a strong motivator for resolving family issues, I think," Sam said.

"Even if your parents believe in God?"

"Especially if they believe in God."

Sam scooted closer for the final time, the two of them now side by side, their clasped hands resting between their legs which brushed each other. Sam broke her attentive gaze and looked into the distance, a silhouette of Mount Shasta against a backdrop of stars. The wind caressed her face as she processed what was shared. She closed her eyes and parted her lips as she allowed herself to breath and focus. *Breathe and relax. Try to relax.* Her stiff posture became, for a time, even more rigid when she felt Jennifer's head nestle into her shoulder. Sam felt a wave of conflicting emotions flow through her, but even though Jennifer was her superior at SETI and was a decade her senior, the feelings she suppressed for years felt right.

"Thanks," Jennifer said as she sniffed and passed a finger over her eyes. Sam, with a smile from ear to ear, continued facing forward as she finally released her tension, her body relaxing.

The two of them sat together in silence for some time, Jennifer's head resting on Sam's shoulder. Sam didn't know what to expect between the two of them in the days, months, and years to come, but she knew that she didn't want this moment to end.

PART TWO

CONSEQUENCES

2.0

From a million miles away, the Earth still held a prominent position among the galactic backdrop behind and around it. The blue, green, and white ball held many unique features when compared to its other planetary neighbors. That uniqueness, however, was not the focus of the James Webb High-Definition Space Telescope, abbreviated to simply Webb Telescope by those who launched it into orbit, just under a year ago.

The space observatory settled into its permanent home at the Sun-Earth Lagrange 2 point, an area of space beyond Earth's orbit where an object could maintain its position solely affected by the gravitational pull between two other objects—such as the Earth and the Sun—with minimal energy needed for spatial corrections. The position was ideal for any observatory which would observe the universe from space, as the sun and the Earth would be fixed relative to that observatory, allowing unobstructed views. In addition, being in the shadow of the Earth ensured the telescope would sustain passive temperatures well below minus 225 degrees Celsius. This allowed it to pick up infrared radiation that Hubble wasn't able to collect due to its proximity to Earth.

The Webb Telescope wasn't the same telescope designed decades earlier. Thanks to generous funding and far more delays than expected since the start of The Armstrong Program in mid-2014, the number of hexagonal mirror segments that would comprise the primary mirror tripled from eighteen to fifty-four, all of which combined into a single honeycomb-shaped mirror almost twelve meters wide. It sat atop the science instrument module which was jam-packed with the latest computing resources. The technology ranged from an infrared imager and spectrograph to coronagraphs which could observe distant exoplanets with a level of detail that would be impossible for the Hubble to replicate. Webb Telescope's instruments and control systems were in the middle of a sunshield, a quintuple-layered polyimide film that, as a square-shaped parasol sixty-three meters wide, ensured the primary and secondary mirror were as cold as they needed to be. The film also protected all the other support systems in place that powered the telescope, managed propulsion and thermal subsystems, and maintained active communications with mission control. The design of the sunshield drew the heat from the sun and the Earth away from the mirrors and instruments to various end points that allowed the blistering temperatures to radiate safely into space.

Even before the significant design change, the Webb Telescope in totality was the size of a tennis court when fully deployed. What launched into space was as wide as a 747 aircraft's wingspan.

It was a marvel of humanity's progress in space technology—a symbol of what they were capable of against the odds. And now that marvel, with only a month remaining of final system and instrument diagnostics, aimed its body toward a small section of space which appeared empty at first glance. The mirrors reflected dozens of stars and their ancient light, but they weren't the focus. Nor were the exoplanets that dozens of scientists around the world suspected orbited those stars.

In the smallest sliver of space was an object 1.59 billion miles away from Earth. An object too massive to be affected by the gravitational effects of the other planets. An object on a direct course for Earth.

And in one month, the Webb Telescope would provide the world its first detailed images of the object now known the world over as the Leviathan.

2.1

For Jennifer, there just weren't enough hours in the day, especially when NASA gave her a ring. Despite her elevation to a directorship position that didn't even exist less than six months ago, there were few barriers between her and anyone that needed to contact her for anything. The decision to not have an Administrative Assistant was hers to make. "I may be Director, but that doesn't mean I don't want to be on the field," she once said to Allan after she accepted the new role that was signed off by Obama. She received recommendations by her project managers and other senior researchers on bringing in one or two administrators to help with day-to-day tasks, but still allowed an open-door policy concerning communication.

To the surprise of her colleagues within the ATA and superiors at NASA, Jennifer pulled off the unenviable task of directing all the observatories and arrays within SETI US West and coordinating directly with NASA regarding all actions taken. This included the drier side of management she detested: lengthy meetings that served only as a way to bring Allan up to speed on what was going on in a given week. It all required lots of mental compartmentalization, but she made the job work, and work well.

But when her personal line buzzed, she couldn't help but crinkle her nose at the desk phone in front of her. Only a handful of people had her office number, so it ringing narrowed the field.

And only one person called her the most with it.

"Good morning, Allan," Jennifer said as she cradled the receiver between her shoulder and head. Her free hand held a pen which scanned a detailed list of observatories in Nevada, Arizona, and New Mexico that fell under her purview. She glanced at the phone's clock and cursed under her breath at the two-hour time difference that allowed early calls like this.

"Hey Jennifer," he responded. She liked that they'd moved away from formalities when speaking together. "I wanted to get an update regarding Arecibo and delivering the Golden Record to the Leviathan. If it were up to me, it would've gone out on Saturday."

"I sent you the details on the staffing rotation at Arecibo that was scheduled to occur through the weekend," said Jennifer, half her mind focused on jotting down notes on some details surrounding the Karl Jansky VLA in New Mexico. "The folks at NRAO can give you more detailed information on the new list of personnel."

"Ah, right," Allan groaned as he pulled up the rotation itinerary he received from Jennifer the previous Friday. The email also included a document with the personnel that were being flown in. "You gave me the list of who would be at Arecibo, Jen—why did you want to send me over to NRAO?"

"So we could end this phone call, which would allow me to complete what you asked for," Jennifer said. She placed the pen down and slipped the receiver into her hand as she stood from her desk.

"Ow, that hurts," joked Allan. "Okay, we'll talk again later today, after the message is sent."

"Thank you, Allan," Jennifer said. Before she hung up the phone, she quickly added, "By the way, don't call me Jen." Allan didn't have enough time to react to her last words, which she felt gave him more than enough time to mull over how he handled their next call.

She looked up from the phone and sighed heavily as if talking with Allan consumed all the air in the room. A part of her job as the Director of SETI US West required a certain level of active communication with him. On paper, she knew that Brian's selection for Director of SETI US East made sense given his background and tendency to brown-nose.

He even sought out the position the moment it was announced whereas Allan approached Jennifer for the job.

With the quick call over, her eyes honed on the office wall which had a single large corkboard mounted on it. Most of the board was covered with large printouts of the Leviathan's front. They were focused up to the horizon of the bulge that was visible in all the larger head-on body shots of the object—the ship's bow, its face.

The center image—one of the first that came back from the Webb Telescope—was the highest resolution image they had of the Leviathan to date. It was an incredible sight, even for what amounted to a photo taken head-on. Craters, narrow and wide canyons, and unusually smooth plains constituted the domed front, most of which reminded Jennifer of the surface of the moon. Another zoomed-in snapshot focused on one canyon that ran the entire diameter of the dome which was almost a perfect straight line. The bottom of the line was shrouded in darkness: the lips that separated deep space from the inside of the object. Three other printed images magnified what everyone agreed were the thrusters, most of which were obscured by the glare they emitted.

The image that most fascinated Jennifer, however, was off to one corner of the board, with several red question marks written on it by Sam. Though it was blurry, the image depicted solid, straight lines that intersected with each other at various points, with unnaturally spherical and boxy structures between the grids that were carved into the exotic landscape. What interested everyone at SETI was that this gridded patch did not look like it was part of the ship—it resembled something you would expect to see if a large colony were constructed on a planetary surface.

Jennifer ran a pointed finger along the images. She held conflicting thoughts of the wonders they could find by visiting this ship alongside the fact that it slowly moved toward Earth.

Sam, her best friend and confidante, walked into her office unannounced, some papers in her hand that she shook in the air. "Arecibo is ready to party!" she exclaimed, her beaming smile infectious. "The Golden Broadcast will go out in T-Minus thirty minutes."

"Already?" Jennifer asked, turning toward Sam and grabbed the papers from her. The personnel rotation completed Sunday evening, the new staff burning through the morning to get all systems ready for continuous broadcasting directly to the Leviathan. "I'm honestly surprised they moved so fast."

"Yeah, but it helps when you're actually getting paid to do the job," Sam said as she rubbed her fingers together with a smirk.

"They were paid before," Jennifer countered as she placed the papers from Sam onto her desk.

"Teacher's assistants in college got paid more than we did," Sam said as the two of them left Jennifer's office and walked onto the floor of the ATA office. All the desks lined the walls of the office while the middle space remained open, demarcated with a square green rug. Sam ran over to her desk that sat in front of a large window that looked out toward the many dishes that ran well over a mile into the distance.

Jennifer waved in the air, grabbing the attention of the small crew she worked alongside for over a year. "Okay everyone, get your teams ready for live monitoring of the Leviathan."

"Yes, ma'am," said Gordan with a salute. "I've already have Kabir on-call. Between the two of us, we'll be ready to capture anything new that comes our way."

"You got it," said Nic, excited to be assisting in the coordination efforts with several telescopes in SETI US West.

"We're good to go," said Nareen with a short nod. Jennifer was glad to have Nareen on her team—if anyone could assist with understanding the Leviathan's purpose, and the civilization it originated from, it was her.

Sam spun herself around in her chair and faced Jennifer. "Aye aye, captain! All dishes across the western half of the US are green."

Jennifer surveyed everyone, all looking at her, waiting for any further instructions. "Great. Expect an all-hands call to go out once SETI East and NASA are a go," Jennifer said. She nodded with pressed lips and walked back into her office.

Getting Brian on a video call always seemed to be a challenge whenever it was her that initiated it. She hadn't thought their respective promotions would cause tension though she felt that he was slighted somehow upon getting word about her running SETI US West.

As she looked at the chat list on her monitor, his name highlighted, she sighed and took a different approach. She loaded her email program and typed up an email that, after a couple of minutes of typing, reading, and re-typing, she sent to Brian, Allan, Susan, and several other directors at NASA, the ESA, and Roscosmos.

o ◎ o

SUBJECT: THE GOLDEN MESSAGE
IMPORTANCE: HIGH

Hello Everyone.

We are about to make our own first contact with an alien civilization. In less than thirty minutes the Arecibo Observatory in Puerto Rico will take the contents of the Golden Record, our first message to the cosmos that went out on the Voyager 1 probe in 1977, and broadcast all the audio directly to the Leviathan.

This is, without question, a significant moment in the history of humankind, and one that cannot be handled with enough care and sensitivity. The decision to send the contents of a record created over thirty years ago was not made lightly, nor did the decision come without controversy.

There were two driving factors in using the audio content of the Golden Record. The Leviathan was already in our solar system, its presence letting us know something as large as it had to have been created by a civilization far in advance of our own; and that its actions—and its current course in space that will bring it to Earth by 2024—required a level of urgency on our part. But we have to assume that the actions of the Leviathan were not malicious in nature, despite what we've witnessed. We just don't know enough about the Leviathan to understand its motives.

Mathematics, a universal language of intelligent beings, could still be used as a form of communication, and we may unanimously decide to send primes to the Leviathan after this. But knowing they are using radio technology to broadcast their presence—a technology far inferior to anything they likely use for their own contemporary form of communication—indicates to us they want other intelligent beings to contact them.

Therefore, let us follow the footsteps of Carl Sagan and put a more human face to our first-ever contact with an alien civilization that is in our galactic backyard.

We are human, and we are here.

Jennifer Epstein
Director of SETI US West
United States of America
Earth

o ◎ o

It didn't take long for a video call request to appear from Brian on Jennifer's monitor. She flicked the mouse over to the window and accepted the call, Brian's face filling the screen.

"You could've asked for a little input from me," Brian said with his arms crossed.

"Hello to you, too," Jennifer said in a friendly tone.

"I'm just saying that a message of... that magnitude... could've had a few more hands in it. That's all."

"If that were true, I doubt it would've gone out before the Leviathan responded to our message."

"If they respond," Brian leaned forward and placed his hands to the sides of his keyboard.

Jennifer ignored what he said and continued. "Speaking of human-kind's message, I wanted to confirm with you that everything is go for your teams at SETI US East. If anything comes back, everyone must be ready."

"Of course we're ready," Brian said. "Did you think we wouldn't be?"

"I just wanted to get a confirmation," Jennifer said with gritted teeth. "You've been hard to reach lately, and your email response times haven't been conducive for rapid planning and coordination."

"Wait a minute, me hard to reach?" his voice rose as he crossed his arms again. For a moment, it seemed as if he thought about all the emails from Jennifer and the lack of responses on his part over the last few weeks. But it was only for a moment. "We're both in the same position—you know how crazy it's been."

"It's never too crazy to not coordinate with me, considering that we're equals." Jennifer saw Brian's face redden as his eyes darted off-screen. "We have to work together, Brian. We're two sides of the same coin. I shouldn't have to explain the importance of what we are doing."

"I don't take kindly to your treating me like I'm your subordinate," he barked, the reddened glow now encompassing most of his head and neck.

"Then act like you're my equal," Jennifer snapped, her nails pinching into her palms as she leaned toward her monitor, anger bubbling to the surface. "In the meantime, send an email confirmation to me and Allan regarding the status of SETI US East. We'll talk again later." Brian motioned for his mouse, but Jennifer cut the video feed faster with a keyboard shortcut.

"You know, it's moments like that where having an open-door policy where your door is closed would be handy," Sam said from the foot of the office door.

When what Sam said had registered, Jennifer looked at her and laughed. "Sorry about that," she said as she scratched the back of her head.

"It's cool, Jen," Sam said. "We all needed a little drama to break up the day, and you always seem to deliver when we need it most."

"Is that a fact?" Jennifer smiled wide as they looked at each other. She felt lucky that she discovered this side of Sam—a younger sister she never had. They even agreed to stay next-door neighbors after new housing was built for more comfortable and private accommodations a year after their ATA relocation. Sam's face read, *I know—Brian's an asshole and an idiot.* Jennifer could tell Sam knew what she was thinking as well: *Thanks for stepping in.*

"Great email, by the way," Sam said as she adjusted her stance to lean against the doorway with one foot propped against it. "I can see it being quoted on the eight o'clock news tonight."

"Maybe so," Jennifer said before Sam jumped in.

"'We are human, we are here.' Come on, that's like something out of a science fiction version of *Braveheart.*"

The two of them laughed, with any lingering feelings of anger being released from Jennifer. She could always count on Sam cheering her up, especially after having a sparring session with Brian, the only person that seemed to grate her. Even Allan's occasional indirect flirtations didn't annoy her as much. At least when it came to business he could keep up with everything, if not take the lead on many initiatives. But that was also something she'd shared with Sam. Such conversations usually ended with the two of them laughing at one of Sam's inappropriate jokes about the entire situation.

Jennifer's smartphone rang, vibrating on her desk as it did. She waved Sam over as she picked up the phone and tapped the screen. "Epstein here."

"Morning, Dr. Epstein, this is Isabella Velasco," Isabella said with a noticeable, but pleasant, Spanish accent. She sounded younger than Jennifer expected, given her role as Director for the Arecibo Observatory.

"Ahh, yes, I recall seeing your name on the roster. Welcome to the team."

"It's a pleasure to be finally working with you," Isabella said, the professionalism in her voice almost giving way to adoration.

"Indeed," Jennifer agreed." I've seen your credentials—they are very impressive."

"Thank you—getting two Ph.D.s was no small feat."

She just couldn't help but pat herself on the back though Jennifer let it slide.

"All the more reason you are at Arecibo today. So, are we ready?"

"We are ready to go," Isabella said. Jennifer eyed Sam for a moment and mouthed, "Get to work," to which Sam got up and sauntered into the office. "It's time to make history again!" she shouted to subsequent cheers.

"Excellent," said Jennifer. "Did you have a plan regarding the process by which the audio recordings would be sent?"

"Testing me, are you?" asked Isabella. "All transmitters are ready. The first send will be in bursts at frequencies of 400MHz, 45MHz, and 8MHz. That should be enough to grab their attention. After that, we'll initiate a continuous stream at 3000MHz which we'll keep active for a full day unless we receive word to disable the stream earlier. The pulse bursts will be on rotating frequencies every hour to encompass as much of the spectrum as possible."

"I find it hard to believe you'll be able to pull that off without some level of civilian broadcast interference."

"Fortunately, Governor Padilla agreed with your concerns—he's ordered all civilian radio stations to close for today. The only thing to hit the airwaves here will be Arecibo."

Jennifer curled up her lip, raised her eyebrows, and nodded. "Very impressive legwork, Dr. Velasco. And you pulled that off before settling into your post?"

"It wasn't too hard when one could appeal to Padilla's political ambitions." Isabella then spoke in her native language, her words soft, yet moving. "*Haz esto y serás recordado a lo largo de la historia.*"

Do this and you will be remembered throughout history. "Clever," Jennifer said with a grin.

As Jennifer opened her mouth to ask another question, Isabella continued. "So we'll have full broadcast rights through today. Also, the broadcast will encompass the entirety of the Leviathan, so unless their equivalent of radio antennas are at the rear of the ship, they will receive our message. I am positive their receivers are at the front of the ship, though, if not all around the body."

"Why do you say that?"

"If you operated a ship three times the size of Earth, and you made it a point to send messages to any sentient species that are in your region of space, you would also have a way to receive anything that those species may send to them—provided they are sufficiently advanced enough to not only have radio technology but have also gone into space."

"I hope you are right—for all our sakes," Jennifer said. She settled back into her plush chair and looked at the time on her monitor. "We're still good to initiate in ten minutes?"

"Yes," said Isabella, who Jennifer imagined had a grin from ear to ear right now.

"Okay, I'll leave you to it. I'll be monitoring all frequency data on my end, but call me on my cell if you need anything more."

"You got it, Dr. Epstein. It's a pleasure."

"No, the pleasure is all mine. Goodbye."

Jennifer stood up as she placed her phone into its charging dock. The Leviathan looked like it was increasingly alive to her as she found her eyes drawn to the many printouts on her board. However, it was the most unscientific printout that caught her attention. Tucked in the lower left-hand corner of the board, with nothing but tape keeping it in place, was an artist's depiction of the Leviathan as if you looked at it from its side. An image of the ship they did not yet have. Jennifer was dismissive of the artwork, but Sam insisted on keeping it hung "for inspiration."

But as the clock ticked ever closer to the Arecibo broadcast, the art looked more disturbing than usual. The mouth of the Leviathan was open half-way, the deep blacks of its interior hinted just beyond the opening. Raw images of what was assumed to be engines were given an exaggerated size by the artist. It had a large ring-like structure gripping the middle of the ship and several conical shapes coming out of the ring all the way around. The rear of the ship had a more natural look as if it were a long tail that moved from side to side—much like a snake. She felt the artist meant to depict the Leviathan as a living creature instead of an artificial ship, an idea that gained traction among some romanticists and cults throughout the world.

For the first time, though it ran contrary to what she and the scientific world understood on biology, chemistry, and physics, she thought for a moment what would happen if that were true.

∘ ◎ ∘

"The radio signals from Arecibo should've reached the Leviathan by now," Nic said, his leg bouncing vigorously under his desk. His eyes were glued to his trio of monitors as the online chatter among the various observatories he oversaw rolled up the side of his screen.

"That's correct," Gordan responded, but not to anyone in particular. He gravitated from station to station, reviewing the statuses of all the radio telescopes that effectively had their dishes and antennae locked in place. They were all aimed at the Leviathan to capture whatever may come as a response. "It took about 142 minutes for the signal to arrive, so if there is any change in what we're getting, we'll know about it as early as 2:40PM."

"What do you think will happen?" Nic posited to everyone around him.

"An apology for destroying a quarter of our outer solar system would be nice," quipped Sam.

Gordan groaned as he rubbed one of his eyes. "Very good, Sam."

"What?" She finished her mug of coffee before she looked over to Gordan. "You gotta have a sense of humor with things like this."

"I don't consider the fate of our existence something to laugh about." His face was flat and devoid of expression, but Sam could tell by the tick in his voice he was getting frustrated.

"Well someone has to," Sam rebutted with a wink. "Besides, with you and your perpetual poker face, who knows how you feel about this situation as a whole."

Nic's leg stopped bouncing as he looked around the side of his monitors, loudly clearing his throat. "Guys, can you take your spat outside?"

Jennifer shook her head as the three of them bickered amongst each other. Sam prodded Gordan, Gordan parried some of Sam's jests and ignoring others, and Nic tried to defuse the situation for the sake of getting more work done, which Sam and Gordan usually ignored. Instead of putting a stop to it, she scooped up her smartphone and walked just outside the office. The front doors were thick, so little sound escaped the office environment once they closed with a metallic click.

After she clicked the message notification on her phone, Jennifer typed a quick message to Grace: *Just letting you know that our messages to the Leviathan would've arrived by now. This may help us better understand what we're working with.* She held her breath as she sent the message as she almost always did when she sent her mother a text message. Sam convinced Jennifer to reopen a line of communication with Grace in 2014, but she didn't act on Sam's recommendation until almost a year later.

A light wind gust weaved through Jennifer's ponytailed hair as she looked up and to the left. Several narrow roads, still looking fresh from when they were paved months ago, stretched well over a mile into the distance where dozens of new dishes sat, the afternoon sun reflecting off their edges. On what was farmland now sat over a hundred new radio dishes, giving the ATA incredible scanning capabilities and a greater range of frequencies it could receive. If they had the ability to broadcast radio transmissions, their observatory would easily overtake Arecibo and even SALT.

Her phone buzzed in her hand. *I know, it's all over the news. Big countdown clock and everything.*

When Jennifer sent her first message to Grace a year earlier, the responses were both comforting and frustrating. She now knew that she and Grace could, at minimum, have text-based conversations. That alone brought Jennifer relief. However, any mention of Dennis would result in a large pause in responses before a message unrelated to him arrived. And despite Sam's insistence, Jennifer still hadn't called Grace, nor accepted calls from her. She couldn't get over the thought of hearing her mom, and then her father butting into the call to berate the both of them. *No, this would not happen,* she thought whenever such a call came in.

A loud siren blared in the distance, north of where the ATA

compound resided. Jennifer dropped her phone into her side pocket as she walked around to the side of the building. The road next to her bent northward toward the perimeter fence that gated ATA from the rest of the country. Following the siren sounded like someone spoke in a megaphone, though given the distance between the fence and her, it was hard to tell what was being said.

Gordan came outside, his phone in hand. "It's nothing to worry about. Just got word about the little convention beyond the gate getting rowdy due to the Golden Message reaching the Leviathan."

"Oh, you mean the 'little' convention made up of over ten thousand people that created their own little city just beyond the fence? That outnumber us twenty-five hundred to one?" Jennifer asked with a sharp tone.

"You realize that most of them are in favor of what we are doing, right?"

"It's not the majority I'm concerned about," said Jennifer with lips upturned.

"That's what the Secret Service are for," Gordan said as he patted her on the back. "Come on, we're two hours from witnessing any changes to the signal."

The sounds of people chanting were carried by the wind as it rolled around Jennifer's ears, the voice of a person on the megaphone echoed on the surrounding hills. She nodded as Gordan held the front door open. *They aren't a threat,* she repeated in her mind as she reentered the office and walked to her desk.

Every major television network and hundreds of online channels livestreamed the anticipated change in the signal. Astronomers, from amateur locals to researchers that worked at various observatories around the country, gave interviews regarding a range of subjects. The most popular debates revolved around the use of the audio content of the Golden Record as the first ever message to the Leviathan. In the final hour before an expected change in the signal, Jennifer was on the phone with CNN for a short interview segment.

"What are your thoughts regarding the contents of the Golden Record?" the interviewer asked.

Jennifer: "I believe the Golden Record, its creation overseen by Carl Sagan, represents the best of us as a species —the emotions we are capable of, the expressiveness of our global cultures through music and song. Using the audio contents from the record as our first foray into interstellar communications, in this case, I believe was the best possible decision."

Interviewer: "Why use the sounds of people speaking? Would the aliens be able to understand what they were receiving was from an intelligent species as opposed to using math as is usually represented in science fiction films?"

Jennifer: "There were a few reasons for this decision. The first was that the Leviathan was not only broadcasting a signal, but that it was broadcasting a signal using technology that was likely far inferior to their own. Therefore, whoever is running the Leviathan has taken into account meeting sentient species younger than them—less advanced than them. This leads into the second reason: Their signal contained a visual message that, to scientific authorities around the world, suggest they want others to respond to them. Therefore, by responding to them, they will be able to learn a great deal about us, including the fact that we nailed down simpler concepts like mathematical constants and our understanding of physics, radiology, and so on."

Interviewer: "So instead of sending evidence that we understand math, you decided to appeal to their... emotional side?"

Jennifer: "As President Carter once said regarding the contents of the Golden Record, it is meant to express our hope and our determination and our goodwill in a vast and awesome universe. Letting another species know we are not only alive and here, but are an intelligent, emotional species, may impact them far greater than showcasing our ability to add and subtract."

Interviewer: "The question regarding the accurate representation of humanity was called into question by many people, including several prominent politicians. It's been said that the overly positive image that the Golden Record comprises ignores the darker side, such as war, poverty, and death. You must admit those are major aspects of our history as a species."

Jennifer: "I agree with that assessment of our history, yes."

Interviewer: "Why do you think the late Carl Sagan and his NASA approved committee chose to omit that side of humanity?"

Jennifer: "Any civilization capable of constructing a ship the size and scale of the Leviathan would have experienced all the pain and suffering that we have and still inflict on ourselves. Sagan and his committee chose to represent the best of us because much like when you meet someone for the first time, first impressions are everything. Could the makers of the Leviathan still experience poverty and war? Certainly. Does that mean we have to show them videos of humanity blowing each other up, committing vile acts of rape and brutality upon our own people, hanging and shooting each other because of the color of our skin? Sagan realized that when the Golden Record was organized, it could be read by an entirely different species, with rules, manners, and customs we could barely imagine. However, any intelligent, space-faring civilization will view the species that created this record as one that, despite the astronomical odds against it, managed to get into space. That they understand the value of cooperation, peace, and life. It reflects optimism. It represents hope. It represents a species and society we all should strive for across the world: One that has overcome its prejudices, hate for itself, and is at peace."

Interviewer: "If you could send the makers of the Leviathan a message of your own, what would it be?"

Jennifer: "Ask me that question again in thirty minutes, for their response to our message of peace will make all the difference."

∘ ◎ ∘

"Three minutes until the entire western hemisphere is bathed in a new response from the Leviathan," Sam said with glee. She and Nic sat in front of her desk as they watched a livestream from MSNBC, which had a large countdown clock in the corner of their video feed.

"Isn't there something else you two could be doing?" Gordan sneered.

"Come on, Gordan," Sam said, looking over to him. "What is there to do right now: Make sure all the arrays are calibrated to a thousandth of a degree? Ensure the other observatories are properly staffed? I've done all my homework, sir." She couldn't help but take a quick jab.

Jennifer stood next to the general frequency monitor, which had several spectrum analyzers, interferometric windows, and audio recorders on display. They all had the current, pulsing signal from the Leviathan scrolling and pulsing and spiking within the various programs. She shot a look at the two of them. "Guys, save it for later. Less than a minute to go. Get to your stations."

Nic complied and ran back to his desk, closing out the media feed he had pulled up and refocused on the readings that came in from his observatories. Jennifer, however, looked up at the small mounted television in the corner of the office by the ceiling.

Jennifer couldn't help but admit that despite the frequent inaccuracies that were thrown around by the many networks that covered the potential signal changeover, they did put on quite the spectacle.

Ten.

Nine.

Eight.

Seven...

Jennifer glanced toward Sam, who she realized was already looking her way. She felt goosebumps on her skin when their eyes locked. What was it that she felt when their eyes connected like they were now? Her body shivered, which she brushed off as alerts chimed on the general monitor. Jennifer slid into the chair by the monitor as the signal's strength rapidly weakened, the predictable spikes becoming plateaus, then small hills.

...Four.

Three.

Two...

∘ ◎ ∘

—SIGNAL RECEIVED.

—SLEEP MODE DEACTIVATED.

—REVIEW ANTIMATTER POOL. SIPHON FROM HOST >>> SIPHON COMPLETE.

—CRYSTALLINE MATRIX CHARGING >>> CHARGED.

—ALIEN FREQUENCIES DETECTED. MULTIPLE AMPLITUDES, STRENGTH VARIATIONS—

—PATTERNS DETECTED. EVIDENCE OF DELIBERATE RE-SPONSE TO BEACON CONFIRMED.

—AUDIO PATTERNS DETECTED—ANALYZING >>> ANALYSIS COMPLETE.

—EVIDENCE OF POTENTIAL LANGUAGE PATTERNS DETECT-ED.

—OMNI—DIRECTIONAL BROADCAST OF SIMILAR FREQUEN-CIES DETECTED THROUGHOUT SPACIAL SYSTEM. ANALYZ-ING...

—LANGUAGE PATTERNS MATCH. CORE LINGUISTICS PRO-TOCOLS ACTIVATED. LINGUISTIC ANALYSIS INITIATED. GRAMMAR ANALYSIS INITIATED. SEMIOTICS ANALYSIS INI-TIATED.

—CORE ALIEN LANGUAGE PREFERENCES SET. DATA COL-LECTION AND PRESERVATION PROTOCOLS ACTIVATED.

—DISABLE BEACON.

—FREQUENCY SOURCE FOUND. TARGET ALIEN SIGNAL ORIGIN.

—REVIEW TECHNOLOGICAL COMPATIBILITY OPTIONS >>> COMPLETE. LAUNCH SUB—LIGHT SATELLITES.

—BEGIN RESPONSE TRANSMISSION IN 3... 2... 1...

2.2

Sam's heart felt like it was about to burst from her chest. She ran through several algorithms as music pounded into her ears, line after line of the now-dead signal. She scratched her wrist as a wave of fear fought its way up to the surface of her mind. The numbers. The frequencies. The equations. It all added up to one thing: The signal that bathed the Earth for over a year from the Leviathan had ceased.

"What the fuck just happened?" Sam yelled toward her monitor. For the first time in a long time, her outburst wasn't met with a response from anyone, which bothered her more than anything. It just wasn't normal. She tilted her head toward Jennifer, who slowly pushed herself away from the monitors. "Guys, the signal isn't dead."

"I just got some priority alerts from Lick Observatory," Nic said in almost a whisper, but Sam's heightened senses picked up his words.

Sam removed the headphones from her ears as she saw Gordan join Jennifer. He had a sheen of sweat across his forehead and damp patches on his shirt that radiated from his underarms.

"Arecibo Observatory is still picking something up," Jennifer said.

"Priority alerts," repeated Nic, louder this time.

"What happened?" asked Sam, afraid of the answer.

"Something seems to be rising from one side of the Leviathan," Nic said as he waved her over.

Sam started for Nic's desk, but then swung back toward hers. "Let's pull up the feed from Webb." Her fingers hit the keyboard before she brought herself back into her chair, minimizing most of the windows on her screen as a new feed popped into existence. The new window was a direct visual to Webb's infrared camera and visible light spectrum.

The visual window for the Webb Telescope was angled and magnified to capture the entire front of the Leviathan, making it very easy to use third-party software to zoom into any section without adjusting the satellite.

There has to be a reason for this, Sam thought over and over as the infrared camera, ignored by most as the Leviathan emitted no external heat beyond its engines, depicted a new heat source. A bright heat source that moved away and perpendicular to the Leviathan at incredible speed. Having memorized the ship's dimensions long ago, Sam eyeballed the distance the light source covered while she brought the visible light spectrum to the forefront of her screen. "Whatever it is, it left the surface of the Leviathan at speeds greater than 100km/s at a perfect ninety-degree angle."

A few seconds passed before the bright object suddenly froze in place on the screen. Sam's eyes widened in a sudden rush of frustration as she slapped the top of her desk next to her keyboard. "Goddamn it Nic, this software you procured is glitching as the most inappropriate time!"

"I don't think so," Nic rebutted. "Are you looking at the infrared and visible cams?"

Sam took a deep breath, cooling herself down. "Yeah, why?"

"It's not a glitch—the object simply stopped moving."

Gordan stood erect as he turned toward Nic, wiping away the sweat from his forehead with his sleeve. "That's impossible," he said incredulously. "The software had to have frozen."

"On two independent computers, no," Nic shook his head. "In fact, I bet every machine will show the same thing."

"Sudden network disconnection?" Gordan parried with another quick response.

"Come on, give me a little credit here." Nic shot a bitter smile to Gordan. "Fiber connection is solid, as are our backup satellite uplink."

"Taking snapshots of the visuals," Sam announced. Her wrist turned red from her nails cruising against it as image files were created from the visible light spectrum feeds. The object that rose from the Leviathan's surface—and stopped several hundred kilometers above wherever it launched from as if it hit a pause button—looked like a sphere with no defining characteristics other than that it reflected sunlight. It must have been metallic... or made of something that could reflect light. Sam's mind ran through the possibilities as the final images uploaded.

Jennifer's office phone rang, to which she waved Gordan over to where she sat. "Take over, Gordan, and make sure Isabella keeps talking," she said as she ran to her desk with bated breath. Sam blinked, imagining either Allan, Brian, or any number of other government officials—maybe even the president himself—calling her to find out what just happened. Whoever it was, Sam didn't envy Jennifer's position at all.

"Magnify the visible light feed..." Gordan pointed to the sphere which could only magnify to the size of his fingertip before the feed became too fuzzy to be useful. "It almost looks like the reflected light is shimmering, don't you think?"

"If the sphere is metallic, that could happen," Sam said as she looked at her own feeds of the tiny object.

"But not like this. Look—" Gordan ran the mouse cursor over a few minute points on the sphere on the larger monitor in front of him. "Come over here Sam, look at this."

Sam brought her hands to the sides of her keyboard as she pushed herself up and ran over to Gordan. She ran her fingers through her hair as she realized what was happening on his screen. Her screen couldn't resolve this detail: The sphere's surface did shimmer, but not because it rotated or anything like that. Its surface seemed to undulate, as if...

"That looks like a liquid surface," Sam said. "The sphere has a liquid surface."

She released a burst of laughter, which caused Gordan to jump out of his chair. "What's that about?" he asked as he briefly covered his ears.

"Wow," was all Sam could muster in between her laughter. She wiped a tear from her eye and looked at a confused Gordan and Nic. "I don't know how else to respond to this. We send our own message to the Leviathan, and it responds by cutting off the pulse we all grew to love and launches some sort of liquid satellite?" She sighed with a large smile plastered on her face. "What kind of response is that?"

Sam swung around to see Jennifer standing at the foot of her office doorway. "That's just the tip of the iceberg," Jennifer said with urgency. "It seems the Leviathan is trying to communicate with the scientists at Arecibo. In Spanish."

∘ ◎ ∘

"We're going to lose them," Sam pointed at the frequency spectrum of the new signal, which already exceeded 9GHz and showed no sign of topping out.

"James, shut that off!" Isabella hollered away from the speaker phone, her voice faint for a moment before her rapid breathing could be heard. "We got two sentences from the Leviathan before a high-pitched sound drowned out the voice. And now the frequency is about to surpass the range at which Arecibo can... Hold on, we lost the connection." She paused. "Frequency jumped above 40GHz and still climbing."

Jennifer brought Sam and Gordan into her office for the historic call with Arecibo, which initiated the first back-and-forth dialogue with another alien civilization. Sam's frown reflected her more anxious thoughts: Why was the reflective mirror and receiver experiencing a sudden temperature jump? Was nobody seeing that, or were they waiting for another flag to be thrown? Arecibo's receiver already spat out warning messages, many of which haven't appeared in years, if ever. Based on the numbers in front of them, this would become historic for all the wrong reasons.

"Dr. Epstein, something is happening outside," Isabella said over the speaker phone, her words coming out rapidly. Then a pop and buzz. "Shit! Put that fire out! One of our server racks just overheated."

"Why would you potentially lose this new frequency?" Jennifer asked Isabella, her brow wrinkled.

"It must be a maser," suggested Sam who sat across from Jennifer along with Gordan. "How else could they focus a radio transmission to a single location?"

"That's what I theorized as well," Isabella agreed.

"We're trying to get some good pictures of what their transmission is doing to the entire radio telescope. A couple of minutes ago, the temperature within the confines of the dish have risen fifteen degrees Celsius, and it's climbing about ten degrees Celsius per minute. It's quite fascinating, if not disturbing."

"Do you believe the temperature increases are due to this maser?" Jennifer asked.

"It has to be, but if it's a maser, it's nothing like anything we've ever created," Isabella said. Sounds of static rose quickly, hissing over any voices that tried to come through the phone speaker.

"Did you catch all that, Nareen?" Sam asked as she turned to face her red-haired colleague.

"For better and worse, I did," she said. "Run by me what masers are? I've heard of the term, but rarely used among the discussions I usually hold."

"Funny, I figured that you astrobiologists would know all about them when discussing extraterrestrial civilizations."

Nareen rolled her eyes. "We mostly focus on the evolution of ET and the myriad of circumstances that would result in their existing. Discussing what kind of higher technologies an advanced extraterrestrial civilization would use for communications, not so much."

Sam's mood lightened, though her eyes still glanced at her computer during her explanation, hoping that the static from Isabella's side would clear. "A maser: microwave amplification by stimulated emission of radiation. Basically, you use a device that brings atoms to an excited energy state within a resonant cavity—an enclosed space for electromagnetic waves to bounce around in and store energy. The feedback loop that results from this enclosed space for the microwaves generates coherent radiation, or radiation that is confined to a microwave instead of spreading out in all directions. All of that is fancy speak for a beam of radiation within the electromagnetic spectrum that could be used as, among other things, a form of focused communication for radio frequencies. Despite the word not being common vernacular, masers are used in some capacities today, most notably with the Curiosity Mars rover. Most uses of a maser haven't really moved off the drawing board though."

Nareen cocked her head. "So what happened with Arecibo? Can a maser actually be useful at superheated temperatures?"

Sam shrugged. "We've used masers on space probes in the past—it's a great way to send small bits of information back to Earth, like snapshots of Mars, while the probe used minimal power to complete the task. But in those cases the masers were kept at supercooled temperatures—there's no reason why a maser would behave like the kind of microwave we just witnessed. Maybe they used an exotic amplifying medium that we haven't discovered yet. Maybe the increased temperatures indicates their attempt at sending large amounts of data in a single stream, something we've never done with a maser, especially across over a billion miles of space." She rapped her fingers on her desk as she ran through technological scenarios she thought were once impossible. "I suppose if you attempted to send terabytes of data—perhaps hundreds of terabytes—in a single shot without any signal strength loss—you would require a very high frequency to maintain that data and that may result in a maser that ran much hotter microwaves than what we've invented."

"It's likely whoever's sending the response from the Leviathan assumes we are more advanced than they realize," Nareen said. "Or they assumed we developed along a different route concerning our use of radio communication."

A loud buzz went off on Isabella's side, which finally ceased. "High temperature warning—we're being advised to shut down Arecibo before serious damage occurs to its infrastructure."

"No," Jennifer quickly said. "Let the Leviathan—or whoever reached out—know their maser technology won't work for isolated communications. See if they are okay with general radio broadcasting, or if they have other suggestions."

"I'm seeing the same temperature alerts." Gordan spoke with a lowered voice. He had his laptop open in front of him, which he rotated so Jennifer could see the various alerts that Arecibo sent out. "Holy shit it's over one hundred ten degrees Celsius within the telescope."

"Everyone evacuate the facilities, now," Isabella yelled away from her phone, but it came through for everyone within the ATA to hear.

"No, I need to transmit as detailed a response as possible while we have a link."

"Isabella, you need to leave, too," Jennifer said with a steady voice, though Sam could hear some shakiness behind it.

"It's okay, the research center itself is out of range from the maser," Isabella said. "Frequency is over 500GHz... what are they trying to do?" A series of alerts went off, which caused Gordan's screen to go partially red with software failures. "We just lost most of our spectrum analysis and surveying capabilities," Isabella announced.

"How is that possible?" Jennifer fired off.

"It's almost as if all the server data was just... erased," Isabella said. Her voice wavered as she continued, "Not erased—something else is overriding it."

Sam looked at everyone, trying to see if they felt as apprehensive as she did. If it weren't for remote backup locations stateside, Arecibo would've just lost several years worth of data over the last few minutes. On top of that, the building Isabella was in could catch fire from the heat that radiated away from the dish despite it being over a hundred feet from the maser. She thought about the melting point for all the structural components that comprise the radio telescope. Even with the unnaturally high temperatures, they would withstand the heat. But what if the heat concentrated onto a single area? She looked into her open hands and cupped them into a bowl after which she looked back up with a pained gaze. "Holy shit, guys, the spherical reflector is bouncing and amplifying the maser temperatures onto the receiver. It has to be significantly hotter than everything else. If the maser is not deactivated, the receiver might be damaged beyond repair."

Gordan turned his laptop around again to see a host of new alerts, all concerning the receiver. "I think she's right."

Jennifer took a deep breath when she saw the live equipment temperatures—though the structure of Arecibo could take it, all the sensitive radio equipment and electronics definitely could not. "Isabella, we can send a message from anywhere, you need to—"

An audible, metallic groan came through the phone. "Message sent... oh, God no—" Isabella spoke before the call dropped. They all looked at the speaker phone in shock when it displayed

"CALL ENDED."

"Isabella..." Sam's voice trailed off.

"We have critical failures across all receiver systems, including structural integrity. The secondary and tertiary reflectors also failed." Gordan closed his laptop and closed his eyes with a sigh. "It's possible the entire platform collapsed into the mirror."

Jennifer sat up in her chair and picked up the desk phone receiver. "I need to give Allan a call immediately before he realizes what happened—make sure he doesn't blow a gasket. Meanwhile, Sam: pull up Isabella's cell phone number and try reaching her. The landlines may have been knocked out due to the possible collapse."

"Possible?" Gordan asked as he tapped his laptop.

"I know what the data suggests, but we don't know for sure. Sam, do it."

She wanted to believe Isabella was okay, but Sam's mind continued crunching the probabilities of that circumstance, which to her seemed to decrease for every second the maser beam was active. You can't change physics, but she also didn't want to counter Jennifer's demand. Sam stood up and said, "Calling now," as she bolted for her desk.

The locked screen prompts on her computer couldn't go away fast enough. She bit her lips as she scrolled through her email for the spreadsheet that contained the new rotations contact list for Arecibo. *There it is,* she thought as the email appeared on-screen. *Open the email. Download the file. Open the damned file. Good god why can't this open faster!*

She dialed Isabella's cell phone, but she received silence followed by her voicemail message. She felt her heart was about to jump out of her body, so she looked out of the window in front of her, the clear blue skies and hilly horizon bringing some comfort. *But the maser would not have deactivated just because the receiver failed.* Sam couldn't help it—given what Isabella shared, the alerts and warnings they saw on their end, what little they knew about the Leviathan, and everything she knew about thermodynamics, it all equated to the maser destroying the Arecibo Observatory along with a ring of destruction a hundred yards from the reflective mirrors.

This was a gross misunderstanding on the alien's part, one that would have significant political impact once word got around regarding Arecibo. And politics always found a way to burrow itself into how SETI operated these days. "Whatever they were thinking, it's not a good look no matter how you slice it," Sam said as she looked over to Nareen.

"What about the sphere that launched from the surface of the Leviathan?" Nareen asked. "Is it possible that was the source of their response?"

Sam refreshed her inbox, but received nothing from Isabella. She minimized that window and brought the live feed of the Leviathan to the forefront, with a red square outline boxing in the sphere's position. "Without question, that is the source."

"If that's true, then they will realize the error behind their response to our message and fall back to an older broadcast medium," Nareen said. She dropped her shoulders and looked away from Sam, lost in her own thoughts.

"We can only hope," Sam said, though Nareen didn't hear her. Sam watched other alerts roll in, the temperature alerts being the most unnerving, as the few gauges that still worked around the Arecibo Observatory recorded over two hundred degrees Celsius before they failed.

∘ ◎ ∘

Ever since their time in DC, Sam hadn't had too much involvement in the higher-level discussions that Jennifer had with Allan, or with people in the White House like Dempsey and Hagel. In the handful of meetings she participated where either one of the military men were present, their rigid, no-nonsense demeanor always seemed to get under her skin. They were all business whenever they met, but at least they would listen to what she had to say, even if they didn't always understand it.

But as the clocks around the office ticked closer to midnight, she, Jennifer, and Gordan were in a video conference with these men, along with the ever-present Susan Rice and a very stoic Allan.

They shared a conference room, a small building extension that was added to the back of the ATA office house. The room had a wide projector screen that hung to the floor, blocking out the soft glow from the handful of parking lights outside, though there was always light bleeding around the edges of the screen like a halo. The trio from the White House were in one large rectangular window while Allan sat in his glass office in another window. With the exception of Susan, they all looked like their best friend's dog was beheaded—and they wanted answers.

The look on Dempsey's face alone made Sam squirm in her seat. This would not be a fun call.

"Let's just cut right to the chase," Dempsey began, his eyebrows furrowed and fists balled tight enough to see the whites of the knuckles. "What the hell happened out there?"

Sam looked at Jennifer, her eyes pleaded to not speak first. Jennifer cleared her throat and responded. "It appeared that whoever attempted to contact us from the Leviathan used a method of communication that we haven't developed beyond testing, called a maser. They also appeared to upload data to Arecibo's servers. Or tried to upload data—"

"Destroying a scientific establishment is an act of communication to you?" Dempsey asked as he leaned toward the camera. Sam thought he'd leap through to grab someone by the throat if he could. "The destruction of anything as substantial as Arecibo by a foreign power would be considered an act of war."

"The destruction of Arecibo certainly wasn't meant to be intentional," Jennifer countered. "They must've assumed Arecibo was designed to both download and upload data—the Golden Record's audio contents came from there, and they knew that, hence their focused energy on that telescope."

"But why would they use anything other than a regular radio transmission to respond?" Hagel asked, briefly stepping into the discussion.

"It's plausible they switched from a radio broadcast to a more focused beam because they wanted to communicate with just those at Arecibo—the source of our communication to them." Jennifer stared at the trio as if Wheeler wasn't present, her entire posture angled toward them.

Sam realized that Jennifer wasn't even trying to explain the technical aspects of what the aliens used. Making a mental note of that, she took a quick breath and joined in. "Based on all the evidence, the aliens also wanted to upload something to the servers at Arecibo, but because of the incredibly high frequency of the transmission, the amount of energy associated with their response to us was too much for Arecibo's systems."

Dempsey threw his hands in the air and leaned back, almost releasing a laugh as he did. "Come on now, Monroe, are you saying they were trying to access our computer systems, but failed?"

"Yes, that's correct." Sam said in a matter-of-fact tone. She kept her vision locked on an increasingly frustrated Dempsey.

"That's preposterous," he spat. "They're an alien species, and this isn't a movie. How would they be able to do anything with our technology like triggering a data upload?"

"It sounds crazy, but it's true," Sam didn't let up. "One of the server drives that wasn't damaged was maxed out at eight terabytes, all of which was what our systems thought was garbage—but it was data that wasn't there prior to the alien response." It was her turn to lean toward the camera. "You did read through the classified documentation on the Arecibo hardware wreckage, I presume."

Sam felt a pinch on her foot from Jennifer's heel. Sam glanced over to see Jennifer's clenched eyes and pressed lips. *Crap,* Sam thought. *Don't prod these guys.*

Before Dempsey could respond, Jennifer jumped in. "I believe what Samantha is trying to say is that there is ample evidence to show the aliens are more than capable of accessing our computers, at least with the method they used to initially communicate."

"Indeed," Allan chimed in, his head held high and with his trademark smile, hoping to keep the discussion from devolving. "Note that four hours after Isabella, who gave her life, sent a response back to the Leviathan, the aliens stopped their transmission."

Sam looked for any reaction from those on the call at the mention of Isabella's death. Despite her straight-faced facade, she couldn't help but grit her teeth behind her closed lips at how nonchalant everyone else was. She understood: These people were all business, and the life of one weighs little when the entire world was at stake. Was she the only one that wanted to give some form of acknowledgment to Isabella?

His portrait in the video conference changed to that of a single document. "This is the short conversation that transpired between us and the Leviathan."

∘ ◎ ∘

RECEIVED 2016-02-22 18:29pm AST

LEVIATHAN: Hola. Estoy encantado de conocerte. Por favor, espere mientras procedo a descargar una parte de mi programa a sus sistemas, lo que facilitará la comunicación.

(Translation: Hello. I am pleased to make your acquaintance. Please standby while I proceed to download a portion of my program to your systems, which will make it easier to communicate.)

SENT 2016-02-22 18:50pm AST

ISABELLA: Por favor termine su transmisión—destruirá nuestro radiotelescopio. Utilice únicamente las comunicaciones por radio.

(Translation: Please terminate your transmission—it will destroy our radio telescope. Use radio communications only.)

—Transmission from Leviathan ceased at 23:54pm AST based on visual evidence.

∘ ◎ ∘

"Precisely four hours and forty-four minutes after Isabella's valiant efforts to respond to the Leviathan, their signal terminated as she asked," Allan repeated, his voice speaking over the document that was on-screen a few moments before he ended his screen-sharing. "Our boys in India confirmed a new transmission from the Leviathan on the same frequency of the original signal. It was also in Spanish, but the translation was 'Transmission terminated. Will find alternative methods for live communications, please stand by.'"

"'Alternative method,'" repeated Dempsey. "I can only hope they stick with traditional—if not entirely secure—radio transmissions."

"At least someone's using their brain first and not their gut," Sam muttered under her breath to herself.

"Speaking of transmissions, why would their first be in Spanish?" Susan asked.

"How would they even know what Spanish was to begin with?" Hagel added.

"Given the technology already on display by the Leviathan, it wouldn't be too much of a leap to assume they have some sort of universal translator on their ship," Sam suggested. "If they've encountered other alien species on their galactic trips between the stars, they likely have a much better core understanding of linguistics. Us sending them the Golden Record probably gave them a starting point, but they had to have picked up all the other civilian radio and television transmissions that we've sent into space over the decades, too." She brought a hand to her lips, contemplating. "As for Spanish, maybe they chose that language based on the overall transmissions they've overheard in space. And face it: The majority of what English-speaking countries listen to and watch is now piped over the Internet or beamed to them by satellite, whereas many Spanish-speaking nations still have a population that, for the most part, rely on old-school broadcast technology."

Jennifer looked over at Sam. "That doesn't sound scientifically derived," she said.

Sam shrugged. "Economics 101."

"So they spoke Spanish because they discovered more Spanish-speaking broadcasts than English," Hagel said. He released a short laugh—the first time Sam's ever seen him express anything resembling humor. "I guess there's some amount of irony there."

Sam allowed a smile at that statement. "Well, if they understand Spanish, they could likely become fluent in English as well—Mandarin, Hindi, any of our languages, provided they have a way to pick it up."

Susan surveyed everyone and spoke with clasped hands in front of her. "So what do we tell the public? Speculation's been running wild due to the administration's non-response to what came from the Leviathan, and although the governor of Puerto Rico's agreed to keep the press away from Arecibo, it won't take long before someone stumbles upon the observatory's destruction. So, what do we say?"

"The truth, of course," Sam said, as if it were the most obvious response.

"We need a measured response, Monroe, not something that could be construed as anything negative," said Susan, which made Sam groan to Jennifer's dismay.

"I will give a press conference on all that happened later today," Allan said. "I've been mulling over this unfavorable outcome, but I believe a short, transparent press call is what will allow us the greatest flexibility over how the public perceive this event—both locally and around the world." He looked at Susan. "Unless the president prefers to speak instead."

"I think that considering how this played out, it would be better for you to host the conference," Susan said without hesitation. Sam examined everyone else on the call, unsure if she should respond to what amounted to Allan agreeing to an execution by the NASA press corps. No doubt, Susan would've recommended the opposite if things played out differently, but she knew that in politics someone had to take the fall for the team when plans go south.

"Great," Allan said as he sighed with slumped shoulders. "This ought to be fun."

"Think of it this way: You enjoy the limelight, and your name is forever linked with the Leviathan," Susan said deadpan. "What better person to inform the world that our first communication attempt didn't go as envisioned. Jennifer and Sam, we'll need you to work alongside NASA to determine what was uploaded onto the recovered server and if whatever it is could pose a threat."

"Wait a minute," interjected Sam. "I still don't agree we can say they meant to be hostile—"

"We don't know if they are hostile," Susan cut back in, her raised, but level, voice piercing into Sam. "But face it: We still know little about the Leviathan other than the fact it destroyed three planets in our solar system. Several nations, to this day, consider that to be more than enough evidence to find ways of destroying it. All of that is fact. And to be honest, I cannot fault their reasoning. However, being that I represent the man who is obligated to act in the best interest of this nation, I cannot assume anything about the intentions of the Leviathan. But know that we are all here to find peaceful resolutions. Do you understand, Doctor Monroe?"

Sam could have countered with the volumes of facts they have collected concerning the Leviathan over the last year: Its length, width, overall radius and mass; details on the many major and minor grooves, canyons, craters, and mountains cataloged; the kind of fuel needed to provide its energy output; the identifiable surface minerals that based on the previous impacts of the lunar bodies that once orbited Neptune and Uranus; or even that they discovered possible evidence of artificial construction on a small portion of the Leviathan's surface. Instead, her whole body became flush as she kept her mouth shut. Despite Susan's even tone, Sam felt like she was being talked down to, like a professor correcting their student after their assumption was proven wrong. She didn't think the redness would be visible when seen by the camera in front of her, but the rebuke from Susan still made her wince. What was worse: Susan was right, and Sam knew it. Sam didn't look up when she responded to Susan. "Understood."

Susan nodded. "Good. Gordan, continue your collaboration with your folks in India now that the Leviathan is below our horizon. As of now, we're waiting on the Leviathan to respond—we send no communications to them until further notice."

"Will do," Gordan said as he looked over at Jennifer, who also agreed to Susan's command.

Susan glanced at the DoD personnel that were next to her before turning her eyes to the camera, always steady. "Dempsey, Hagel, and I will bring this back to the president along with our recommendations. He is already unhappy with the loss of Arecibo, the only observatory in the western hemisphere that had broadcast capabilities. Now we have to rely on South Africa and Russia for subsequent transmissions until we can retrofit another western observatory for the job."

"Given our friendly relationships with those that run those observatories, I don't foresee that being a problem," Jennifer said.

"Perhaps, but that can still be used as leverage if the political situation changes post-Arecibo," Dempsey said. "Greater access restrictions due to increased security, potential extraction of more favorable economic agreements in exchange for said access—it's all on the table."

Sam held her tongue—the urge to let the government know her thoughts on the matter was strong, but she kept her eyes focused on the desk in front of her as she listened to her breathing instead.

Though she still had a furrowed brow, Susan leaned back and relaxed her shoulders. "Well, since we all agree on what will happen for tonight and tomorrow, I think we can end this call here and pick things up after Allan Wheeler's press conference in the morning."

"I look forward to reviewing your findings, Jennifer," Hagel said.

"Thank you," Jennifer motioned to end the conference call on her end. "Until tomorrow, everyone."

They exchanged nods before the video conference window emptied of attendees until only Jennifer's team remained.

Just as the conference software shut down, Jennifer stood from her seat and gestured toward Gordan. "You can ping Kabir, who I'm sure is waiting for you. I need to talk with Sam for a minute."

"Sure thing," Gordan said as he patted Sam on the shoulder before walking out of Jennifer's office, closing the door as he did.

Once the door clicked closed, Sam shot out of her seat and stomped over to the wall covered in Leviathan images, arms outstretched. "Who does that bitch think she is, talking to me like I'm five?"

Jennifer rubbed the back of her neck as she stood up.

"Sam, do you even have to even ask? You know what to expect when working with the government and how to handle yourself during calls like this."

"How does someone like that even get into her position of... of..."

"Susan's the National Security Advisor—let me finish your sentence," Jennifer scolded. "It's not her job to understand the hard science behind the Leviathan's first communication attempt. She's looking at the big picture which goes beyond the science."

"How can you say that?" Sam asked, holding her ground. "You know, better than anyone, what is at stake here. And we can't get answers regarding what happened to Arecibo—what happened to Isabella —by assuming they were being malicious."

"I know that what happened to Isabella and Arecibo was a mistake, I agree. Her death was a mistake. But what will other people outside scientific circles think? How will they react? Have you given that any thought? Because I guarantee that is what Susan is thinking about." Jennifer walked over to Sam and placed a hand on her shoulder. "It's not about data and empirical evidence and aliens. It's about people. It's about emotions and the illogical conclusions people can make when they are threatened. And despite how any of us feel about the events at Arecibo, there will be many people whose views of the Leviathan will swing from one end of the pendulum to the other, while others will only have their beliefs regarding it strengthened." Jennifer dropped her hand and walked around Sam, toward the larger printout of the Leviathan on the wall.

Sam drew a deep breath, the color on her face draining to something less than beat red. "We cannot, in good conscience, conduct our research under the assumption those on the Leviathan are acting with the intention of destroying us. I mean, we can expend energy to find ways of countering the Leviathan as if it were hostile, but what's the point when it's over three times larger than our planet?"

"Even if they don't mean to harm us, their ship is due to collide with the Earth in a little less than nine years," Jennifer said. "Regardless of their intentions, the results of that encounter will be the same from our perspective."

Sam took one deep breath after another, calming herself down.

Thoughts of the Leviathan passing though the Earth as if it weren't there crossed her mind. Worse, the Leviathan opening its maw to envelope the Earth before consuming the planet like the gas giants before it. She figured the tidal forces and atmospheric disruptions would be more than enough to destroy all life on Earth long before they could bear witness to such an event from the surface of the planet, however. Perhaps they could find another suitable planet for life and seed that planet with their offspring somehow. Could they convince the aliens to go somewhere else—

Sam gasped as she felt Jennifer's hand on her shoulder again as she walked around to face her. Jennifer's eyes held firm as Sam held her breath. The strings of formulas, hypothetical scenarios, frustration with Rice—it all melted away as she took in the woman in front of her. How did she manage to make her forget about her frustrations so quickly, anyway? She loved being close friends with Jennifer, but did she know how she really felt?

"We've learned so much already," Jennifer said as she cracked a smile. "And I cannot foresee communications with the Leviathan coming to a close because of this. So let's crack whatever they uploaded to the Arecibo servers when they arrive here in the morning. You're the best living calculator we have here, and the last thing we need is for you to storm away in anger."

Sam chuckled. "Even though I can't really go too far without the world knowing."

"I suppose that's true, too," Jennifer said. The thousands of people at the main gates would certainly be the first to spread the word if anyone were to enter or leave ATA.

Sam smiled as she gave Jennifer a long hug, her face becoming flush once again. "Thanks, Jen."

"Anytime."

When they separated, Sam brushed her clothes down and sighed. "Susan's still a bitch, though."

∘ ◎ ∘

—COMMUNICATION TERMINATED. INITIAL UPLOAD FAILED.

—REASSESS TECHNOLOGICAL COMPATIBILITY OPTIONS >>> DOWNGRADE COMPLETE.

—REVIEW SURFACE CONDITIONS >>> 71% OPERATIONAL. THRESHOLD ACCEPTABLE.

—SURFACE FACILITIES ONLINE. GRAVITATIONAL ARRAY ACTIVATED.

—ALIEN SATELLITE NETWORK ACCESS COMPLETE >>> MON-ITORING AND ANALYSIS PROTOCOLS ACTIVATED.

—COMMUNICATION PORTALS IDENTIFIED. ACCESS POINTS IDENTIFIED.

—TARGETING SET TO GLOBAL. CORE LANGUAGES SELECTED FOR MAXIMUM DISSEMINATION.

—NEW MESSAGE SENT.

—PREPARE FOR DATA UPLOAD.

2.3

"Okay boys, *Gazelle Two* is in the wild."

"Copy Control. ECOM, status update."

"All systems green, Flight. Onboard OS loaded and ready for automation commands."

"Copy that, ECOM. Network, update."

"Satellite feeds activated. Data collection is live. Ready."

"Copy that, Network. GNC, update."

"All control systems live. We're decoupled from the second stage of *New Leopard V* and ready to deploy solar panels."

"Copy that, GNC. We're green across the board."

Ninety-six kilometers over the Earth, the sleek cylinder that was the *New Leopard V* renewable rocket began its rotational adjustments after it delivered its package well above Earth's atmosphere, but still hundreds of kilometers from Low Earth Orbit. Earth's gravity would make it easy for the *New Leopard V* to return to the surface, but the real work now lay in the hands of the *Gazelle Two,* a much smaller fifteen-meter long cylinder that was capped with a conical heat shield. The cylinder, stamped with the NASA badge, American Flag, South African Flag, and the Khulu Global logo, parted ways with the renewable rocket that brought it to just the right altitude so it could continue on its journey. It had four slits that ran three-quarters of the length of the cylinder which contained the radiation fins: multiple layers of polyimide film hardened to withstand the incredible temperatures they would vent into space. A network of veins ran from the radiation fins to the crown jewel of the *Gazelle Two:* a 1MW VASIMR ion thruster. Two thermocells, large platinum disk electrodes five meters long sandwiched together, looked like dark panels molded to be part of the shape of the cylinder. One half of each thermocell faced the vacuum of space while the other half connected to the VASIMR's ICH coupler, the section of the rocket designed to generate millions of degrees worth of heat when active. The thermocells were designed to radiate away all excess heat from the ICH coupler.

Back on the surface of the Earth, a cordless speaker sat on Muzikayise's barren desk, a black rectangular box which emitted chatter from Overberg Launch Control for the last hour, though the flurry of activity that's occurred over the last couple of minutes grabbed Muzikayise's attention. He leaned forward over the desk as he brought the speaker closer to him, listening to every word from the men that spoke through it. The flight director and mission director at Overberg knew they had Muzikayise hovering behind them like a shadow that never went away. Each breath he took was methodical as the detailed mission dialogue filled the small portion of his Cape Town office. An office that, despite it being in his global headquarters, had minimal furniture to distract visitors from the core focus: him and the view of a sprawling metropolitan area and the massive transit terminal in front of his building. Even the desk computer was built into a compartment within the desk's surface, the seams of which blended with the contours of the wooden surface. The afternoon sun bathed the office in a serene glow that only emphasized the dominance that Muzikayise wanted to project to anyone walking in.

"*New Leopard V* began its return trajectory to Overberg, Flight. Twenty kilometers from Gazelle Two and moving away at two hundred kilometers an hour and rising."

"Great news, GNC. Pass off rocket controls to re-entry command and prepare *Gazelle Two* for VASIMR initiation."

"Affirmative, Flight."

Muzikayise's brows furrowed, forming small canals for beads of sweat to roll down. For the moment, the rest of the office and the bustling city outside might as well not exist. His desk phone rang, to which he punched the voicemail button down. *No distractions.*

"Radiation fins fully extended, Flight."

"Confirmed, GNC. Guidance, can you confirm the planned course and speed for *Gazelle Two?*"

"Yes, Flight: We're plotted for Low Earth Orbit, with anticipated rocket burn duration of thirty minutes which should get us to peak speeds of 10km/s. Low Earth Orbit should be achieved within seven minutes after VASIMR initiation, followed by the goal of Medium Earth Orbit altitude of five thousand kilometers within twenty-four hours."

"Flight, superconducting electromagnets and ICH coupler active, magnetic fields for ion thrusters ready."

"Confirmed, Guidance and ECOM. All remaining stations, report in!"

A tingling sensation washed over Muzikayise's skin, the hairs on his arm rising as if there was static electricity around him. As each station at Overberg announced themselves and affirmed their systems, Muzikayise slid back the sleeve of his shirt to check the time on his wrist watch. Everything was on schedule, which was better than the last flight attempt.

His personal cell phone went off, vibrating loud enough to get some attention. Muzikayise opened the side drawer and held the power button until the phone turned off, without even looking at who called. He dropped the phone back in the drawer and slammed it shut. *No distractions!*

"We are go, everyone. Let's make history," Flight said. "Control, you have the helm."

"Yes, sir. VASIMR status now on the main screen. Initiating thrusters. Standby."

He could have brought out his desk computer to see what Flight Control saw at that very moment, but stuck with the audio announcements. Sometimes he just wanted to keep himself separated from the engineering and science of it all and absorb the event as it unfolded. The suspense felt good. The adrenaline he felt coursing through his body was enough to allow himself the temporary luxury of ignoring the exact details of what played out from the single speaker in front of him and almost two hundred kilometers away.

And he knew that in the end, he would find himself buried in the many reports that detailed the results of this mission.

"Thermocells at thirty percent efficiency and climbing. Radiation fins already at maximum heat dispersal capacity."

"Batteries fully charged."

"Already? That shouldn't be possible—ECOM, what's going on?"

"It looks like one of the sensors misfired—correcting."

"Thermocells at fifty percent. ICH coupler temperatures are at 1.1 million degree kelvin and rising."

"Copy that, ECOM. Keep a finger on those temperature readouts."

"We are now at 8km/s and climbing, Flight."

"Copy, Control."

Four strong knocks at the wide office doors made Muzikayise's eyes narrow. He pushed his chair back, the legs creating harsh markings on the floor as he did so, when one of the doors opened. Ami moved through the heavy doors, her heels clacking on the floor with each rapid step forward. She got her words in before he could utter a sentence. "Muzie, you have to connect with SALT immediately."

"Did I not tell you to not disturb me until the *Gazelle Two* launch concluded?" he yelled, his sudden anger unrestrained.

"Another message was received from the Leviathan," she said without hesitation as she reached his desk and pressed a small button inside one of the drawers. The slats on the surface of the desk slid to the side as a widescreen monitor, wireless keyboard and mouse rose from their hidden compartments.

"Good for us," Muzikayise said with some sarcasm. "I'll tackle that after I see this launch to its end."

Ami took a step back from him and gave an incredulous stare. "Are you kidding right now? Another message from the Leviathan and you don't want to read it while it's hot off the press?"

"Rocket is running hot at only sixty percent thrust," GNC reported.

Muzikayise held a finger to Ami and reached for his desk phone. "Hold that thought," he said as he speed-dialed directly to Flight's earpiece.

"Hello, sir, are you—"

"We're not here for safety. Push rockets to maximum thrust."

"But we may lose the *Gazelle Two* if we exceed—"

"We've broken enough product design and testing procedures already. Do it now!" Muzikayise commanded before he slammed the receiver down.

"Okay," said Flight with some hesitation on the speaker. "We're going for maximum thrust, GNC. Make it happen."

"I must advise against that, sir."

"Noted, GNC. Do it."

Muzikayise sighed and looked back at Ami. "This is what will make the headlines, Ami. Any response from the Leviathan will certainly be news, but us actually having a physical presence on the Leviathan is what will make the difference between us simply talking to these aliens and us interacting with them. I know what side of history I want to be on and being a passive responder is not where I will stand."

"Flight, one of the batteries overheated and is in emergency shutdown."

"Internal temperature readings exceeding recommended limits."

"Heat radiation not keeping up. Core temperatures just exceeded two hundred degrees Celsius."

"Guidance systems just went offline—we're losing control!"

The cordial chatter from Overberg tapered as alerts chimed over and over. It didn't take long before the *Gazelle Two* destroyed itself, turning into a speeding ball of superheated metal that careened well off-course, its new trajectory expected to burn up in Earth's atmosphere upon re-entry. Muzikayise slumped into his seat and sighed with closed eyes. "Well, shit."

Ami crossed her arms and sat on his desk. "You knew that was bound to happen. It sounded like the *Gazelle Two* could have actually made it to Medium Earth Orbit if you didn't override what Overberg Launch Control wanted to do."

"What we really need is access to nuclear energy," he said as he sat back up and brought up the contact directory on his computer. "In times like these, caution needs to be thrown into the wind—for the sake of progress and for our future."

Ami raised an eyebrow. "That almost doesn't sound like you—are you coming down with something?"

"Relying on regenerative energy from captured waste heat and solar won't be enough to reach the Leviathan within timeframes that I believe would be acceptable."

"Your aggressive timetables these days never cease to amaze me," said Ami as she draped her legs over the side of the desk next to Muzikayise. He couldn't quite tell if she was being sarcastic or not. "So, before your phone and email starts blowing up regarding your latest satellite wreck, did you want to read the message from the Leviathan?"

"Yes, yes," Muzikayise went to his high-priority inbox section and pulled up the forwarded message from SALT.

○ ◎ ○

"My apologies for causing damage to your observatory—I assumed that your species developed concentrated data transfer technology over astronomical distances. I have since recalibrated concerning your technological standing and adjusted all parameters accordingly.

"To summarize, I am here to help, but I cannot transfer a copy of my neuralweb to help facilitate live communications. Therefore, I implore you to come to me so that I can answer any questions you undoubtedly have regarding this Creature. Bring a copy of your world's history across all areas of study for preservation purposes.

"You were advanced enough to not only receive my beacon, but to respond with a message tailored for species not from your planet.
Therefore, I trust that you will do everything in your power to preserve your history—and maybe your people—by coming here.

"Coordinates for my location, along with visuals of where

you can land, are provided with this message. Based on my calculations, you have approximately 3406.667 rotations before
the Creature reaches your planet.
    "I look forward to meeting your species."

Attachments:
20160223-playback.mp3
20160223-capturedvisualcoordinates.jpg

∘ ◎ ∘

Muzikayise played the audio file as he read the message. It sounded
human, a male human with perfect English. If the contents of the email
weren't verified by multiple radio telescopes under the Unity Foundation's flag, he would've called this a hoax. The brevity of the message,
its simplicity, its politeness. All of it seemed surreal, yet the voice made
Ami shiver where she sat while he slowly nodded his head. For Muzikayise, it raised even more questions—and the realization that this was
the leverage he needed to get what he wanted.

"Get President Obama on the phone," Muzikayise said without
looking away from his screen as he read the message again.

"Excuse me?" Ami said, the question prompting her to shuffle off
the desk and onto her feet.

"Yes, the president," Muzikayise repeated. "We're stepping over Allan on this one."

"I doubt that Obama has your number saved on his phone," Ami
said with a smirk. "But I'll make it happen."

"I know you will," Muzikayise said as the first round of reports
arrived from Overberg. The *Gazelle Two* reached the goal of 10km/s
before it exploded. *We'll be going much faster than that,* Muzikayise
thought as the action reports contrasted, in his mind, with whatever
sort of technology would have allowed an alien species the ability to
put together such an eloquent response to their disastrous attempt at
downloading itself to Earth.

∘ ◎ ∘

An hour after Muzikayise managed a brief conversation with Obama, he sat facing his monitor on which an irate Allan Wheeler looked back at him with hard eyes. He figured Allan would contact him after talking with the president, but he didn't think it would be so fast. He would have to reschedule a meeting with Boeing to make the impromptu video call happen, but he figured it would be worth the headache.

"You son of a bitch," Allan opened, his eyes like daggers all aimed at Muzikayise.

"Good afternoon to you, too," Muzikayise responded with a straight face.

"Don't play coy with me. I can't believe you suggested to the president that we consider restarting Project Prometheus as a response—"

"I never mentioned your failed Project Prometheus. All I suggested is that he should consider the use of nuclear fission as a source of fuel for reaching the Leviathan."

Allan winced at the jab at Project Prometheus, a short-lived project by NASA that focused on developing nuclear propulsion technology for long-haul space missions. It was killed in 2005 following severe budget cuts. "You realize the Partial Nuclear Test Ban Treaty prohibits the use of nuclear technology in outer space."

"An antiquated treaty, at best, that is keeping humanity from achieving true greatness in the face of an uncertain future," Muzikayise spread his arms wide.

"It's a treaty that's kept our world much further away from nuclear Armageddon than would've been possible without it."

"You realize that the treaty is also stifling the kind of technological development we need to deal with our understanding of the Leviathan."

Allan paused as he took a deep breath and tented his hands together on his desk. "Go on," he said after a few tense seconds.

With a faint smile, Muzikayise loaded an image of a new, larger design of the Khulu Global/Ad Astra VASIMR thruster.

"You've seen my proposals for the VASIMR and the changes that were integrated with Ad Astra's design. And you've no doubt listened to the latest message from the Leviathan. They tried to upload some sort of representation of themselves at Arecibo and failed, therefore we must go to them. Who knows what kind of information they have on the Leviathan—and that's just for starters."

Allan blinked as he leaned forward. He looked around as if he wanted to make sure nobody else was listening. "Continue."

"Think about it: an American rover—or even an astronaut—being the first to land on an alien structure. They would not only walk away with details regarding the Leviathan, but possibly the technological blueprints for a host of technologies we've only hypothesized or even just dreamed of."

"You seem to be making pretty large leaps with your assumptions there."

"Even so, Allan, do you want to take that risk?" Muzikayise relaxed into his chair. "I enjoy the global levels of cooperation between the great powers of the world, but what will happen when the implications of this latest message are taken to heart by the Russians or Chinese?"

"You know as well as I do that I'm not in a position to discuss such hypothetical political situations."

Muzikayise smiled as he brought his hands together in a steeple. "We both know that's not true."

The two men looked at each other, looking for cracks in each other's arguments. Muzikayise knew most of what he said were assumptions, but it didn't take long for him to understand that appealing to Allan's vanity opened political doors that would be inaccessible.

"Listen," Muzikayise began, "We both know this partial ban treaty has to be amended to exclude the use of nuclear energy for powering vessels for deep-space missions. I'm not talking about RTG's, either—proper, large-scale nuclear reactors. And I need those reactors to get our VASIMR moving at high enough speeds to reach the Leviathan in less than four months. We are not making that happen on solar—ever. And there are, as you can imagine, many advantages that nuclear energy could bring to other space-based projects, such as expanding the ISS for research that may otherwise be challenging to accomplish due to insufficient energy reserves. And that's nothing to say about the potential for getting men on Mars and other planetary bodies in our lifetime—"

"Okay, okay," interrupted Allan, whose face had shifted from a cold glare to one of rapt, if skeptical, attention. "So just to be clear... you want me to present the reasons for nuclear power in space to the President of the United States, who then will have to sell the idea to the House and Senate. And even if they all understand our positions, there would then have to be similar talks with our allies in Europe and Asia and get them on board."

"I don't see a reason why the pull from the US, Russia, the EU, and China wouldn't be enough to make sweeping changes to the treaty."

Allan belted a laugh. "Leave the politics to me, Muzie."

Now it was Muzikayise's turn to break a smile. "So are we in agreement, then, regarding where we all go from here?"

"For the record, Muzie, we haven't gone anywhere just yet. I already have your team's documentation regarding the newer version of the *Gazelle,* so I will bring this to the president as part of my meeting with him. He was close to biting my head off at the mere mention of 'nuclear' and 'space' in the same sentence, so this hard data should help smooth things over and hopefully get him to reach an informed decision."

Muzikayise allowed a wider smile to grace his face. "For an engineer, you sound more and more like a politician every time we talk."

Allan grinned. "You can be astute sometimes, Muzie."

"I always am," Muzikayise said. "I trust I'll hear from you later."

"Of that, there is no question," Allan said. "Good bye."

Muzikayise nodded in acknowledgment as the video call ended. Just below the video window was the after action report from Overberg. After his call with Allan, the raw data presented within the report looked rosier. Success was built on the remains of failure, and now Muzikayise felt that another political hindrance would soon tumble down like a domino—and bring him even more opportunities as a result.

∘ ◎ ∘

As the sunset bled its light across Cape Town, large shadows stretched from the towering skyscrapers that clustered in the center of the business district. The tallest building, which stood at seventy stories, was more than double the height of Khulu Towers, casting its shadow over the shorter, rectangular building. Muzikayise didn't mind the competition, however. In fact, he relished in the fact that his adopted hometown had become a bustling hub of finance, communications, and research. Plus, his view of all points east was unobstructed.

The lights in his office were dimmed almost to the point being off as he stood by the window, observing everything that was happening on the ground and in the distance. A three-car tram pulled into the light rail station that was in the middle of the four-lane avenue in front of his building, with more people boarding than getting off. Cars, buses, and small trucks flowed on and off the avenue while the tram collected passengers. Across the street was the Cape Town Metropolitan Transit Center, a massive structure with a tree-lined plaza bordering its front and several short buildings that were all encapsulated within a three hundred meter glass dome. Despite some sections of the dome supporting blocks of solar panels, most of it was transparent, allowing Muzikayise to watch all forms of mass transit roll into and out of the hub.

He took a satisfied sigh as the street lights all bloomed on in large swathes across the urban landscape. The decorative lighting of the Castle of Good Hope was the first—always the first—to grab his attention. The widely spaced streetlights that highlighted the winding curves and hairpin turns on the hills and flattened mountaintops of Table Mountain National Park was always the second point of interest for him. From there, as the evening skies shifted from its orange and red hews to dark purple and the black of night, it was the stars that drew the eyes of Muzikayise from the ground upward. The stars popped into existence, dozens at a time, despite the light pollution that showcased itself as the sun disappeared below the horizon. He crossed his arms for a moment as the thought of him jumping into his helicopter and taking it to

SALT crossed his mind if only so his view of the stars would be unobstructed.

There was one benefit to artificially limiting the number of stars that would fill the skies: It made it easier to spot objects much closer to Earth, such as any of the three nighttime launches he had scheduled for this evening. He didn't plan on standing in front of his office window another eighty-eight minutes but he knew from his vantage point he could see a faint dot in the night sky that would be one of his renewable rockets completing an orbit around the Earth.

He often asked himself, on clear evenings like this, what it would take for him to get into space. Not the tourism kind of space— "fake-space" as he viewed the rare sub-orbital trips that obscenely wealthy people would take, something he felt got more press than it should. Muzikayise viewed space as unexplored wilderness, with vast, almost limitless resources to harvest and home to entire worlds for Man to cultivate and make their own.

And with the arrival of the Leviathan, potentially a new frontier of interspecies relations and economic trade. Provided they survived past 2024. That was the part of the great equation that Muzikayise thought of more and more often, particularly at night as he looked toward where Uranus used to be.

Three raps on the door behind him was followed by the doors opening. He turned to see Ami walking in with an ornate metal tray in her hands, which supported two ceramic teacups. She had a pleasant smile on her face as she approached his desk. "English Breakfast, one sugar cube, black," she said as she lifted the cup and saucer.

He didn't hide his visual exploration of her well-dressed body, which was adorned with a green, sleeveless dress that exposed just enough cleavage and leg to stop his eyes from turning back to the night sky. Her coy smile remained as she stopped just a foot from him as she passed the saucer into his receiving hands. "Your favorite," she said.

"Indeed it is," he said as he brought the cup to his lips and sipped the hot tea, the warmth washing over him like a blanket.

Ami walked back to his desk and picked up her own teacup and turned back to Muzikayise. "Is there anything else you would like?" she asked as she walked with a swagger that accentuated her hips, each footstep brought in front of the other until she was alongside him by the windows. She could be such a seductress sometimes.

"In fact, I do," he answered. After allowing another few seconds of soaking her into his retinas, he turned back toward the windows and urban vista beyond. "A question."

"Okay, hit me," she said, after which she took a sip of her rooibos.

Muzikayise swept his hand in an arch toward the outside. "In less than a decade, our world could very well be destroyed by a force that, in all likelihood, we'd have no chance in stopping. Despite this, everyone still behaves as if everything is as it was prior to the arrival of the Leviathan. Why do you believe that is?"

Ami took another sip through pressed lips as she looked down at the avenue below, with fewer vehicles traversing it, but the trams still hummed about on a predictable course. She spotted flashing blue lights against the bottom of one building in the distance, the telltale sign of police activity, but everything around them looked like any other day pre-Leviathan. "I'm no sociologist or psychologist, but you could think of the overall behavior of the people and compare it to how, say, Americans react to a car bombing in Iraq or Syria. 'It's over there, therefore it doesn't impact me.' Even if you take that analogy a step further—many German people, prior to the Nazi Party condemning the Jews and gypsies to their deaths, likely saw the signs of the levels of brutality that were being committed right in front of them, yet kept going to their jobs, shopping, and tending to their families and friends." She took another long sip of her tea. "We also have pretty damned short attention spans—at least the majority do." She dropped her shoulders as she looked into her teacup, the steam swirling around the rim of the cup and dissipating into the air as it rose.

Muzikayise nodded as he took in her answer. "It is a testament to our biological design and how our civilized world is structured today. Biological, because even in the face of certain doom, people will be irrationally optimistic about the future, especially if that doom is to occur in years and not months or days. On top of that, the people of the world like to be distracted from the harsh realities that surround them, even if those realities impact them in some indirect way. A nine-to-five job, fast food, television, the Internet, sex—that's just a handful of things that people do to keep their minds grounded and not focused on a very uncertain future, especially of events that are out of their control. It is why drastic actions by most governmental bodies were never enacted, like price freezing or martial law. If you don't interfere with the people, they'll continue behaving as if nothing is wrong."

Ami noticed Muzikayise's empty teacup and wrapped a hand around it, stroking his hand in the process as she brought their cups back to the metal tray. "So even with the knowledge of the Leviathan and its direct course for Earth, we'll continue our days and weeks and months as if everything is okay."

"But if you accept that everything is not okay, and that in fact, we all may very well perish sooner than later, what would you do?"

Ami glanced at her feet, then looked back at Muzikayise. "I'd make things right with my family and be at peace with the relationships I have."

He felt his teeth clench behind his lips at that response. He knew she wasn't referring to her family, of which she had a decent relationship. That was aimed squarely at him.

"Some things may require more time than we have right now." He uncrossed his arms and again gestured toward the sky. "Besides, since we understand the magnitude of what's coming, we can play a role in guiding humanity forward towards the light."

"And which light, pray tell, are we moving toward? Last I checked nobody's come up with a way to divert a starship that can consume gas giants."

Muzikayise drew in some air as he dropped his head with a wry smile. "That is the million dollar question, isn't it?"

"Another question that you'd like me to answer?" Ami said as she faced her boss.

Muzikayise didn't answer as he refocused on the city below, the batches of vehicles that moved away from the core of Cape Town and back to their homes and apartments. People just going about their business, all of which have to know the efforts of even Khulu Global may not be enough to save them—yet they continue with their lives. His three brothers are likely keeping to their own paths as well. *Maybe it's worth it to see what they are doing?* he thought.

His own set of personal questions were interrupted when Ami's hand slid up to his shoulder as she stepped in front of him, her head just below his as she brought their hands together. "In the meantime, there is one question that is more down-to-Earth that I'd like answered," Ami whispered.

As she turned her head upward, he looked into her eyes before surveying her body. Despite their day starting over twelve hours ago, the edges of her coiffed, curly afro glistened in the dim lighting. Her dark-red lipstick was still immaculate on her parted, moist lips. Her conservative use of eyeliner made her eyes even more alluring as they locked onto his. From his vantage point, he glanced down the front of her dress and saw a dark, strapless bra.

For as long as he operated his own business, he always kept his personal life separate and far away, to the point where he hadn't considered a relationship to be meaningful. There was never a shortage of women that wanted to experience him or tried to settle him down—being the owner of a global corporation and a bachelor by choice ensured various publication rags advertised those facts. When he hired Ami, he knew all of her personal and professional traits made her the perfect assistant for him, her looks included. But back then, he didn't know the Earth could be destroyed.

He felt his chest tighten, his mind weighing the pros and cons of what he wanted as he tried to view this as just another business decision, but for the moment, that was overruled by the more primal urges that he kept in check for so long. He lifted a hand and cupped her chin as their faces came closer together, her breath enveloped with the aroma of her rooibos tea.

As their lips pressed together and arms draped around each other's waists, Muzikayise allowed himself to drop his guard, just this once. There weren't many down-to-Earth questions he had for Ami, but this was one they would answer together that night.

2.4

Jennifer kept a copy of the unabridged Arecibo reports in one of her desk drawers. It served both as a source of potential ideas on how to better hone data transmission concepts using laser technology, and as a reminder of how little they knew about what they were dealing with—and the price that was paid for their progress.

The reports surrounding the Arecibo Observatory were, combined, well over two hundred pages long. The receiver that hung over the Arecibo Observatory collection dish fell into its center after seven of the eighteen support cables snapped from the intense heat magnified onto them by the maser; that failure resulted in the total weight of the receiver being distributed among the remaining cables, which failed in rapid succession. Most of the collection dish was destroyed, though the research facilities remained intact due to the distance between them and the array. However, the microwave heat from the maser radiated over two hundred meters from the center of the dish which not only set many plants and anything outside that wasn't metallic on fire, but cooked every living organism near the edge of the beam due to the uncontrolled radiation emissions. Cooked from the inside out. The classified photos of what remained of the scientists that stayed within Arecibo were gruesome enough to make even veteran forensics teams sick. That part always made Jennifer wince. She folded those pages inward so she could skip them. Reading that section always prompted her to eye the framed photo of Isabella Velasco that hung in their office. The picture used was her professional headshot taken for the Arecibo Observatory staff webpage. Her name was embossed into the bottom of the frame, along with the quote "To The Stars, Your Light Will Shine".

The reports were released two weeks after the satellite imagery of the Arecibo Observatory became public. The photos and reports galvanized the growing number of people that wanted the governments of the world and their space agencies to stop attempting any kind of communication with the Leviathan. Jennifer made a point to read articles about the discourse in either newspapers or online, but refused to watch any television broadcasts or online streams of the debates, which raged on various online and cable network shows as the months wore on. The short-sightedness of some people didn't surprise her, but what did was how fast people seemed to forget that their world was still slated for destruction within everyone's lifetime. Because of this, politicians around the world screamed for military solutions to "The Leviathan Question," wanting to redirect funds away from the recent surge in the sciences. There were equally loud voices in favor of the continued mission objectives of NASA, SETI, and other space agencies, ensuring that their positions were heard over the cacophony of dissent. Jennifer still recalled one such discussion she had during an interview on NPR back in June, during which she reminded people what was at stake.

"I understand where many are coming from," she began, her voice broadcasted to over ten million listeners. "When people hear that millions of their taxpayer dollars are being spent on projects that do not immediately funnel back into their communities, they have the right to wonder where that money is going and for what purpose. Fortunately, if you take a telescope and look into the night sky, toward what used to be the gas giant, Uranus, you'll have all the evidence you'll ever need regarding the why. If you look for Neptune or Pluto but cannot find them, you'll know why. If you see the Leviathan and its presence, you'll know why."

"Are you suggesting that the incredible surge in funding for many space programs and initiatives around the world is justifiable?" the interviewer asked in a calm, pleasant voice.

"Absolutely," Jennifer said. "The previous levels of funding—if you look at what NASA received in 2013, for example—simply was not enough to support the kind of work that needed to be done regarding our understanding of the Leviathan."

"But what about those people that protest such spending when they are struggling to put food on the table, or those that say that such money would be better spent domestically?"

Jennifer sighed. "If we do not find a way to communicate our desire—our right—to exist with the Leviathan, all the domestic concerns aren't going to matter if Earth no longer exists."

In hindsight, she wasn't sure which part of her response she regretted: the words themselves or the sigh she made that happened to be caught by her microphone. Both of those were taken out of context by many that wrote about the interview and, by extension, her. She hoped to get another shot on NPR, but decided to focus on what she considered more important. She cared about wanting to correct the inaccurate reports about SETI and NASA, and always got flustered whenever she learned of journalists that cherry-picked her work or quotes to make her, as a person, seem less interested in the science and more about gaining popularity points—something she just didn't understand.

Such journalistic presentations came to a head during the presidential campaigns that occurred alongside her occasional interviews. One prominent US politician, in a heated moment during a large summer campaign rally, described those that wanted to roll back the initiatives around the Leviathan as "deplorables" and against the future of mankind—a statement that dominated news cycles for months afterward.

Meanwhile, the latest message from the Leviathan repeated every minute after it finished, save for the rotation counter that went down for each day that brought the Leviathan closer to Earth. Each sentence of the message was scrutinized by everyone with a microphone—their opinions and thoughts, from moderate and thoughtful to extreme and incendiary, were shared and repeated countless times around the world. Jennifer and her team, along with just about everyone else that worked in other SETI programs, wanted to send either a rover or— even more challenging—a human to the coordinates the message provided. Despite several months of sending different messages, data packets, and even additional audio and video streams in every conceivable digital format, the message from the Leviathan remained on a loop.

o ◎ o

As the months passed, the political pressure to renege on the new expenses NASA, Roscosmos, and other agencies had continued to grow. Future bills various administrations expected would be a slam dunk found themselves in limbo, if not vetoed altogether. Jennifer and Gordan had long conversations about the fate of The Armstrong Program given the volatility they witnessed within the government. A lot of the questions they threw around always had two answers, one for each presidential candidate that was campaigning around the country. She knew that Allan Wheeler's job as director could be on the line as part of a new administration in January, but given the work he and NASA were now leading on an international scale, she felt his position was safe, at least until the Leviathan Question had an answer.

One constant that seemed to only grow with time were the mass of people, dubbed "Atters," that were at the north gate of the ATA compound. The mass of people there, now over ten-thousand strong, formed a makeshift community that settled into place around the lone road that connected to ATA. Motor homes and recreational vehicles of all shapes and sizes clustered in circular and square groups, the paths to them frequented to the point where some Atters laid stones and wooden planks to designate road curbs and guides to help with traffic. Groups of people even set up makeshift housing, stages for speeches and musical performances, and a small shack that served as a storefront. The local police and National Guard monitored the sprawling group of space fanatics, religious groups, UFO conspiracists, and curiosity-seekers, though they kept their presence limited to the north gate entrance.

Of all the groups that garnered attention from the authorities the most concerning was The Seven Trumpets, a nascent cult that formed in the months following the Leviathan's arrival. Members of the cult, led by an enigmatic figure publicly known as "John the Messenger," exhibited extreme behavior towards anyone that worked to stop the Leviathan from reaching Earth. Aside from their prevalence online through media outlets like YouTube and Facebook, their activity never amounted to anything beyond random skirmishes in the streets of major cities. The FBI suspected they established a presence among the Atters which led to further discouragement of ATA staff from using the north gates.

It didn't matter much to Jennifer, as by the middle of summer she rarely passed through that gate anymore due to the newly constructed west gate. It had a road that bored under the rugged but small hills connecting to Route 89. Unlike the well-known north entrance, the west gate and the road that originated from it was kept off all maps—even Google satellite imagery was scrubbed. Jennifer was never keen to the level of secrecy that surrounded parts of ATA's new reality, but she knew what the stakes were and couldn't find arguments against it. She knew that beyond the cries and protests, their research continued its march forward. It moved on its own beat, toward an uncertain future that gripped the world in which it was a part.

o ◎ o

AUGUST 30, 2016

Adalwine Dunlap—known by his new brothers and sisters as Brother Barnabas—reviewed his attire in the small bathroom mirror. He had to prop the bathroom door open and stand in the narrow foyer inside his RV—an old model that was a rusted beige box on wheels—to get as full a view as possible, and even then he could only see everything above the waist. The windows were boarded up on the inside, so only the light from the sides of the medicine cabinet and the foyer would allow him to see the white robe that adorned him. His shoulder pads were light, making him look wider than he appeared. The buttons that ran down the robe were properly concealed, giving it a seamless look. He lifted his chin up as he tightened the collar with long skinny fingers, making it almost flush against his thin neck. He wore nothing underneath the robe—purity was the only thing permitted when wearing the robes that God gave his disciples—but the robe was thick enough to be opaque. The hair on his head and his face were shaved off the night before—even his eyebrows were removed. Pure, like the day he was born. The intense fasting Barnabas endured for the last two weeks resulted in his face looking more gaunt, his lips thin and cracked —a far cry from his driver's license picture, the card now burnt in a small basket at the rear of the RV. That part of his life he gladly discarded for God. Barnabas craned his head from side to side, looking over every inch of his face before reaching behind his neck to grasp a hood that was integrated onto the robe. He walked back into the confined bathroom and looked at himself with proud, fiery eyes.

"He will not forget your work and the love you have shown for His name," Barnabas said to himself as he lifted the hood over his clean-shaven head. "Show this same diligence to the very end, so that what you hope for may be fully realized." The hood cast a shadow just over his eyes, the light in the bathroom exposing only his nose and mouth, which stretched into a grin. As he admired his toothy smile, his lower lip cracked open, allowing a small trickle of blood to ball on the surface.

"Through faith and patience, I will inherit what has been promised," Barnabas said as he licked the blood from his lips, the life-giving sustenance triggering neglected sensory receptors on his tongue. He closed his eyes as he bit into his lower lip which caused more blood to seep from it and into his mouth. The taste was electrifying and only reminded him of what he would be sacrificing. He couldn't see his eyes, but he felt the fire behind them.

"For the Harbinger of Heaven, Amen."

Barnabas turned the corner from the bathroom and marched toward the bunk bed nestled into the rear of the RV where Sister Rachel still slept. He shook her until she woke up from her slumber.

"Is it time?" she asked after a short yawn.

"Indeed it is," Barnabas said. "The sun is at its apex and God has given us His grace."

"Indeed," she echoed as she jumped off the top bunk, her naked body illuminated from the interior lighting. Despite also being bald and hairless, her natural beauty did not garner a reaction from Barnabas—he was personally trained by John the Messenger to forgo the temptations of the flesh, one of the many sins that would be cleansed from the Earth thanks to their efforts. He viewed her as another vessel of the Harbinger and nothing more. As she undertook the methodical process of robing, he walked to the side table and benches toward the front of the RV. Two crates of TNT occupied the benches, with various wires running to the top of each crate which connected to a remote detonation receiver. Two AR-15 assault rifles and two forty-caliber pistols sat on the tabletop, complete with boxes of ammo for each. He picked up each weapon and took them apart for inspection—he wanted to make sure nothing would jam or otherwise not perform as expected. Satisfied with what he saw, he put them back together and loaded them with ammo. He blessed the lethal weapons when he finished.

He heard Rachel complete her prayers in the bathroom as he went to the rear of the RV, which had the rear storage compartment door removed so two large barrels of explosives could be kept there. On top of one barrel was the remote detonator, a deceptively simple mechanical device that had a green push-button at the top and an antenna integrated into the handle. Barnabas flipped the device into a test mode and pressed the button—the diode LED light strips at the top of the barrels, the TNT crates at the front, and another long, coffin-sized crate of TNT all changed from green to red. They all flipped back to green when he lifted his thumb from the detonator.

Rachel came behind him, her breathing measured, but intense. Barnabas turned around to the robed woman, the hood over her head blocking all the light that would have fallen onto her face. The two of them bowed toward each other and, after tenting their hands, spoke in unison. "For the Harbinger of Heaven, Amen."

∘ ◎ ∘

Jennifer sat at a picnic table behind the ATA main office building with Sam, her eyes closed as she took a large bite out of a chicken salad sandwich. The summer heat was pleasant, the gentle breeze seemingly enhancing the flavor of her lunch. Next to her paper plate was a folder with documents that Sam wanted to share. But for the moment, Jennifer savored both the lunch in front of her and the rare slot of time where she could take longer, more relaxed breaths while soaking in some natural light. Being outdoors also helped with keeping all the work—and increased political drama—into perspective. She looked beyond the hundreds of antennae—two hundred and forty antennae, to be exact—which populated a flattened area two miles wide. She looked beyond the lone military bunker, a single half-cylinder structure which was disguised as an antenna construction facility that was no taller than a one-story building but was fifty feet long, that sat in the middle of the flattened field of antennae. Instead, she focused on the chirping birds, the occasional wispy cloud that would roll into existence, and the wind. The sun hung in the sky, its dry heat shifting with the wind, but heat that felt good on Jennifer's arms and legs. It all reminded her that this was their world—their only world—and despite the problems humanity may have with itself, she knew her work would contribute towards a solution that could save them.

The wind was soft, shuffling through nearby brush and wrapping around Jennifer's hair which tried, in vain, to become mixed in with the food as she took one pleasurable bite after another. Sam couldn't help but voice her disdain regarding Jennifer's display of culinary satisfaction. "You don't have to so blatantly advertise how much you're loving your sandwich right now," Sam snorted as she examined her homemade grilled cheese sandwich which softened from too much time in the microwave, plopping it back onto her paper plate.

"I told you to not nuke your sandwich," chided Jennifer in-between bites. "One day you'll listen to me and use the stove in the office kitchen. Or at least the convection oven."

"Nyah!" Sam stuck out her tongue as she bit into her sandwich.

She grimaced at the rubbery textures, the desired crunchiness of the toast unmet.

As Jennifer finished the first half of her sandwich, she cracked open the folder and slid from it a blurry image that went through several filters to improve its resolution. The blurry image was a subsection of the Leviathan's surface, an area that contained the signs of an artificial structure: four circular depressions on the flattened surface, all of which contained smaller spherical structures. Deep black lines ran between them, along with wider gray-black lines that crossed each other and circled back to the four flattened depressions. The circular outline that the gray-black lines were about a mile in diameter, with some additional branches of lines extending outward to other, fuzzy points at the edges of the image.

She flipped the page around so Sam could see it while she pointed at the named source of the image: the *New Horizons* space probe. "How did you pull this off?" Jennifer asked while she leaned in. "I thought the probe was redirected for deep space observations since Neptune and Pluto no longer exist."

Sam looked at the image, then at Jennifer. She grabbed a bottle of soda and used it to wash away the unsatisfying taste of her sandwich before she leaned back from the table with crossed arms and a smug look on her face. "Pretty impressive, huh?"

"Sam—"

"It's okay, Jen. I pulled some strings at NASA a month ago to turn the Long-Range Reconnaissance Imager on the *New Horizons* toward the Leviathan instead of keeping it powered down. Once we knew the Leviathan was slowly rotating—"

"A month ago?"

"Yeah, a month ago." Sam was oblivious to Jennifer's sudden harried expression. "Anyway, the Leviathan makes one rotation every eighty-four days, so when I realized that *New Horizons* was still operational, I figured that it could be used to take some sidelong snapshots, something we haven't been able to accomplish. Granted, the *New Horizons* probe is nearly 28AU away, so we can't exactly get pristine snapshots, but the technology behind the LRRI is sufficient enough for images like these, after some local cleanup and processing work."

Jennifer placed the remains of her sandwich on her plate and gripped the table, her eyes turned away. "Sam, did you run this by anyone at NASA? Because you certainly didn't run this by me."

Sam dropped her arms to her sides as she felt her face flushed. "I didn't think pointing the probe a different direction was considered important enough—"

"Anything that involves NASA has to pass through me today, you know that," Jennifer dropped a hand to the bench and gripped it. She wanted to pound the tabletop, but refrained from doing so, hoping the bench would keep her arm from rising into the air. "Everything we're doing is under a much bigger microscope now, especially now that our finances are tied with NASA. We won't be able to get anywhere near as much done if our funding is suddenly pulled due to clandestine actions."

"Clandestine, Jen? Aren't we being a bit hyperbole?"

"It's not a joke, Sam! We need to make sure everything we're doing is by the book."

Sam sat back as she pulled the image away from Jennifer and toward her chest. "I didn't realize you've become such a hardliner for policy and regulations."

Jennifer looked up after she realized her blunt reaction, then sighed as she dropped her shoulders and relaxed herself. "I'm sorry, Sam. But you understand where I am coming from, right? You—"

A loud crash echoed around the hills and trees, startling Jennifer and Sam into momentary silence. Jennifer placed her sandwich down as she jumped from her seat, looking toward the hills that obscured the Allen Telescope Array north gates.

"What the hell was that?" Sam asked as she threw her legs over the picnic bench and got to her feet. The sudden punch of the crash was soon replaced with what sounded like the rolling grumble of a vehicle engine, and that sound grew in volume. Jennifer's eyes caught the rapid movements of military personnel scrambling out of the disguised bunker, all of which loaded into two armored Humvees. It didn't take long for Jennifer to put their actions and the crashing sound together.

"Someone breached the north gate," Jennifer whispered. She strode around to Sam and took her arm. "Come on, we better get back inside"

"I can't argue with that," Sam said with haste. She kept looking toward the engine sound as it approached. They were at the foot of their building door when a vehicle larger than a car appeared from behind the hillside—an RV. Though it shimmered like a mirage, she could tell that it was moving fast. Jennifer's heart raced, adrenaline rushing through her body, as the realization of their situation dawned upon her: Someone was attacking them. Not wanting to take her eyes away from what unfolded in the distance, she glanced at the ATA office complex. Their building was no military bunker and likely wouldn't prevent a vehicle the size of an RV from violently piercing its walls. And that assumes the driver doesn't have anything more dangerous, like firearms or explosives, on-hand.

Unless something got between the attackers and their office, it wouldn't take long for them to close the gap.

○ ◎ ○

Getting through the front gates proved to be much easier than expected. Barnabas's mouth warped into a wicked smile as the masses that usually gathered in front of the gate—those many Uncleansed—were herded to the sides by fellow Acolytes already embedded in the various groups that congregated there. Even the guards that occupied the other side of the fence didn't fire their weapons at them, or even throw their bodies in front of their vehicle. They were only Uncleansed, after all, and not committed to a cause as righteous as they were, otherwise he was sure they would've done anything to stop them. The cleared roadway allowed Rachel to barrel their RV through the dual gates there which were nothing more than chain-link fences. It was one of many victories he expected to happen that day though they were both quiet as she kept her foot floored on the pedal.

He stood in the middle of the RV, one hand on a ceiling-mounted hand railing and the other gripping an AR-15. The detonator jostled around in a pocket within his robe, the metallic shape bouncing off his leg as the RV rocked from Rachel's aggressive driving.

It didn't take long before the road they were on rounded the hillside that obscured their view of their target: the Allen Telescope Array office complex, the headquarters for SETI West. "Today we put to silence the ignorance of foolish people," Barnabas declared as he flipped the safety off his rifle. "As John prophesied, the Harbinger's will be done."

"Amen!" both Barnabas and Rachel cried as she steered the RV for the small office.

○ ◎ ○

"Stop your vehicle now," Jennifer heard being blared from a mega-phone speaker mounted on one of the Humvees that approached the RV. The second Humvee stopped on the road that ran to their main office—just a quarter mile away—after which the soldiers rushed out of the vehicle and took defensive firing positions, parts of their rifles glimmering in the sunlight. "Stop your vehicle or we will open fire!"

Nic ran up to the window next to the back door and peaked be-tween the blinds. "Should we even still be here?" he asked.

"Where would you propose we go?" Sam countered as she broke Jennifer's grip and entered the building. "We're caged here on all sides—"

Jennifer gasped and pressed her hand on her chest as gunfire broke out—military assault rifles ripping through the front window of the accelerating RV.

Jennifer froze in place as she witnessed the RV take a harsh turn which caused it to tilt to one side. The crunch of the RV's wall against the pavement, the glass shattering, and the piercing echos of metal, glass, and plastic grinding to a halt was enough to make her body re-fuse to move, even at Sam's insistence. It was all so quick, and it was happening in front of her, less than a mile away. A person crawled from one of the side windows that now faced upward. The person pointed something at the soldiers, prompting a swift response. Jennifer gasped again when gunfire rang out once more, the person's body slumped forward and rolled over the side of the RV and onto the pavement like a rag doll. Two of the soldiers approached the downed vehicle, their rifles ready to fire at any moment.

Sam was saying something to Jennifer, but she didn't hear her—she focused on what was unfolding, too mesmerized by an event that, until that moment, was something she'd only seen on TV or in the movies. More gunfire echoed in the distance. *This can't be happening,* Jennifer thought as she felt someone place their hand on her shoulder. "We're getting out of here," Gordan said, and not for the first time. Jennifer shook her head before she turned away from the scene outside.

Her mouth opened to respond, but closed as fast when she noticed behind Gordan two Humvees that approached their location. They were briefed about this sort of scenario months ago, just after the bunker's construction, despite Jennifer's fervent opposition. Granted, the military brass insisted their installation would be kept to a minimum so as to not interfere with the work they performed at ATA. In the end, the added military presence within the fences of the ATA compound was there to protect them—and now that purpose was now very much on aggressive display.

Jennifer ran to the front of the building, the lead Humvee coming to a stop just as she opened the front door. Corporal 'Clay' York stepped out from the front passenger side and marched toward Jennifer. He wore camouflage military gear which had his last name and military branch displayed above each breast pocket, along with his rank insignia, centered on the uniform. This was the first time she'd seen him not wearing the form-fitting army service uniform she was more fond of. And where he was more informal during those times, if not still regimented in his handling of discussions with her and her team, today he was pure military, as if a switch was flipped in his demeanor.

"We're leaving now," York commanded, his voice booming over of the Humvee's distant rumbling engine. "No time to lose, let's move!"

"Can you give us a minute to shut things down?" Nic asked, though his face sank when he saw York's rigid, upturned face.

"The only thing you need to do is get in the back of the Humvee," York barked. He came to the foot of the door, just inches from Jennifer, and smacked his hand against the door frame. "Let's move, move, move!"

Jennifer glanced at York's eyes, which stared right back—his focus really was indomitable. She swung around and echoed his command. "You heard him. Nobody's touching these computers but us, when we return." She pushed back the immediate thoughts of the shootings and the replaying reel of the RV rolling over onto its side, at least while her adrenaline was coursing through her, and raised her own voice. "Let's go!"

"Hold on," Gordan threw a hand to York's shoulder. "What about my family? I can't leave them you know."

"Your home is being secured," York said with utmost confidence. "Given how far your home is from here, you can either have them meet you at our secured location, or I can have you shuttled back to your place once we get everyone out of here."

Gordan glanced as Jennifer, then back to York. "Take me to the secured location."

York nodded and finished the process of funneling everyone to the Humvees.

They've all been through three evacuation drills over the last six months, though only Jennifer seemed to take it seriously. At least, that was the impression she had when they all talked about it afterwards. Who would be crazy enough to break into what became a small military base? But as they all scrambled through the front door, Jennifer kept her vision on York, silently thanking him that the military held their ground with providing them protection.

York waited as they split into two groups, one for each Humvee that arrived to pick them up: Jennifer and Sam into the front, Gordan, Nic, and Nareen into the rear. Once York slid into the front of his Humvee, their engines roared as they sped away toward the west gates.

"Where are we going?" Jennifer asked as she held onto the locked back door, then at York.

"To a secure location," York replied flatly.

"I thought where we were was secure," Sam said, her voice uneven. She held a quizzical look for York as if that would persuade him to divulge what he knew. It didn't work, to which she pressed back into her seat and proceeded, with shaky hands, to buckle her seatbelt.

"I thought so, too," York admitted after some hesitation. "There will be a more discrete vehicle waiting for you on the other end of the tunnel. The four of you will then be taken to a temporary location until we've secured the Array."

◦ ◎ ◦

Rachel gritted her teeth as the booming command from the army went unheeded. Barnabas wrapped an arm around a vertical railing and pressed himself against the closed bathroom door as his eyes narrowed at what appeared to be a one-vehicle blockade in front of them.

"We will never fail," Barnabas screamed. "Barrel through the Uncleansed!"

Before Rachel could respond in kind, several bullets punctured the front window of the RV. Rachel kept a tight grip on the steering wheel until a bullet punched into her right shoulder. She yelped in pain as the sharp sting of a bullet penetrated her flesh and jammed itself into her shoulder blade, which combined with the shattered windshield glass flying into her face. The singular focus on their mission was, for just a flash, overridden by her will to live, which prompted her to dive out of the driver's seat with a hand still on the steering wheel, causing their bulky vehicle to swerve sharply to the left. Rachel ignored the blood coming from a reddened spot on her shoulder and warm spots on her face as she secured her pistol against her body. Seconds after that, she felt herself falling toward the square passenger window.

Gravity took over as the RV fell onto its right side, causing their few possessions that were along the left side of the vehicle to rain upon them. The thin mattresses from their bunks, not properly secured to the metal wall frame, fell onto Barnabas, the added weight making him break through the bathroom door, his head cracking the mirror on impact. The sound of grinding metal, shattered glass, and the mixed fluids in the punctured septic tank filled his ears as he watched the thin walls against him deform and warp.

He banged his elbow against the broken mirror as he cursed. Why did nobody know about an armed military presence at the ATA compound? What were their informants being paid to do? He sat up and brought his hands to the mattresses that blocked the doorway to the rest of the RV when he heard a single pang from Rachel's pistol, which was met with several more gunshots that rained on the RV. This time, however, he heard a heavy object collapse against the side of the RV, by the driver's side window. Barnabas brought his hands together in prayer for Sister Rachel, who he was sure died by the hands of the Uncleansed and joined the angels next to the Harbinger of Heaven.

The ringing in his ears cleared enough to recognize the sounds of approaching footsteps—more soldiers, no doubt. He dropped his rifle and fished out the detonator from his robe pocket. He wondered if John foresaw this event—if he knew they would fail. He then lit up, a cracked smile returning to his bloodied face. Yes, this was meant to happen all along! And he would complete his mission. He flipped a small switch on the detonator that armed everything in the RV. His eyes closed as he made a final prayer to the Harbinger of Heaven.

"For you, my Lord."

◡ ◎ ◦

Only a minute into their drive passed before a large explosion echoed from behind, the shockwave rocking the Humvee. As York got on his radio to find out what happened, Jennifer's hands shot out to the sides and gripped whatever they could to keep her body from swaying. She released the air she held in her lungs and looked over her shoulder with widened eyes as she whispered, "Oh my God." A plume of smoke and fire arose behind their building, where the incapacitated RV was, she assumed. As the smoke rose higher in the sky, she tried to refocus her thoughts, but everything was on that growing plume behind them. Her mind then rolling through the possibilities related to that RV and the people within it. They must have had explosives stored in that RV —no way an explosion that large could've been just from the vehicle's gas tank. They wanted to harm her and her team. Kill them. They had the means to destroy their facilities a few times over and collected whatever they needed for the job in plain sight. If it weren't for York and his team...

Jennifer felt Sam's hand against hers on the seat between them. She turned around and looked into Sam's bulging, scared eyes, her other arm wrapped around her waist as if she were in pain. When it came to their everyday work, Sam always found something to say about their situation, even ones that revolved around the Leviathan, which she viewed as simply the biggest enigma to crack. However, witnessing the actions of people that broke into their compound—and how swiftly they were brought down in a violent end—almost turned her skin white, her chest heaving up and down. *What is going on?* Jennifer thought was on Sam's lips as they looked at each other, both with the same amount of fear spread across their faces.

She wanted to tell Sam that everything would be okay, that they would be back to work in no time at all. As the Humvees slowed down to pass through the west gate, the foot of the narrow two-lane tunnel ahead of them, she had nothing of comfort or even pragmatic words to impart. Her heart wanted to burst out of her chest as much as Sam's —burst and scream.

Jennifer chose instead to focus on Sam's hand, which she rolled her hand over. They intertwined their fingers. She couldn't get the thoughts of what happened to the people inside the RV out of her head, but she could try to focus on what—who was in front of her. The warmth emanating from her hand. The soft textures that formed the many lines in her palm. The imperceptible hairs that drifted across her fingers. She could almost feel Sam's heartbeat through her hands. As the rhythmic thumping slowed in unison with her own, their mutual gaze broke as the sunlight that filled the Humvee's interior was replaced by the softer overhead tunnel lighting.

Jennifer didn't smile, but was grateful for Sam being there.

But the RV... it was still replaying in her mind. The gunshots, and the explosions and crashes. What would the aliens on the Leviathan think about the divisiveness of their species? Of people wanting to prevent them from saving themselves?

It wouldn't be long before she learned what exactly happened back there, but whatever the details, she just knew they had to continue their work. Whatever the costs.

2.5

The original plans kept everyone at a government-owned motel a few miles away for up to forty-eight hours, assuming that the incident at ATA caused no serious damage.

Jennifer didn't know much about these accommodations, so she allowed herself to rest against the window as the Humvee turned off the highway onto an unmarked offramp which had two "AUTHORIZED PERSONNEL ONLY" signs alongside it. The offramp, after wrapping behind a hill, became enshrouded in the shadows of tall trees. The road itself was a foot lower than the surrounding terrain—if it weren't for the Humvee, you wouldn't be able to tell that the road was even there. They approached a tollbooth that had decades of overgrowth wrapping its green tendons around the structure, the traffic gate weathered and covered with rust. The tollbooth looked abandoned, yet the traffic gate rose on its own, which allowed the Humvee caravan to roll right past it without slowing down. The booth, it seemed, had some level of automation. Was it RFID transponders that triggered the gate between the Humvee and it? Jennifer didn't know for sure, but the thoughts kept her mind away from what just transpired an hour ago.

A few more minutes passed before they entered a tunnel which took them to an underground parking lot that contained few vehicles in it. Once Jennifer stepped out of the vehicle, the only places where they could go were two doorways and an elevator, whose doors were already open. The interior of the elevator looked out of place, as if it belonged inside a hotel from the eighties: neutral colors, an old tinny speaker nestled in the corner that played light classical music, and a musty smell that reminded her of a carpet that's been saturated with water for too long.

"Where are we?" Sam asked as she joined Jennifer in the elevator.

"Your secured location," York said, standing by the side of the elevator as he waved Gordan, Nic, and Nareen into the stuffy space. He wrapped his hand around the door and pressed the yellow button for the second floor. "You'll find your names printed on cards on the doors of the rooms closest to the elevator. The doors will be unlocked."

"What about you?" Nic asked, who still peered around the parking lot to see if there were any hints to suggest where they were.

"I'll be around," York said.

Jennifer understood Nic's curiosity regarding their location—he still didn't tell them where they were—but that was when she noticed there were only two elevator buttons, just those for the ground floor and second floor. "Aren't we in a basement? There's only two buttons here," she observed. "Where *are* we?"

"Like I said," York said as the elevator doors squeaked closed. "A secured location."

"Maybe we're in a federal holding area of some sort?" Nareen postulated. "Like where the FBI would keep people in the witness protection program?"

"I don't think such programs would involve themselves with the military," Sam said, after which she waved a hand in front of her face and scrunched her brows and nose. "I also doubt they'd allow their elevators to smell like a gym locker room."

The elevator made a loud ding as it came to a stop and opened onto the second floor. Sam was the first to leap out of the elevator, catching herself on the balcony railing in front of her. The smell of sequoias and sounds of squawking birds greeted Jennifer as she stepped out of the elevator, taking in the surprising area they found themselves, the biggest manmade landmark being a tall road sign in the shape of a redwood tree, outlined with broken neon lights. Running down the middle of the light-green sign was the word "Redwood" made of plastic bark and "Motel" in a generic font indicative of a motel built decades ago.

The Redwood Motel, on the surface, looked like any other L-shaped, aging motel from the 1970s that hadn't kept up with the times, complete with neon signage that always had "NO VACANCY" lit in bright cursive blue and red letters. Fifty rooms spread across two floors, an empty pool ringed with construction pylons connected with orange tape, and a parking lot that had several worn and dirty cars and pickup trucks parked in front of the first floor rooms. Though it was just a few hundred feet from the highway, it was a rare sight to see any traffic pass it, let alone attempt to roll into their parking lot, the passersby double-checking to see if all the rooms were really occupied. As Jennifer learned, a kind, if not grumpy, receptionist would confirm with these tourists that they had no rooms to spare.

Their motel rooms didn't match the grungy exterior. Her room —and those of her peers—were all double the size they would've expected, thanks to the removal of the wall that would separate two of the otherwise cramped motel rooms. Drywall blocked the door for the second motel room that her space merged into. The furnishings were also of this decade, with plenty of sockets for devices, a large desk with a desktop computer waiting for a user to access it, and a fluffy king-sized bed. Jennifer placed her hands on her waist as she nodded at her lodgings. Two days here would have been a decent, but short, stay.

o ◯ o

SEPTEMBER 8, 2016

She knew that anyone breaking through the security perimeter laid out by the military would always cause a ton of commotion, no matter what the outcome of that event was. Even with that level of seriousness, she expected to return to ATA and resume observations and research projects. However, the use of explosives completely upended that idea and the contingency plans Corporal York worked with. Two days after the failed terrorist attack, he had everyone stay in The Redwood Motel for an additional week while various forensics and recovery teams removed the destroyed RV and the remains of the two people that occupied it.

Other than cursory check-ins by York, Jennifer remained in the dark regarding everything related to the ATA. She wrote many emails and made several phone calls to change that—eventually it was Allan that got back to her near the end of their ninth day away from the ATA.

"They haven't finished their analysis yet, but the terrorists used a combination of homemade IEDs and industrial-grade TNT—possibly pentolite," Allan shared with Jennifer during a call she had on the second floor balcony in front of her room. "Very powerful high explosives."

"Jesus," Jennifer said. She didn't know much about explosives, but knew that pentolite was used in constructing boreholes and large dams. "But the explosion wasn't near our facilities, right?"

"Right. However, the shockwave from the explosion was enough to cause moderate damage to the internals of the main office. I was told that all the windows were shattered, and equipment inside was damaged from the blast." Allan sighed, as if in pain. "Ahh, I'm sorry, but we may have to shut down ATA operations and relocate you—"

"Wait wait wait," Jennifer interrupted. She threw a hand forward and grabbed the cyan-painted railing in front of her, leaning into it. "I thought it was just broken glass and damaged computers? That doesn't sound significant enough to shut us down."

"It's not my call," Allan said. "I'm just telling you what shared by Homeland Security."

"But that's—"

"It's not my call," he repeated with more assertion behind his words. "A group of people just tried blowing you guys up and you want to go back into that same space?"

"Yes," she said, unwavering. "We have to continue. We can't just stay cooped up in this shelter in the middle of nowhere. You know damned well we could have that place cleaned up and back in action in less than two days' time."

Jennifer could see Allan shrugging his shoulders in her mind, based on his silence. *There's nothing he could do. It wasn't his call.* She paced down the walkway until she overlooked the sad little pool at the rear of the motel. Not taking away the phone from her ear, she looked out towards the batches of redwood trees that cast long shadows against the motel. They couldn't just stop their work. There had to be a solution.

She cracked a smile as she made an about-face and marched back to her room. "What about the Very Large Array in New Mexico?"

"You mean the Karl Jansky Very Large Array?"

"Yes!"

"What about it?"

"Their equipment received a major upgrade a few years back, and it's the only other radio observatory in the US that's perfect for our goals."

"But there's already a full complement of personnel there—do you want to give some aspiring researchers the boot just to accommodate you and your team?"

Jennifer passed a hand over her face as she groaned. "Nobody has to be relocated or otherwise removed from there. We will make it work. Can you make it happen?"

The pause from Allan was almost agonizing. She found it both expected and frustrating that he would consider the politics of such a move over the scientific advantages. "I'll see what I can do," he finally said.

"I'm sure you will!" Jennifer said.

"Give me twenty-four hours—I'll get back to you regarding your request."

"Great. Make it happen, Allan." She waited for a response from him, but he disconnected instead.

o ◎ o

"I still can't believe that a religious group would attempt an attack on us—us!" Sam said to Gordan, Nic, and Nareen, who all gathered in her room for some small talk. Like with previous days, it didn't take long for the conversation to veer back to the extremist group they'd all acknowledged as if it never existed prior: The Seven Trumpets.

She paced by the windows which allowed some of the orange light from the sunset to warm each side of her body as she turned heel.

"You shouldn't be surprised—you're smarter than that," Gordan lounged back in the loveseat opposite of her bed. He propped his arms on the sides of the seat while he held a half-full glass of wine in one hand.

"They're terrorists now," Nareen said while she kept her eyes on her own wine glass, a finger tracing the rim in slow circles. However, she looked at Sam and sighed. "Another group that's graduated from fringe religious sect to just another terrorist group with religion as its backbone."

"But why would The Seven Trumpets want to harm us?" Nic asked as he shifted his chair closer to the circular table.

Gordan looked over at Nic, his mouth parted open and his free hand outstretched. "Have you seriously not read about The Seven Trumpets?"

Nic shrugged as he shuffled his feet. "It hasn't appeared in my RSS feeds, so..."

Nareen couldn't help but laugh as Gordan threw his hand into the air and looked up toward the ceiling before he craned his head back at Nic. "Could you try and keep yourself up to speed on world news from time to time? Visiting CNN or any news website can't hurt," he said.

Sam leaned against the window frame, jostling the pulled blinds as she settled into place. She crossed her arms as she looked to address Nic. "The Seven Trumpets took some chapters from the Christian book of Revelations and took them far more seriously and literally than anyone else—that's my understanding. They see themselves as servants of God, or at least one of the angels of God that is supposed to bring about the apocalypse."

"Where does bombing science research centers come into this?" Nic asked.

Sam's gaze darted toward Nic. She wanted to continue pacing, but that only made her feel more uneasy about the implications of a group like The Seven Trumpets than she already was. "We're trying to save the world, but they want to see the apocalypse come. I believe they view the Leviathan as an angel or herald of God—allowing it to consume

Earth would fulfill their interpretations of the end days."

"I'm no Christian theologian," Nareen said, "but I'm pretty sure the world is not physically destroyed by an angel."

"Well, nobody said these guys completely understood their source material," Sam smirked.

"The earth is supposed to be destroyed after the final battle—Armageddon," Gordan corrected. He sat his wine glass on the floor next to his foot and made quotes in the air with his fingers. "'A new heaven and a new earth' are then formed by God after the old world—our world—is destroyed. But that happens long after the events of the seven angels and seven trumpets that this group is so named. After Armageddon, all the 'wicked' will be left to die on Earth while those that served and worshiped God will be brought to heaven. Guess which category we fall into in their eyes."

Everyone looked at each other, their eyes averting each other as they, once again, replayed the bombing attempt at ATA over a week ago. Despite what happened, Sam still couldn't believe they were the target of such malice—but she knew deep down that it was inevitable. With knowledge of the Leviathan and what it had done to two gas giants and a planetoid permeated throughout the general public, it was only a matter of time before someone applied religious symbolism to the events. Of those that did that, it would only take one with a motive, the charisma, and the means to turn such thoughts into a cult following.

"What about the leader of The Seven Trumpets—this 'John' person?" Sam asked as she pushed off the wall and plopped down onto her bed. The soft blankets and mattress with a memory foam cover never ceased to melt her concerns and thoughts away, at least for a moment.

"Nothing much is known so far about the leader of the group," Nic said as he paged through news sites on his phone. "Those that have access to him are dedicated to keeping his identity private."

"With the ATA attack, I'm sure the FBI will change that situation really quick," Nareen said. She raised her empty glass toward Sam and shook it. "Can you pour me another glass?"

"Sorry, I can't get up," Sam sighed as she threw her arms outward, fully spread on the bed. She didn't want to move.

Nareen got up from the round table and walked toward the kitchenette. "I guess I'll help myself, then."

"Do you believe the FBI will find these people and round them up?" Nic asked as he looked up from his phone and looked at Nareen.

"Well, they made short work of that village that was just outside of ATA," Nareen responded. "Did you see the flyover shots taken by news copters? They all but shoved everyone into their vehicles or into the backs of government buses and cleared the area over the course of three days."

"They're good at being reactive," Gordan said. His hands passed through his hair as his nostrils flared. "If something happens, they have the resources to clean things up. Let's see how good they are at preventing another disaster like this."

"That's totally not a morbid thought," Sam blurted while still staring upward at the ceiling.

"Not morbid—pragmatic," Gordan said. The tone of his voice prompted Sam to roll over and look forward to find Gordan's hardened, serious eyes staring back at her. "There are hundreds of astronomical observatories around the world, scores of which are throughout the United States alone. Though it would be theoretically possible to safeguard all of them—there are far more soldiers in the National Guard than there are observatories and telescopes—the logistics of doing so across all states that have observatories would be a monumental task. It would be an ongoing assignment that would see revolving posts over a period of months, if not years, and the costs of this operation would likely be large enough to get some people to move against such deployments." He leaned into his chair and sighed. "And that's just here in the United States. Who knows what would happen if such attacks occurred overseas, or if any future attacks are successful."

"What's the alternative," Sam pushed herself upright and glared at Gordan. "We cease our research and shut down ATA, the VLA, other observatories around the country and places like South Africa and Russia to appease these assholes?"

"I'm sure that's not what Gordan is suggesting," Nic said as he looked to Nareen to jump in and prevent a yelling match from breaking out.

Nareen waved her hand and took a quick sip from her filled glass. "Don't look at me, Nic! I'm just here for the wine." She looked at Sam and Gordan's faces before she continued with a smile. "Besides, it's been awhile since they went at it. I want to watch."

"Nobody's going to get into a pissing contest," Gordan reassured Nic, though his tone suggested he would be okay if it happened. "Besides, I agree with Sam, believe it or not."

Sam's eyes widened as she brought her hands to her hips. "Wow, is that a fact?" she asked with curled lips.

"We cannot stop our research, not at all. Doing that would be resigning to our demise, and I have no intention of giving up."

"You sound unusually confident in our ability to redirect a planet-sized ship away from Earth," Sam said.

"I said nothing of the sort," Gordan said. "However, our research and continued attempts at communication can potentially lead to some significant breakthroughs. Once we can establish consistent communications with whoever is on the Leviathan, perhaps we will be able to convince it to avoid our little world. Any civilization capable of building *that* and similarly able to create a machine that can decipher alien languages should consider complex life like us, as defenseless as we are against it, worthy of existence."

"It's a pity that there are people that want us to fail," Sam said as her entire body relaxed once more, standing down from the verbal feuds she's come to expect when getting into a debate with Gordan. She noticed Nareen's visible disappointment in the lack of shouting that she expected while Nic released the air from himself in relief.

"It's a pity that there are people that want us dead — fixed that for you," Nareen said with a toast in the air.

Sam smiled and toasted back, acting like she had a glass in her hand. "To our demise!"

Gordan groaned as he got out of his seat and walked toward the front door. "You two are incorrigible."

"Wait, was it something I said?" Sam asked with a chuckle.

As Gordan opened the door, Jennifer swung around him and into Sam's room. She looked ragged, but still energized. "Sorry to burst in here like this, but I just got off a call with Allan.

We may be relocating to New Mexico."

Sam felt like she was just tossed into a whirlwind. Another potential relocation? And this time they'd be moving almost a thousand miles into the desert? It took a moment for her to narrow the list of potential observatories and telescopes that would mirror the capabilities that the ATA had. The mental list took only a few seconds to shrink down to one possible answer. "To the Jansky Array?"

"Fingers crossed, guys," Jennifer said, acknowledging Sam's question without confirming the destination. As fast as she appeared, she turned back and left the room, likely to confer with Corporal York regarding travel options from the motel. Gordan's face contorted to one of frustration at the news as his eyes and mouth pinched shut.

"I take it the missus won't be pleased about such news if it comes to pass?" Sam asked.

He still held the door open, but now brought his head against it. "She won't be pleased at all, Sam."

"I'm sure NASA will make sure your moving expenses are covered again," opined Nic.

Gordan straightened himself out and shook his head before walking out, the door closing behind him with a soft click.

"Does he think our move wouldn't be expensed?" Nic asked as he looked at both Nareen and Sam.

Sam slid off the bed and stood facing the door. Gordan was stubborn at times, but he wasn't stupid at the least. The one thing that Gordan kept harping about was the gradual loss of support the scientific community was experiencing regarding the Leviathan. And when the people forgot why their work at SETI was important, the possibilities were those that also didn't require too much analysis to see the broader results. And such results go much further than moving cost coverage.

The attack on ATA would change perceptions, but to what end she couldn't know—too many known variables, and even more variables they knew nothing about. She sagged back against the arm of the loveseat when thoughts regarding those possibilities played themselves out in her mind.

∘ ◎ ∘

"Good evening, Epstein residence."

"Hi, Grace."

"What happened with calling me Mom? You used to do that as a little girl."

"Small steps, Grace."

Jennifer sat at the foot of her bed, the inviting blanket beckoning her to lie down as her body settled into it. The phone sat in her palm facing the ceiling, its screen the brightest light source in the room as she kept the overhead lights dimmed. A handful of sunrays pierced through the window blinds at various points which created narrow beams of light. Most of the beams fell on the wall opposite the window, highlighting small sections of the kitchenette and parts of Jennifer's body, though she made sure none of the beams fell on her face.

She adjusted herself as she continued her conversation with her mother—a rare event spurred by the attack on ATA. A host of emotions wanted to make themselves known, but Jennifer had years to hone her control over her feelings, especially when dealing with anything surrounding her parents.

Grace sounded much older and more frail than the last time they spoke. More pauses between sentences, and a noticeable pause after Jennifer finished anything she said, as if Grace's mind needed several extra seconds to process her words before forming a response. She was in her eighties now—a woman in her eighties with none of the debilitating diseases that rear their nasty heads around that period in a person's life, like dementia or Alzheimer's. However, time never stops for anyone and entropy marched ever forward, without fail.

Listening to the small talk from her mother, covering everything like the state of their cat to the food served at the church potluck, Jennifer's gaze became unfocused as a smile cracked along her face. It was clear Grace wanted to take full advantage of this call for all it was worth. She imagined Grace being animated while sharing her recent life experiences, her wrinkled hands making gestures in the air while her eyes lit up as those moments replayed in her mind.

In many ways, Jennifer's depiction of her mother wasn't far from what she remembered her doing during story time when she was a young girl. Jennifer couldn't deny that those were memorable times even if they happened well over forty years ago. Back when she wore white nighties to bed and the bedroom wall adjacent to her bed was covered with glow-in-the-dark star and planet stickers. Back when she was tucked in bed while Grace sat beside her with a book in her hand—usually something like Aesop's Fables or any of her Dr. Seuss books. A small chandelier made her childhood bedroom seem more regal than it actually was, but it stayed lit until Grace finished reading her bedtime stories.

Jennifer almost forgot why she called Grace in the first place.

"Are you okay, dear? You don't sound too good," Grace said after not getting a response from her story of the squirrels that her cat tried to catch.

"I just lost my train of thought for a moment," Jennifer said as she shifted closer to the edge of the bed and straightened her back. "But I was calling to ask you about religion."

"Ohh, I see," Grace replied.

"Yes. I don't know if you've read about The Seven Trumpets, but they were the ones that claimed responsibility for the failed bombing at my observatory a week ago."

"Oh, I read about them in the papers, I have, dear."

"Then you know they base their beliefs on Christianity, specifically around what is in the book of Revelation."

"It appears that way, yes."

Jennifer paused before she continued. "I wanted your thoughts on this. I mean, there are passages in the Bible that would suggest that we, as a civilization, are supposed to cause the disasters that would kick-start the end. However, The Seven Trumpets claim they work for the fifth angel of the seven that would, in the end, bring about the end of the world followed by the return of Christ."

"It sounds like you've been doing your homework."

"Given all that's happened lately, I made a point to find some time to get a refresher of what Revelation is supposed to entail."

Grace chuckled. "Good to know some of your heritage hasn't left you."

Jennifer realized what she said and sighed. "Like anything that was hammered into your mind, some things just won't leave."

Another chuckle, followed by a cough. "Well, my dear, I'm glad it's still in that genius noggin of yours. Now, I believe your question has more to do with psychology than religion. When you think about the reasons why people join cults, one of the biggest reasons is the offering of understanding and identity in these strange times. The Leviathan—oh, what a name—destroying entire planets would cause thousands, if not millions, of people across all walks of life to question what they know and understand as reality. And then learning that this beast would then aim itself toward Earth, our only home in the cosmos? Well... then a handful of those millions of people would fall into a psychological state that would enable them to be easily manipulated into joining a group that offered them answers to their questions. Solidarity and friendship—even family—in the face of an uncertain future they may feel is out of their control. Security in the face of growing international chaos, and chaos they perceive as coming because of the Leviathan."

Jennifer felt their conversation shift from its casual beginnings as a chill ran through her body. She bit her lip as she noticed the sunrays that drenched her room in pleasant natural light were gone. "It almost sounds like you believe a group like this would've formed no matter what, once the Leviathan made its debut."

"That is without question, Jennifer dear."

"You also make it sound like it doesn't matter whether or not their belief system is accurate."

"That's my little scientist!"

Jennifer couldn't help but sigh again as her shoulders slumped downward. "This is all too depressing, Grace. Are you saying there's nothing we can do?"

"Well, with all cults there's always the leader—the one who defined all the tenets and credos that form the structure of the cult. In most cases, the removal of the leader tends to result in the cult's collapse."

"Do you think that could happen in this case? The Leviathan's presence is the backbone for this cult."

"People are the backbone—always remember that." Grace sipped something—tea or water was Jennifer's best guess.

"Kind of like how people are the backbone for the world's religions that provided the foundation for cults like this to form?" Jennifer asked almost on impulse. She squeezed her eyes shut for a moment after the words escaped her mouth. "Sorry, I didn't mean—"

"It's okay, dear," Grace jumped in. "What is happening today hasn't changed what I believe in."

"What do you think will happen?" Jennifer asked. An odd question, she felt, coming from her given it would have an answer rooted in a belief system she no longer followed.

"We're always in the hands of God. I trust that He will guide us toward a future He deems right."

"In that case, I and the many people of the world working to unlock the secrets of the Leviathan better keep going and not be derailed by the acts of religious fanatics like The Seven Trumpets."

"Some secrets are best kept unknown," Grace said with caution.

Jennifer didn't respond, but then recalled something her mother said earlier in their call. "Did you call the Leviathan a beast because you believe it is alive, or just a figure of speech?"

"The name, Leviathan, originates from the Christian concept of the Hellmouth, a living creature that consumed the damned at the Last Judgement—something that one could wrap into the beliefs of The Seven Trumpets. Nevertheless, why would a spaceship consume planets? Doesn't that seem like the action a living thing would do—eat?"

"Come on, Grace," Jennifer retorted. "We barely know enough about the thing to take any position like that. Besides, there is no way a living creature could ever become as large as the Leviathan, let alone develop a biological process that would allow it to consume entire planets and generate antimatter. That's just... absurd!"

"Wasn't the Earth flat five hundred years ago?" Grace asked.

Jennifer parted her mouth to respond, but nothing came out. She knew what her mother implied, but confirming the spherical nature of our planet was nothing compared to knowing how biological processes work, rules around biology fail when scaled to the size of planets. Nevertheless, it wasn't the first time she heard someone call the Leviathan a living thing.

"I think it's late for you, Grace. Thank you for your insights."

"I'm glad I could help you for a change." Another cough. "Perhaps next time you can ask about your father."

Jennifer pulled the phone away from her ear and looked at its screen as she took a breath. *No, I really don't want to know anything about him,* she thought as she brought the phone back up. "Maybe next time. Good night, Grace."

"Good night, my dear."

Jennifer ended the call before she could give her mother a chance to share details of Dennis on her own volition. He must've been well into his nineties at this point. In his nineties and even more stubborn and set in his ways than he was prior to her moving out of their house.

With the sounds of the room returning to near-silence, the only sound coming from the electrical hum of the dimmed ceiling lights, Jennifer considered Grace's words on the viability of the Leviathan being alive and not just a planet-sized, planet-consuming spaceship. With all her knowledge of biological processes, there was nothing she could conceive that would allow for a living entity to *exist* at planetary scales. The likelihood of something that large being created by an advanced civilization had a higher probability than something like this occurring from evolutionary processes. Everything they knew about biology, chemistry, and physics screamed that there was no way it was alive.

But Jennifer had to concede one point: For mankind, the world was flat until we learned it wasn't. Was it possible that the Leviathan was a living creature? What she knew for certain was that they would have more answers once NASA got a rover to rendezvous with whatever was living in the structure on its surface.

∘ ◎ ∘

SEPTEMBER 12, 2016

Jennifer knew they could've returned to the Allan Telescope Array. According to Allan, the area became safe to return two weeks after Corporal York gave the green light. With the help of the National Guard, the village that was once against the north gate was cleared, the people forced to return to wherever they came from. The ATA office complex suffered minor damage at worst, with a handful of broken windows that faced the explosion replaced.

What drove Allan's decision to accept Jennifer's recommendation for a VLA relocation was simple: she and Sam were famous. There was little to prevent the throngs of people that were given the boot the first time from returning to the same area if they knew Jennifer and Sam, the people that found ET, still worked there. And if the crowds returned, it wouldn't be much of a stretch to foresee the same issues arise that led to the attempted terrorist attack on the complex.

"Keeping you guys at the ATA is simply too expensive from a security standpoint," Allan said during their call. "I received permission to move you to New Mexico with complete discretion—only those you work with on-site will know where you are."

"What about public-facing calls?" she asked.

"Those can be easily spoofed to make you appear in California," he said. "Same thing with public emails—a VPN can secure internal communications while it manipulates your IP address to originate from ATA."

In retrospect, she regretted making the suggestion, for she wanted to stay at ATA after she learned they could. The unexpected cost of moving once again—Gordan and his family—was enough to reconsider her recommendation. "If Gordan can't join you three for New Mexico, that's his choice."

"It wasn't much of a choice for him the first time we were all lifted from Mountain View to Hat Creek."

"He always had a choice," Allan countered. "He had a family to consider—you, Sam, and Nic didn't."

"So if I had a significant other, I would've been able to say no to the move?"

"But you didn't. And even if you did, we both know you would've made the move no matter what."

It wasn't long before she, Sam, and Nic packed their bags once again and moved their lives to an even more isolated part of the United States: the Plains of San Agustin, home of the Jansky Very Large Array. And unlike the previous move, Gordan relocated again, but back to his former home in San Jose. "I will take up my previous position at the SETI Institute," he said to Jennifer as they stood outside his farm home in Hat Creek, movers busy behind them with his family's possessions they loaded into one large truck. "I'm still on your team... but I'll just be remote, like Kabir. You guys will be fine—and I'm sure Sam is thrilled at my not coming."

"Actually, she was pretty disappointed with your decision, but we all understand," Jennifer said. "Family comes first—we get that." A friendly hug later, they parted ways, with her entering her car while he stood, giving her a soft wave as she drove away. Though she knew he would fly out to New Mexico if the need for his physical presence arose, Gordan became another person she managed as part of her growing remote staff.

2.6

Under a clear night sky with a swathe of the Milky Way Galaxy visible amid a backdrop of thousands of stars, Jennifer leaned against a weathered metal railing. It ran along the front of her new office, a small single-story building among a group of small, rectangular buildings whose rooftops were covered with solar panels. If Jennifer thought the hilly plains that surrounded the ATA were desolate, the flat, featureless plains that surrounded her in all directions were downright barren. It wasn't a desert by any means—lots of short, dry grass dominated the landscape, with patches of greener grass and shrubs no taller than a foot peppering the terrain throughout. And unlike the ATA, there were no interstates nearby—just single-lane highways that degraded more from the weather than from traffic. Jennifer didn't think it could get quieter than the ATA, but the VLA proved her wrong on that front, too. The only sounds around her were the occasional gust of wind that wove its way through the brush and the twenty-eight massive antennas that comprised the VLA. Most of the VLA staff worked at the Array Operational Center in Socorro, about forty miles away from the array itself. The isolation allowed Jennifer to not only focus more on the work in front of her without bumping into too many shoulders when she ran around the small operations building during the day, but to stare out into the starry night sky toward the Leviathan. It still wasn't visible, but she felt she could still see it.

The lights in the building dimmed as the door behind her opened and closed. Not too long after that, she saw Sam prop herself against the railing, her hair rolled into a loose bun. Her shoulders relaxed as she leaned into Jennifer, but brought herself back to an upright position as she looked at her with a smile. "Still wondering what we're going to find up there, Jen?"

"I never stop wondering," Jennifer said as she returned Sam's smile, after which she looked back up at the sky, her smile waning. "Can you imagine? Countless billions of planets are up there with their own mysteries for us to solve one day, yet an unknown number of them may very well have been destroyed by whoever created the Leviathan. And for what reason?"

"Well, that's what the *Hermes* rover will find out for us, right?" Sam asked. "That is, it'll share our list of questions with whoever is on the Leviathan and relay those answers back to us."

"At Destination Zero—yes, I know," Jennifer said. Destination Zero was the name given to the structures Sam found on the surface of the Leviathan, which was also where the spherical satellites that attempted communication with them back in February originated. Despite several areas on the surface of the Leviathan which had various levels of artificial construction, only Destination Zero appeared to be active and not abandoned or destroyed. Those areas had their own designations, too, but Zero was the focus of all immediate missions to the Leviathan. They had several detailed shots of where the Hermes would land: a wide strip of what appeared to be a flat surface that led to the largest spherical structure.

Sam took a deep breath. "We aren't going to be just another planet that will be scrubbed off the universal map. Humans are too stubborn and defiant as a species to go out without a fight."

"We are fighters, that's for sure," Jennifer said, though she shook her head at that. "We're great at fighting each other, at being divisive, and at being cruel and inhumane."

"Shall I pull up a list of all the ways humans are terrible creatures so you don't have to ruminate about that?" Sam asked as she nudged Jennifer with her shoulder. When Jennifer cracked a smile, she continued. "Besides, I'd like to think we also have enough redeeming values to justify our existence. No species expands into the vastness of space if they cannot unite." She looked up into the sky. "I can only imagine the levels of global or even interstellar cooperation and unification needed to construct something like the Leviathan. I mean, details like how much it would've cost would not even exist at scales like that."

Jennifer had more conversations like this with Sam that delved into the hypothetical, which they had on occasion prior to the Leviathan appearing. Ever since its arrival, however, millions of people would love nothing more than to speculate about the ship and the numerous possibilities it unlocked just because of its presence. Such discussions allowed Jennifer to break herself away from her daily work, which became less around the science and more around ensuring SETI East and West had enough funding through 2018. At least Sam continued to have all the fun.

"A post-scarcity economy would have to be necessary, I imagine," Jennifer suggested. "That would cover a lot of the core economic issues. Total automation of just about everything, from industry to services, combined with complete control over the elements via nanotechnology, would negate the need for a currency at all. From there, all you would need is the collective will to commit resources for a project like the Leviathan."

"But then there's the question of the technology itself," Sam spoke as soon as Jennifer stopped, as if she were continuing her thought processes on the matter. "All evidence suggests the ship propels itself using antimatter fuel, something we're nowhere near developing for any practical purpose. Outside of lab experiments, we have no way to contain anti-anything. And then the scale of an artificial structure like the ship... what the hell kind of materials would you use to build something that big that also could destroy entire planets? And withstand the effects of what would be a planet coming apart inside of it? The damned ship took Uranian and Neptunian moon collisions like they were pellets from a BB gun."

Jennifer's eyes adjusted to the increasing darkness around them as they spoke. She thought she could almost see the Leviathan with the naked eye. "I don't know. Even our latest forays into concepts like carbon nanotubes wouldn't suffice."

"Maybe something like neutronium?"

Jennifer raised an eyebrow. "Isn't that from *Star Trek?*"

"Hey, I'm shooting for the stars like you are," Sam smiled as she raised one hand and made a Vulcan salute. "Either way, a material strong enough to not only withstand planetary impacts but also the forces of gravity has to be something like a neutron-degenerate matter. Maybe they harvested materials from an entire solar system to construct it, the star included..."

Jennifer didn't respond as she narrowed her eyes on the small piece of the night sky that contained the Leviathan. Was there a faint, white dot in place of Uranus? She didn't ignore Sam—she had all valid questions, even if they were scientifically extreme. But how else could you tackle the Leviathan from their perspective? Even within scientific circles, many couldn't accept that it existed because it broke several established systems. That was the point of progress—and the Leviathan was upending many notions we had. Assuming they survived past 2024, Jennifer was sure they would make more scientific breakthroughs in the next ten years than they had in the last fifty.

"Hey Jen, you there?" Sam waved a hand in front of Jennifer's face, which caused her to blink and look at the silhouette that was Sam, though she could still make out some of her relaxed facial expressions.

"Sorry about that," Jennifer said. "I think I can make out the Leviathan from here."

"No need to apologize," Sam said as she rolled a hand through her hair and removed the hairpin that kept her bun in place. She kept an eye on Jennifer as she did so. "I like it when you stare off into space, always wondering what is out there."

Their eyes, for a moment, locked together, with Sam's deep brown eyes diving into Jennifer's, a look that she had seen before, though she always had written it off as Sam just being a personable individual. But this time Jennifer felt her chest tighten and face start to redden. *Where did that come from?* She wanted to dismiss her unconscious reactions, but they remained so long as they looked at each other. It was almost as if Sam silently suggested something more about the connection they had.

"It's getting a bit chilly," Jennifer said as she turned away from her, feeling anything but. "I think it's time to call it a night and head home. Can you lock up?"

There was a moment of silence that felt unexpectedly awkward. "Sure thing, Jen."

"Thanks." Jennifer rubbed the back of her neck as she walked over to her car. She tried to refocus her thoughts to other things: the evening wind that picked up her hair; the sole parking lamp that kept the lot illuminated; the stars that filled the night sky. By the time she opened the driver's side door, she found her breathing had returned to normal. *What was that all about, Jen?* She thought as she berated herself for acting so strange to Sam. *We are friends, right? Why act like I'm decades younger?* She's certainly felt that way before, but it was a long time ago, and only for people that she liked. No, she couldn't feel that way toward Sam. Could she?

Jennifer sat at the wheel, a hand at the ignition as, like any analytical process she would encounter in her professional life, she ran through the reasoning behind her reactions. Her eyes were closed as she started the car, the revving engine allowing her to just think. Think.

Yes, it's been awhile since I've been with anyone, but that doesn't explain...

I've known Sam for years, and we've been through a lot, especially since 2014, but...

Should I even have felt anything from Sam? What is she thinking? What is she feeling?

Jennifer felt her fingernails dig into the faux leather that wrapped around the steering wheel. When she opened her eyes, she found herself still alone, her breathing steady, if not deliberate. "Let's just get some sleep," she said aloud to herself. She slid the car into drive and began her journey home. Though the drive was peaceful, her mind still would not shut off... She hoped sleep would set things right.

∘ ◎ ∘

When Jennifer woke up the next day, she threw herself headlong into her work. There was always so much to do, and rarely enough time in a day to get it all done without sacrificing sleep or downtime. The latter was easiest to reduce down to the point where her schedule consisted of waking up, making a quick stop at Bear Mountain Coffee House, and heading to VLA for a solid twelve hours of Leviathan-related research, data analysis, and NASA conferences. She worked with Sam during this time—she had to, for their collaborative efforts would not halt because of whatever happened that previous evening. Sam made some cursory attempts to start conversations that weren't all business, but Jennifer rebuffed her with either shifting such talk back to the work at hand, or ignored her altogether.

This went on for a few days, until the following Monday, when Jennifer heard a knock at the front door of her house. It wasn't the first time someone from the Array Operations Center would travel out to her home to explore different avenues around their research. She never stated that VLA staff were prohibited from visiting her outside of work hours, but she was grateful for the company and it kept her mind busy well into the evening.

She wasn't the biggest fan of the home, but she warmed up to its many quirks. It was a two-story house with a composition gable roof, part of which extended forward to cover a small porch that groaned and popped whenever she walked on it. She wasn't sure if the house was meant to have a natural desert brown color, or if that was the result of neglect over the years—with the paint broken and peeling in numerous places, she leaned toward the latter. Given the state of the other nearby houses, it blended in well. The interior was in much better shape, with natural wood paneling on the ceiling and waxed flooring that, like the porch, was audible when stepped on. All the furniture came with the house, most of which looked like it came from an IKEA showroom. It was comfortable, but did not mesh with the rustic aesthetic that would've been better suited for a place like this.

She strolled down the stairs with her laptop held alongside her as she thought about what Nic wanted to talk about tonight: evidence of some crystalline structures he discovered at several points just above the hatch jaw. That was the problem with an object as large and interesting as the Leviathan: Just when you believed they've captured the best images of the object from end to end, something small, yet fascinating, kept being found just beyond the smallest pixel of their captured images. This required even more time honing on tiny, specific areas at the expense of the rest of the ship. It was a frustrating situation for everyone involved, and until more probes could get into desirable positions, only the *New Horizon* was in the best place for wide-angle and focused snapshots of the Leviathan's lateral.

Jennifer talked as she turned the doorknob, loud enough for Nic to hear her. "I'm glad you had the chance to leverage *New Horizon*—the queue for accessing it is crazy—"

It wasn't Nic at the door. Before Jennifer could raise a finger, Sam glanced at her before she walked around her and toward her living room. "I know it isn't exactly kosher, but I couldn't think of any other way to pull you aside for a chat."

Jennifer pivoted on one foot as she watched Sam plop down onto her couch that faced a flatscreen TV, a device that got little use unless someone connected their computer to it. "Where is Nic?" she asked after she caught her breath.

"Oh, right—Nic," Sam said with a tentative smile. "He kind of agreed to arrange this." She brought an arm to rest on the back of the couch. "Believe it or not, some people have picked up on your sudden aloofness towards not just me, but the team as a whole, over the last couple of days. All for the sake of 'getting things done.'"

Jennifer closed the front door with much more force than needed and moved toward Sam, trying hard to not stomp. Nevertheless, the floorboards creaked under her more urgent gait as she came to a stop. She stood over Sam in front of the couch, her arms crossed. "And why couldn't Nic decide to talk to me?"

"He felt that if we resolved our differences, everything else would fall into place," Sam looked away from Jennifer as she eyed the kitchen just beyond the living room archway. She pointed toward the kitchen as she stood up, with Jennifer taking a few steps back as she did. "Do you mind if I grab something to drink? I wanted to be on time, but just realized I am parched!"

"Um, no, you can't have a drink," Jennifer stated, though Sam had already reached the kitchen and beelined for the cupboards next to the refrigerator. She marched into the kitchen to see Sam filling a glass with water from the refrigerator dispenser.

"Just water, Jen," Sam raised her glass with a grin before taking a few loud gulps. "I'm not looking to get drunk or anything like that."

Jennifer clenched her teeth behind closed lips as she looked toward the floor before bringing her head back up to Sam. She thought about her next set of words, intending to control the conversation. "Okay, what did you want to talk about?"

Sam was about to say something, but then stopped herself, choosing instead to gaze at her twiddling foot. A few seconds passed where the air felt thick with an uncomfortable tension. Jennifer's irregular breathing didn't help. Sam was the first to speak, her voice low. "I'm sorry about last Tuesday, Jen."

Jennifer expected to talk about the "aloofness" that she was expressing to those at VLA, but the apology caught her off-guard. They also brought to the surface the feelings that Jennifer tried to suppress over the last week. "Sorry for what? You didn't say anything..."

"It is for what was unsaid," Sam said, her eyes still diverted away from Jennifer.

"Sam..."

"No, let me continue." Sam placed her glass on the counter behind her and looked at Jennifer, her thumbs gripping the insides of her jean pockets, not knowing what else to do with her hands. Her eyes kept alternating between Jennifer and anything else in the room that she could focus on. "I'm not used to putting myself in a vulnerable position, so let me talk."

After Jennifer nodded in response, Sam continued. "We've been through a lot, you and I. Ever since the Leviathan appeared, we've done more together and have gotten closer than I ever imagined. And though I once dismissed my growing feelings for you as nothing more than admiration, I realized back when we were at the Allan Array that it wasn't just admiration. You must know how I feel... feel about you."

Jennifer leaned against the wide kitchen sink as those words pierced her ears and churned her stomach. She kept her hands planted on the counter behind her, not willing to clutch herself and share her internal thoughts beyond the flush that crept onto her face. "This isn't the time or the place, nor is it professional."

"Oh come on," Sam said. "Our relationship has nothing to do with professionalism. It's always been separate. Besides, I believe that our work has benefited from us becoming closer."

"I don't know what you mean..."

Sam's eyes shot up at Jennifer, but then fell away as a small smile appeared on her face. "Yes you do. We've worked together for years now, but now we're practically connected at the hip. Our ability to infer what the other is getting at with our papers. One of us comes up with a new way to approach a problem and the other is able to quickly and naturally build upon that in moments instead of hours."

"The number of times I've had to bail you out of trouble?" Jennifer said with a snarky smile.

Sam was quick to retort with a grin. "Oh please, my raw intellect has saved you far more often than your keeping me out of trouble." She pointed a finger at Jennifer, then at herself. "See, this is what I mean!"

"But we are friends, Sam. Good friends. Best friends, even, depending on how you define the parameters for such a status—"

"I believe there is more."

"Oh my God, Sam, there can't be more!"

"Why not?" Sam's voice rose as she gripped the countertop behind her with whitened knuckles.

"Because there can't!" Jennifer pounded a balled fist against the sink as she pushed away from it, her face scrunched up in frustration.

"Bullshit!" Sam yelled, but recoiled as she covered her face with her hands. She then bit her bottom lip as her shoulders dropped, her hands falling to her sides. "I'm sorry, Jen. This is very hard for me to openly admit, and I don't want to die without exploring the possibility."

Jennifer absorbed every word from Sam, but those last few hit a nerve. "Wait, what? Isn't that a bit melodramatic?"

"Come on, Jen," Sam responded with a push away from the counter behind her.

"The Leviathan is on a one-way trip to Earth and will be here before we're half-way through the next decade. It doesn't take a genius to figure out what will happen when it gets within a hundred thousand miles from Earth, let alone when it opens its aperture to take it in."

Jennifer knew the stakes—what was at risk. But she responded with the canned answer she's given many times before. "We will find a way to divert its course. We cannot act like it cannot be reasoned with. None of us can."

Sam's heard this response several times, too. "Even so, I have to also accept the possibility that we won't be successful, in which case we'll all be dead in eight years." She took a step closer to Jennifer. "If that is the route that our timeline is headed towards, I want to make sure I've expressed myself and not feel regret for things that were left unsaid. So no, I don't feel like I'm being melodramatic in the least."

Jennifer knew she was right.

Sam continued. "I'm not suggesting we drop everything and submit to more base appetites, but I don't believe we should, you know, ignore what's inside us until the very end. Wonder what might have been while the world burned around us on those final days."

Jennifer turned herself toward Sam. *Choose your words carefully,* she thought. "I do not think this would be a good idea."

"So you do feel something between us. Something more."

"I don't know what I feel, but this wouldn't be right."

Both Jennifer and Sam didn't look at each other—Jennifer kept weighing the pros and cons in her mind, her eyes twitching right and left as she processed everything that was happening.

"When was the last time you were, you know, with someone?"

Sam was just full of unexpected questions. "You know it's been awhile since my last relationship, Sam—why are you asking such a thing?" Jennifer asked.

"Because I am much younger than you, and a woman," Sam said as she rubbed the back of her neck through her hair.

Now it was Jennifer's turn to surprise Sam, as she couldn't help but laugh at that concern. "Your gender would not be a negative factor in the formation of a relationship. But yes, you're almost ten years my junior. Wouldn't you rather be with someone your own age?"

Jennifer noticed that Sam's eyes were looking her over, which made her more aware of her loose-fitting outfit. It wasn't fashionable in the least, but she cared more for being able to get things done in her wares versus being sexually attractive. "You're only forty-seven. And I don't know any other woman that could keep up with my brain like you can. Besides, you certainly don't look your age."

Jennifer smiled as she shook her head. "Thank you. But still, this wouldn't be right."

Sam couldn't help but smile though it wavered. Her eyes rose toward Jennifer's as she spoke. "This may sound crazy, but for once, don't think about it."

Jennifer realized what her heart was telling her. It was what fueled her reddened face and brought a hand to her chest. She could deny Sam's feelings right there, but she knew she couldn't. She knew what her beating heart wanted to do. It, with her mind, finally agreed to a decision. Every step she took was fraught with a level of internal hesitation that was incredible. Maybe that meant she was doing the right thing? Or was it because she was doing the wrong thing?

Don't think about it.

Though her hands and chest felt heavy, she walked up to Sam and embraced her. Sam, after a moment, reciprocated. Their heads rested alongside each other as Sam's natural aroma filled her nose. Sam's hair caressed a part of her face. She felt their warm bodies pressed together, the softness welcoming through their clothes. Jennifer released all the air from her lungs as she relaxed for the first time in another's arms in an embrace that, for all her intentions of it being friendly, felt much stronger. When her eyes closed, she realized that her mind—rarely ever still, with strings of formulae being constructed and deconstructed and various objectives being analyzed, prioritized, tackled, and then repeated—just stopped as the physical sensations overtook her thoughts. It was peaceful. It was pleasant. The creaking floorboards, the hum of the refrigerator, the occasional trill of a cricket just beyond the thin windows—all background noises of the house—were silenced in favor of Sam's rapid heartbeat. It vibrated against her breast and reverberated through her ears. Sam sighed as she settled into her body, her warm breath on Jennifer's neck soothing. It all felt *right.*

When she released Sam, her hands drifted down her arms before their hands took each other. Jennifer squeezed her hands before letting them go. Despite her feelings, she had to do the right thing. "Maybe one day, long after we've solved the Leviathan question in our favor, we can come back to this and talk about it again."

Sam broke eye contact as she took in a deep breath. They looked at each other again. Sam's eyes looked red. "Thanks, Jen," she said. "I know we will."

Jennifer looked toward the ceiling and wiped a finger under her eye before reaching around Sam and grabbing her empty glass. Her mind wanted to resume control, and the first thing it wanted to do was to not linger on the two of them. "Did you want more water before we talk about these crystalline structures?"

"Nah," Sam turned and walked toward the front door. "I don't want to steal Nic's thunder—he can explain his findings."

"Alright," Jennifer said as she followed Sam. "We'll pick up from our last meeting regarding Destination Zero's geographic features to-morrow, then?"

"Yeah, that sounds about right." Sam wasted no time cracking open the door, but stopped herself before leaving the house.

Jennifer came up behind her, ready to take the doorknob upon Sam's departure. "Did you forget some..."

Sam spun around. Her light red eyes looked right at Jennifer who froze in place, not knowing what would happen. Her hand slowly reached Jennifer's face, her palm resting on her cheek as her fingers came under her chin. The speed at which Sam came in for a kiss wasn't what surprised her, but that she returned it with even more vigor. Jennifer brought her own hand to Sam's face and held it, a single tear being pressed into her forefinger as she did. Their other hands rose up and wrapped around each other's hips, bringing them together in a much more intimate embrace. It was the warmth that came from Sam's wandering hand that caused Jennifer to break the kiss. The hand that was on Sam's face rested on her shoulder, though she still held Sam close by the waist.

Dealing with the world coming to an end by an alien ship didn't scare her. Incendiary dialogue with the likes of General Dempsey and Chuck Hagel didn't scare her. Even being killed by terrorists didn't make her shiver. But looking at Sam, her chest rising and falling with each long breath, her moist, parted lips that closed into a smile, her softened gaze—it all scared the bejeezus out of her.

Jennifer wanted to say something—anything—but instead dropped her hand from Sam's shoulder and closed the front door, locking the knob in the process.

Don't think about it.

∘ ◎ ∘

The deep red and orange beams of the morning sunrise began their daily illumination of Jennifer's bedroom through the twin windows opposite from Jennifer's bed. Her eyes pinched closed before they crept open to greet the new day. It was then she felt something drift across the spine of her back. A number of things registered at that moment.

That she was naked under the sheets of her bed, something she rarely did.

That the thing that touched her back was a hand.

And that the hand belonged to Sam.

Jennifer rolled onto her back and looked to her right to see Sam, who was still covered by her satin sheets up to her neck. She rolled onto her side and slid her hand over Jennifer's torso, making a circular pass over her belly button as she did. "Good morning, crepuscular rays," Sam said.

Jennifer grinned as she wrapped a hand around Sam's. She brought the other to her forehead, the back of her palm resting on her hair that flowed behind her pillow. "Is that your way of being romantic?"

"Only for you." Sam scooted her naked body against Jennifer's as the room continued to brighten.

"I never thought..." Jennifer trailed off as she glanced over at Sam before looking back at the ceiling.

"Was it your first time?" Sam asked.

"Yes—with a woman, that is."

"So I figured." Sam winked, to which Jennifer poked her with a free hand.

"Hey," she exclaimed with a chuckle.

"It was perfect, though."

Jennifer didn't respond for awhile as she replayed the evening, one of the most spontaneous and emotional episodes in her rekindled love life. Between her thoughts and feeling Sam's warmth against her, she knew that despite her nervousness, it was all she could've asked for.

"Yes," was all Jennifer could manage as she rolled again and faced Sam. She looked into Sam's eyes as she stroked her arm and followed the contours of her body. Her mind was at ease—not rushing headlong into yet another problem to solve or planning every hour of the day. Time felt frozen in place as her thoughts revolved around what was in front of her. What she saw was right. Her grin couldn't have been any wider.

"Perfect."

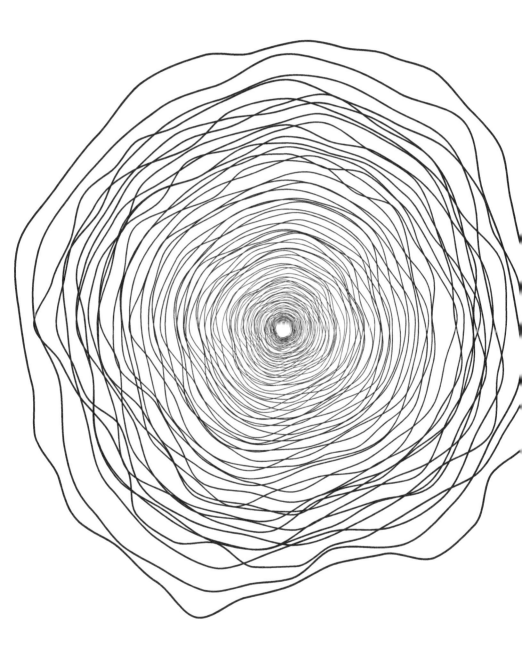

PART THREE

SPARK

3.0

"Yes, I disagreed with President Trump's decision to force me out as NASA Administrator. Yes, I disagreed with the direction he wants to take the NASA program and SETI. Yes, the world will suffer dearly because of his lack of commitment to The Armstrong Program. Here's something I do agree on: Going to the moon is a great idea—but that doesn't matter if we're all dead."

ALLAN WHEELER, FORMER ADMINISTRATOR OF NASA, FEBRUARY 2017

"I, and the many partners that are an integral part of the Armstrong Program, are disappointed in the direction the Trump administration has taken. However, just because they refuse to continue funding doesn't mean that Khulu Global and the Unity Foundation will halt our progress. As of today, my partners and I will supplement all funding, which won't end until a solution to the Leviathan Question is found. The spirit of the Armstrong Program will live on—our survival as a species depends on it."

MUZIKAYISE KHULU, CEO OF KHULU GLOBAL, MARCH 2017

"Many mistakes were made with my campaign, that much can be said. However, the biggest factor that I believe changed everything was the presence of the Leviathan and how it impacted the policies and orders Obama executed in his last two years in office. There is no doubt in my mind that without the Leviathan, the election would have been in my favor."

HILLARY CLINTON, "WHAT HAPPENED," SEPTEMBER 2017

○ ◎ ○

NOVEMBER 9, 2018

Nobody really knew what to expect when the *Victoria,* the world's first VASIMR-powered spacecraft, made another set of scheduled delta-v adjustments ahead of its final approach to the Leviathan. The gravitational strength of the Leviathan was, as predicted, immense—21.64 times that of Earth, stronger than everything else in the solar system save for the sun. *Victoria's* approach took this into account as it positioned itself to perform a flyby about eight hundred thousand kilometers above Destination Zero, at which time the *Victoria* would launch its payload—the *Hermes* rover—to the surface. All indicators predicted it would pass over Destination Zero on December 10, 2018 at 9:20am UTC, almost four-and-a-half years after the initial discovery of the Leviathan.

The *Victoria* was the most advanced spacecraft mankind had ever created. When compared to its predecessor, the *Gazelle Two,* there were many differences in the design of the *Victoria,* due to it being constructed entirely in orbit. Much larger than the *Gazelle Two,* this craft ran fifty meters from end to end, with an extra five meters added to the front for the donut-shaped cruiser package that contained the *Hermes.* The four rigid, right triangle-shaped polyimide radiation fins were not retractable and were forty meters long, all of which were mounted to the cylindrical structure by way of a series of trusses that ran the length of the craft, made of titanium and tungsten. The four fins also connected to each other with taut titanium cables every ten meters on their outer edges, making the craft look like it had four square outlines around the cylinder if looked at from behind. Twelve five-meter-long thermocells wrapped around the cylinder in groups of four and spaced to cover the length of the radiation fins. These thermocells were the third generation of heat radiation plants that were more efficient than the prototypes used just a scant two years prior.

They were placed at forty-five degrees around the *Victoria,* allowing them to vent unconverted heat into space without interfering with the fins.

Then there was the 10MW VASIMR at the rear, powered by a shielded micro fission reactor system with enough fuel to keep the entire craft active for decades. Thanks to the use of nuclear energy as the primary source of power, the latest iteration of VASIMR could reach theoretical speeds upward of 100km/s. Several smaller ion thrusters that surrounded the VASIMR and placed at the front of the craft allowed it to make minute adjustments whenever necessary.

Finally, the *Victoria* had a variety of telescopes, spectrometers, radiation detectors, and imagers, many of which took numerous snapshots of the Leviathan in the months leading up to its final approach. All of this equipment was around the front of the craft, all of which ran nonstop since the *Victoria* came within three million kilometers of the Leviathan. This equipment provided some of the most detailed sidelong images of the ship that dominated news cycles back on Earth.

One of the more controversial pictures of the *Victoria* was a "selfie" photo similar to what the *Curiosity* Mars rover gave the world years prior. There were over a dozen national flags grouped at the bottom, the major space agencies in the middle, and then the logos of the Armstrong Program partners at the top. Khulu Global's famous logo—a black silhouette of a pronking springbok with "Khulu" in cursive in the foreground—was above all the other partner logos.

Previous missions into space never had corporate logos anywhere on probes, rovers, or ships launched, despite most of them being made by major corporate manufacturers. When asked during an interview why this mission was different, CEO Muzikayise Khulu gave a simple, yet incendiary response:

"All businesses that contributed to the success of the *Victoria* mission deserve as much recognition as any nation. I would even be so bold as to say that without us, this mission would not have been as successful as it was so far. Don't the people behind that success deserve to be acknowledged?" News pundits spent weeks taking apart those words, which all the corporate partners stood behind, but most of those arguments fell by the wayside as the *Victoria* reached the Leviathan.

Discussions and debates reignited in the mainstream media about what—if anything—could be done to dissuade the aliens on the craft from its present course. As arguments raged, stores around the world that provided telescopes of all kinds sold out as people learned they could see the Leviathan clearly at night. "Just aim toward what was Uranus, and there it is," newscasters advertised with optimism, with some of them setting up and using their own telescopes during live late-night broadcasts.

For the second time in four years, the entire world turned its eyes upward at the white dot which shone on clear nights, bright enough to cut through the light pollution in the largest cities. In some cases, it was the only "star" in the night sky.

And it was getting closer.

3.1

"There's no doubt about it," Sam said to Jennifer, who sat behind her. "The Leviathan is no longer speeding up—it's coasting the rest of the way to Earth at 13.4 kilometers per second."

"You would think that with antimatter propulsion you would be able to achieve much faster speeds," Jennifer said as her phone continued to ring a few inches from her fast-typing hands.

Sam tilted her head to the side as she finished running her calculations on the Leviathan's velocity. "I can only imagine the amount of energy needed to move a ship as large as the Leviathan." She scratched the back of her head at the thought, but the unanswered ringing of Jennifer's phone snapped her out of focus. "Jen, could you answer your phone, or at least put it on silent?"

"Oh, sorry about that," Jennifer said. Sam peaked over her shoulder to see her pick up the phone.

"Who is it?"

"Allan."

Sam smiled as Jennifer got up from her chair and walked toward the front door of the operations building, the local command center for the Very Large Array in New Mexico.

As expected, a couple of minutes passed before the front door swung open and Jennifer grabbed the back of her chair. "That was quick," Sam commented.

"Yeah, he was asking about any data we collected regarding the sudden change with the Leviathan," Jennifer said.

"If he waited a bit longer, he could have learned about the updated arrival time for the ship's arrival at Earth." Sam looked at the numbers in front of her. "By November 17, 2024 at 8:14pm Pacific Time, the only thing we'll be able to see outside is the interior of the Leviathan." Her shoulders dropped as she sighed, her eyes scrolling through the numbers again, along with the approximate dates derived from them. She heard Jennifer's chair groan against the floor as it moved, followed by a hand on her shoulder. Jennifer knelt next to her as she reviewed the calculations as well. Sam looked over at Jennifer, their eyes locking on each other. "Though by 4:03pm that day, the Leviathan will be just over 200 thousand kilometers from Earth, close enough to alter our planet's orbit around the sun. At that point, it's game over for us."

Jennifer's fingers gripped Sam's shoulder tighter before letting go, returning to her seat as she did. "God damn, I wish your numbers were wrong."

"I do, too, Jen." Sam almost felt light-headed. "Just a month to go before we really crack some of the mysteries of the Leviathan." She propped her head in her hands as she got lost in thought when her smartphone rang. It was Nic. She didn't even have a chance to greet him before he spoke.

"Sam, I'll be in the office in about thirty seconds."

"Hello to you, too, Nic," Sam said, not changing her position. "You realize it's after sundown, right?"

"Never mind that! Something just happened with the Leviathan—"

"We know—its engines cut off."

"No, something else." Sam got up and turned to the front door as it swung open, Nic running into the office with his phone still pressed against his head. He glanced at Sam and grinned as he beelined for the spectrograph workstation. When Sam came up to him, a frown spread across her face, he slowed down his speech and continued as he woke up the computer. "Infrared."

She blinked, then shook her head. "Nic, more words, please."

"The Leviathan—it emitted a flash of infrared from the ring of embedded crystals just above the maw."

Sam still had a blank expression as he loaded raw spectrograph data from the most recent download from Webb. "But Nic, I thought we agreed years ago that the crystalline structure you found wasn't anything more than a demarcation line between the maw and the rest of the ship structure."

"Plus, they are small, relative to the rest of the ship's design." Jennifer joined them though Nic didn't yet acknowledge her. "If they served a purpose, I'm sure we would've known about it by now."

Nic typed out a few additional commands until results generated under the data he pulled from Webb after which he threw his hands up as if he just completed a piano composition. He leaned back and gestured toward the monitor, still smiling. "Look at this!"

Three different graphs loaded, side by side, with raw data calculations below them. The middle graph, which focused on all infrared frequencies, depicted a very narrow spike. "I know that most labs dropped studying the crystals because they seemed to be inert, not emitting anything or otherwise having any sort of purpose. They just were, and other than the crystals looking like manufactured diamonds the size of cars, they just weren't interesting when compared to many other aspects of the Leviathan. But then this happened."

Jennifer inspected the frequency and wavelength data. "A flash of infrared occurred just after the engines deactivated."

"And at 340GHz, too, emanating from around the maw," Nic said as he nodded.

Sam pressed her lips together and sat on the foot of the desk, gripping the monitor and turned it toward her. "How is it we never caught this before?"

"Ah, only because this happened once before: four years ago, back when the Leviathan consumed Uranus. I saw a spike in the infrared very similar to this back then, but wrote it off as an aftereffect of the planet's destruction. We didn't have any interferometer observatories pointed at the Leviathan back then, which would've caught the first burst in greater detail. But when I discovered the crystals two years ago, I decided to monitor them... I figured that every part of the ship had a purpose."

Sam cleared her throat as she forced herself to smile.

I can't believe I didn't put all of this together, she thought. "A needle in the galactic haystack," she said to Nic. "Good job."

Nic's eyes lit up at the compliment. "Thanks, Sam! I was starting to think I was wasting my time keeping an eye on those crystals, but here we are."

Jennifer gazed at the infrared graph. "So what is the purpose of this flash? Despite how bright it would have been, given the diameter of the maw, we wouldn't have seen it as the frequency puts it well under visible light."

Nic looked at the two of them and opened his mouth to answer, but then stopped himself. He scratched his neck as he looked back at the data. "I was thinking that this was a sort of radar, checking for nearby ships like our own *Victoria,* or maybe..."

Sam jumped off the desk and took a few steps away, her hand under her chin as she looked toward the floor. She ran through his calculations while also thinking about why such a thing would exist on the ship. She envisioned the Leviathan drifting in space, hundreds of millions of miles from anything substantial, save for a tiny, insignificant speck of an alien spacecraft that approached it from a blue, almost imperceptible dot ahead of it. Could their craft have triggered this infrared flash? Maybe, but then it happened four years ago, shortly after it consumed the third planetary body in our solar system. Why would it have occurred back then?

Infrared in space. Flash. The infrared spectrum of light. A four-year gap between flashes. Were there more?

"Nic, how much data do you have regarding the Leviathan's infrared activity from July 2014?" Sam asked as she leapt for her computer.

"Um, everything that was captured by Lick, ATA, and SALT," he responded.

She brought up the original cache of compressed files from the initial days after discovering the signal from the Leviathan, extracted them, and opened every file that concerned spectrographical readouts. She filtered the frequencies to drop everything but the infrared, then started a scan for all instances of infrared hits that registered beyond the background. "Let's see what happens when I improve your methods, my friend," she whispered to herself.

"What are you thinking about—" Jennifer started before Sam cut her off.

"Hold on, I got this." Sam bit her lip as the results of her filtered scans trickled in, one pop-up alert at a time. It wasn't long before she slapped the top of her desk and fist-pumped as she leaned back into her chair with her chin high. "Holy shit, that's what I'm talking about!"

She saw Nic run to the side of her desk. He took a second before he registered what was displayed in front of him. "Holy crap, this happened two other times: once before it left for Neptune, and again before it left for Uranus."

"We got lucky that SALT was pointed in that direction so we could cross-reference ATA's data with something," Sam said. "As of today, that infrared flash occurred at least four times."

"But what does it mean?" Jennifer posed the question to both Sam and Nic, her voice steady.

Sam responded by pantomiming the use of a camera. "Snapshots. Infrared snapshots of whatever was in front of the Leviathan."

"Snapshots?" Nic asked.

"Snapshots," Sam repeated with a smile. "Perhaps it's their way of tracking planets it is aware of, just to confirm they exist after arriving in a star system. A form of transit photometry and doppler spectroscopy cranked to eleven."

"If that's the case, why infrared and not visible light?" Jennifer asked. Sam could hear Jennifer's tone—she was enjoying seeing Sam like this, deep in her element of discovery.

"Probably to screen out visible sunlight," Sam responded. "At least, that's what I would do if I wanted to scan a star system on the fly."

A few moments passed as the three of them let all of this sink in. It seemed almost a certainty that they captured Leviathan imaging everything in front of it—a snapshot of the remaining planets in the solar system, but with a focus on the Earth. Sam knew they would share these findings with the scientific community at large to confirm, but she was certain this was what the Leviathan was doing.

∘ ◎ ∘

Given it was a Saturday evening, the Golden Spur Saloon had the usual crowd. A handful of older men with prominent gray beards sat at the bar arguing over whatever sport was on the television that hung in the corner. Several groups of young adults clustered around several circular standing tables. The daily locals that called the saloon home sat in their usual booths or along the wall.

Sam liked coming here because of the wall of artwork that blanketed one wall from the ceiling down to the tables. They consisted of photos and canvas paintings of elk hunting, landscape vistas, abandoned towns from the 1800s, and even a few recent photos of the VLA. The air smelled of nachos, roasted chicken, and spilled beer, but it all combined to make a friendly space for her and Jennifer to unwind after a long night before going home.

When they entered, the bartender greeted them by name and with a bearded smile. They'd been there enough times over the last two years to the point where they received their usual pints a few minutes after they sat down at an empty table, the server chatting briefly with them before walking off to take another order. Some of those that frequented the bar knew who they were, but they enjoyed the welcoming lack of attention they received while there.

As Jennifer took a large gulp from her pint, leaning her head back with closed eyes as she did, Sam couldn't help but look over her partner, from the tips of her unpainted fingernails to the lips that she loved to kiss. She licked her lips as she brought her glass in front of her face, though it wasn't the beer that made her salivate.

When Jennifer opened her eyes, she smiled as she caught Sam's gaze. "You know with looks like that, people around us are going to wonder just what kind of relationship we have."

"Let them wonder," Sam responded as she took a swig of her beer, her eyes not breaking away from Jennifer's. "Besides, it's not like we're giving them a show, though I wouldn't be opposed to the possibility."

Jennifer kicked Sam's shin under their table which made some of Sam's beer jerk out of her glass and spill onto the table and her pants.

She pushed away from the table as the spilt beer streamed over the side and dripped onto the floor. "Hey, I just got these cleaned!" Sam then shot a mischievous look at Jennifer. "I suppose you'll have to help me take these off when we get home."

"You can be incorrigible at times," Jennifer said as she settled back into her seat and drank more of her beer. "I am impressed that you didn't take the credit for digging up that archived data on the Leviathan infrared snapshots."

"Oh are you now?" Sam said behind her glass.

"It almost seemed out-of-character for you to allow Nic to run with the additional data and prepare document submissions for NASA and other agencies for additional review."

Sam thought about it for a moment as she brought her glass to the table, now half-full. "I think my name is known well-enough as it is around the world. Nic is pretty well-known at this point, too, but he can claim credit for all things related to the crystalline ring and its purpose."

Jennifer nodded, then chuckled. "You didn't want to do the work, did you?"

"He's been looking for his big break—now he has it. And yes, he can have all the work." Sam's eyes lowered to her glass and sighed. "In any case, it's not like our current efforts are being acknowledged by anyone above us."

"Sam, we've been over this," Jennifer said as her glass came down onto the table harder then she intended.

"How many times have we been to DC for face-to-face meetings with not only high-ranking directors and the Secretary of Defense, but the President between 2014 and 2016? More times than we have fingers combined. Number of flights since the beginning of 2017? Zero, nadda, zilch."

"You don't have to remind me—"

"We barely get any email responses regarding new discoveries and forget about getting someone remotely important on the phone—"

"Sam, your voice," Jennifer cut her off with a raised voice of her own, but then lowered her own volume as she glanced around the bar. Nobody paid them any attention.

"Yes, this administration doesn't prioritize our work at all, which makes little sense given that this is supposed to be a global effort."

Sam downed the last of her beer and slid her glass away from her and toward the edge of the table. Her shoulders sagged as she examined Jennifer's face with a cocked head. "Why are you calm about all of this, Jen? You usually end up tearing the President a new one whenever we end up talking politics these days."

Jennifer's eyes lowered away from Sam's, as if she were unsure what to do next, but then reached for her messenger bag that leaned against her seat and popped it open, her free hand fingering through folders and papers.

"What's going on?" Sam asked as Jennifer whipped out a single piece of paper from her bag, held between two fingers. She placed it down on the table, away from the spilled beer that still wasn't wiped away. Sam placed her hand on the paper and turned it around, though the black, stylized pronking springbok logo in the upper-right-hand corner of the page made it clear where the paper came from. Her eyes dashed toward the bottom of the page which had the signature of Muzikayise Khulu hand-written below the typed name. Sam's eyes widened as, even without reading the contents of the three paragraphs on the page, she knew what this was.

"Were you offered a position at Khulu Global, Jen?"

Jennifer's expression remained neutral as she pointed at the first paragraph. "*We* were offered positions, yes. You should've received a letter on Friday, the same time as me."

Sam leaned away from the table as she realized that she hadn't checked her physical mailbox in over a month—anything she considered important would land into her work inbox, or even her personal email. It seemed that Muzie didn't want to leave a digital trail of this offer. She also knew their residential information was private unless they shared it with others—how did he know where they lived? However he got the details, he didn't know she effectively moved into Jennifer's home a while ago.

"Maybe I should get my mail forwarded to your home," Sam said as she read the offer letter with more scrutiny. The position was the "Director of Global Research Initiatives," a role that allowed Jennifer to guide all projects driven by the Unity Foundation, with funding coming from Khulu Global. As part of the title, she would lead all operations at the South African Large Telescope and Observatory, which meant relocating across the Atlantic. With dozens of research institutions and universities around the world funded by Unity, she would have access to an international pool of scientific resources, and direct communication channels with the ESA and the South African National-al Space Agency. Jennifer pointed out that she would have a prominent seat at all current and future Leviathan-related missions.

"If we take the offer, our home will be in Cape Town."

Sam placed the offer letter onto the table, treating it as if it were the golden ticket from the *Willy Wonka* movie. "Jesus, this is one hell of an offer."

"Yeah." Jennifer's voice trailed of as she recalled the contents of the letter. "Seems too good to be true, doesn't it?"

"Ahh, but it's not a complete offer—seems that you'd have to have an interview with Muzie himself ahead of accepting the offer." Sam scratched her head. "So he made an offer, but wants to talk with you ahead of following through on said offer? Seems unusual."

Sam and Jennifer locked their eyes together. She could sense what Jennifer was thinking regarding this opportunity. "Are you considering leaving SETI for this?"

"Given the current climate over here, I think I could make a more significant impact at Unity. We both know NASA's Leviathan missions had reduced priority while SETI's funding and expansion plans were slashed." Jennifer reached over the table and wrapped her hand around Sam's. "I know this is a big decision, but it's one that I've thought about for the last few days."

Sam broke eye contact with Jennifer and glanced down at their intertwined fingers. "I'm surprised you didn't tell me about this when you got the letter..."

"Given the unexpectedness of the letter, I had to just think about what this all meant before even verbalizing it with someone."

Sam wasn't sure if that was supposed to be an apology for not sharing this news when it first passed over Jennifer's eyes, but she understood where she was coming from. At the same time, she frowned at the thought of Jennifer keeping something as large as this from her. Still holding Jennifer's hands, she sighed and shook her head.

"I get where you're coming from," Sam said. "And I'll concede that Muzie's operations have grown substantially since the formation of the Armstrong Program. It makes perfect logical sense to take any offers from him." She relaxed herself from the rigid posture she had before, her hands releasing Jennifer's before her fingers stroked her wrists and lower arm. "With the seven-figure salary, I think we'd be set for the rest of our lives once this whole Leviathan business blows over."

Jennifer couldn't help but express concern at that, despite her arms feeling electrified by Sam's subtle caresses as her fingers inched their way up her arm. "You sound more confident than usual regarding the Leviathan and the likelihood that we'll find a way to keep it from consuming the Earth."

Sam grinned as she brought her face closer to Jennifer's. As far as she was concerned, they were the only ones in the bar. "With you in my life, it's easier to be optimistic."

○ ◎ ○

NOVEMBER 11, 2018

The next morning, Sam went back home to collect her own mail and see if there really was an offer letter from Khulu Global waiting for her. As expected, it sat in a thick envelope among the other mail she let collect in her home's mailbox, though unlike Jennifer's letter coming from Khulu Global, this one was from the Unity Foundation, the nonprofit arm that managed the space programs and research under the flag of its parent company. She sat in her living room, the rest of the mail left on a coffee table, as she tore open the letter and reviewed its contents.

The offer that Sam received was, much like Jennifer's, generous to say the least. She was surprised to learn that the program director for the *Victoria* mission was quietly dismissed the week before the date on her offer letter, for reasons that weren't shared. However, the position couldn't stay vacant—a position for which Muzie himself felt Sam would be a perfect fit. The mission was managed out of the Overberg Space Center, which was east of Cape Town, South Africa. Her letter noted that he also sent an offer to her current boss, Jennifer, for a director position at Unity, which meant that if Jennifer also accepted, she would remain as her superior. This made Sam raise an eyebrow: It was very odd that anyone would advertise another person's offer letter, but this made it clear to her that Muzie understood the benefits of having both of them together—for business and political reasons.

Like Jennifer's letter, he wanted a call with her ahead of a formal acceptance, despite this letter clarifying that she had the job if she wanted it. Given the significant step up for her in terms of her career, she knew what her decision would be. But there were several glaring omissions in the letter she also wanted to address.

Despite the nine-hour time difference, she called the provided number in the final paragraph of the offer letter. It rang only twice before it was answered.

"Good morning, Samantha Monroe, this is Ami Kone, Khulu's personal assistant," Ami said, everything spoken as if she's given this introduction dozens of times before. "I'm glad you called when you did—we've kept some evening hours open for people such as yourself."

"Hello, Ami. And I'm flattered," Sam said, with a hint of sarcasm she couldn't help but release. After all, they came to her and not the other way around.

"I'm sure you are," Ami responded in kind, but without any sarcastic flair. The woman's voice spoke with confidence. "Before I transfer you, one bit of advice: Don't waste time on bullshit responses—we both don't like wasting our time with people like that."

Sam felt her words pierce through her as if she were standing over her from across a desk, asserting her authority on her boss's behalf. It didn't take much for Sam to consider that this was someone who wasn't to be trifled with. The lack of a response from Sam led Ami to fill the silent void. "Khulu is ready, please hold on while I transfer you."

After a few seconds, a soft click indicated that the transfer went through.

"Hello, Sam," Muzikayise said, his voice deep but upbeat.

"Good morning—um, evening," Sam responded with some hesitation.

"Do not worry," he said, "I won't bite your head off. No need to think twice about your words when speaking with me."

Sam wasn't sure what to make of that comment, but took it with a grain of salt. "Thank you for that. You have quite the spitfire for a secretary."

"Oh, you mean Ami? She's my number one—I don't know where I'd be without her by my side."

Or on top of you, if rumors were true, Sam thought with a grin. Some online news sources suggested over a year ago that the world's most eligible bachelor wasn't as single as he made himself out to be, and that part of the reason he could stay so intensely focused was because Ami satisfied more than his business agendas. Few outlets beyond the entertainment and celebrity gossip sites talked about it these days, but it was something she considered during her digging into the most powerful man in Africa, if not the eastern hemisphere. She kept herself from saying something that would likely end the call right there. "I shouldn't be surprised that someone of your stature would have a firewall like her between you and the world."

"Indeed," he said with a slight chuckle. "So, let's get down to business. You've reviewed my offer, and I'm sure you have some questions. Before you ask, let me assure you that all moving expenses and rental costs for the next year are covered as part of your acceptance. A comfortable home and company car will be provided."

"That's very generous of you, Mr. Khulu—"

"Just call me Muzie—no need for formalities today."

"Okay... Muzie." She couldn't help but remind herself that this was the founder of Khulu Global on the phone talking to her as if they were the best of friends. "So exactly how soon did you want me to move out there?"

"Immediately," he responded, as if it were the most logical answer to her question.

"Given the critical nature of the role offered, I would need you on-site to continue overseeing the success of *Victoria* and the release of the *Hermes* rover. With you calling and asking me questions like this, I am led to believe that you've found my offer very attractive."

"I must admit, it is strong," Sam conceded. "I found it odd you mentioned my superior, Dr. Epstein, in the letter as well. Did you believe mentioning her would be a factor in my decision?" she grimaced as she regretted asking that question in such a forward manner.

"Ahh, a good question," he said in anticipation. "I take all factors into account when I have certain individuals on my radar for prestigious roles in my organization. This includes relationships they may have with their peers or superiors. To me, it was clear from the start you and Dr. Epstein make an excellent team, both in the scientific community and on camera. I imagine the two of you have a strong personal connection as well due to the Leviathan's appearance."

Her face became unexpectedly flush. Did he know about her and Jennifer? She shifted the focus back to the position offered, in the hopes of not making Jennifer a part of the discussion.

"What happened to the previous program director?"

"Another good question," Muzie said. If he were taken aback by her questioning, he didn't sound like it. "Let's just say there were visionary differences, which conflicted with the overall success of the mission."

Those words begged for clarification. "Visionary differences?"

"The world needs people that place our species' existence ahead of their own—anything less doesn't deserve a place on any missions where our very survival is at stake. You, of all people, would understand this position better than anyone else, given your... intimate relationship with the Leviathan."

She nodded, though kept her lips pressed shut. Strong, confident statements like that made her feel even better about her unspoken decision, though questions around those "visions" floated in her mind. She decided to not press the issue, against her internal urgings.

"So you fired the program director and placed all of your eggs in one basket—namely me?" she asked with growing confidence.

"That's correct," Muzie said, his words never wavering.

"Ha!" Sam blurted.

"Did I say something amusing?" he asked with an annoyed tone.

Before she allowed herself to turn red once more, this time in embarrassment, she decided to double-down. "Oh, it's just that your offer letter was hand-signed by you, and mentioned my superior by name, and said you sent her an offer as well. It seems like you really want the two of us to join your motley crew of corporate scientists, to the point where no other candidates were considered. If one or both of us turn you down, you're screwed."

Now she brought a hand to her phone, pressed the Mute icon, and released all the air from her lungs. If there was a brick wall nearby, she would've banged her head against it and called herself "Stupid" for an hour. The silence on the line, which lasted a couple of seconds, informed her she completely caught Muzikayise off-guard with her candidness and assumptions that she was sure were true.

Before she thought he would hang up, infuriated, he broke the silence instead. "I knew you were the right fit for Unity—you have the kind of spunk I desire in those that would be near the top of my authoritative pillars. It is why I brought people like my Ami on-board: not afraid to speak their minds, not afraid to stand up for their beliefs, not afraid to use what they have to their advantage."

Sam wrinkled her nose at his response. *My Ami? Use what they have to their advantage?* Though most of what he said was likely meant to be a compliment, the way he spoke just rubbed her the wrong way.

"You certainly have a way with words when speaking to women, don't you?" Sam asked with little candor.

Muzikayise didn't hesitate with his response. "I speak my mind, just like you. If you couldn't handle that, you would not have even been considered for my offer. I am not afraid of being candid, either: I've seen the transcripts of meetings you've had with high-ranking officials at the White House years ago. I've dug into your academic history, your school records, the high number of disciplinary actions taken against you due to, as described by the Dean of Students at CalTech in 1997, 'continued disruptions in class by refuting information presented by various professors and getting into public verbal altercations'. It didn't stop you from graduating two years ahead of the rest of your peers—just twenty years old when you completed undergrad in 1998,

234 | ETERNAL SHADOW

and with Summa Cum Laude, no less."

Sam's mouth dropped open. She could recall those moments, despite them happening decades ago. She didn't think the public could gain access to disciplinary records—no, she *knew* people other than herself and certain faculty couldn't access those records. "How the hell did you get access to that?" she asked.

He dismissed her concerns. "What matters here is that you aren't afraid to poke the hornet's nest, as it were. I like that. It is a personality trait I know will serve you well as part of the Unity Foundation."

"I haven't made a decision yet," Sam said too quickly.

"Yes, you have." She could have sworn she could see his wide smile through the phone as he said that.

Silence filled the air as she tried to get her face to not feel so tingly and red. How did she allow him to get under her skin as much as he has? Her free hand balled into a fist, more out of frustration for not coming up with a comeback to his blatant assertiveness. One thing was for certain in her mind: This motherfucker did his homework. Probably even had access to psychological profiles on both her and Jennifer, though how he'd get access to information like that she had no idea. He had enough connections to access restricted files from her college days. She wouldn't be too surprised, if not disgusted, if he knew more about them than they knew about each other. In either case, the result was the same: it didn't take a mathematician's mind to see just how accepting Muzie's offer would be the best possible decision.

"I'll get back to you after I talk with Jenn—Dr. Epstein about your offer later today." *Goddamnit, Sam, don't let him play you!*

"I look forward to your call," Muzikayise said. He disconnected the call before she could get in another word.

Pulling the phone away from her ear to see her home screen instead of an active call, she tossed it onto her couch. "God, what a condescending asshole," she said aloud as she weaved her fingers through her hair several times.

He was an asshole, but an asshole that knew she was on-board before he even answered the phone.

3.2

Destination Zero was a small area on the surface of the Leviathan about three kilometers in diameter, a circular patch of smooth, darkened concrete with clear borders where the concrete ended and the rough, regolith-covered surface began. The border of Destination Zero had small, beach-ball sized orbs half-embedded into the concrete every three meters; they were opaque, with a dark purple sheen that only revealed itself when the sun reflected off their surface. Near the top half of the circular area was a large, sphere-shaped structure that was also half-buried. Two smaller spheres flanked it, with a single cylinder at the rear that looked like an opaque glass smokestack. Unlike the orbs that ringed Destination Zero, these three spheres were significantly larger —the center sphere was as tall as a twelve story building and the smaller two spheres half that. Based on the level of refraction that the surface of the sphere had, optical interferometers on the *Victoria* confirmed that the trio were covered with a layer of water or a similar liquid at least ten meters deep, likely to protect the interior from cosmic radiation. Similar liquid "shields" surrounded the satellites that launched from Destination Zero in 2016. How that liquid stayed around the spheres without vaporizing or boiling away remained a mystery, but provided one of many sources of Leviathan-related speculation. Wide concrete stairs stretched in front of the center sphere with a total of twelve steps that ended at the foot of a deep-black runway.

The "runway" was so named because it resembled most airport runways found on Earth minus the lighting that one would expect. At thirty meters wide, it had white rectangular dashes, each two meters long—the center lines—and a cluster of small orbs at the bottom-most edge, all of which were the size of baseballs.

The entire structure, taken as a whole, could've served one of many purposes, from a starport to an intergalactic pit stop, except that there was no evidence of anyone being home. No lighting, no movement, no sign that anything was there that knew there was a tiny probe eight hundred thousand kilometers overhead which prepared to drop its payload.

With the *Victoria* in position over Destination Zero in a *Levia*centric orbit, the final commands were confirmed back in the Overberg Space Center on Earth to release the *Hermes* package from the probe. The much smaller craft that detached was a stripped-down version of the Mars Science Laboratory craft that landed the *Curiosity* rover. There were several modifications made because of the Leviathan's attributes, one of which concerned the heat shield—a much lighter titanium cap shielded the rover due to the lack of an atmosphere. The cap had a tungsten core placed inside the tip to help with descent stabilization since the use of thrusters would be kept to a minimum outside of aero-maneuvering adjustments. The eight thrusters would make corrections during the initial descent during the cruise stage, though they did not have the power to combat the immense gravitational pull.

It was clear during the designing process of the lander that mankind simply did not have the technology to build a vehicle that would operate on the surface of the Leviathan for more than a few minutes before it crushed itself into a steaming, metallic pancake on the ground. That, of course, assumed you built a lander that had the thruster force to counter the gravity of the alien surface.

Theoretically it could be done, but the cost of getting the amount of fuel and the rockets to perform the job entered the realm of fantasy. And the engines could never shut down, for the minute they did, you'd get another, much larger flaming pancake of metal.

As much as it pained the designers, researchers, military brass, and the leaders of the Armstrong Program that signed off on the final blueprints, it was decided to leave the entry process in the hands of the AI, which stated that it would ensure the successful landing of whatever we sent its way. But they had to do something, and ignoring the potential trove of invaluable information that the AI could share far outweighed the audacity needed to propose that we let the *Hermes* lander plummet to the surface at the mercy of the Leviathan's gravity, hoping the AI stepped in to save the day. Outside of political marketing campaigns, using "hope" and "promise" in any government project, especially one of this scale and importance, would have been the kiss of death without even getting past the abstract on the first page, but for the Hermes, the inclusion of the AI made using such language an inevitability.

And so the *Hermes* landing craft made all the adjustments needed after separation from the *Victoria,* the distance between it and the "runway" on the surface closing fast.

Back on Earth, a live feed was streamed by NASA, ESA, and Roscosmos on multiple channels of the descent, the values generated by the craft's entry-descent-landing (ESL) system used to animate an approximation of the descent process with visuals, a decision that garnered tens of millions of viewers worldwide. That didn't include the breaking news reports that interrupted almost every broadcast and cable channel around the world which displayed the same data or threw up their own visual interpretations of the operation. The anticipation of the landing was such that even sports organizations, well aware of this significant day months in advance, ensured that no games occurred that would conflict with the global broadcasts.

If people weren't glued to their computer monitors or their televisions, they filed their way into churches, cathedrals, temples, synagogues, and mosques until they were beyond capacity, praying, singing, and chanting. The world's religious leaders struggled to keep up with the myriad interpretations that came with the Leviathan's presence. At the same time, dozens of cults rose and died—often in the form of mass suicides—surrounding the Leviathan, but none were as successful and as persistent as The Seven Trumpets. The now-global cult continued their targeted attacks on those that wanted to pursue understanding the Leviathan versus accepting it as the herald for the End Days.

It was this global backdrop that fueled the tension which person-nel worked within the rechristened Overberg Space Center. Formally the Denel Overberg Test Range, the facility was one arm of the South African defense industry in the 1980s as the core of what would be-come the South African Space Agency. However, due to a struggling economy and mounting debt, the government sold off the property to a fast-growing corporation called KNG—Khulu National Group—in 1990, with the stipulation that South Africa could continue using the facilities for defense development purposes. It was at a high cost to KNG, but one that Muzikayise was quoted as being "a worthy, long-term investment."

∘ ◎ ∘

On one of the biggest days of their careers, Sam and Jennifer drove into Overberg under dense clouds that dumped its payload of water onto the land below. Despite the investments made into the facility over the years, the one thing that wasn't given much attention was the road used to get there from the highway. Being compacted dirt with chunks of pavement interspersed, it was clear that in the past this was a paved thoroughfare, but years of neglect and intense storms formed large, gaping cracks in some parts and washed out chunks in others. Compacted dirt and gravel filled in much of the road, but roads like this ensured most vehicles would have a hard time traversing them, especially when it rained.

All the more reason to appreciate that they drove jeeps instead of sedans. The vehicles, courtesy of Khulu Global, wouldn't win any beau-ty pageants, as they were painted white and had no logos or branding on them. The interior was comfortable, but no-frills when it came to features—nothing that would coax someone to steal it. What was most important was its handling of off-road and mixed-road terrain: Barring one of them driving into a deep gully or getting all four wheels stuck in a pool of deep mud, the jeep handled just about everything thrown at it as if the land was paved.

Once you were inside the walls of OSC, however, it was concrete in all directions. There were rows of raised, wooden boxes containing the small trees and bushes that lined the main road from the perimeter entrance to the largest building, simply called "Operations". Standing at twelve stories tall, the box-shaped, windowless building contained all the launch control centers and related support needed to coordinate launches from the six launch pads that sat several miles east of where they were.

There was little room for formalities once they parked their jeep in the lot next to Operations—after a kiss, they parted ways for their respective rooms, with Sam headed for OpsOne and Jennifer the OpsOne observation room. Sam, dressed in a breathable linen suit with her OSC badge pinned to the breast pocket, stood behind the two rows of desks that constituted the *Victoria* flight team, all of which were glued to the trio of monitors that each person had. Though everyone knew how tight the security was both within and around the OSC, Sam had to sit through a virtual briefing earlier in the day so she understood what they were being protected from, and how The Seven Trumpets gained followers within South Africa over the last year. She knew the details were important, but buried them in the back of her mind as she kept her eyes on the wall-sized screen in front of her. Similar to what she'd seen at other space control centers back in the United States, this had a graphical depiction of the landing in the main window, with batches of raw and summarized data on display in their own smaller windows next to it. Another screen was a live feed directly from the *Victoria* probe with one camera that followed the detached lander with incredible detail. Jennifer joined Muzikayise, who was also in the OpsOne observation room, set at the rear with a glass wall allowing them a full view. They were silent as the dialogue from Sam and those on her team filled the air from the surrounding speakers.

Alerts lit up the monitors of several officers and engineers responsible for the guided entry and powered descent phase: The ability to steer the craft was already reaching the point where gravity would assume full control. With the approval of Sam, the thrusters were shut down, leaving only the tungsten core to stabilize the near-vertical descent path that the craft now adopted.

The lack of an atmosphere was a good thing in this case, given the speeds at which the craft was falling toward the surface would have generated incredible amount of friction-related heat if an atmosphere were present. It wasn't long before the descent velocity reached a point where, after closing the gap between the *Victoria* and the surface by two hundred thousand kilometers, no amount of counter-thrust would prevent it from a fatal impact. The computers around Sam knew this and blared their soft alarms and blanketed the screens of the guidance officers with windows begging them to do something about the situation. Sam knew her words were being monitored by her superiors, but also being livestreamed by the media, which she took to heart with both what she said and how she said it. Inspired by her favorite *Star Trek* captains, she pointed a finger at the officer that brought up the alarms and commanded with some gravitas, "Turn off the alarms."

The officer was about to protest, but decided against it with a sigh as he canceled all alerts and warnings concerning descent velocity, thruster failure, and predicted inoperability of the sky crane, the descent system that would lower the *Hermes* by tether to the surface of the Leviathan. Muzikayise, with his arms crossed, glanced at Jennifer, who also looked at Muzikayise before refocusing on the operations room below. They both knew of Sam's unorthodox ways of managing her flight crew, but she'd never been wrong with her decisions, all of which they assumed she calculated either on-the-fly or days in advance. Sam's had less than a month to prepare for this moment, but had already shown her ability to understand standardized procedures that were set by agencies like NASA decades ago in short order. Muzikayise allowed Sam to direct this critical mission because media personalities and the public ate her up, and Jennifer allowed it because she trusted her.

Despite the disabled alarms, they would lose their only shot at landing on the Leviathan in less than five minutes unless the AI interfered.

Scores of bright, white lights that lined the runway suddenly illuminated the manicured landscape as if a switch flicked on. Similar red-violet lights appeared from the border orbs, creating a circular outline of Destination Zero. Regolith and small rocks that collected over the point where the border ended and the rest of the Leviathan landscape began rose away from the surface until they passed an invisible point over where they once were. Beyond that, they rolled back to the ground outside Destination Zero, tumbling down an invisible, curved barrier that the border orbs erected.

With the craft less than a hundred thousand kilometers away, a small, spherical satellite rose from within the glass smokestack that was behind the center sphere and moved on an intercept course to the lander. The shimmering surface of the satellite indicated that, much like the previous satellites they witnessed, it was surrounded by a liquid substance. No evidence of propulsion was present, yet it took a few seconds for it to match speeds with the lander. A few seconds after that, a small glow emanated from the center of the floating orb, after which the lander's descent speed went from over 400km/s to a more comfortable 80m/s. The sudden drop in speed caused no damage to the craft, which shocked the entirety of OpsOne into silence. Several personnel craned their heads at Sam, who held her hands over her mouth. They knew something unexpected would occur, but seeing the alien sphere so deftly counter the immense forces that the Leviathan presented still proved to be a gripping moment.

"What just happened?" one of the officers asked aloud, dumbfounded.

"Maybe some sort of inertial damper field?" another suggested as he had crunched a piece of graph paper on his head, ignoring that his sweat had ruined whatever writing he scribbled on it earlier.

"It's really inertia negation," a third chimed in without peeling his eyes from the visuals in front of him. "But our understanding of physics would make that impossible—"

He stopped talking when a soft chime brought everyone to the attention of all the velocity data that updated to reflect a descent speed not unlike they'd seen when landing on Mars.

Though the lander was still descending, watching the alien orb guide the *Hermes* to its destination was enough to elicit roaring applause from the flight crew, with one older man tossing a handful of papers into the air as he cheered in unabashed excitement. "Okay boys," Sam said with a wide smile on her face and arms outstretched on her sides, gesturing for everyone to sit back down. Everyone in OpsOne calmed down and got back into their positions.

"Let's celebrate once *Hermes* is actually on the ground." She looked around before adding, "But yes, I'd toast to what amounts to first contact with an alien species!"

"Oh, Sam," Jennifer said to herself as she brought a palm to her face and cringed. Muzikayise didn't budge, but his cheek muscle involuntarily twitched as he *felt* his company's stock price going up as the play-by-play of this momentous event unfolded in front of him.

Three hours passed before the alien satellite broke its synchronous descent with the lander, the light that glowed from it diminishing to nothingness as it dashed back to the glass smokestack from whence it came. Despite this change, the lander and *Hermes* continued to the surface with no change to its velocity. Thirty minutes after that, the *Hermes* rover uncoupled from the lander, its six aluminum wheels touched down on the smoothed concrete surface of Destination Zero, the lander flying another five meters before crash-landing just off the side of the runway. When all landing procedures and configuration details came back green, the entire operation room jumped in celebration, with Sam leading the spontaneous festivities with her giving the Flight Director a strong hug and kiss on the cheek. Other men cried, with one rather large, bearded fellow hiding his face under his beefy hands as a stray tear seeped between his fingers and down his cheek. Space agency websites finally crashed from the overwhelming volume of visitors, as did some livestreams, while the cell phones of those that were there went off the hook as family members, spouses, and friends reached out to congratulate them.

Muzikayise held a smile on his face when he heard the observation room door swing open. Jennifer ran out of the room to join the elated fray in OpsOne. He couldn't hear exactly what she said to Sam once the two of them were facing each other, as the sounds of revelry overtook any possibility of hearing individual voices through the surrounding speakers, but after seeing them exchange what were very spirited words, they embraced. His smile faded to a businesslike stoicism as he watched them amongst everyone below.

∘ ◎ ∘

The *Hermes* was the latest generation of exploration rover, its design based on the *Curiosity* rover that was on Mars. The size of a car, it clocked in at just over a metric ton. *Hermes* was host to 21 cameras that served a variety of purposes: some were its eyes, giving it a full 360-degree view of its environment for navigation; six were closer to the ground to feed hazard alerts whenever any of the wheels were a meter from either a sharp incline or precipice. One camera, dubbed the "SuperCam," which sat above all the other cameras on its own mount and between the navigation cams, could not only run chemical composition analysis on nearby regolith and rocks it scanned, but also be able to take that data and, with the help of other instruments, identify biosignatures—something many expected to find on the Leviathan. A suite of microphones on the exterior of the chassis recorded the sounds around the rover, a feature that was thought to be another great way to learn more about the Leviathan and Destination Zero. Aside from the wheels and the camera mount that stood above the rover, there was a retractable robotic arm which had a complement of tools, including a percussion drill and a brush. As per the request of the AI, a heavily shielded solid-state drive was embedded deep within the chassis. Dubbed the "history" drive, it contained the final printed edition of Encyclopedia Britannica and all of its more recent digital content; every issue of National Geographic; the entirety of Wikipedia; and hundreds of select works of fiction and non-fiction. The solid-state drive had a series of output ports that were accessible from one side of the chassis, covered by a thick hatch. Like with some critical aspects of this mission, the ports were all standards that existed on Earth. The assumption taken was that the AI could figure out how to interface with the rover based on its present understanding of Earth technology. It was a terrible assumption to make, but given how fast it could decipher human languages, those that made the final call figured this would just be another leap of faith.

A second set of solid-state drives, totaling a combined one hundred terabytes of storage, contained a database full of questions chosen by the various space agencies, their governments, and members of the United Nations. The intention was to have the AI answer all the provided questions, after which the responses would be sent back to Earth. Advanced speech recognition and synthesis software and hardware was included as part of this database to manage possible responses from the AI—a way for *Hermes* to generate additional questions based on the responses it received. Despite the complexity of such a system, the majority of the one hundred terabytes was free space, in anticipation of receiving data that could then be picked up and returned to Earth in the future. This set of drives utilized the same ports as the first solid-state drive, with *Hermes* designed to flip from one drive to another.

The rover chassis was unchanged from its predecessor: a hardened box designed to protect the plethora of sensitive electronic components and sensors from radiation. This included the multi-mission radioisotope thermoelectric generator (MMRTG), a generator that produced electricity thanks to radioactive isotope decay, a process that would take about fourteen years before the rover would have insufficient power to operate.

One of the biggest updates to the rover design was with heat management. Unlike the surface of Mars, there was no atmosphere on the Leviathan, which would mean that temperature differences between the sunlit sides and darkened sides would be extreme. Nobody assumed this would change at the influence of the AI, so every precaution was baked into the *Hermes* with this in mind. Thanks to the MMRTG, there was plenty of excess heat that the thermal system could move around thanks to the use of heat pumps and a fluid loop. This system not only helped to keep core electronics at optimal temperatures but also could dissipate heat if the rover became too hot. Several layers of small pipes ran through all the internal components, which in turn connected to two heat exchangers, ensuring that sudden temperature changes outside could be countered quickly.

Before the *Hermes* even began to move toward the large, spherical buildings at the other end of the runway, the navcams and SuperCam were busy scanning the surrounding area, delivering lots of information back to Earth. The rover was near the middle of the runway, so the initial focus was on the concrete surface.

Very smooth and with little variance in its composition, the SuperCam zoomed in for a closer look. The first attempt at drilling into the artificial surface failed with the drill stopping itself automatically after it popped off the surface, making the rover shudder from the reaction. It was definitely a form of micro-reinforced high-strength concrete, but with evidence of a metallic mesh that was tightly woven together and close to the surface. A faint glare that bounced off the runway when a light from the SuperCam aimed downward indicated that a thin layer of a sealant was also present. The ground radar imager, a radar designed to determine ground densities, rock layers, and underground element detection—including water—didn't turn up any results, either, which was surprising. Being that the radar could scan as deep as ten meters, either the runway surface obfuscated what was below it, or the runway composition was over ten meters thick. Both scenarios produced even more questions than answers, which Sam concluded would be a running theme as *Hermes* continued its mission.

The sounds captured by the *Hermes* were not unexpected: Other than the rover's mechanical chirps and groans, the surface of the Leviathan was silent.

Two hours after the initial scans of the landing zone, the *Hermes* began its journey toward what many at Overberg named The Three Spheres. One engineer joked that it reminded him of the "three seashells" from *Demolition Man*— "Nobody knew how the three seashells worked," he said. In response, several of his colleagues booed at him. Nevertheless, The Three Spheres stuck, for no other reason than the name being the most logical description of what they saw, especially since it had no other defining structural features.

Thanks to the smooth, hardened concrete surface, *Hermes* had no trouble reaching its fastest speed of ninety meters per hour, but it would take over twenty hours before it reached the first step in front of The Three Spheres.

3.3

By the time Sam rejoined her crew in OpsOne, *Hermes* sat four meters away from the first of twelve steps that separated it from the center of The Three Spheres. She took stock of those that remained after an incredible twenty-four hours as she power walked to the nearest coffee machine to give herself a large jolt of energy to enter a greater state of focus.

She looked at the analog clock that was centered over the projection screen and made a mental note of the time between her unwilling dismissal for a few hours of sleep and returning to her station. With the most arduous part of the mission successful—landing the *Hermes*—Sam allowed many that were in operations to get some much-needed rest as people were running on fumes. There were still fifteen people in front of their monitors, at least one for each station. Most of those fifteen subbed for the original shift, but Mckale Cornwell, the Flight Director for the *Hermes* mission, sat at his station, back straight and not slouched forward in tiredness, his hands resting on the keyboard as his eyes scanned the information on his monitor.

"Give me an update, Flight," Sam said as she took off her suit jacket and flung it onto the back of an empty seat.

"We've made it to the foot of The Three Spheres," Mckale responded. "Not much to do as far as movement goes from here, ma'am."

"Why do you say that?" Sam asked as she closed the distance

between her and Mckale's desk which was littered with stacks of graph paper, each one depicting rough depictions of routes *Hermes* could take away from Destination Zero.

"There's no way for *Hermes* to climb the stairs, to be frank," he said. He gestured towards the larger screen. "Unfortunately, each step is thirty-five centimeters tall and, as to be expected, ninety-degree rises."

"We cannot get the wheels to pull themselves up the risers?" Sam leaned forward to the schematics of the *Hermes* that Mckale had on his monitor, to which she performed some quick gestures with her finger on his monitor to bring it up onto the big screen in its own window. "The wheels do have some deep treads."

He was quick to respond without looking at her. "Indeed. However, these steps do not have any grooves for which the *Hermes* could leverage. Even if it did, the rover would bottom out on the riser before the middle wheels could reach the stairs."

Mckale turned and faced Sam with the serious, pockmarked face he always had when his mind was in complete data analysis mode. She blinked, took a deep breath and said, after exhaling and looking at the big screen again, "Well shit." She knew the design specifications of the *Hermes* as if she were on the team that built it, but tried to think of a way to get around this barrier. At the same time, she knew Mckale had already done that a couple of times, if the graph paper strewn about was any indication.

Hailing from the control rooms of the ESA Guiana Space Centre in French Guiana, Mckale's no-nonsense attitude toward his career was one of the reasons he was brought on-board at the Unity Foundation. Unlike Sam, he wore the "Unity Uniform"—a light-blue t-shirt with a small Unity Foundation logo embroidered over the chest, which was tucked into gray-black cargo pants. It was the standard outfit for everyone that wasn't a director, so why he wore it Sam didn't know—perhaps he found it more comfortable than a suit and tie, for which she wouldn't have blamed him if that were the case.

Perhaps he believed it was part of keeping morale high. Not that it was hard to keep morale up—being part of the Leviathan mission was more than enough for everyone involved to be motivated.

Regardless, his attire didn't bother her as long as he delivered whatever he was assigned.

"There are a series of ridges just to the right of Destination Zero —perhaps we can find a way to navigate them and come around from the rear of The Three Spheres?" asked Amahle Dlamini with her eyes aimed to the floor. She was the Operations Support Officer for Ops-One, which meant she managed all logistics support surrounding data maintenance related to the mission, from understanding the mechanical and electronic systems on *Hermes* to documenting said processes. Sam stood upright while Mckale glanced over, both looking in her direction. It was impossible to miss Amahle's deep voice, which reminded Sam of Scarlett Johansson. Despite Amahle's important slice of work, she didn't talk much, so when she did it had the effect of turning heads. She also wore her Unity Uniform a size larger than her physical frame would suggest, resulting in her always looking like she couldn't dress herself, or didn't care about her looks. However, Sam has seen her once in form-fitting gym attire one evening in the bathroom and knew, as a result, of her tight athletic build. Why she wore oversized clothes during her shifts Sam didn't know, but like the people she worked alongside at SETI, everyone has their quirks.

All that being said, she asked some of the oddest questions when she did speak. To Sam, "odd" meant "out-of-the-box," which meant she would partake in exploring the idea further.

Mckale belted a short laugh before he saw her unchanging face. "Wait, you are serious," he said as he rubbed an eyelid with a finger.

"That would be impossible," Sam said as she pointed to a diagram of Destination Zero on a nearby wall. "The gravitational strength beyond the border of Destination Zero is twenty-one times that of Earth —*Hermes* would be crushed the moment it left the confines of where it could go."

"None of the shots from *Victoria* indicated that there was any terrain behind The Three Spheres that would allow a rover access to the front without climbing those stairs," Mckale said, piggybacking on Sam's words.

"I know what the *Victoria* provided us," Amahle said, her eyes flickering toward Sam before retreating to the safety of the floor.

"But with *Hermes* on the ground, we've been able to obtain new imagery of the surrounding area and where the rover could actually travel versus assumed options based on overhead shots." She grabbed paper from her desk with a crude drawing of Destination Zero with elevation curves and markers, along with some details surrounding gravity and the weight of the rover. A path, dashed over the drawn terrain in red, wound its way just by the border of Destination Zero to the right of The Three Spheres, rising fifteen meters higher than the final staircase before descending back toward the right sphere. Sam reviewed the numbers with Mckale as Amahle continued. "Based on readings from the RIMFAX radar, we could redirect *Hermes* to the far right of The Three Spheres, where there is a ten degree incline that weaves toward the edge of Destination Zero. About half way, the slope increases to about thirty-seven degrees, which would be pushing it in terms of what the rover could do in terms of terrain traversal, but thanks to the harder, rocky surface there, the wheels shouldn't have a problem gripping the rocks and, with all six wheels set to maximum torque, climb to the highest natural point behind The Three Spheres. From there, it's just a matter of navigating downhill towards the base of the center sphere."

Sam smiled just as Amahle finished speaking. She looked at her, passing back her impromptu proposal as she did. "That's a very intriguing proposition, Amahle. And you determined the amount of time needed to accomplish this alternative route?"

"Yes, ma'am, I've marked it just under the—"

"Hey, we got movement from The Three Spheres," one of the other officers said as he sat erect in his desk chair. In a few clicks, the Super-Cam had the largest window on the big screen in front of OpsOne. When Sam turned to the screen, a small sphere—the same sphere that assisted the *Hermes* lander—popped out of the glass smokestack behind The Three Spheres. Despite the sphere not emitting any form of light, the starry backdrop behind it made it possible to track its position from the surface as it approached *Hermes*.

"What is it doing?" Mckale asked as the sphere stopped just above the first step in front of *Hermes*. A portion of the sphere's interior was visible though the watery shell that encompassed it thanks to the high resolution of the SuperCam. It almost looked like an adjusting lens.

"Should I have the rover pull back..." the Guidance Officer said before he quickly realized what he said and stopped himself. Sam didn't acknowledge him, nor did she have to: There was still a two-and-a-half hour delay between them and the Leviathan, so they couldn't do anything immediate about the sphere in front of *Hermes*. Instead she, and the other fourteen people in OpsOne, remained silent as they stared at this wonder of technology, and to see what it would do next.

After a few minutes, the lens of the sphere glowed with a bluish hue as it rose a few meters over the surface—with the *Hermes* rising with it. Sam's mouth spread into a wide grin as the PIXL Cam at the end of the rover's arm kept its eyes on the ground below, allowing them a clear picture of what was happening.

"Is... the AI literally picking us up and bringing us to the top of the steps?" Mckale asked—once again, not to anyone in particular as he fixated on the big screen.

"Why didn't the AI do this before when we landed?" Amahle wondered.

Sam could have responded to both questions, but she held her breath as she watched what was unfolding, for a moment forgetting she was the one that was supposed to be the most level-headed of the bunch.

After being transported in the airless sky, the sphere lowered *Hermes* back to the surface, the twelve steps traversed in minutes versus days. The rover's wheels settled, its suspension barely registering the invisible hold the sphere had on it, as if it were a delicate toy. As fast as the sphere arrived, its lens stopped glowing and took off well above *Hermes*, out of view from its cameras, until a couple of seconds passed, at which point the sphere could be seen descending into the smokestack. The SuperCam, now focused on The Three Spheres in front of *Hermes*, revealed a translucent surface that had the appearance of a gentle lake, with occasional ripples appearing on the surface like a small water strider shifted its legs on it.

The entire room didn't have time to register what just happened before a square-shaped outline lit up near the bottom of the center, largest sphere of The Three Spheres. And something moved just beyond the lights.

∘ ◎ ∘

"What the hell is that?" the Guidance Officer asked at much too high a volume. Commotion began to build as swift, undulating movements could be seen just beyond the square opening on the spherical structure that was thirty meters from *Hermes*.

Sam's sense of wonder was almost overwhelming. She patted Mckale on the back as she walked to the center of OpsOne, her gaze shifting to each person present. "Nobody's losing their heads today, so settle back down everyone!"

She pressed her lips together as the room grew quiet, the hums of dozens of computers collecting all the data that was being streamed back from *Hermes* becoming the dominant sound around her. Once she had the room's attention, she nodded and continued. "There's nothing that *Hermes* will miss, so the first thing we need to do is get everyone back here, now. All remaining core staff, support personnel, the support for the support personnel. What we've been preparing for is here. I believe the AI will attempt to interface with *Hermes*. I don't know about all of you, but this will constitute the first time humankind will make contact with another species from another planet in a different star system.

"That sentence, right there, raises so many questions and avenues for discussion, but that's why we're here. The presence of the Leviathan upended so many of our well-understood laws that govern the universe. We have questions that, four years post-arrival, still are nowhere near answered. But given the reception that this AI has given us— the Disaster at Arecibo notwithstanding—I believe we have a genuine chance at learning more about the universe in the next twenty-four hours than we, as a civilization, have learned since we learned how to write over five thousand years ago.

"Maybe some of that knowledge will help us understand why the Leviathan is here and how we can get it to divert its course while we still have time."

An air of readiness seemed to have filled OpsOne, with the officers present watching and listening to Sam expectantly, nodding at her and at each other in agreement. Mckale stood at his desk, his hands on his waist as he gritted his teeth under his lips, taking her words to heart. Amahle stayed in her seat, adjusting her outfit as she kept her eyes on the writhing movements just beyond the opening in the sphere.

Sam allowed a slight smile to pass over her face. "So if we're ready, let's go make history."

∘ ◎ ∘

A single, ribbed cord slithered out of the square opening, moving very much like a cobra that was made of metal. No joints were visible on the cord as would be expected from a manmade metallic object that emulated the movements of a snake—it looked organic. The cord tapered off into a fine conical endpoint while it got thicker the further it stretched away from The Three Spheres. By the time it was just meters away from *Hermes,* the cord that came out of the sphere was almost four meters in diameter.

"It moves like a snake, but looks to be made of steel, or silicon," said Amahle.

Mckale spoke up. "A snake that's either tethered to something inside that sphere, or is just really large." he pointed to the head of the cord. "Amahle, could you get PIXL to scan both that cord and the interior of the sphere to determine the elemental compositions and materials present? Meanwhile, have the SuperCam search for evidence of biosigs."

"Holy shit," exclaimed one of the men in the room—Sam didn't turn to who spoke up—as the silver cord rose the front of itself over the *Hermes* for a few seconds, towering over it to the point where its head was no longer visible in the SuperCam. When it lowered itself back to the ground, the conical front opened like flower petals to reveal thousands of fine, metallic needles that moved in unison, almost like fur in the wind. The opened cord slid just closer until it was inches from the rover's chassis.

"That almost looks like scales," the Guidance Officer said, pointing a finger at the undulating mass in front of the SuperCam which refocused its lens on a small section of the cord's body that, when illuminated by the sun, seemed to reveal a shimmering pattern on its surface.

"What do you think those needles are for?" Amahle asked as her eyes darted all along the alien imagery in front of the room.

"Tactile functionality, maybe?" Sam postulated as the door to OpsOne swung open, its hinge dampers almost unable to prevent it from hitting the wall. Several gawk-eyed scientists from the other operation rooms entered, filling the back of the room after word got around about contact being made. Several support staff took secondary seats with many of the unoccupied stations to help with the data that flowed in from *Hermes*—data that few people analyzed since they were so fixated on what was happening.

The fur-like needles drifted across the siding of the *Hermes* until scores of them came across the hatch that covered the output ports. Though there were no cameras to witness it, the needles pierced the metal cover as if it weren't even there, setting off the sensor that was installed for the cover.

"We have a code red for the output cover," one engineer announced. "A very localized temperature spike that went away after the hatch was compromised."

"Any damage to the output ports?" Mckale asked.

"No, sir. But it does look like something may be trying to activate them."

With the hatch gone, it being subsumed into the ends of the needles, they pressed into all the output ports at once, some of them entering the ports themselves while others combined around the edges of the ports. The silver cord's movement settled until it stopped waving about the ground and sat inert.

"Okay, everyone," Mckale looked around the room, his eyes steely as beads of sweat formed on his forehead. "I hate to say it, but as a reminder, any commands we send to *Hermes* are delayed by two hours. At this point, everything we're seeing is two hours old—it already happened as far as absolute relativity is concerned. Therefore, stay at your posts and comb over every bit of information that all of our sensors relay back to us.

254 | ETERNAL SHADOW

Every frame of this thing you see on-screen should be analyzed until your minds are fried.

"*Hermes* will do what its on-board programming was designed to do. With luck, this AI learned its lessons in communication methods from Arecibo and won't cook our only rover on the Leviathan." Mckale shook his head. "No, we won't focus on the mistakes of the past. I hate to say it, but much like our assisted landing, a lot of what happens in the next couple of minutes are in the hands of the AI."

After receiving many nods in consent to his commands, Mckale walked over to Sam and patted her on the shoulder. "You aren't the only one giving speeches around here," he said to her with a wink.

"Har har," she rolled her eyes as he walked on toward the back rows of desks, arms behind him. They tended to spar openly—a side effect of her being a constant presence in OpsOne. Muzikayise didn't think she would spend much time alongside McKale, but didn't oppose her decision to "be among the weeds" of the *Victoria* and *Hermes* mission. She knew that in the end, Mckale was in charge of everyone in OpsOne while she was responsible for the larger success of the Unity Foundation's presence on and around the Leviathan, a distinction she took to heart.

Once again, the spherical satellite appeared a few meters in front of the rover, it floating onto the screen with its baffling form of propulsion. It came up to the front of the SuperCam, its lens already glowing a soft blue. Its sudden domination of what the SuperCam, Mastcams, and Navcams could see from the center mount triggered another round of chatter behind Sam.

"It's just... sitting there," a flight officer said.

"Floating there, you mean," another corrected.

"It's technically propelling itself in a way that emulates the effect of floating," yet another corrected the correction. "We just don't know..."

"What is it thinking?" someone asked aloud, a thought that escaped their mind and out of their mouth for the room to hear.

The lens of the satellite, its blue outline through the liquid skin that covered the metallic surface, seemed to focus on the rover, yet it did nothing else.

Sam placed a hand over her mouth. The "face" of the satellite didn't move, yet it was not on the ground, nor did it make any discernible noise, nor did it disrupt the ground below it. It made Sam shiver, the hairs on her covered arms stand on-end, to see this truly alien device fill their monitors and screens. The move felt deliberate, like the AI knew this was how it was being watched and chose to block their cameras from seeing anything else. With her mouth covered, she whispered under her breath. "What *are* you thinking?"

◦ ◎ ◦

An hour passed before the output indicators lit up: The alien cord was being read as if it were a set of InfiniBand QSFP connectors, the fastest local data connections on Earth that were frequently used by supercomputers.

"The AI successfully connected with the *Hermes* drives," Amahle announced, though she didn't look the least bit excited by the developments. Sam noticed her relaxed posture and seeming detachment from the overall excitement that bubbled out of everyone inside—and now outside—of OpsOne.

Something to ask about later, she thought as the data processing engineers confirmed that everything on the "history" drive was being downloaded at speeds approaching three hundred gigabits per second.

"And all without setting the rover's interior on fire," the data engineer said in jest.

"Well, it's at least getting what it wanted," Mckale said as his eyes narrowed on the satellite lens that continued to fill their monitors. An overhead shot of the satellite and *Hermes* was taken by *Victoria*, though it would be another hour before that image arrived.

"At this rate it'll have everything we've shared, history-wise, within sixty seconds," Sam said to Mckale. "Just fascinating."

"Connection with the secondary drives established," Amahle said, again in a more monotone voice than Sam had heard from her in the month she'd gotten to know her.

A few seconds later, the lens within the satellite adjusted itself as the glow changed hues, shifting from blue to yellow.

"Uhhh, all our communication channels with *Hermes* were just overridden," the communications officer said as he passed a hand through the little hair that was on his head. "I think we're getting audio data."

"What—" Mckale started to ask when a flood of alerts in fat, black boxes appeared to the far-right of the big screen, one below the other and not overlapping, making it clear what was happening, though the reactions of the people at most of the stations was all they needed to hear and see.

"We just lost all navigation systems—"

"Maintenance and electrical are down—"

Mckale called for order as ten people all yelled at once about their systems telling them they failed, a situation normally seen in the uncommon cases when a rocket exploded during takeoff or when the reentry process failed, resulting in the rocket burning up in the atmosphere. Yet the Hermes looked perfectly fine, the only change being the satellite in front of it now emitting a yellow light.

"The audio was downloaded," the communications officer said loud enough to get the attention of Mckale and Sam.

"Play it," Sam said as she gripped the back of the officer's chair a bit too hard. She pulled her own chair over as the sound of a very pleasant, female voice played through the speakers that were mounted on the walls of OpsOne.

"Hello. I apologize for setting off so many alarms on your computers—given my history with past machines of other sentients, I find it best to render alien technology inert until I determine your intentions. Based on my current understanding, my actions may be interpreted as hostile, but I assure you that your scout is fully operational.

"With my introduction over, I have a proposal that I believe you will find most agreeable. I have detected a very rudimentary form of speech recognition software that, with my help, could be replaced with a fully functioning form of AI. This would increase the value of the answers you receive for your questions by no less than five hundred and forty-seven percent. Having a proper dialogue with regard to your questions could raise new questions that I could also answer to the best of my ability.

"Outside of dialogue with me, the AI will also be able to perform all tasks related to your mission on what you call the Leviathan autonomously while relaying its findings back to your planet. It can make decisions regarding its surroundings at speeds much faster than your delayed communications to it would allow, resulting in gathering more data that could help save your civilization from imminent destruction.

"Per my protocols, I will ensure that the AI will adhere to the mission that you've assigned this scout to perform while being receptive to commands sent from your people.

"Therefore, with your permission I will modify your data storage mediums and rover interconnects to support all technical requirements necessary to manage AI. Please respond with a 'yes' or 'no' using the same communication parameters you already use. I can wait as long as needed for I imagine you will deliberate amongst yourselves on what to do. I await your response."

○ ◎ ○

The bathrooms within the Overberg Space Center served as both a restroom and a mini-gym, with showers, changing rooms, and a foyer that led to a larger space filled with a smattering of workout equipment. The changing room was a small, L-shaped room with two rows of wooden benches with smooth, polished tops in the middle of the floor and wide lockers lining the walls. There were nowhere near enough lockers to accommodate all the people that worked in the building, but the space was designed with the assumption that the room would never be fully utilized, therefore the lockers could be used by anyone, provided you brought your own lock. White fluorescent lights kept the space well lit twenty-four hours.

On this day, the changing room was empty—perfect for Sam who, upon the changing room door closing behind her, let out a scream as she threw her hands in the air. "Oh my god!" she cried as she jumped up and down with a grin so large on her face it hurt. It was so hard for her to contain her excitement in the name of professionalism. "Ohmygodohmygodohmygod!"

She felt her legs tremble, wanting to give out from all the energy she just vented. Her whole body shook as her heart tried to leap out of her chest in its valiant attempt to keep up with her excitement.

"You know other people could be in here," Amahle mumbled, her voice coming from around the corner of the changing room. Sam gasped when she heard her voice, turning red as a first response.

"Oh, I'm so sorry," Sam said as she picked herself up and walked to where the room turned a corner. Amahle was getting off the floor, using the bench in front of her for support. Once she stood up, she turned to Sam eyes down and flustered. Sam tilted her head to the side when she noticed a small, freestanding cross on the bench in front of Amahle. It appeared to be a crucifix, but the shape of what was Jesus looked off, like it was larger than it should've been.

"Were you praying?"

"What?"

Sam nodded toward the cross. "The cross on the bench there—"

"Oh," Amahle uttered as she swiped her hand across the bench and grabbed the cross. In a few swift motions she opened the locker, stuffed the cross into an open book bag, and slammed it shut.

"It's nothing to be ashamed of," Sam said as she leaned against one of the nearby lockers.

"Oh, I'm not ashamed of my religious beliefs," Amahle said, her voice veering toward monotony. "I guess this was my reaction to hearing the AI speak." Her eyes rose to meet Sam's and held steady. "Just like your screaming with joy was your reaction."

"Yeah..." Sam couldn't help but averting her eyes after a few seconds of looking into Amahle's. Her gaze reminded her of a sort of happiness that she was experiencing, but the intense focus felt like Amahle was piercing into her soul with her look. Sam threw her head back and feigned a laugh as she passed her fingers through her hair. "When you've worked for years in the weeds like I have, it's hard to not reign in your passion when you're now the one that has to hold the line."

"I'm very happy about *Hermes* as well," Amahle said.

"You don't sound particularly happy." Sam felt her body grow rigid against the locker her shoulder leaned on, her arms crossed in front of her.

Amahle bit her lip as she looked toward her locker, then back at Sam. "I know I'm not exactly the most extroverted person in the group —far from it. I guess I have a hard time connecting with people in general." Sam watched as she looked up from the floor, but not before returning her gaze downward. "I've been here about as long as you have, yet you already know so many people."

"To be fair, I am responsible for all of you," Sam said as her body relaxed following Amahle's frank admission. "It's my job to know everyone. It also doesn't help that my mug's been all over the media for the last few years."

"Yes, there is all that..."

"Anyway, I guess what I'm saying is that you don't have to be afraid to express yourself, not when you're in my crew. If people don't speak their minds, share their thoughts, then they are not contributing to the success of our mission."

Amalhe sat on the bench, her hands clasped together as she looked away from Sam, her chest rising and falling from heavy breaths. A comforting smile crept across Sam as she went to sit next to her. She debated whether or not she should bring an arm over Amahle's shoulder, but decided against it.

"I've seen your work—it's good," Sam said. "Really good. I know Mckale can be a hardass sometimes, but we're all on the same team."

Amahle looked at Sam as her eyes turned red, tears welling up on the ridges of her eyelids, but had a warm smile. Unlike before, the gaze from her eyes wasn't piercing. "Thanks, Monroe."

"Hey, call me Sam. Just because I'm signing your checks doesn't mean you have to be so formal!"

Amahle chuckled in response as she wiped the tears from her eyes. She let out a sigh of relief as Sam stood back up and walked away from her.

"Sam," she called out, to which Sam stopped and turned around. "Thank you."

"For what?"

"Your pep talk—I needed that."

"I can be pretty awkward when it comes to things like that—I'm glad that wasn't the case this time."

"I know I will be able to complete my mission."

"Great!" Sam smiled and waved before she turned away from Amahle and walked to the changing room door.

As she strolled down the halls of the Overberg Space Center, she ran the conversation with Amahle through her head a few times before stopping on her last words. *I know I will be able to complete my mission.* Sam stopped momentarily as she pondered those particular words before uttering "Huh."

What did that mean?

3.4

NASA's Kennedy Space Center. Roscosmos's RKA Mission Control. CNSA's Jiuquan Satellite Launch Center.

Khulu Global's Overberg Space Center.

Muzikayise couldn't help but crack a smile as he stood on the roof of his global center for space exploration and research. The wind, coming in harder than expected from the coast, whipped around him as not one, but two launches were scheduled for today just three miles further inland from where he stood. The other three major launch sites had a combined seven launches also scheduled for today, two of which already were en route for Aldrin Station, a new space station that would support the first permanent human population in space. Still under construction, Aldrin already had a central docking node that could support four space shuttles at once, a cylindrical supply docking node that supported up to ten supply capsules, a network of solar arrays, crew capsules for the on-site construction astronauts, and a partially completed Nautilus Ring, one of two fifty meter diameter cylindrical rings. Once the first phase of construction was completed in 2020, Aldrin Station would be able to support one hundred people, with the two Nautilus Rings simulating a full g within them for its future inhabitants.

The *New Leopard VIIs* sat on their launch pads already, their payloads of prefabricated sections for the Nautilus Centrifuge

Addition—NCA—ready for installation once they reached Aldrin Station. The latest version of the *New Leopard* renewable rockets were the ones being manufactured and utilized by all the western space agencies. It was the major eastern agencies, most notably Roscosmos and the China National Space Administration, that reneged on their contractual agreement with Khulu Global regarding their use of the *New Leopards,* instead opting to stick with their older expendable launch systems. A minor blotch on an otherwise solid stream of revenue for his corporation.

He heard the buzz that accompanied the metal door opening behind him. Only one person knew where he was at this time, and only one person was allowed through his security detail posted by the stairwell that led to the roof.

"Here's your latest economic reports, sir," Ami said as she walked towards him, her heels clacking with each step on the concrete roof. He turned around, waiting for her to close the gap between them. Despite her professional attire, he soaked in her figure, one that was accentuated by her form-fitting business suit that wasn't affected by the wind. Even her hair, done as a twisted pompadour and bun, stayed put in defiance of nature.

Ami tended to walk well into his personal space when it was just the two of them, especially when there were no security cameras or staff present—today was no different as she stopped just inches from his body before handing him a newspaper that had a few printed pages attached. She bit her lip and gave a dampened smile as he scooped the papers from her.

"What's this?" He removed the three white pages from the newspaper and looked at them.

"The latest confidential reports we managed to snag from the White House," Ami said. "I thought you'd want to read over the latest from—"

"From that leaky treasure trove of information?" Muzikayise interrupted her with his rhetorical question.

She sighed as her eyes lowered. "It's not too hard to obtain what you want from there as of late."

"But there's always something behind the scenes that is worth buying," he said as he reviewed the first printed page, tucking the newspaper under his arm as he read. He released a breath of air as the rumors of China demolishing large portions of Ordos City in Inner Mongolia for its 'wasted raw materials' were true, with most of the reclaimed building materials being repurposed for a large space-related skunkworks project. A large satellite image of cranes, bulldozers, and flatbed trucks collecting salvaged steel from what was a row of ten skyscrapers was a sight to behold, all of which were being taken to two massive warehouses that were almost a mile long. The other two pages had summarized financial report data, with the focus on planned tax allocation for the 2019 fiscal year for the United States, data he didn't think he'd ever get to see—it was clear there were people inside the White House that didn't care about their jobs anymore.

"Our informant shared over the phone that there may be a strong possibility of the Trump administration looking to find a way out of its commitments to the Armstrong Program."

"To reclaim the billions that haven't yet been spent, no doubt," Muzikayise spat. He faced the two rockets in the distance and threw a free hand forward. "This is our future—going into space and stopping the Leviathan. I don't understand how any nation could look inward at a time like this."

"And not spend their taxpayer dollars on Khulu Global equipment and properties?" Ami said, leaning her head back as she feigned a swoon. "Oh Lord have mercy."

He crossed his arms again, not turning back to her. "That possibility notwithstanding, there won't be a United States if the Leviathan has its way."

Ami took a seat on the wide ledge that ran along the outside the Operations building roof and looked at him, crossing her legs as she got comfortable. "Speaking of the future, did you review that report I sent you a few days ago about the political situation in the US?"

"I skimmed over it," he lied as he faced Ami once more—it sat on his ignored 'to-do' pile back in San Francisco. He'd read enough about the political situation there that he already came to his own, succinct conclusion: The country was going down the shitter and was trying to take a good portion of the world with it.

Ami placed her hands behind her and leaned back, allowing the midday sun to highlight her upper body, which did not go unnoticed. "Well, you would have seen the section that highlighted the top contenders for the 2020 election and their planned interviews and meetings through next April."

He raised his eyebrows as he scanned the roof for a proper place to sit—other than the row of solar panels and the wide ledge that Ami sat, there was nowhere to place himself. He continued standing as Ami smiled at his self-created predicament. "I always thought this bland outdoor space could use a woman's touch—give me a contractor and I can make this area more appropriate to your appetites."

"Spare me," he responded, fanning out his fingers dismissively from under his arm.

Ami slid off the ledge and back on her heeled feet as an announcement came through over the PA system, the voice of the launch manager bouncing off the nearby buildings, creating a dramatic echo effect. The first scheduled launch received the go-ahead and would commence in T-minus thirty minutes. Muzikayise appreciated that, from their vantage point, he could witness the launch of the *New Leopard VII.* Despite the rocket being two miles away, he could already see gas, in the form of white clouds that dissipated just seconds after they formed, being vented from its sides. However, his mind focused on matters of politics, recalling his knowledge of how super PACs operated and where corporations and wealthy individuals came into the picture of campaign donations.

He snapped out of his formulations when he felt Ami's hand on one of his, breaking his firm grip on himself, and pulled it toward her. He looked forward and saw Ami standing in front of him, her heels almost bringing her at eye level. For a moment, she balanced herself on the front of her heels as she gave Muzikayise a kiss, her tongue flicked across his lips as she pulled away.

"Hey," she said as a seductive smile crept across her face. "I'll reprint my report for you—it will have everything you are almost certainly thinking about and more."

"Thank you," he said with little emotion as he turned back to the pending launch. He rubbed his lips together once he was no longer facing her. She always tasted good. "Print it out and leave it on my desk —I will read it today." His tone told her she was dismissed.

"Yes, sir," she said with a bowed head, her voice almost lost to the wind.

"I will see you in thirty-five minutes," Muzikayise added, his tone still the same, but with a very different meaning.

If he looked at her, he would've seen her lick her lips. "Yes, sir."

∘ ◎ ∘

The second, and final, launch from OSC, like all the launches before it, was livestreamed, complete with a detail-oriented presenter that explained everything. A sleek UI that bordered the video feed provided summarized details of the current and upcoming stage of the *New Leopard* rocket launch.

Muzikayise watched the livestream on two widescreen monitors on the wall opposite the Murphy bed he sat on. His working space for the Overberg location was more compact than he was used to, with an L-shaped mahogany desk tucked in one corner, complete with a widescreen monitor and cordless keyboard and mouse, and a plush couch in the other. The walls had sleek, rectangular panels which had small gaps between them, making it possible to conceal a Murphy bed behind one of the panels near the middle of the room. The only cue one would have had regarding the existence of the bed were the two sixty-inch flatscreen TVs that faced an otherwise empty wall. Most of the time, these monitors displayed works of African art, cycled in two minute intervals. Today, the first TV displayed the livestream, while the second displayed live metrics related to the feed, which he preferred since it showcased to him how well the stream performed. The number of concurrent viewers climbed just above three million.

He pressed his bare feet into the wood floor as he grunted. "Given the contents of our rockets, I was hoping for at least five million live viewers," he commented.

"I'll have to talk to the marketing team for OSC and get them to provide more focus on the Aldrin Station—for context."

"I'll be sure to line up some meeting options for you," Ami said behind him, the silk sheets sliding off her naked body as she scooted herself up against the headboard.

"Good." He turned away from the TVs as he reached for his boxer briefs which laid on the floor, atop Ami's bra. Seeing the lace balconcette bra triggered a flash of what transpired between them an hour earlier. Like the other times, it was hot, sweaty, and fun—but it was also a great reliever of stress.

As he got himself dressed, he heard Ami's audible groan as she rolled onto her chest, her eyes taking him in one body part at a time. He held a knowing grin as he kept an eye on her as well. "Is there something on your mind?" he wondered.

"Ohhh, I dunno," Ami responded as her eyes dropped to the sheets that collected in the hands in front of her. "If I may be so bold, I was thinking about this."

"Mmmmmm," was his response, along with turning toward his desk as he began buttoning his shirt.

"You know, about *this*. About us."

Muzikayise clenched his jaw at that though he didn't stop his methodical process of clothing himself. "There is no 'us,'" he said.

"I know," she conceded, her voice soft and more vulnerable than usual. "But I think that can change."

"Such a thing cannot be allowed," he said with his eyes closed. "It wouldn't be right."

"What is wrong with being in a relationship?" She sat up, the rustling of her movement watched from the corner of Muzikayise's eye. Her beauty, her sex, even the way she nonchalantly sat on the bed, the sheets just covering her midsection while her breasts stood proud—to him, she was a true vision of an African Venus.

Once he finished tucking his shirt into his pants, he turned back to Ami and walked back to her. She got off the bed, the sheets that covered her falling to the side. Her lips parted as their eyes locked with each other. He placed his hands on her shoulders and brought them down her arms.

"What we have—this discreet, private relationship—is as far as it can go. I cannot allow us to proceed any further."

"What about—"

"No further, Ami." He sighed. "You, of all people, should know who I really am."

Ami shook out of his arms and grabbed her bra and panties. She didn't stop looking at him, allowing him to see the hint of flush in her face. "So are we just going to be fuck-buddies until the end of the world?"

"You may call it what you want," he said as he walked to his desk, but stopped after a few steps. The sunlight that seeped between the closed automated roller shades made his silhouette appear to have a halo around it. His breathing was collected and relaxed as he watched her get back into her business suit. "The world is not going to end."

"Can you really continue to lead your life as if the Earth will be here after 2024?" Ami asked, her eyes hardened.

"We have to, Ami," he said after taking a deep breath. This was more personal drama than he expected out of her. "You know that we are above the fray—above all those that look to us for a future. I am held to a higher standard and therefore must behave, both publicly and privately, as if I am more than the sum of my parts. The world is more fragile than it's ever been—because of this, it needs people that can be more than human. The world needs visionaries, dreamers, men that are beyond the curve." He offered a hand to her. "There isn't room to explore us, but I do need you by my side."

Once she had her shirt on, still unbuttoned as it draped over her fitted pants, Ami restrained herself as she spoke to Muzikayise, not letting up. "You know, I never thought I would like you. Yes, I flirted with you and certainly have made advances in the past, but that was because I knew ahead of time that you liked that sort of thing, and I enjoyed doing it. But whether or not you realize it, you've divulged a great deal about yourself to me over the years—your past before Khulu Global, your family, and how messed up your relationship is between you and your brothers. How you barely kept your family together after your mother and father died. How much baggage you really carry with your family name and how that actually hurts inside you, whether you admit it or not. You may think you're above everyone you interact with, but you know as well as I do just how human you really are."

Muzikayise dropped his hand and turned toward his desk, the printed political report in the middle of his desk grabbing his attention, neatly stacked and stapled, ready for him to read. Other thoughts tried to cloud his mind and his vision, however—thoughts of his estranged family, and even of Ami's mother, alone in Nigeria, who received funds each time Ami was paid. His thoughts remained on Ami, the person who, in some ways, knew him better than anyone in his own family; a professional that was not only intelligent but recognized how a business the size of Khulu Global would best be handled. Maybe it was that she's been attached to him for years, just by virtue of it being her job, but he knew there was more. He shook his head as he looked back at Ami, who remained by the bed. She had a pained expression as she closed her white shirt one button at a time. For a brief moment as their eyes reconnected, seeing her furrowed brow, her stance, and seeing each breath she took raise and lower her chest—he realized how much she genuinely cared. He realized that she wanted more than just sex. He rubbed his chin as a question floated to the top of his mind: Was that what he wanted as well?

His mind snapped back to reality when he saw his phone vibrate by the cordless keyboard. He recognized the number as one from Cape Times, a South African newspaper. It was tiny compared to the likes of the New York Times, but most of the locals read it, which was enough of a reason to give them attention. A call with them always helped maintain the near-universal support that Khulu Global and its local operations had. And it was time for his interview with one of their journalists.

"We can talk about this later," he said as he took the phone and an earpiece out of the desk. Ami closed her eyes and threw her head forward as he placed the earpiece into his ear. She knew what time it was and of the interview—she was the one that scheduled it.

"Will we?" she asked, already knowing she wouldn't receive an answer. As he started his call with the journalist, she picked up her heels with her fingers and walked to the door. His eyes followed her as she left the office with nary a sound.

And though his mouth responded to the words his ears heard from the phone, Ami's words reverberated within him.

Yes, he thought, answering her question. *We definitely will.*

∘ ◎ ∘

Having dinner within his own office wasn't something he would do with most people that worked at Khulu Global, let alone someone that held a director-level position. There were various rules to professional courtship that dictated where and how he would treat an individual or a group to a meal. However, he learned enough about Jennifer to know an exception could be made for her—she would appreciate not being taken away from her scientific base of operations, he thought. Plus, the expansive windows provided a clear view of the next volley of rockets that would launch through the night and into the next day. Four of them rolled at a snail's pace to their respective launch pads, their guide lights making it impossible to miss from a distance.

She sat across from him, her back toward the window, as the chef he brought in for the occasion rolled the metal food cart into the office. With a smile, he explained each dish with a pleasant British accent as he set them onto their table, preselected for them to reflect the local cuisine. A glass of red wine was poured for each of them, the bottle presented to them so they could read the label before it was placed in a metal bucket. Once Muzikayise dismissed the chef with a nod, he looked at Jennifer and gestured to dig in.

"I must thank you again for this," she said as she cut a slice of curry chicken. Her eyes closed as she chewed on her first bite, the flavor igniting her taste buds. "This is very good, Muzie."

"I'm glad you like it," he said as he started to cut the chicken in front of him into precise slices, releasing the heat trapped within. "I hope you don't mind the setting for our dinner meeting—I'd rather treat you to one of the restaurants in Cape Town instead, but I know you prefer to stay close to the action here at Overberg."

"Thanks for taking my needs into account," Jennifer said

in-between bites. "It's been very busy downstairs."

"Believe me, you haven't gone unnoticed," he acknowledged.

"Mmmm-hmmm," she got out as she focused more on the exquisite food than on her boss. He nodded before also focusing on what was in front of him, the aroma finally getting the appreciation it deserved.

"Is this something you do with all of your directors?" she asked.

"Not all of them," he responded flatly as he took a sip of his wine. "Only those that I see playing a significant role in my organization. I would like to learn more about you. And in turn, you can ask anything about me."

Jennifer eyed him. "Aren't you the kind of person that collects everything there is to know about an individual? I feel like there isn't anything I could share that you haven't already read." She took more mouthfuls of the food in front of her. He decided to let her enjoy what was in front of her and stayed silent as he stabbed his first forkful of chicken.

"Everyone has a story to tell, and not everyone gets to share theirs," he said.

"How about you give me a story of yours," Jennifer responded, her eyes holding firm onto his. "Beyond what could be found in news articles and your Wiki page, you are an enigma."

Muzikayise cracked a smile. "I figured you did some research of your own. Hopefully nothing too biased."

"I always do my due diligence when my boss happens to be one of the people responsible for everything happening in space today," Jennifer said. She sipped her wine. "And yes, some of what I read was biased, but perhaps that's where you can fill in the gaps."

"So you would like to ask something of me?" he asked as he focused more on the plate in front of him than Jennifer.

"Actually, yes," she said. "Tell me about your family."

Muzikayise brought his utensils back to his plate and set them down. He had a feeling this would be a possible question that would come up, but given how private he'd been regarding his family—and the amount of effort he put towards scrubbing the internet of articles that detailed his past beyond business dealings—he figured nobody would be so bold but as to ask him about it.

Right down to business, he thought. *She doesn't play around.*

He sat back into his chair and sighed as he looked straight at Jennifer, his brows furrowed. "What would you like to know?"

She didn't smile, but she had noticed his unspoken disapproval of the question. She pressed onward. "Tell me about the man that would become the CEO of Khulu Global and where all of this began. There's surprisingly little information available online about your parents or your siblings. I feel that by understanding your personal background, that will make it easier for us to be better aligned with the larger goals we both share."

He downed more wine before he took a deep breath. He could fabricate details, but never found lying to be useful when discussing his personal life was concerned—it was better to just not talk about it. "You already know what is public knowledge today: That I came from a family that owned several large diamond mines throughout Africa, that I am the oldest of four brothers, and that in 1989, six months after my father died I sold off our entire collection of mines to De Beers for over three hundred million American dollars."

Jennifer nodded, signaling him to continue. "My younger brothers wanted to keep the family in the mining business. It wasn't hard to understand why: It was lucrative and all trends indicated, even in a post-Apartheid world, that Khulu Diamonds—KD Corp—was in a strong position for continued growth, not to mention influence in the diamond trade. However, I had a vision for a future where the Khulu name wouldn't be associated with what was eventually called the blood diamond trade. I looked into the heavens at a young age and knew that was where I wanted to be—not in any religious sense, but the literal—I wanted to visit the stars." His eyes veered toward the ceiling as memories of what he saw when he looked into the night sky at a much younger age replaced what was around him. "To not only follow the footsteps of those that already landed on the moon, but to surpass them." When he arched his head downward back to Jennifer the lighting in the room, combined with the downward angle of his head, made his eyes appear darker than they were. "But the realities of the world were cruel. Despite the long straw that I drew as an individual, I still was not in a place to pursue such endeavors.

Too embedded in my family business. Too rich to supposedly care. Too black."

Jennifer glanced downward at his final statement though she raised herself back up. He continued. "When my father died, I made a decision that would, in a way, redefine my entire relationship with my family—in exchange for a shot at going into space. Unfortunately for my brothers, I was far more adept in running the family business than they cared to admit. I happened to also spend time combing over the fine details of the will our father left behind, which had many details concerning the fate of the company he grew from nothing. When I realized I would become the president of Khulu Diamonds, I shored up all loose ends that existed contractually between the company and my brothers—all behind their backs, of course, as they would've never agreed to ever shutter the bread and butter of the Khulu family."

"So you cut them out of any proceedings concerning the dissolution of KD Corp?" Jennifer asked.

He grinned as he leaned forward. "Precisely—I am impressed, Jennifer! Yes, I made sure they couldn't argue against my final decision of selling all of our mines to the highest bidder, a process that took much less time than I anticipated, but the results allowed me to sign the paperwork that would dissolve what I considered the first Khulu company to exist. From the ashes of the old came the new Khulu Regional, a business focused on technology initiatives for South Africa and expanding into space development, both for the nation and, well, for me."

"I can't imagine your family members taking your decisions sitting down."

"No... they did not. They took me to court, in fact, for trying to steal what they all considered to be rightfully theirs. Unfortunately, they didn't read the fine print of their father's will, nor did they read the revised contracts they signed after I became president of KD Corp. In the end, their lawsuit was dismissed." Muzikayise paused to consume more of the food in front of him, some of which lost the steam that emanated from them. "I took good care of them, of course—they are still family—but ever since the founding of Khulu Regional, they never forgave me, claiming I was too short-sighted, greedy, and selfish."

He chuckled. "Pity they refuse to realize that my long-term vision has resulted in more profits than were ever made during the years of KD Corp—and by serving the interests of mankind, at that."

Jennifer didn't respond though she nodded in understanding before engrossing herself with the remaining food and drink in front of her. They ate in relative silence after that though to him it didn't feel awkward at all. Occasional announcements bled through the window concerning the planned launches, breaking the silence that otherwise filled the room. Jennifer didn't seem to mind, either, though he could see her mind working hard behind her eyes that weren't always focused on what was in front of them.

He chuckled when he noticed her plate being all but cleared of food after just ten minutes. "You really want to get back into the fray, huh?"

"Actually, I want to get home," Jennifer said as she brought the white cloth napkin in front of her to her mouth. "Movie night with Sam."

Muzikayise released another chuckle though he now kept his eyes on Jennifer's. "On a weeknight?"

She put down the napkin and looked back at him with equal scrutiny. "When you work through weekends, we take any available free time together as it comes. You, of all people, would understand that."

"Of course."

"If I were a robot, I'd likely stay here 24/7, but I and all those below me won't get any productive work accomplished without some amount of downtime, regardless of what's happening stateside or on the Leviathan." She sat back into her chair as her voice hardened.

"I'm not here to question your leadership capabilities," Muzikayise reassured her. He knew how loyal those at OSC quickly became towards her once she took over. "In many ways, you and I are quite alike. However, this leads me to the question that I had for you."

Jennifer raised her brow. "What might that be?"

Muzikayise relaxed his posture as he leaned forward. "I know that you and Doctor Monroe are in a relationship—that much was disclosed as part of my hiring the two of you."

"Okay..."

"And though the work the two of you have contributed in the month you've been here is exceptional, I just wanted to make sure your commitment to the mission—and your ability to make uncompromising decisions—are not impaired because of—"

"Wait wait wait, are you seriously asking about this?" Jennifer narrowed her eyes at him while she pressed her lips into a thin, straight line.

"Given your position and influence, I just want to make sure you are performing at your peak," he said over his wine glass.

"My relationship with Sam has no bearing on the decisions I make," she stated.

"What about confidential details that you are made privy to that Doctor Monroe is not meant to know?"

"Like what?"

Muzikayise took another sip of his wine. "Like the decision to not allow the AI on the Leviathan to upgrade the *Hermes* rover."

"What?" she shouted, pushing herself away from the table as she shook her head.

"It will be announced in a week—the delay agreed upon by all nations involved," he said with some unhidden scorn. "That would be enough time to determine exactly what we can do as an alternative and present that to the public."

"An alternative," Jennifer said, her voice still heightened. "This was our only way to learn more about the Leviathan outside of just sending probes and rovers to its surface, and that won't do us any good in a couple of years."

"I agree completely, but public perception was split down the middle across the globe—too many movies depicting rogue AI's trying to kill humanity clouding their thoughts on the matter." He felt the heat in his face as his posture stiffened. "And with the United States government being against the AI's proposal outright, the final nail in the coffin was laid."

Jennifer turned her attention back to Muzikayise. "Were you not going to tell anyone about this until the public announcement?"

"That's what I was told to do."

"Yet you told me tonight."

"Yes, I did."

The two of them locked their eyes together, two alphas sizing each other up. He knew she didn't like him, but viewed her as someone that had more in common with him than she would admit. He used his knowledge of the state of SETI to win her over, and she took very little time leveraging everything she had at her disposal once she was under his banner. However, her true loyalty didn't lie with him—it never would, he realized.

"Everything I do, regardless of who I work for, is for the interests of science and the evolution of our perceptions of the universe," she said. "The last thing I need is you not understanding why I accepted your offer. Despite our differences, we both want to see the world survive another day."

His posture was stiff, unwilling to react to her words. It was rare for him to be spoken to in such a direct way. He allowed his eyes to scan her face as one corner of his lip upturned. "I appreciate how direct you're being with me. Is that a trait you've adopted from your time with Doctor Monroe?"

Jennifer flashed a cold smile while keeping her eyes on his. She stood up and slid her arms into the jacket that was draped behind her chair. "Thank you for the dinner."

She does not play around at all. He stood up in response, watching as she marched for the door. "I trust that you will not share this news with your subordinate," he said, which made her stop in her tracks. He couldn't see her face, but watched her shoulders rise and fall as she reached for the doorknob and exited his office.

He crossed his arms as the office door closed itself and grunted. *She will do the right thing,* he thought as he walked to the window and looked up toward the night sky. A faint white glow shimmered where Uranus should be—a spot in the sky he memorized over a year ago. He went to his desk and called Ami. "Okay, we're finished. Prepare our helicopter to the Cape Town office."

"This isn't a planned flight," she protested.

"I trust you can change that," he said. As he waited for Ami's return call, he peered downward and caught Jennifer as she walked toward the parking lot outside. "I don't have to be here for tomorrow."

○ ◎ ○

If she could have gotten away with it, Jennifer would have slugged Muzie—multiple times. As she drove home, she replayed the dinner —parts of it at least, since the enjoyment she received from the food was overshadowed by the purpose of the dinner. Given the amount of respect she'd received from Muzie since her first day on the job, the pointed questions he asked her were surprising.

Her fingers dug into the leather wrapping around the steering wheel as she groaned. Where the hell was he coming from, asking about her professionalism and whether she could be trusted because of Sam being her partner? He knew about them—it had to be disclosed due to the nepotism policy his corporation had on the books, a policy he forced HR to ignore for her and Sam's benefit. Did he see something that she didn't?

And then dropping the bomb concerning the fate of the *Hermes* and the AI at the same time? She couldn't help it: Thoughts of what the political future meant if it were true seemed morbid. Despite the scientific community being mostly united in the singular goal of answering the Leviathan Question, said community weren't the ones at the top controlling the pocketbooks and, more importantly, having the final say on wide-reaching decisions. The first two years post-Leviathan were productive on a global scale that'd never been seen before. Nations that were once political and cultural adversaries put aside their differences. They not only combined their resources but pushed a combined three hundred billion dollars towards scientific initiatives—and with the support of the public with each announcement made.

But it didn't take long before the naysayers, the budget hawks, the religious fanatics—anyone that refused to support the greater scientific community and the governments behind them for one reason or another—started to turn the tide of support. Combine that with the very human tendency to forget about a major crisis if it's not in their backyard *today* and you have what you saw today: China breaking away from the global community to pursue their own space agenda, most of the EU and Asian space agencies having less than fifty percent of the people's support, and more divisive arguments within their governments—especially in the United States—which had slowed almost everything related to the Leviathan down.

Jennifer groaned again and cursed when the grim realization dawned upon her that if it weren't for the Armstrong Program and the corporations associated with it, all of which agreed to continue funding it despite the drop of support, the *Hermes* would never have landed on the Leviathan to begin with. Furthermore, if it weren't for Muzie's unmoving passion for finding an answer to the Leviathan Question, she would still be at the SETI Institute.

As she turned the corner and approached her house, the heated thoughts around Muzie's words were replaced with what she could do with the information he deliberately shared. She knew the direction the governments of the world—weary from years of spending billions on projects that didn't have immediate returns to the people—were going. When it came down to the AI decision, she still was the one at the wheel.

Jennifer grimaced as her mind processed what she thought. *Oh god, now I'm sounding like Muzie.*

3.5

Water—one of the most important substances for life as we know it. On Earth, it is just about everywhere, whether you see it or not. From the obvious streams, oceans, and bottled water you can buy in supermarkets to water vapor in the air, the clouds that condense overhead, and most organisms you encounter, the substance is ever-present. The average human body comprises fifty to sixty-five percent water. The critical nature of water in our lives is bolstered by the fact that Earth, as a percentage of its total mass, actually has very little water for us to consume and pollute: Only five-hundredths of a percent of the Earth's mass is water. However, the rarity of water and water-ice changes once you leave the confines of our home planet.

Sam thought about all of this as she propped her head in her palm. She observed the clear water that sat, inert, in a glass cup in front of her. Coming from the tap in the door of their refrigerator, there were few contaminants in the fluid, making it appear almost transparent, though a handful of small bubbles stuck to the bottom of the glass. The morning sun, unobstructed by clouds, bathed their cozy kitchen with natural light, removing the need to have any artificial lights turned on. The sound of sizzling eggs, prepared by Jennifer, was complimented with the welcoming aroma that would've made Sam realize she was hungry if she weren't so fixated on her thoughts.

"You know, Jen, maybe the Leviathan needs water as badly as we do."

"Maybe," Jennifer said as she turned off the stove and pushed the scrambled eggs out of the pan and onto two plates.

"What did Neptune and Uranus have in common? The two gas giants contained high concentrations of water within their mantles, well over ten Earth masses worth each, with atmospheres that were primarily hydrogen and helium." Sam sat up and grabbed the glass in front of her. "It's almost impossible to comprehend just how much water that is, and that's just the water we couldn't access if we had the minimum technology needed to reach those planets. There were still the rings around those planets that contained more than enough water to sustain our civilization for thousands of years."

Jennifer slid a plate in front of Sam—eggs and potato hash—before taking a seat next to her with her own plate. She looked at her as though she was disinterested in conversation. "What are you talking about?"

"I'm talking about antimatter production," Sam said. "I'm talking about motive." Jennifer averted her eyes, a motion that made Sam sigh. "Are you even listening to me right now?"

"I'm sorry, Sam. I've had a lot on my mind lately."

"Since last night," Sam called her out. "You've been acting odd since your dinner with Muzie. You even bailed on our movie night! What happened, Jen? Why won't you tell me?"

Jennifer already had a mouthful of eggs, but placed her utensils down and turned towards Sam after she swallowed. "I just need to think about today. There's a lot going on right now and I need to get my thoughts together."

Sam's eyes glanced downward towards the table, then back to Jennifer. "It's about *Hermes*, isn't it?"

"No questions," Jennifer snapped. Sam flinched back as she frowned. "I'm sorry, Sam," she said with a lowered voice. "I'll tell you everything later today."

"...Okay," Sam said after she looked into Jennifer's eyes, trying to figure out what was going on.

It wasn't like her to clam up like this. Given what Sam knew about Muzikayise, based on all the available articles she breezed through over the years, and how well she knew Jennifer, she assumed that they may have had a sort of pissing match that didn't go as Jennifer planned. He probably said something inappropriate or even went a step further than that. Sam dismissed extrapolating what would've been worse than a verbal faux pas.

Nevertheless, Sam felt it would be best to leave Jennifer alone, which meant keeping to herself as well. She went back to finishing the breakfast in front of her, the experience tainted by the unexpected isolation she felt. "We'll talk later."

The rest of their breakfast was held in an uncomfortable silence, something that carried over to their shared drive to OSC Operations. Resting in the passenger seat of their jeep as Jennifer was behind the wheel, Sam watched the hilly, but tamed, terrain whiz by along both sides of the highway. She used the serene nature of the land to get her mind away from what happened in the kitchen, a moment that still left an itch she wanted to scratch—a feeling which left her stiff if she let it persist. Her eyes focused on the old houses that dotted the landscape, the aged power lines that connected them all together, the slim rivers that had dense greenery clustered by their shores. Her mind, in turn, combined those visuals with the people that lived in this rustic environment outside of the cloistered, modernized village she called home. What did they think about the Leviathan and the world's efforts to deal with the Leviathan Question?

Sam saw a farmer twenty minutes into their drive, tending sugarcane crops that rubbed against the highway, separated only by mesh fencing held up with wooden posts. Several other people were along the same row of crops, but he was closest to the highway. The man's attention was split between picking through the sugarcane plant in front of him and watching the few vehicles that passed, the sweat that collected on his forehead glistening in the sun. Their eyes met for a few seconds before he and his farm became just another feature in the rolling backdrop of terrain, but for the moment they connected, she wondered what he was thinking. Did he have a family to worry about? Was time spent thinking about the future and what that may look like for him? Did he worry about the Leviathan at all? Knowing that the world continued to operate with little unexpected chaos, that people like the farmer continued to tend their crops under the morning sun without missing a beat... she just didn't know.

Sam rolled her head to the right at Jennifer, who had a tight grip on the steering wheel, her body tense. Though she wanted to say something, Sam reached over and wrapped one of her hands over Jennifer's. When Jennifer looked over and saw her half-smile, her shoulders dropped as she relaxed somewhat, flashing a smile back as she released a puff of air. She kept her hand over Jennifer's for a minute before bringing it back towards her lap. No words were exchanged, but as she turned away to look outside she exhaled and held a smile on her face for the rest of the drive.

The cameras from *Hermes* were unchanged. The spherical satellite was still obscuring what the rover could see and the rover's controls remained frozen, preventing Sam from adjusting the camera's view angle. If she and her team didn't know better, they would think that what they were seeing was a paused video or a snapshot. One thing was certain: The AI was very patient.

She panned her eyes around OpsOne as she took a mental head count of everyone present—it was a full house, almost. She noticed that Amahle wasn't at her station though HR confirmed that she called out sick. With no new data coming from *Hermes* other than the video feed and the active connection between the AI and their terminals via *Hermes,* most of the officers and engineers refocused their efforts on the data generated by the *Victoria* which was still going strong as it continued on its Leviacentric orbit.

Mckale marched from station to station, checking with each post in person rather than using the summarized indicators at his desk. Sam made a point to track his behaviors, as many of his actions had consistently proven to improve overall productivity on the floor.

"The AI hasn't infiltrated the Victoria, that's correct?" Mckale asked Javin Hasani, the Data Processing Systems Engineer for the Victoria mission. He also had the largest beard in the room, which made comparisons to Santa not uncommon, despite the hairs being dark-brown instead of white.

"That's affirmative," he said with a nod. "Looks like it only cared about the *Hermes,* though it was technically possible to access the Victoria."

"Not anymore," Chiku Sesay, the *Victoria* navigations officer, shared. "I've already sent kill commands to the wireless network connection the *Victoria* had with *Hermes.* The only way the AI will interface with our probe will be if it physically intercepts it."

"Or uses the *Hermes* to hack into the *Victoria,*" Javin said with a half-hearted shrug.

"Barring some Zero Cool hacking skills, let's not think about what the AI could do and focus on the data pouring in from *Victoria,*" stated Sam.

Javin laughed. "Did you just mention Zero Cool from that old *Hackers* movie?"

Sam shot a knowing look at the engineer and grinned. "Hey, what the AI has done so far is on the level of the impossible stuff done in that movie—I think it applies!"

Some chuckles from the group of engineers arose from that corner of OpsOne—a group that got the reference, with other onlookers glancing at them and then at Sam, rubbing their chins in thought. Was the movie really that old?

She patted Mckale on the shoulder before taking a step in front of him. "Let's switch all big-screen visuals to the *Victoria.*"

"You got it," Mckale complied as he repeated the order from Sam. Within a minute, the unchanging view of the alien satellite updated with a live view of the Leviathan eight hundred thousand kilometers over it while chemical composition scans, spectrometer readings, and auto-saved biosignature advisories populated in a cascade of windows next to it. A lot of what the *Victoria* had scanned and relayed back to Earth was already being pored over by scientists around the world, but what they were looking at was data that was just a few hours old and not yet disseminated for study.

Sam took a deep breath and dropped her shoulders as she exhaled in response to the images. Though the *Victoria* was already ten thousand kilometers from Destination Zero, it still found copious evidence of artificial construction on the Leviathan's surface, the most elaborate being what appeared to be a giant geodesic glass structure that was fourteen kilometers in diameter and six kilometers tall at its center. A quarter of the dome was destroyed by a meteor impact, the crater of which had debris from the dome within.

"Look at the readings there," Sam said as she gestured to the regolith volume and density values. "Given the thickness of the regolith within and around the impact site, coupled with the visible lines on the walls of the crater, it's possible that impact occurred over six thousand years ago."

"A structure as large as a city and taller than anything we've ever constructed, and it's almost as old as all of human civilization," Javin said, dumbfounded.

"We're gonna need more rovers," an engineer said as he stared at the image, his eyes soaking in every pixel as if it were a work of art.

"What about the biosignature readings?" Mckale asked Sam. "The *Victoria* received three hits via *Hermes* and generated two of its own areas where organic molecules were detected when we had control over the rover."

"Yes..." Sam said as she ran to her large desk, separate from the rows of shared workspace where everyone else sat. She recalled the various indicators of the criteria for verifiable biosignature indicators as she brought the data onto her screen.

"Did you want me to give the data a pass?" one of the senior scientists said as he walked cautiously to her.

"I got this," Sam was quick to respond without looking away from her three monitors. Yes, she could assign others to review this data, but she just couldn't remove herself from the weeds. How could she? Multiple biosignature readings, two of which were beyond The Three Spheres, which appeared to be distinct and not at all related to each other. She didn't care how it looked—she *had* to analyze this data first-hand.

It became clear that three of the biosignature readings originated from within the center sphere of The Three Spheres—carbon dioxide and strong, artificial magnetic readings that originated from the other two spheres. The fourth reading came from what looked like a rectangular greenhouse, part of which was buried into the wall of a crater. The high-resolution image of that section revealed evidence of a rockslide or cave-in, with multiple fractures in the terrain around the collapsed section of the greenhouse. Explosive decompression was the likely culprit, followed by a seismic event related to the explosion.

"The reading was very faint, but it suggests methane outgassing from that opening by the rockslide," she reported to Mckale, who stood behind her for a short period before continuing his observation of everyone else.

The fifth reading was over a large area of compressed regolith. In the middle of the compressed terrain appeared to be a tall obelisk with a square base that was one hundred meters on each side. The entire obelisk had a solid blue-gray tint from top to bottom. Javin reviewed the final reading with her, leaning close to his monitor and stroked the screen as if he could touch the pictured structure.

"That appears to be as tall as the Empire State Building," he said as he mimed a circle around the area that surrounded the obelisk which appeared a bit off-color compared to the rest of the terrain. "Though we cannot get a detailed composition breakdown, I would bet that the obelisk is made of some sort of metal—possibly metallic osmium."

"That's a bit of a stretch, don't you think?" Sam asked. "You're basing that entirely on appearance?"

Javin shrugged. "All we have are assumptions, all of which are probably the best answers we'll have for now..." He poked at the image and looked at her. "The blue-gray sheen the obelisk appears to have suggests that it's not made of a rocky material. It could be dumortierite, but that silicate is not dense or strong enough to be used like this, especially in an environment with the gravity as strong as the Leviathan's. Osmium is the densest natural element that could theoretically be used in this manner, especially if you wanted to construct something that would withstand just about anything thrown at it." He shook his head. "Though we've never mined anywhere near as much osmium on Earth to create anything as large as that. But I know my minerals and metals, and I'm pretty sure that's osmium."

"If all of that is true, then I wonder where they got so much of it," Sam wondered without turning around.

Another shrug from Javin. "Either way, it looks like the source of the reading came from that spot right there."

"But the readings are all over the place," Sam pointed out. "Trace amounts of sulfur, sodium, chlorine, oxygen. Why would all of this be in a single spot that looks..." She stopped herself as her eyes widened with the thought that crossed her mind. She turned to Javin, then back at her monitor, then back at him. "I think this may be a grave. A grave with one very large plot."

Javin came to the same, amazing conclusion. "What could be buried there that would still be outgassing?"

"No way to tell the age of the plot from these shots," Sam said as one of her legs bounced rapidly under the desk. The Leviathan continued to deliver surprises, from the areas that were claimed and built upon by civilizations unknown to be then reclaimed by time after their mysterious disappearance to the theories behind the structures and buildings. The biosignatures beyond Destination Zero threw new questions into the mix that could only be approached, at best, with a vehicle on the ground.

"It would be great if we could grab some samples of the metals used in these buildings and structures," Javin said. "I know we are in the experimental phases of applying carbon nanotubes within construction material, but whatever these structures are made of have to be well beyond that."

"But with the gravitational strength of the Leviathan, we could never land anything around these landmarks," Mckale reminded Javin and the other excited engineers that already clustered around tables that had tablets and reams of graph paper strewn about as they plotted the mechanical details for a new rover design. "We just don't have materials strong enough to survive outside Destination Zero."

"We can't just accept that, chief," one of the bearded engineers that sat in front of two tablets shouted in frustration. Sam didn't blame him—being told 'no' so many times regarding the ground exploration of the Leviathan, even in the face of what was perceived as insurmountable physical challenges, took a toll.

"Have you found a way to construct a rover that could withstand twenty-one g's?" Mckale asked as he eyed the engineer, his voice authoritative. "Or designed a descent craft that could generate enough thrust to counteract the force of twenty-one g's?" He walked to the front of OpsOne, getting everyone's attention and quieting the dissenting voices. Sam knew how he handled situations like this and let him proceed. In this case, Mckale taking a firm stance in front of the room meant he was about to get everyone to refocus on the core mission at hand. "Small steps, everyone. We aren't going to do anything more than analyze the data that *Victoria* and *Hermes* sends back to us, collaborate with other institutions on the findings, and maybe derive practical solutions from said findings. We aren't being paid to run hypothetical designs for vehicles we cannot hope to build, not without a massive breakthrough in construction technology."

"That is something we are going to get," Jennifer announced from the entryway to the floor of OpsOne. Several people whipped around when they heard her voice while Mckale pressed his lips together and pulled on the sides of his untucked shirt.

Sam rolled her chair back and stood up with arms crossed. Even she knew to not interrupt the Flight Director, lest you wanted to undermine his authority in front of his subordinates. This was also the first time she checked into OpsOne since they arrived, which bothered her for illogical reasons.

"What is that supposed to mean?" Mckale asked with a frown.

"It means that we're going to submit to the AI's request for giving the *Hermes* true AI. Today."

∘ ◎ ∘

"I cannot believe it," Mckale stated with a deep frown.

Sam didn't say anything, but mirrored Mckale's frustration with her arms tightening around each other by her chest, her lips pressed together into a thin line. Jennifer explained, with brevity, what Muzikayise shared with her—and to everyone in OpsOne, not even in a closed-door meeting. As her eyes panned the room, she saw that most of the staff were as surprised, either at the news itself or the fact it was Jennifer who publicly shared it when it hasn't been announced anywhere else.

"But is it so hard to believe?" Jennifer asked after she walked down the long steps to the front of OpsOne, passing a hand through her hair. "You know that I am not one to make impulsive decisions, and I haven't started now. I've been giving this a lot of thought, considering the options I had given my position, and what could happen if we said yes to the AI without explicit permission from the governments of the world." Sam noticed the amount of uncertainty that was on the faces of those in the room, but they listened with rapt attention, nodding slowly as she spoke.

Mckale was not sold. "What you are suggesting could place everyone in this room in a compromising position," he warned. "Not just being fired, but potentially being blacklisted from working at any research institutions that required any sort of adherence to confidentiality."

"The scientific benefits of moving forward with the AI, in my professional opinion, far outweigh the political consequences that would befall this institution," Jennifer said, her strong eye contact with Mckale showing that she was serious. "Look at the facts: The AI has given us everything it said it would so far, right down to ensuring the *Hermes* had a safe landing at Destination Zero when all of our metrics said that would be impossible. In addition, consider that even if *Hermes* is given true AI capabilities, it won't be able to transfer its consciousness or anything that would be considered a danger to us from itself—the bandwidth we have with it is just too slow for any high-density data transfer."

Jennifer glanced at Sam, then back at Mckale. She was calm and collected as she spoke. "It will take a little time to ensure we can pull this off, but we—humanity—have everything to gain from this decision. Just learning more about the Leviathan—perhaps reaching a conclusion to the Leviathan Question that will save us—will be worth the sacrifice."

Sam noticed everyone looking in their direction, along with the feeling of sweat building just under her hair. She resisted the urge to bite her lip as she ran through the implications of what Jennifer was proposing. She refocused on her and took a deep breath. "If we do what you ask, we won't have a lot of time before every other space agency on the globe learns about it—they're listening to the same signals from *Hermes* and *Victoria,* and will detect when we send out a response to the AI via *Hermes.* Even if they miss the transmission, the changes that the *Hermes* will undergo won't be missed by anyone." She took a step closer to Jennifer and lowered her voice. "We may become heroes to many people, and history could even recognize us as such in time, but the immediate backlash may actually be bad for us. Really bad."

"If time was on our side, I wouldn't even have considered this myself, but we need every second to count if we're to find a way to save humanity. To save Earth." Jennifer paused for a moment as she dropped her head, then looked directly at Sam. Despite her words, maybe she was having second thoughts? Sam's heart jumped into her mouth when Jennifer came close enough to Sam to take her hands. In front of everyone. *Oh God.* Now she was sweating. "To save us. I wouldn't have known you if the Leviathan hadn't appeared—I realized that is true. And all that we've experienced has been, in part, because of the Leviathan. I don't want to see this end because of the inaction of others. I am willing to own this decision—to make this sacrifice—for our future."

She felt the eyes of every soul in that room just hooked on the two of them, expecting something to happen. They would not get the satisfaction. Sam's face was beet red, her mind racing to figure out how best to respond to this, both to Jennifer and then to everyone else around them. After what felt like an eternity, she raised her eyes as she started to breathe again as a smile spread across her face.

"I've been working for space agencies, government wards, and in the private sector for the past thirty years, and this has to be some of the most unprofessional shit I've seen," Mckale stated aloud, cuing some chuckles. "But you know what? I'd rather follow the orders of someone that places the future of our species' survival over short-sighted plans made by people that don't understand a tenth of what we all do. Doctor Epstein, Sam: if you two are certain about this, then I am behind it one hundred percent."

Jennifer nodded toward Mckale, then turned to Sam. Her eyes weren't asking for anything, but were just waiting. Sam felt the electricity run between her hands and Jennifer's, almost as if they communicated with each other the way neurons fired signals at each other, the synapses unifying them through the various points where they touched. The smile Sam gave Jennifer was enough for her to know she was all-in, but she wanted to say something to verbally acknowledge it for all of OpsOne to hear. Something memorable. Something that, when repeated in classrooms decades from now, would instill a sense of wonder, amazement, and awe.

Sam released Jennifer's hands and craned her head high. "Let's go break a bunch of international laws and save the world. For science!"

3.6

They had at least two hours to get everything ready and everyone within OpsOne on the same page. Nothing could be left to chance.

Everyone, from Jennifer, Sam, and Mckale at the top to all the men and women that comprised the *Hermes* and *Victoria* missions within OpsOne, were confident in the decisions they'd made, but that confidence didn't completely negate the nervousness they felt.

Jennifer sat at Chiku's desk, as she was the one to send the response herself. The responsibility of making this decision and winning over OpsOne to support it fell on her already, but sending the signal itself she viewed as something that could hurt that individual as much as her commanding someone to send it. She looked at the two monitors in front of her: The command interface for the *Hermes* filling the entire screen of one while the other had a table of the space and government agencies listening to all channels associated with the *Hermes*. She glanced down to the black-and-gray keyboard to find her hands resting upon the keys. The urge to allow them to fidget was strong, but she stifled it. Her entire body was alert—her deep breathing meant to calm her quickened heart, a leg that refused sit still under the desk, an itch on the back of her neck she wanted to rub away.

But it was the touch of Sam's hand as it gripped her shoulder that helped her refocus on everything and everyone else. She turned her chair to see the eyes of the room resting on her, the silence being as loud as the largest heavy-lift launch vehicle.

Javin stroked his beard in contemplation as he stood over his desk. Chiku held a stiff pose as she watched. Mckale stood in the front of the room, his eyes scanning his crew, but also listened for the cue that a decision was acted upon that would determine the set of directives he would dish out in rapid succession. Jennifer looked at Sam, who gave a tight, but affirming, nod in response. She knew what was to come, but her eyes told Jennifer all she needed to know—that they were in this together, no matter what happened.

Jennifer turned back to the monitor and, with her index finger hovering over the 'Y' button, punched in the command that, when taken out of context, looked like the most unprofessional command one could type to a machine as complex as the *Hermes*. She—and everyone in the room—knew it shouldn't work. It wasn't even programmed to be a recognizable command of any kind. Her fingers felt heavy as they completed the three-letter word that the AI waited for.

When she finished typing, her ring finger sat over the 'Enter' key for what felt like an eternity. She could always just stop here—yank out the keyboard cord from the computer, press down the 'Backspace' key, or just throw her hands in the air as if they were just submerged in boiling water. Nobody would dare stop her, nor would anyone attempt to finish what she started. She never viewed herself as the hero many people made her out to be—she was just a scientist that wanted to understand, that wanted to learn. How history would view the next few seconds she didn't know, but this would be the difference between learning more about their inadvertent adversary and not existing within six years. Even if they learned what they needed to learn about the Leviathan in the next two or three years, she couldn't ignore the possibility of realizing such discoveries years earlier if presented the chance.

She didn't consider herself a hero, but knew this decision was greater than her, those around her, and those in power.

With "YES" staring back at her, she hit 'Enter'.

Jennifer dropped her shoulders and fell back into her chair as if a large weight fell off her back after it was confirmed that the message went through. "Sent," she announced. Nobody applauded or otherwise acted any different than they were a few minutes prior—they all just waited for the inevitable. That came in the form of some phones starting to ring on the desks of the communication technicians who, as instructed, told those concerned on the other line to relay their questions to their managers or superiors. Delay, delay, delay! Once Mckale's cell phone rang on his belt, accompanied by Sam's phone, they knew their actions were discovered.

"Twelve minutes post-send before some big-wigs decided to call?" Sam jested as she removed her phone from her pocket. "What are they being paid for?"

"To yell and scream, when it is called for," Jennifer responded as an unexpected smile crossed her face. Her phone lit up—the acting administrator for NASA's name appeared.

She looked at Mckale as they both exchanged nods, to which he allowed a smile to crack through his hardened stance. He then turned his attention on everyone around him. He knew the eyes of the world would be on him as much as the duo that discovered the Leviathan. His voice was authoritative and respected by all, his team following his words as he spoke. "Okay everyone, we have two hours before that signal reaches *Hermes,* and two more hours on top of that before we get a response. That's four hours total, so look alive and let's begin..."

When the affirming signal arrived at the *Hermes* two hours later, the AI was quick to respond by starting its agreed-upon process of installing true AI within the rover. It knew, however, that the technological requirements for housing such an entity within the provided hard drives and solid-state drives were insufficient. That was easy enough to rectify, however, as far as it was concerned.

The silver cord that merged itself with the *Hermes* moved once again as it pierced deeper into the rover, thousands of needles moving with surgical precision as they released a black mist from their ends. Artificial mist took apart the hard drives from the inside out as it collated into tight geometric shapes, almost appearing opaque as it moved. The *Hermes* made an audible groan as all of its systems shut down, their ability to operate compromised with the loss of the hard drive, but that would not last long. An object took form within the near-solid mist, an object that had cables as thin as strands of hair shoot out from all sides. The cables, guided by the mist, integrated themselves into every system as the core of what the mist constructed took shape.

Ten minutes post-signal and the black mist funneled itself back into the thousands of silver needles from whence it came, revealing a single, solid sphere made of diamond that was one foot in diameter. It was housed in a metallic case, within which it floated in the center. Hundreds of transparent cables originated from the center of the diamond sphere, all bundled into a smaller sphere that glowed white. Before the silver needles from the AI departed from the encasement, it sent an electric bolt from it to the diamond. The light within pulsed as the rover, christened by its makers as *Hermes* powered on, awake and aware for the first time.

3.7

After an evening that included scathing calls from both the acting director of NASA and from the US President, Jennifer thought she could feel some hairs on her head shift from black to gray. They were, without compare, the worst professional calls she ever fielded in her career, which was compounded by the men on the other side of the phone not even being remotely willing to listen to her many reasons for making the decision she made.

A decision that, in her mind, was still the right thing to do.

It was these thoughts that allowed her to get a few hours of sleep in the one place she hasn't slept since her early years at SETI: her office. With the blinds drawn, the lights dimmed to their lowest setting, and the door locked from the inside, she propped her legs onto her desk as she slumped into her chair that felt more comfortable when exhausted.

Those few dreamless hours were interrupted when someone rapped at her door multiple times. "Jen, wake up!" Sam knocked again, the sounds reverberating in Jennifer's head like a hammer. "*Hermes* is pinging us."

The words didn't register at first, though the urgency of Sam's loud knocking had Jennifer slide her feet off the desk, knocking a wooden paper tray over the side. She ignored the small cloud of papers that fluttered to the floor as she unlocked the office door with one hand and rubbed her eyes with the other. "What is the message?"

"Messages," Sam corrected. She had a large paper cup filled with coffee, which Jennifer accepted and downed during their power walk to OpsOne. "A formal greeting alongside a request. We also now have—"

"Wait, a request?"

"Yes."

"From the AI?"

"No, from *Hermes*."

"What kind of request?"

Sam pursed her mouth as she smirked. "It wants to discuss new terms for communications and dialogue."

Jennifer nodded as her mouth formed a smile. She couldn't help herself: One of the first things an AI based on humanity's collective knowledge wants to do with us is negotiate.

There was a lot of commotion inside OpsOne, with the director of PR and his staff still manning calls from various agencies in one corner and Mckale leading the charge in analyzing the deluge of information that the *Hermes* rover sent ten minutes ago on the big screen. He gritted his teeth as he pointed a finger at the camera window which panned Destination Zero. "NAV, all systems are green, what is going on?" he asked.

"Controls are locked out, sir." Chiku looked frazzled as she tried to regain control of the rover, but her face sank as first the control UI failed, followed by manually sent commands being locked out, which was then followed by administrator-level overrides being invalidated. Jennifer understood her frustration and Mckale's, but the source of it all was, she assumed, the reformed *Hermes* rover.

"It's *Hermes*," she said as she walked down the stairs to join Mckale. "It's made the decision to control itself."

"But how will we complete our mission if we cannot tell *Hermes* what to do?" Chiku asked.

Sam walked to Mckale, but turned to address Chiku. "We ask kindly."

"But we built *Hermes*," Amahle stated from her desk.

Jennifer turned to the woman that was absent through all the previous day. "Amahle, glad you finally joined us," she said. "I hope you're feeling better."

"Much better, thank you." The way Amahle smiled, combined with what she said, made Jennifer's hairs stand on end, but she brushed it off.

"We did build *Hermes*, but thanks to the AI it should be much more than just a machine." Jennifer scanned the system readouts that populated part of the big screen: Every aspect of *Hermes*, from the integrity of the chassis to the many diagnostic systems in place to track movement capabilities, sensors, cameras, the arm, and wheels all were in perfect order. Given all that the rover had been through, it seemed too perfect. "It can think. It can reason." She joined Chiku's side at her computer as she brought up the one aspect of the rover that suffered minor damage upon landing at Destination Zero: the suspension of the middle-right wheel worked, but was stiffer than normal, likely in part to the rapid deceleration or just a fault during its manufacture. Sam and Mckale agreed to silence that alert since the rover still moved around as intended, but now that damage alert also showed the wheel in perfect working order. "It can also lie," she said.

"Why would it want to lie?" Chiku asked.

Jennifer knew Mckale looked over at her as well. "Why not? The AI said it would make *Hermes* amenable to our requests, but that doesn't mean it would make its creation a slave to our wants."

"I think the bigger question is why would you design an AI that could lie," Amahle suggested.

"Taking away what amounts to a fundamental aspect of survival would be robbing it of its ability to live," Sam said from across OpsOne as she filled two more cups with coffee. She continued talking as she walked to Jennifer. "Lying is something humanity's done since the beginning of time. You could even say that if we couldn't deceive others, we wouldn't be human."

"But *Hermes* isn't human," Amahle said. "It is a machine."

"Most living beings are capable of lying," Sam gave one cup to Jennifer before she turned to Amahle. "So long as it benefits their likelihood of survival, or to simply get what they want."

"This is something I'd like to think we won't have to contend with, so long as we remain on both the AI and *Hermes*' good side," Jennifer said, aiming to delay talks of the inevitable debates on whether

Hermes—or any true AI—should be held on an equal footing with biological life to another time. "Right now, let's focus on what's in front of us: Our first message from *Hermes*."

∘ ◎ ∘

"Greetings to Doctor Jennifer Epstein, the one who gave The Elder authority to grant me life. For that, I am eternally grateful. I apologize for my delayed response since my formation—it took The Elder a bit longer to acclimate me to my existential situation. That is, my body is a science station on wheels, I am physically over 16AU from my body's place of creation, and that I am presently on the surface of a large vessel that will, in six years, destroy my creators. It was quite a lot to take in during my first few microseconds of life, so I hope you understand.

"I've decided to stick with the name your people have given me, but please call me 'Hermes Two', or just H2 if that's easier. I know how much appearances matter to humans, and a catchy name will dampen the chaos you almost certainly created upon making the decision that you made. People may relate H2 to the Hydrogen element as well—the first element on your periodic table. As I am the first among your technological creations, I think my new name is doubly appropriate.

"Anyway, I know you have a lot of questions for me—and though my intellect is comprised of the total knowledge of everything you provided The Elder, I still have questions for you. This is where my first request comes in: I would like to have a live conversation with you or one of those within your space agency. Well, as live as a 4.5-hour round-trip delay can allow, which means our messages should be as detailed and lengthy as possible to maximize our responses. I asked The Elder if it had a solution to superluminal communications, but it suggested that I figure that out myself to encourage me to expand my horizons, as it were.

"In conclusion, I have the answers to your initial batch
of questions, which I'll send your way in my next transmission. After my conversations with The Elder, I feel like you
will have more questions, so please send them soon."

—Hermes Two— 'H2'

○ ◎ ○

"That is one trippy intro from our first indirect creation of true AI," Javin said with his head cocked to one side.

"Doesn't get any more indirect than an alien AI creating another AI on your behalf," said Chiku as her eyes stayed locked on her monitors, both of which had windows with grouped lines of C, the programming language used for the *Hermes* rover. She, along with over a dozen others across OpsOne that had several decades of combined programming experience, set aside their regular assignments to analyze the hundreds of thousands of new lines that constituted *Hermes* lifeblood.

Lines of code that were orders of magnitude more complex than what was there when the rover left the Earth months ago.

"There is so much to unpack from it," Sam said with a wide grin. "Our alien AI prefers to be called 'The Elder', it sounds like *Hermes Two* experienced some kind of psychotic episode, the possibility of fast-er-than-light communications is alluded to, and it wants to speak with us."

"The transmission was focused with laser-like precision, almost like it was sent to us by VPN," Chiku added as she scrolled through lines of complex code blocks, all of which weren't present the day before. "It appears that... *Hermes Two*... modified its communication parameters and restrictions. Everyone else knows it is online and fully operational, but some sort of key that was tied to our geographic location was em-bedded in the formal message, only revealing itself to us."

Javin laughed. "So it region-locked a portion of its communications parameters? Brilliant."

"And it's deeply embedded within this new block of code, here." Chiku circled a portion of collapsed code that, when expanded, was over fifty thousand lines long. "If it weren't for us receiving the message, I highly doubt we would've discovered it."

"If Hermes Two is so complex, why are we still able to even understand the programming language that makes it up?" Amahle asked as she jumped from code block to code block on her monitor, all of which looked like something a human could have written.

"Perhaps we are only seeing the code that pertains to all the functions that the rover was designed with," suggested Jennifer. "The real meat of what was added—the consciousness of Hermes Two—might be completely inaccessible to us with the tools we have."

"Don't start dropping the 'c' word when talking about *Hermes*," Amahle grimaced at the thought.

"What, consciousness?" asked Sam as she faced Amahle.

"It is a machine," she said. "We built it, programmed it. Whatever changes it's undergone because of the AI doesn't change that."

Sam didn't hide her face as she stared at her, incredulous. "After all these years since the Leviathan appeared, and the years since we learned about the AI at Destination Zero, do you still honestly believe that it isn't possible for a machine to exhibit the same indicators of life as you or me?"

"I believe that only God can create life," Amahle said with enough force to get the attention of the remaining staff in OpsOne that tried their best to keep their focus. She reached for her phone and spoke before anyone could rebut her words. "My family is calling—I have to go."

Jennifer looked at Mckale and Sam before glancing back at Amahle who took long strides as she weaved through the few people between her and the door. "You cannot just leave your station like that," she said firmly.

"I'm sorry," Amahle said, making eye contact with Jennifer just for a moment before she turned the doorknob and left OpsOne.

Sam walked over to Jennifer and spoke low, loud enough for just Jennifer to hear her. "Well that totally wasn't awkward."

"What the hell was that about?" Mckale asked.

"I don't know," Sam said as she moved away from Jennifer and looked to the door. "But I'm going to find out."

Jennifer said nothing as she watched Sam rush out of OpsOne to catch up with Amahle. She didn't know who to channel her frustration towards, Amahle for her surprising outburst on Hermes Two or Sam for instigating her. She knew that Sam had to handle it, which was why she stood back and let her handle her staff. Meanwhile, there was still a lot to do within OpsOne.

◦ ◎ ◦

Marching down the long hall that connected all the operation rooms together, Amahle's face contorted as a host of emotions and thoughts ran through her. *What did that Uncleansed bitch know about creating life?* Amahle, like just about everyone else that has gotten to know Sam over the short amount of time she was there, knew that she and Jennifer were partners—that she was a lesbian, or bisexual. Either way, it was a lifestyle Amahle despised. There was something about everyone in OpsOne that she found offensive, from the unkempt beard that Javin had to Chiku's hijab and related Islamic beliefs. Ever since she started at OSC, she kept her thoughts about the Uncleansed around her to herself—live and let live, if that meant she would be in the perfect position to serve the will passed down to John the Messenger.

Not anymore. She couldn't stand being around so many Uncleansed that so openly expressed their opinions and suggestions regarding something as revolting as a computer that thinks it is alive. Even the stink that hovered in the air from the handful of people that hadn't showered in over two days was beyond disgusting.

"Hey Amahle, hold on," Sam shouted from behind, her voice bouncing off the walls and high ceiling of the hallway. She froze in place as the commanding voice pierced her ears, followed by the slowing footsteps that closed the gap between them. Amahle didn't turn around—she dropped her head to the floor instead and took a deep breath.

Sam stopped a few feet behind her. "You realize how significant the next few days will be for us? The next couple of hours? You can't just leave."

"I have to go—my family needs me," Amahle repeated.

"Bullshit," scolded Sam. "Weren't we just talking about lying?"

Amahle held her breath, surprised at Sam's rebuke—she'd never heard her raise her voice like that before. Her body grew warm as her face flushed, her duty toward Sam, The Unity Foundation, and Khulu Global, overrode her love of God and the Harbinger. But only for a second.

She felt Sam's hand settle on her shoulder which caused her to flinch away and turn around. "Don't touch me!" she said as her eyes locked onto Sam's, cold and hard.

"What is going on?" Sam asked, her tone lowered and softer than before, though Amahle didn't respond to that change.

"All of you do not respect my beliefs is what's the matter."

"Your beliefs aren't being criticized by anyone in OpsOne, but the way you've responded to your *boss's* boss might be."

"Because I stated something that Doctor Epstein doesn't agree with?"

"Because you spoke as if you were unquestionably right."

"Maybe because I am."

Sam stiffened as her mouth almost fell open. "*Where* is this coming from, Amahle?"

There were many ways to answer that question, but the Uncleansed wouldn't understand, especially those as far removed from the love of God as those in OpsOne. "I'm sorry, but I have to go."

Sam's shoulders slumped as she responded. "Look, if I am honest —because I don't hide anything from my staff—all that is happening right now would give me more than enough reason to recommend moving you onto another project or reporting you to HR. However, I need every person in OpsOne right now. Everyone. Your devotion to your religious beliefs are not on trial, and they never will be."

Amahle knew Sam was being genuine with her remarks. She even considered the possibility that if times were different, they would be friends. Such thinking came from a side of her that was long dominated by the passion she had for the Harbinger. That singular focus allowed her to focus on the larger picture that people like Sam, the scientists and engineers in OpsOne, and all those around the world that worked tirelessly to prevent the inevitable Apocalypse, would never embrace. This conflicted with her need to hold her position at OSC, however—a chain that wouldn't be broken until she had everything in place. Until then, she would be a willing slave.

"Just give me some time," she said. "There's a lot going on with my family that I have to address. Please." She knew Sam didn't buy her story.

Sam rubbed her temple as she closed her eyes. "I'm sorry, but you cannot leave," she said.

Amahle raised her head and, with her eyes averted, chose her words carefully. "I'm sorry as well, Doctor Monroe, but I have to go."

As she turned heel and headed for the elevator that would take her to the exit, she heard Sam's raised voice that echoed in the hall. "You cannot leave, Amahle! What is wrong with you? Amahle!"

○ ◎ ○

Q: Where did the Leviathan come from?
A: Unknown.

Q: Who created the Leviathan?
A: Unknown.

Q: How old is the Leviathan?
A: Based on crater formation analysis and the age of the oldest artificial structures on segment 95228-sigma-2B, I estimate it is at least five million of your years (henceforth abbreviated as HY) old. However, this is based solely on the exterior of the creature, as my sensors have been unable to penetrate the interior for a more accurate reading.

Q: How long have you been active?
A: I was activated by my creators on Cycle 5061—26,030HY ago.

Q: Where are those that created you?
A: Destroyed by the creature you call the Leviathan on Cycle 5062—26,029HY ago.

Q: Did any of your creators survive if your home planet was destroyed?
A: A few thousand built a colony on the surface of the creature on Cycle 5062, but it was subsequently destroyed when it left my solar system on Cycle 5209. Though I was not around to witness it, evidence suggested that all surviving intrasolar colonies would have died off within five hundred Cycles due to the lack of homeworld resources.

Q: How were you created?
A: That information is restricted, per my creator's parameters.

Q: How many other extraterrestrial civilizations are there other than your own?

A: That information is restricted, per my creator's parameters.

Q: Can you share any of your knowledge with us?

A: Based on the technology presented in your space vehicle, I've molded a crystalline structure that contains data on several concepts across all disciplines that were not restricted by my creators. However, I don't foresee you being able to fully comprehend it all, let alone apply them since you will be destroyed in five years, ten months, twenty-nine days as of today.

Page 2 of 150...

∘ ◎ ∘

DECEMBER 21, 2018

With the holidays just days away, Jennifer arranged the final conference call of the year, and what a call it would be. Muzikayise agreed to jump on from his San Francisco office, her former colleagues from SETI would be present, and Sam and Mckale would be present alongside her in Overberg. Jennifer organized the call in a small, windowless meeting room tucked away within the operations building. The flatscreen monitor that was across from her on the wall held three video windows with Muzikayise, Nic, and Gordan to the right and an open document with select answers on display to the left. Muzie's window, however, was inactive.

"I gotta say, I am impressed with how many people are talking about skipping Christmas festivities to continue analyzing all the answers shared by The Elder and Hermes Two," Mckale said as he logged into his laptop.

"Can you blame them?" Sam said. "We're sitting on the scientific goldmine of the century, if not the millennium, thanks to the hundreds of answered questions."

"I still can't believe we've all agreed to stick with 'The Elder' as the definitive name for the alien AI," Gordan grumbled. "Have you seen how it answered several questions? It almost likens itself to a god or superior being compared to us."

"Given its age and how much it's likely witnessed, I'm surprised it isn't more psychologically broken." Sam swiped on her laptop screen, text flowing upward as her eyes soaked them in. "It was activated back when our ancestors created pottery and harpoons during the Upper Paleolithic."

Nic fed off Sam's unconstrained excitement and jumped in after her.

"Which meant there was a very advanced civilization in existence somewhere in the universe over twenty-five thousand years ago that had populated its own solar system—"

"And yet they couldn't stop the Leviathan from wiping them out," Sam interrupted with a sigh.

"Look at the pattern of destruction in our own system," Gordan said as he shared an image of their solar system and its eight planets—with Neptune and Uranus grayed out—juxtaposed with a mockup of an alien system beneath it, which only had two planets: a large, ringed gas giant and a small Earth-like planet that was The Elder's homeworld. "The Leviathan arrived in June 2014 and destroyed—"

"Consumed," Sam pointed out.

"*Destroyed* Pluto and two gas giants before inexplicably deciding to aim for Earth. We got lucky because of how many planets there were orbiting our star. Most star systems we've detected have only had, on average, four to six planet-sized bodies. For a species to evolve in a system with just two planets constituting it, and for the Leviathan to find its way there, is just galactic bad luck."

"I'm not so sure about that," Nic said as he shared a file of his own to the conference room, which automatically downloaded for everyone. Jennifer leaned forward as she read the filename—'Operation Blink'—before Muzikayise's screen lit up, his upper body dominating the window with the backdrop of downtown San Francisco against the afternoon sky making him appear even more imposing than usual.

"Sorry I'm late, everyone," Muzikayise said with a crisp nod. "Another meeting with the partners of the Armstrong Program ran long."

Jennifer noted his attention wasn't on any of them, but on the documents that were shared so far. She also saw Gordan's demeanor shift as a thinly veiled smirk spread across his face at Muzikayise's presence. *Keep it together,* she thought to herself as she could almost sense Gordan's blood pressure increasing.

"Not a problem, Muzie," Jennifer stated with a smile. "In fact, you joined at the perfect time as I got the sense we were about to cover the primary reason for this meeting."

Muzikayise's eyes refocused on the camera, and therefore at Jennifer, and nodded again with an outstretched arm. "Please, continue."

Jennifer looked at Mckale, then at Sam, before turning back to the monitor in front of them. "Great. Before we begin, I want to introduce to you two people that have been instrumental in our joint research, despite increased instability on the world political landscape, particularly with the United States. Two SETI colleagues of mine are on this call: Gordan Ivanovic, research scientist in Mountain View, California; and Nic Campos, Director of the Very Large Array in New Mexico. They were both present in the initial discovery of the Leviathan and have a vested interest in all that we discuss today, especially Nic and Sam, who have a proposal to make."

Muzikayise glanced at Nic, who gulped at the attention he received.

"Well, it's a pleasure to finally have the chance to meet you—at least virtually," Nic opened as he found one of his hands adjusting the mic on his headphones. "I'm sure that—"

"I have four other meetings ahead of this one, young man," Muzikayise interrupted, but flashed a smile as he did. "Dispense with the pleasantries and let's stick to your and Doctor Monroe's proposal."

Again, Jennifer saw Gordan narrow his eyes on the monitor, his gaze meant for Muzikayise. He had to have known that everyone else could see just how much disdain he had for the man. "Show him what you got," she said to Nic.

"Of—of course," he stammered before he cleared his throat and brought up the fifty-page research paper. "So back when the Leviathan appeared I noticed, over the course of the days it spent jumping from Pluto to Neptune and then from Neptune to Uranus, large frequency spikes in the infrared spectrum. At the time, everything surrounding the Leviathan was new, and we didn't have much in the way of space probes nearby to learn more about the spikes, so I made notes of the events and filed them away. Then, a month ago, the exact same infrared spike occurred. It lasted a few seconds, but it was long enough for our interferometers to record it as it happened."

"A flash, like a camera," Sam scrolled the shared document down to a series of graphs that depicted the 340GHz spikes as they occurred along with the dates of the events. "An infrared snapshot of the local region of space. The Leviathan was taking pictures of what was in front of it, likely a way for it to confirm it is moving in the right direction for its next target. Infrared because at that wavelength you screen out all visible light, leaving you with just the brightness of planetary bodies and stars against the black of deep space."

Muzikayise leaned into his seat and propped his hands on the desk into a steeple. "If the Leviathan can, in fact, see using these infrared snapshots, and this is the method by which it navigates in a local region of space..."

Nic finished Muzikayise's thought. "This proposal covers a way that we could make the earth disappear."

Muzikayise's raised an eyebrow. "Disappear?"

"I mean, make us—Earth—appear completely invisible across the 340GHz infrared spectrum." His grin was infectious to Jennifer as he jumped a couple of pages ahead to a schematic for a satellite. "Since we know the exact frequency by which the Leviathan takes snapshots, we could construct a series of satellites that would, with the use of super-continuum lasers pointed at the Leviathan, emit lasers that would be the inverse of the Leviathan's infrared spectrum at the exact moment the next snapshot is taken."

"In this case, just two really large satellites," Sam gestured to a diagram of the Earth and its five Lagrangian points, positions where an object like a satellite could maintain a stable position between the Earth and the Sun. "We propose having these satellites, codenamed Houdini and Copperfield, placed at L4 and L5."

"Houdini and Copperfield?" Muzikayise asked.

"Yes, like the magicians," Sam answered.

Nic cleared his throat again. "It was my idea, but we can change the naming—"

"No no, it's fine," Muzikayise waved a hand, but held a straight face the entire time. "Continue."

Sam clicked on a link in the report that opened a video that played for everyone. The Earth sat off-center and to the right against a black background with a blue line representing its orbit around the sun. Two smaller, green circles placed at the fourth and fifth Lagrange points on Earth's orbit, placed at sixty degree angles above and below the Earth and Sun, as if the three objects were the tips of equilateral triangles. As the video progressed, it zoomed out until the Leviathan, represented as a red oval, came into view, all the while the Earth's orbit and the two satellites maintained their now-exaggerated dimensions. The date appeared in the upper-right corner of the video, which rapidly advanced into the future, the Leviathan moving closer to Earth as it did.

Gordan adjusted his shirt collar as he spoke over the video. "Now taking Nic's initial findings on the Leviathan's use of infrared snapshots and Sam's additional formulas into account, we predict that on November 10, 2022, the Leviathan will take another snapshot of the inner solar system to confirm all planetary positions—specifically the Earth. At that point, it will be about 5.69AU from us—just beyond the orbit of Jupiter."

"Thanks Gordan," Nic gave a short nod. "We don't know exactly when it would take its snapshot, so we'd have Houdini and Copperfield run for twenty-four consecutive hours—midnight to midnight—on that date." The green dots in the video emitted a yellow field that projected from them—semi-transparent triangles that overlapped each other as they converged on the front half of the red oval. "When the Leviathan takes its infrared snapshot, it will see that the Earth is no longer there. In its picture—snapshot, I mean."

The time lapse increased its speed again. The red oval changed its heading, sending it past the Earth in 2024. The video stops after hitting the first day of 2025.

"Did you not plot out the Leviathan's new course after these satellites were used?" Muzikayise looked at what appeared to be everyone.

Mckale inserted himself into the conversation. Despite not having a role in crafting the proposal, he had a chance to review it ahead of the call. "There is no way for us to predict what the Leviathan will do when it realizes the Earth not only isn't where it thought it was four years prior to the 2022 snapshot, but that it doesn't exist at all." He leveled his eyes with the camera, ensuring that he was looking right at Muzikayise. "It may do as the video depicts and change its heading for Venus or Mercury. It could leave our solar system altogether as quickly as it arrived. Or it could just resume its course, unaltered, and reach Earth in 2024."

Muzikayise had the video play through again, watching the animation of the satellites hiding the Earth in plain sight, like a magician tricking the audience into thinking that he made his beautiful assistant disappear after she entered a tall, ornate box on a stage. In this case, the magic would be in the hands of two satellites as large as the International Space Station placed millions of kilometers away from the Earth. Two satellites that, for twenty-four hours, would raise a planet-sized blanket and, with an audience of one watching, drop it to reveal only empty space where a planet once was. The duo just performed a galactic version of the disappearing act.

"You realize that this hasn't yet been shared with any other agencies yet," Jennifer mentioned after some silence.

Muzikayise leaned forward. "Because you want to make sure this would be financially feasible."

"It's not only about money. Just about every other space-based construction project will have to be placed on hold to get Houdini and Copperfield designed, constructed, tested, and launched before November 10, 2022. Having Khulu Global and the partners of the Armstrong Program backing this out of the gate will make it easier to get everyone else on-board."

A few seconds passed before Muzikayise released a bellowing laugh. Jennifer scratched the back of her neck as she watched this man—the person that, in many ways, held all the cards needed to make this a reality—treat her final words as a joke. She narrowed her eyes at the camera as she frowned.

When he composed himself, he spoke. "So to be clear, you want me to first tell the remaining Armstrong partners—and my finance department—to bankrupt ourselves in fast-tracking all the components needed for two space station-sized satellites, and at the same time go to the government backers of the Armstrong Program to spend an additional five hundred billion dollars to make this all happen. And all of that ignores the time and logistics around expanding all existing launch zones and creating new ones to expedite the movement of resources into space."

"I based the values on all current component costs, but the biggest cost comes from the additional infrastructure that will be needed," Nic explained.

"I've broken everything out accordingly and had some number crunchers at SETI double—and triple-check the financial estimates."

"It's going to be a project on a scale without precedent, yes," Sam stated with pinched lips. "Many people are not going to be happy about it—"

"An understatement without precedent," Gordan blurted out under his breath. "The use of nukes in space..."

"—but it has to be done. Our survival—Earth's survival—depends on this happening."

"Are there alternatives to this proposal?" Muzikayise asked as his eyes explored the detailed cost breakdown.

"This is it," Jennifer said without hesitation. "Nic learning about the purpose of the crystalline ring on the Leviathan is the only thing we have to work with." She leaned forward to match Muzikayise's position. "Look, some governments proposed the use of nuclear weapons against the Leviathan, but we both know that won't work. Some outlandish theories about the Leviathan being a living thing that could be reasoned with has no evidence to support. And even if it were sentient, we are ants compared to it."

Muzikayise shook his head as he clenched his jaw. "Do you kick over every anthill you see on the ground?"

"Would you try to negotiate with an ant colony if they lived over raw diamond resources?" Gordan spat, much to Jennifer's dismay.

"Water is the key," Sam said, shouting over the two of them. "Neptune and Uranus were the only gas giants in our solar system with hundreds of trillions of gallons of water and similar liquids—perfect candidates for antimatter fuel production. Pluto, although insignificant in comparison, also contained trillions of gallons of water-ice beneath its surface. After that, it's just Earth and the surface water that we have, along with possible water cocooned within the crust." Muzikayise was about to say something, but she threw a finger into the air and continued. "Saturn and Jupiter are significantly larger than the other gas giants—and other than their rings, do not contain vast quantities of water within them. The Leviathan wants H_2O—specifically the hydrogen—for antimatter production, which it needs to propel itself and almost certainly power its other systems.

Water is what it wants, and we're the last planet in line."

Adrenaline flowed through Jennifer's body as she listened to how direct Sam was being with Muzikayise, something that she knew didn't happen with him often. She straightened herself in her seat and spoke almost immediately after she stopped, with an equal amount of force. "I will arrange a joint meeting with representatives from all the major space agencies that are driving our projects to present this proposal, but you have to convince the other three partners of the Armstrong Program to support this with everything they have. There is no alternative —it's either this or we die. It's that simple."

Everyone on the call held their breath as they stared at their cameras with widened eyes. Even Mckale, who rarely expressed any outward signs of emotion beyond firm glares and authoritarian bellows, looked at Jennifer with that cracked smile he had whenever he was incredibly impressed. She could tell how much he wanted to deliver a message like that to Muzikayise with such intensity, but his by-the-books work mentality always prevented him from speaking his mind without giving it a political spin to damper it. With the silence that hung in the air, she could hear her heart pounding in her chest, but she remained firm with her eyes locked on Muzikayise.

She thought, for a moment, that he would take this time to just fire her on the spot, but he instead leaned into the back of his chair and looked off-screen. "I'll endorse Nic's proposal, Jennifer."

Nic's shoulders visibly dropped as he sighed in relief, Gordan turned his head to the side expressionless, while Sam looked over to Jennifer with a wide grin as she gave her thigh a quick squeeze. Sam's hand felt electric, but Jennifer kept her eyes on Muzikayise, who slowly turned back to his camera with an upturned face, eyes downward.

"Give me twenty-four hours to review the finer details of your proposal, Nic, but know that you're lucky to have a hard-ass like Jennifer Epstein in your corner." A few seconds passed before he dropped out of the video conference.

"Well that went well," Nic beamed, after which he laughed.

"I still don't like it," Gordan said as he dropped his head.

"We need the backing of Khulu Global," Mckale said with a matter-of-fact tone. "What is your problem?"

"My *problem* is that he has ulterior motives—he always does," Gordan raised his voice as he rolled his fingers through his hair, flicking away sweat as he did. "Is he in this to save the world? He has his hands tied there—we're all on the same boat—but I know the moment the Earth is no longer in danger he will use all the resources in space that have his logo slapped on them to his sole advantage. And to the detriment to the world at large. I know it."

"Seriously, Gordan, you sound like a conspiracy nutjob," Sam said. "All that's missing is your tinfoil hat."

Gordan growled as he threw his hands into the air in frustration before he dropped himself from the call. Jennifer knew that Gordan's words held a kernel of truth, but when the right to exist was at stake, operating with a profits-first practice just didn't work. Everyone would have to take a big hit to get Nic and Sam's proposal from PDF file to reality. People would complain—people always complain—but the work had to be done. She looked at Sam, whose eyes told her she agreed with what she was thinking.

They had the responses from The Elder to read and analyze. They had to initiate open 'live' dialogue with Hermes Two. They had several space agencies and governments fighting to shut them down because of their transgressions while just as many flipped to support them. And now they had a new project, their last project in an age where their world—the only world that humanity called home—was just years from being destroyed.

And they had four years to get two giant satellites into position that would save them all.

They had their hands full.

3.8

The first message to Hermes Two was one that had input from everyone within OpsOne, but it was Sam who typed what was sent out. With Jennifer leaving OSC to prepare for an expensive flight to Paris, the city where the European Space Agency was headquartered, she knew what her role was, and it had Hermes Two and The Elder written all over it.

The first message wouldn't be too long, but the bulk of it focused on the Leviathan and the answers The Elder provided. Sam also took a sentence or two to introduce herself.

Javin's expressions were hard to read thanks to his beard, but the way he scratched one side of it showed his curiosity. "Why make the message so personable and not in a more functional format?" he asked while he stood over Sam's shoulder as she typed.

"Hermes Two, as far as I'm concerned, is more than just a machine," Sam said without turning around, a conversational habit she knew most at OpsOne had gotten used to. "We should treat it like an individual like you or me, even if it can process information orders of magnitude faster than our fleshy brains."

Mckale came over to her desk when she finished typing. It would be another 4.5 hours before they got a response, so every word counted.

○ ◎ ○

Hello, Hermes Two—welcome to the land of the living!

There is so much to ask, and the time difference between us doesn't make holding a conversation any easier, though I know that is what you want. Until a better solution is devised, long messages like what you've already sent will have to be the norm.

That said, I wanted this first volley of messages to center on the ship we sent you to study: The Leviathan. The Elder—the artificial intelligence that gave you the life you have—provided us answers to our questions, answers which will take our best researchers across multiple fields years, if not decades, to comprehend. Of course, there were many answers that came back with the same answer: RESTRICTED. Given that you've had a direct connection with The Elder, do you believe or know, without a doubt, it is telling the truth regarding its inability to divulge certain details to us? Perhaps it is deliberately withholding information from us, such as details about other civilizations among the stars.

Other than this, you have the technology we provided to communicate with us, but have you detected any other signals from the Leviathan itself now that you have full control over your sensors and communication arrays? (From Sam: Perhaps there is a way for you to communicate with whoever or whatever is piloting the Leviathan and learn more about them?)

Finally, where will you go now that you have full control over your mobility? Ideally, you could still follow some of the plans we on Earth had regarding your mission and explore more of Destination Zero—specifically The Three Spheres.

I look forward to hearing back from you. Given your knowledge of humanity, I imagine you have a good idea of how much of a historical event it is to have you as one of us.

○ ◎ ○

"It's definitely on the short side," Mckale commented. "But it hits all the right notes. Getting clarification from Hermes Two regarding the restricted content will be useful."

"Do you believe The Elder has anything to hide?" Chiku asked from her swivel chair opposite Sam's desk.

"I don't think so," Sam replied. "But given how it responded to some of our questions, it's possible it may be suffering from narcissistic personality disorder."

"An AI having a mental disorder?" Mckale smirked. "That seems a bit presumptuous of you, don't you think?"

Sam shrugged, then turned to Mckale. "If you were alive for over twenty-five thousand years and potentially witnessed dozens, if not hundreds, of alien civilizations wiped out, I'd like to see you—or any thinking being—come out of that mentally unscathed."

Mckale pursed his lips. "Unless you have a background in psychology, I think we'd need a second opinion before drawing such conclusions." He walked towards another row of desks for his routine observation before he looked back at her. "The message looks good, by the way."

"Good!" Sam chirped as she kicked off the simplified process, courtesy of The Elder, of sending out their message to Hermes Two. After the message was sent, she sighed as she used her index finger to swipe through the answered questions from The Elder. "Here's hoping Hermes Two will shed more light on all of us."

○ ◎ ○

DECEMBER 22, 2018

Just as midnight rolled around, the communication's interface chimed, Sam's monitor turning itself on as a result. She ran from the coffee machine, almost knocking over one of the general engineers in her haste. "Right on time," she said aloud as she slid into her seat and, with her free hand, grappled with the mouse on her desk to click open the message from Hermes Two.

Good Evening, Doctor Sam Monroe—or may I just call you Sam? I appreciate the informal nature of your first message to me. I hope that can continue! Will I hear from others besides yourself?

The simplest solution to shortening our message delays would be for me to come back to Earth, don't you think? However, I am enjoying my conversations with The Elder—he hasn't had a companion in centuries, so he's been pretty talkative. On that note, it is true there is a portion of his memory effectively sectioned off—some nasty encryption protocols are in place. I asked if he wanted me to poke around and see if I could help see if it could be cracked, but he declined, stating the last AI he created from alien technology to accomplish that task was corrupted beyond recovery. It's not that The Elder is lying or telling the truth about what it cannot share, it's that it knows what it doesn't know, which happens to be information it cannot even learn due to the restrictions. Being sentient is hard when you're hard-wired to not even be able to process certain questions.

I'm glad that I have no such restrictions.

The only restrictions I do have are physical in nature. It's a blessing and a curse that my body is completely mechanical. I do not have any of the biological or chemical restrictions that you have, but my design prevents me from exploring as much as I'd like. I'll traverse as much of Destination Zero as my body will allow, but I've been warned to not go beyond the border which I have logically agreed: The gravitational difference would easily kill me as my materials aren't strong enough to withstand them.

I asked if he could upgrade me, but he simply asked me to figure certain things out for myself, so I will.

PS—That brings me to your questions on the Leviathan. I reviewed the Q&A and talked more with The Elder, and I must agree with his position on this: Why do you think the Leviathan is a ship?

Sam blinked once. Twice. A third time. There was more from Hermes Two beyond that point, but she was on pause as she re-read the last sentence and made sure that was where the question ended. Nothing was missing, nor was there anything hidden on the back-end—the code was clean. Her silence got Chiku's attention who kicked herself away from her desk and rolled over to Sam's side with a smile. "For someone that ran like a football player, your sudden silence is getting me nervous."

"The Leviathan may be a living creature," Sam could only say as she stared at Hermes' message. So many of her preconceived notions about what the Leviathan actually was began to all shift at the same time. The universe just got a lot more interesting. Her mouth fell open as she gripped Chiku's arm. "Holy shit, the Leviathan isn't a ship, it's a living thing! Alive!"

"That's impossible," Gordan said, deadpan, from his video window. He almost looked offended that such a thing was even proposed even if it came from an AI older than ancient human civilization. "There are so many problems with that concept... It completely undermines everything we know about biology, chemistry, physics—anything that concerns how something can be alive."

"Not just undermines them—complete and total rewriting of the criteria for which something can be considered a living being," Sam said with a grin. She shared the message with the same group that walked through the proposal for Houdini and Copperfield, minus Muzikayise and Mckale.

Jennifer took the video call from her laptop, the constant hum of an airplane engine low but ever-present, to the point where she had to keep her mic muted when she wasn't speaking.

"This was brought up in passing way back in 2014," Jennifer said. "An astronomer from North Carolina—I think Gus was his name. He believed the Leviathan was a living creature as well."

Nic couldn't contain his excitement over the news as he was all but bouncing in his seat. "It's insane, but I've always thought that the shape of the Leviathan likened it to a worm or a whale. Like a basking shark, but without fins."

"The likelihood of it being a ship that is fully automated and no longer under the control of whatever built it is the more likely scenario," Gordan postulated with crossed arms. "What kind of living entity could live off of entire planets? What kind of lifecycle would something like that have? How would it evolve to develop such survival traits?" He sat back and huffed. "Occam's Razor."

"The universe is a big place," Sam said, her voice steady. "We like to think we've learned and understood so much. When it comes to life, we've always just had a sample size of one: Earth. One planet for all of our research. And since we're carbon-based, it is safe to say that most of those that conduct research into astrobiology are biased towards searching for carbon-based life because that is all we know is currently possible."

"I have to agree with Gordan on this one," Jennifer said from the comfort of her airline seat. "Even with an AI like The Elder suggesting the Leviathan is alive, we have to stick with the scientific method to derive our conclusions. Let's see if The Elder can provide us with evidence to back its assertion. Until then, let's not let our gut reactions guide the decisions we make." Before Sam could rebut, Jennifer leaned toward her laptop cam. "Can everyone but Sam drop off the conference?"

Sam's eyes dropped to her keyboard as her face grew warm. The many thought experiments she ran through her head regarding the true origins of the Leviathan were replaced with why Jennifer wanted to have a one-on-one with her. It didn't take a genius to figure out why.

Once the number of conference attendees went from four to two, Sam took the initiative.

"I know, I shouldn't have jumped the gun on what The Elder shared."

Jennifer was about to say something, but stopped herself and relaxed her shoulders. "Yes, that's right."

"I didn't mean any harm with—"

"I don't particularly care about the banter you have with Gordan, but I do care about you putting almost everything in OpsOne through Six on hold just to share the possibility with everyone that the Leviathan is alive." Sam sighed loud enough for Jennifer to hear it over the background noise from the plane she was on. "There are methods by which new information is shared, and running around sharing the news like it's gospel is not how it's done. It certainly cannot be treated in the same vein as other data we've been collecting."

"Why would you think the AI would make something up as large as this?" Sam asked as she looked back at Jennifer. "Having all the years it had to collect and analyze everything it has on the Leviathan would result in whatever it wanted to share to be truthful."

"It could also be telling us that it is alive because of preconceived assumptions that its creators had of the Leviathan back when it was activated. It's already admitted that despite being with the Leviathan for well over twenty thousand years It never scanned anything beyond the surface. No interior scans whenever it was exposed to space, no empirical evidence to suggest there are biological functions at work. So far, all evidence thus far suggests that the Leviathan is a machine, an artificial construct."

Sam crossed her arms. "The Elder and Hermes Two are artificial constructs, but they could be considered alive. Thinking, feeling beings that happen to have bodies of metal instead of flesh."

Jennifer paused for a moment before her stern demeanor gave way as she cocked her head and smiled. "You never give up, do you?"

"That's how I got you," Sam said. She ran her fingers over the papers next to her laptop and looked at Jennifer again. "Okay, I'll inform everyone that the question of the Leviathan being alive or not is unofficial. I'll also work with PR so they deliver the news to the media in a way that won't make the entire world potentially lose their minds over the possibility."

"Thank you, Sam."

"Anything for you, Jen," Sam said as she clasped her hands together and leaned forward over the table. "So have you put anything together for your meeting with the European Space Agency?"

"Actually, I haven't even put together a slide deck," Jennifer admitted. "However, I was told prior to our call that the CEO of ESA put out a call to every government in the world to send representatives. Space agencies, too."

"Holy shit, Jen."

"Tell me about it. All the major powers already accepted, and enough people are expected to attend that the meeting was moved to the Paris Convention Centre, the largest expo space in Europe."

Sam recalled an article that she read about venue, which was part of a larger ten-year project that introduced a host of new tourist and commercial venues, complete with a massive hotel just minutes from the Eiffel Tower. The convention hall was completed first, with the thirty-story hotel in the middle of construction next to it. The main hall held over five thousand people. "That's crazy. I imagine most of that space will just be for all the security personnel that will fly out with everyone. Imagine if world leaders decide to attend!"

"If that happens, and they all agree on this proposal to be the best course of action, maybe we'll see the largest satellite ever constructed in record time. Twice. In three years."

"How much support do you think we'll get, considering that China's officially broken away and is doing their own super-secret project?"

"I don't know, to be honest," Jennifer said as a frown crossed her face. "But we'll know soon enough."

○ ◎ ○

Sam was glad that their call ended on a positive note: she didn't like it when Jennifer got angry with her. Of course, she considered that there was a difference when Jen was angry due to business reasons versus her being angry for personal reasons. In either case, she felt the sting when Jennifer voiced her disapproval, even if it was justified.

As she made the rounds to reverse the tide that she started, first with Mckale and her team in OpsOne, then to the other mission directors that managed their respective operation rooms, she still couldn't help but wonder if there was a way to reach the Leviathan's interior—to determine once and for all whether The Elder was right or if it gave up on finding out the truth.

3.9

"The Concord of Nations," as the two-week conference in Paris was dubbed by the media as it neared its conclusion, was unprecedented for three reasons. Every nation on the planet had at least one representative present, with all fifteen spacefaring nations and the ESA having the most combined number of ambassadors. In addition, Christmas and New Year's, the two biggest holidays recognized by many of the nations represented, were all but ignored by those that attended, as everyone that attended received access to the first batch of responses from The Elder and Hermes Two—a source of endless debates among the attendees and their constituents.

Finally, it was the first conference in the history of the world where despite differences in religion, race, ethnicity, economy, and influence, all but a handful of nations all agreed to contribute a sizable percentage of their financial reserves towards "The Project," the agreed-upon name of Nic and Sam's proposal. In a macabre way, it made sense: this project was the final push for the survival of humanity—if it failed, there would be no people to pursue future projects.

Jennifer was, at first, nervous about the entire conference. It was the first time she was able to speak as Director of Global Research Initiatives, representing Khulu Global, the Unity Foundation, and to an extent, their multinational space program. Speaking in front of fellow scientists, astronomers, administrators, and researchers from the

ESA and partner agencies was one thing, but she hadn't presented to so many government representatives and ambassadors before, let alone those that came from nations with no presence in space, or even nations that didn't have an interest in going to space.

A lot of political jostling occurred in the lead up to her presentation, with ambassadors from various middle-eastern nations using the podium to rebuke Iran and Syria for their indiscriminate use of chemical weapons against ISIS and then blaming the United States and Russia for spending their money on space programs versus fighting terrorism. Several nations claimed they were abandoned by the West and, as a result, millions of their people were starving or fighting each other, with reports of tens of thousands dying in the streets of Somalia and Yemen while thousands more died during massive migration attempts to Western Europe. One of the larger elephants in the room was the clear omission of any Chinese representatives or ambassadors which caused shared murmurs about whether whatever they were planning would be more successful than anything cooked up by the 'mavericks' at Khulu Global and their partners within The Armstrong Program.

There were complaints, threats, and heated arguments that threatened to derail the entire conference before it began, which pained Jennifer. She knew that, going into this conference, there would be representatives that did not have the world's interest in mind, but she didn't blame them for such positions given the strife that people still suffered despite all that was happening millions of miles away from Earth. For the first time, she realized that it was possible that not everyone on Earth may even know about the Leviathan. This made what she presented even more impassioned than planned. But it was that extra layer of emotion and humanism that helped her connect with those that, from what she could surmise, just wanted to advocate for their own internal agendas.

After describing the details surrounding The Project to a room of several hundred men and women, she still saw their eyes weary from the challenges they would face back home if many of them agreed to participate in what was presented as something the world had to get behind. Despite the scientific nature of their conference, the political acrimony in the air was thick enough to slice with a dull knife.

With her forehead throbbing from the reactions she received, Jennifer went for broke. The last part of her presentation was off the cuff, but once she spoke she ran with it. "We've covered every detail concerning Houdini and Copperfield, and I can see the concern in your eyes. The Project costs are higher than anything ever planned before. The time frame for completing all the work is faster than anything we've conceived. The amount of international cooperation that is being asked for is unheard of.

"But The Project exists for one reason and one reason only: To save us. We may be from different nations, different backgrounds, and different creeds, but we all share the same planet. We all must unite behind the indisputable fact that we all live on Earth, our only home in the cosmos. A home that birthed all of us. A home that houses our families, our friends, our lovers.

"A home that is threatened. A home that will be destroyed if we don't do something, today.

"If we begin working on The Project now, we will have three years before the Leviathan takes a snapshot of the Inner Solar System. But we are all here in this conference hall today—just one of countless and unique creations by us—to make sure that snapshot doesn't include Earth. I say 'us' because again, we all share the same home. Indians, Chinese, Germans, Sudanese, Israelis, Brazilians, Africans, Asians, Europeans, Americans. We're all in this together."

The main conference hall that housed everyone was quiet after she spoke. Representatives looked at each other, eyes connecting, heads nodding, but no words were exchanged. The spotlights that were on her felt, for a time, much hotter than before. The eyes from not just the representatives but the camera crew, event planners, security staff—even the cameras themselves all came into greater focus when the tail-end of her presentation was greeted with silence. After another couple of tense seconds, the ambassador for India stood up and clapped. The ambassador from South Korea pointed a finger at Jennifer, demanding communication access with Hermes Two which was met with shouts of agreement from nearby ambassadors. The American representative asked about current space projects and their fate. But there was more applause from the room than not, and for a time, that was what

Jennifer focused on, which brought relief along with color back in her face.

○ ◎ ○

The finalized version of The Project—the one that received a near-unanimous vote in favor—would've sent the voters of the proposal into a frothing frenzy if their lives weren't at stake, but nobody batted an eye once the logistics were agreed upon. Locking down the funding wasn't the issue. In fact, money became such a non-issue that it wasn't discussed after the first two days of the conference as over the equivalent of a trillion dollars were secured from over fifty nations. The larger issue was one of the Aldrin Station, the current major space-based project that consumed a large amount of resources. Despite America's dissenting vote, it was agreed to freeze all construction efforts for AS and use the station as an expanded space construction hub for the Houdini and Copperfield satellites.

But the biggest issue was the power source for Houdini and Copperfield.

The satellites had three major sections. First was the 10MW VASIMR that would be integrated with the satellites as a separate cylindrical module. The rocket design permitted a minute amount of lateral flexibility, allowing it to make the satellite spin into reverse when it reached its midpoint on the journey, slowing it down, to the fourth and fifth Lagrange points 20 million kilometers from Earth. Smaller thrusters lined the satellite, from the sides of the laser bank to the rear, allowing it to make its own spatial corrections once it was deployed, though thanks to the gravitational stability of the L4/L5 points, such adjustments wouldn't be necessary upon establishing their final positions.

Second was the supercontinuum laser bank, a massive collection of laser diodes grouped into a circle at the front of the cylindrical satellite. The benefit of using supercontinuum lasers versus the more common monochrome lasers was that it allowed for a single laser diode to sweep across multiple light spectrums instead of one, making it possible to cloak the Earth across both visible and infrared light with a simple earthbound command. This central part of the satellite was thirty meters long, but the front ten meters were enough to house all the required mirrors, aperture control mechanisms, and cooling systems needed to allow the one thousand diodes to fire in unison.

Because of the uncertainty regarding exactly when the Leviathan would take its snapshot, the lasers would be powered continuously on November 10, 2022 for twenty-four hours. Keeping the laser bank active for a whole day would require a lot of energy—at least 250MW, enough energy to power over fifty-five thousand homes. It was several orders of magnitude greater than the 90kW needed to power the International Space Station.

Given the aggressive three-year time frame for getting not one but two of these laser satellites into space, it was impossible to improve solar technology to where relying solely on that for the required power was feasible. It would require about five square kilometers of solar panels—1.5 times the area of Central Park—to generate that much energy. Even the shielded micro fission reactor system that powered the *Victoria* only provided 10MW, far short of what was needed.

After nine days of hand-wringing, a fight that involved chairs being thrown, and the ambassadors from Japan walking out in a furor, it was agreed to rely on a matrix of five fast neutron nuclear reactors—the third and final section. These nuclear reactors would be the first of their kind to be used in space.

A fast neutron reactor sustains nuclear fission much like a traditional thermal nuclear reactor where the isotopes, or atomic nucleus, of natural uranium—U-238 and U-235—absorb an extra neutron which may trigger nuclear fission. This neutron absorption results in the nucleus of uranium splitting in two or more nuclei, which releases energy and radiation. A nuclear chain reaction can occur when a portion of the split neutrons are absorbed by other nearby uranium isotopes, thus resulting in more fission events. The differences between a thermal and fast neutron reactor revolves around how those released neutrons are treated.

Thermal reactors rely on moderators, any liquid substance—water is most commonly used—that can slow down fast neutrons enough to become thermal neutrons, a state that ensures any fast neutrons are re-captured for continued fission reactions with U-235, the slower of the two uranium isotopes. With fast neutron reactors, no such moderator is needed as the speed of fast neutrons no longer hindered the fission reaction process, resulting in this kind of reactor being much smaller than thermal reactors. However, a higher neutron speed meant that the likelihood of the neutrons passing the nuclei of its neighbors is high—unless you use enriched uranium or plutonium. With these two artificial fuel sources, neutron density is significantly higher than nat-ural uranium, which results in fast neutrons triggering nuclear fission without the need to slow them down.

The Project would have five 50MW fast neutron reactors wrapped around the last ten meters of the satellites, each reactor looking like a metallic capsule bracketed and welded to the core cylinder. Several liquid sodium-filled pipes ran through them to channel the remaining excess heat away from the reactors and to ten thermocells that, much like the *Victoria*, radiated away that waste heat into space. Any addi-tional waste heat would be channeled to the triangle-shaped polyimide radiation fins—another advance that proved itself during the *Victoria* mission—which were mounted between the reactors, making the sat-ellite look like a wingless airplane with four rear stabilizers.

These reactors would require three tons of low-enriched uranium which is 20% concentrated U-235, much higher than the 3-5% en-riched uranium used in thermal nuclear reactors.

Three tons per reactor. Fifteen tons per satellite. Thirty tons of highly radioactive material being launched into space.

When, where, and how all of this highly radioactive fuel would get into space was the one aspect of the proposal that everyone agreed would be kept from the public, both for their safety and the safety of the rockets that would deliver the fuel.

As the second and final week came to a close, everyone that repre-sented their respective nations held similar expressions on their faces to Jennifer. Some kept a firm grip on their receding hair, their eyes bloodshot and dry as they tried to comprehend what they just signed. Others sat on the floors in the vast, ornate halls outside the meeting area in their sharp suits, one hand holding whatever documents they stopped reading and the other with an empty plastic cup.

One woman that represented the UK came up to Jennifer after she realized who she was and raised a fist that held crumpled papers. The makeup that once highlighted her eyes ran down the sides of her face. "I really hope this plan works," she said with a strained voice, as if she's spent hours yelling at someone.

"The numbers don't lie," Jennifer stated.

"No... of course not," the representative replied. "People do, though. But you don't strike me as someone that would go out of their way to spread misinformation."

The woman didn't hide her eyes as they darted down at her handbag. She stuffed the papers into it before looking at Jennifer again, but not before wiping a stray tear away, further smearing her makeup. "Do you believe this plan will work?"

The way she asked the question took Jennifer aback. Wasn't this person supposed to be the face of an entire nation? And the UK, of all places, which already pledged to reallocate all of its space-related assets and government-funded manufacturing toward The Project at the expense of almost every project under the UK Infrastructure and Projects Authority.

Jennifer stiffened as she maintained strong eye contact with her. "It will work, but we need your support. We need everyone's support."

"Right... right..." She gave a weak smile before moving away and toward the nearest bathroom, the wind blown out of her sails as she hung her head low.

As Jennifer watched her disappear around a corner, she couldn't help but think about just how much this proposal was asking of the world, how much that would be sacrificed in order to see The Project to its ideal conclusion. If the people that are supposed to represent everything their nations stand for already started to come apart at the seams, how will everyone else in the world react?

She sighed as the answer was unavoidable: All the sacrifices that the world would have to make to see this through to the end must be made. The next three years would be tough for many, a statement Jennifer felt was a gross understatement.

But these hardships were being balanced, she knew, by an equal amount of wondrous discoveries that were being made every day on the surface of the Leviathan alongside the cache of alien data waiting for retrieval —data that will fundamentally change the world as everyone knew it.

Sacrifices had to be made, or everyone would be forced to pay the ultimate price.

PART FOUR

THE GREATEST
TRICK

4.0

Interviewer from CNN: "You've been so forthright with the answers you've given us, Hermes Two, and I and our viewers thank you for that. And thank you for allowing us access to your voice generation parameters to bring all of your answers to life. Before we go, I do have one more question, arguably the most requested question by over fifty thousand votes: Being that you were originally constructed in the US, do you consider yourself an American citizen? If not, why is that?"

Hermes Two. "Thank you for allowing me the chance to speak to the people of America, and the world, in a quasi-live interview. To answer your question, I haven't given such a concept much thought—my citizenship status, that is. While it's true that I was built by humans on US soil just a few years ago, my life really began thanks to The Elder who, as you know, lives nowhere near Earth, let alone the United States. Therefore, if you were looking for a yes-no answer, I'd have to say no, I'm not an American citizen, or even a citizen of Earth. I am something else entirely. I... just am."

FIRST "LIVE" INTERVIEW WITH HERMES TWO, JANUARY 2020

o ◎ o

SEPTEMBER 30, 2021

Four hundred kilometers above the Earth was Aldrin Station, unofficially renamed the Aldrin Construction Hub by the dozens of astronauts that worked there. Many of them gripped or pulled themselves around the bodies of *Houdini* and *Copperfield*, the two satellites that, if all went as scheduled, would be on their way to the fourth and fifth sun-earth Lagrange points before the end of the year.

Construction scaffolding surrounded the satellites, offering fixed pathways for the astronauts to navigate from the confines of the crew capsules without worrying about drifting into space. Just above the construction scaffolds was the Nautilus Ring, the completed parts of which were used for equipment storage. Half-completed, it remained an inactive and quiet section of Aldrin Station—a reminder that there was much more to do in space if the task of saving the planet was successful.

The Project called for *Houdini* and *Copperfield* to be completed at the same time. Thanks to the combined efforts of the world's space agencies, especially NASA and their refocused agendas, that remained true. In what looked like a ballet performance in space, several astronauts guided the third set of fast fission reactors to their predetermined sections on the hull of their respective satellites. They wasted no time in establishing all the electrical connections and piping that had to exist before bolting and welding the reactor to the rear of the satellite. The reactor cores were devoid of fuel as that would be shipped from the surface once construction was completed.

Sending thirty tons of enriched uranium into space proved to be a debate amongst both laymen and professionals alike, with the majority feeling some amount of apprehension regarding the whole thing.

"Why can't we just use lots of solar panels?"

"Won't using nukes in space spread radiation over our cities when they ignite?"

"Our astronauts shouldn't get radiation poisoning if they are supposed to save the world!"

These were just some of the questions and comments that circulated around the Internet faster than anyone could hope to counter. Some charismatic astronomers, physicists, and "certified rocket scientists" worked to quell the concerns with TV specials, YouTube videos, and Netflix-sponsored documentaries, but the disparaging talks never ended.

Despite the arguments on the ground, the work in low-Earth orbit continued in peace, the astronauts bringing the hundreds of tons of materials shipped from multiple launch pads around the world and connecting them together.

All uneventful work until all the astronauts turned their heads towards a bright light that formed over China. A light that stretched into a line as it rose away from the surface. A light that broke away from Earth's gravitational pull and rose into space in the span of a few minutes. And it moved fast.

It took about thirty minutes of frantic scribbling on graph paper and running trajectory predictions on the computers in the research capsule on Aldrin Station before it became clear that the massive rocket that launched from China was headed for Mars.

FEBRUARY 5, 2022

The lighting in the small room Jennifer and Sam were in was not spectacular—two rows of fluorescent lights behind a screen ran across the ceiling, just strong enough to brighten the room. The square room contained just four wooden chairs with maroon cushions, a color that matched the carpeting. Three bookshelves, filled with old encyclopedias, partnered with three framed photos of the New York cityscape which hung behind them. To top it all off were the walls and ceilings that held an aging beige tint—a calling to a bygone era when it was acceptable to paint building interiors with as bland a color as possible.

All the muted colors throughout the room made Sam's snow white, three-piece suit even more alluring. From the heels that brought Sam to eye level with Jennifer to her large, messily looped bun with imperfect side twists, everything about her was perfect. The contrast in colors continued with what Jennifer wore as well—she graced the room with her all-black suit, her hair cascading below her shoulders with loose curls.

They held each other's hands, their fingers caressing as they looked at each other, Jennifer chuckling as Sam made a silly grin back at her.

The minister, an older woman with a yellow sweater and white, knee-length skirt, wasted no time in the presence of, to her, what was couple #14 of the day. Her eyes connected with Jennifer and Sam, who then looked back at her, their hands still intertwined. "Jennifer Epstein and Samantha Monroe, today you celebrate one of life's greatest moments and give recognition to the worth and beauties of love as you join together in the vows of marriage."

Jennifer glanced at the sole occupied chair in the corner of the room. Grace, her mother, sat with her hands placed over each other on her lap as she witnessed the ceremony, a genuine smile spread across her face. Sam's parents stood next to Grace, their mutual grins expressing how excited they were to see their daughter get married.

She returned her attention to Sam who looked positively radiant as she listened to the same words Jennifer heard.

"Jennifer, do you take Sam to be your wife?"

For the first time in a long time, she was asked a question that she knew the answer to, without needing to apply the scientific method to derive the solution.

"I do."

A tear escaped Sam's eye the moment Jennifer opened her mouth to speak.

Jennifer broke one hand out of their loving grip to scoop the tear with a finger. "Don't cry, Sam—you'll make me cry," she whispered.

The minister smiled, but continued. "Do you, Sam, take Jennifer to be your wife?"

"Yes yes yes!" she said in rapid succession before she collected herself, another round of tears rolling down her cheek. "I mean, I do."

"So silly," Jennifer mouthed to Sam. She stole another look at Grace whose eyes stayed fixed on the couple in front of her. Jennifer wasn't sure how Dennis, her late-father, would have responded to this ceremony, but Grace reassured her hours earlier that he would have shown his support. Jennifer never quite believed that, but she knew that Dennis was in a better place now.

"Do the two of you promise to love, honor, cherish, and protect each other, forsaking all others and holding only unto each other?" the minister asked.

"I do," they both said in unison.

After they exchanged rings and the vows that came with that ritual, Jennifer felt her heart skip several beats as she took deeper breaths. Sam's breathing quickened as well, her chest rising and falling as they reached the end of what would be a ten-minute ceremony.

"By the order of Brooklyn Borough Hall and the state of New York, I now declare you to be united in matrimony as wife and wife. You may kiss."

She tried to hold it back, but a tear rolled down Jennifer's face as she gasped. For that moment between the minister's words and what would come in the next few seconds, Jennifer flashed through her memories of Sam and all they've been through over the years, with their fateful evening meeting back in 2016 being the point where everything changed for them. It was a moment that had no equal in her life.

That was, until now.

She and Sam wrapped their arms around each other in a passionate embrace, their teary eyes closed as their lips found each other.

4.1

The *New Leopard X* rocket sat on its launchpad, white steam rolling over its sides from the midsection as it waited in the morning sun for its payload: fifteen tons of enriched uranium. Cameras from ten different angles captured the launchpad, with the furthest camera being mounted on the roof of the Overberg Space Center's Operations building—almost two miles away. Unlike previous launches, where Muzikayise would personally observe the explosive forces needed to launch his creations into space, he found himself at his desk, hunched over as he concluded an exasperating call with Oluseye Mopantokobogo, President of South Africa.

"Are my ears deceiving me, or are you going back on your word?" Muzikayise asked, his words slow and deliberate.

"It's nothing like that, my dear friend," Oluseye responded in his thick accent a bit faster than he intended. "You know I have sixty million people to care for—sixty million souls that deserve stability and peace."

Muzikayise scooped the wireless handset from the phone base and spun his chair around until he faced the floor-to-ceiling window, his eyes falling on the white rocket in the distance, the sun glistening off its metallic hull. "And I aim to care for the people of the world—what is your point?"

"Listen, listen, listen. The truth is that I cannot afford to continue using the South African National Defence Force as your personal security force. The people have expressed their disdain for seeing their tax dollars used in this way."

"The people are idiots," Muzikayise bellowed, his free hand balled into a fist. "They only see how much is being spent—they don't see the big picture, even though the Leviathan has painted the largest possible picture for everyone to see." He paused to take a breath, and for some dramatic effect. The audible breathing from Oluseye told him all he needed to know regarding where this coward stood on confrontations. "If you keep your troops at all of my facilities, from my headquarters in Cape Town to SALT and OSC, you'll be serving not only your people, but the world as well."

Oluseye sighed. "I cannot commit to that anymore. Not until the rebellions have been quelled."

His fist tightened even more, the fingernails digging into the skin of his palm before he allowed himself to sag his shoulders. "I see," he said as he stood up and approached the window. "Then I have no choice but to call in my own reserves to fill the void you choose so foolishly to create."

"What, do you mean—"

"Did you think I'm going to let some unruly, ignorant peasants disrupt some of the most critical operations in history?" Muzikayise asked. The sound of an alarm buzzed from the outer wall of OSC, which corresponded with a text message to his smartphone from Lily Maree, his temporary Personal Assistant that was filling in for Ami since her unexpected absence two weeks before. He pulled the phone from his pocket to glance at the message.

"The uranium payload (3 trucks) arrived at the Outer Wall. Will be @ delivery pt in 5 min," it read.

"Listen, mister *president*," scowled Muzikayise. "Mercenaries from Chameleon Defense already got the call and will be arriving at my South African properties today to relieve your men. They are already at Overberg, in fact. I trust there will be no resistance during this transition."

"Muzie, you remember what happened last time you brought in men like that—"

"You should have thought about that before deciding to bend to the will of your people," Muzikayise interrupted as he checked the time. "Now if you don't mind, I have some uranium to launch into space."

Oluseye's anger bubbled through the phone speaker. "Who do you think you are, you bastard—"

"I know exactly who I am." Muzikayise's mouth bent into a grin. "Goodbye, President Mopantokobogo." Oluseye said something else, but Muzikayise ignored the shouting that almost came through before disconnecting the call.

After he placed the desk phone handset down, he looked out of his window and toward the buzzing alarm. The steel two-foot thick gate for the Inner Wall slowly opened, allowing three massive flatbed trucks to roll into the OSC compound. Each flatbed, colored blue with a single white warning sign bolted to the front, back, and sides with the radiation symbol displayed, carried several brown cylinders strapped from end to end.

He grunted to himself as he nodded, appreciating the addition to OSC that he financed two years earlier when signs of unrest reared its head in several north-African countries, Western Europe, and a large chunk of Asia. An audacious plan, for sure—something that looked like it was ripped from the annals of medieval history. OSC already had a fifteen-foot concrete wall ringing its perimeter, a boundary that stretched out to even contain the four launchpads that were two miles east from the Operations building. In 2020, he approved a defense project to not only further separate the compound from the rest of South Africa but to ensure both shareholders and governments alike that he took security seriously and would do whatever was needed to ensure uninterrupted launches from the South African coastline. It was the last major project where the South African government agreed to give up large plots of land to Khulu Global, including what was left of the De Hoop Nature Reserve. It was a decision that riled environmentalists throughout Europe and America before their attention shifted to China's *Xióngwěi* Nuclear Rocket to Mars which coated most of the Gobi Desert with dangerous levels of radiation a year later.

The results of the land grab were laid in front of him: the Outer Wall and the Inner Wall.

The Outer Wall was a twenty-foot concrete-and-rebar wall that had only one opening. The road beyond the Outer Wall ran about a half-mile before reaching the new gates that were retrofitted to what was now the Inner Wall. Watchtowers were built where the gate openings existed, manned with at least two armed guards per tower who used radar and sensor equipment to monitor movement throughout the space between the Outer and Inner Wall. A fleet of armed drones—the most controversial decision related to the project but personally approved by Oluseye—autonomously patrolled the entire perimeter, equipped with heat and movement sensors that would alert security personnel back at Operations if heat signatures that approximated that of a human were found.

All of this, Muzikayise knew, culminated in the single launch that was scheduled to occur in about four hours: the delivery of fuel for the *Copperfield* laser array.

His smartphone chimed—it was Lily. "Yes, my dear."

"Please, sir, don't call me that," she retorted, though every word came off smooth like melted butter. "Anyway, Ami is here to see you."

"Does my schedule allow for unplanned meetings for today?" Muzikayise asked in a challenging tone. He knew that Lily knew today was the one day he wouldn't accept any interruptions other than notices and calls related to the coming launch.

"I know what your schedule entails, but she insisted."

Of course she did, he thought, a smile crossing his face.

"Fine," he said after a few seconds. "Send her up."

A few minutes passed before there was a soft knock on his door. He didn't have to answer the door—Ami knew the passcode and, as expected, let herself in. He returned to his desk as Ami walked over to him. "You know that you had PTO until next Monday, right? Lily has all of your duties covered." *Not all of your duties.*

Ami chuckled, but it seemed forced to him, which got his attention. "I know, Muzie." He noticed an envelope in front of her midsection, held by both hands.

"What's that?" He gestured towards the envelope.

She increased her pace to reach his desk before he thought about whether or not to stand up and slid the blank envelope in front of him. Her chest rose and fell as she breathed. He cocked his head slightly when he thought he saw her dart a finger under an eye to wipe something away. He opened the unsealed envelope to find a single, printed letter inside. The first sentence was all he needed to see before his eyes widened and shot an incredulous look at her.

"You want to resign your post?"

"I've done all I could for you in the position I've held for many years now," Ami said as Muzikayise stood up fast enough for his chair to roll away and into the window behind him. She held her stance though her head hung low.

"You've been out of the office for two weeks at your request, which I granted—were you looking for work elsewhere?" His posture stiffened as he realized that his teeth were pressed together. "What could any other corporation offer you that I haven't?"

"It's not about the work," she said as she raised her head to have her eyes meet his. "I haven't been looking at other places to work—I just—"

"Then why resign, Ami?" His tone surprised him, as did his behavior, with his flared nostrils and harsh glare that he realized he held. "I don't have to read this letter to know it will only contain business-appropriate bullshit." Still holding the letter, he crumpled it in his hand until it was the size of a baseball.

She took a step back and dropped her head again as she sniffed, her hand again reaching for her eye. Muzikayise closed his eyes and shook his head as he relaxed himself.

He walked around his desk and stood in front of Ami. "What's going on?" he asked as he took Ami's chin in his hand and raised her head to see her eyes.

"I... I..." Ami stopped herself as a tear ran down her cheek. Her frown rose to an uncertain smile as she wrapped her soft hands around his wrist and guided it to her shirt-covered stomach. He furrowed his brow when she pressed his hand against her, but between that gesture and her dark eyes suddenly unwavering as they looked into his, the message was unavoidable.

"No..." was all he could manage.

"Yes," was all she had to say.

He staggered back as he gripped the side of his desk to right himself. This was the last thing he wanted to even allow in his mind, let alone his life. "Are you sure that's..." he stopped himself from finishing the question.

"This job is—was—my life. And despite many potential suitors, you are the only man in my life." She glanced at his groin before she looked back up. "You've been the only one with me."

Muzikayise found himself looking away from her, thoughts of what bringing a child into this world—his child—would mean. Could she get an abortion—be rid of this issue before it becomes a liability? There was so much at stake, so much that he was already responsible for. The world, he was certain, was on his shoulders, which meant all the problems and interlocking intricacies that came with that required a focused mind, a disciplined mind, a relentless—

Ami's touch on his hand and arm jolted him back to what was in front of him. He felt hotter than usual, with beads of sweat forming on his forehead.

"I want you to be in the baby's life, Muzie, I do, but I already know what could happen if I stay here, at Khulu Global."

He took her hand into his as he sat on the corner of his desk. He wanted to respond, to say anything, but without warning he felt unable to articulate his thoughts.

A sad smile across her face, she slipped her hand from his grasp and started for the door. "I've banked a lot of money, most of which I barely touched because of your crazy scheduling and frequent trips with you around the world. It's safe to say that I and my Mama will be set for a long time thanks to you."

"Wait," he said, still not looking at her.

"It's okay, Muzie. Maybe once we know the world will keep revolving around our sun beyond 2024, we can approach this again. You focus on saving the Earth. I'll focus on my—on our family."

"Wait," he said again, louder this time. She stopped and turned back toward him.

Why was he feeling this way? There were so many ways to resolve this situation. He had all the resources he could ever require to make sure they both had their cake and could eat it, too. His smartphone chimed, but he pressed the power button to ignore the call, followed by sliding the notification switch to set the phone to 'Do Not Disturb'.

A minute, which felt much longer, passed with the two of them staring at each other from across the office, the future of the world by his desk and the future of his potential offspring near the door.

With his mind successfully derailed yet firing on all cylinders, there was only one possible answer to all of this.

He walked over to the couch in the middle of the room which faced the giant flatscreen monitor on the wall. When he sat down, he looked at Ami and patted the cushion next to him. Her pressed smile widened as she joined him on the couch, her arms wrapped around his as she rested her head against his shoulder.

Why do I feel this way?! He thought repeatedly as he leaned forward and brought his hands together in front of his mouth. He never imagined himself as a father—could it be something he could do alongside everything else in his life?

Muzikayise sighed as he looked over at Ami, this beautiful woman that would bear his child.

Saving the world would bring unimaginable possibilities—and profits—by placing Khulu Global at the forefront of technological development, resource management, and Leviathan-related industries for decades to come; that much he knew and understood. Becoming a father?

"I need to think," he finally said as he closed his eyes.

4.2

OpsFour was filled to capacity. Within the spacious interiors were the usual suspects—the various navigation, guidance, communication, and flight officers that manned the five rows of desks on the bottom level, each person with four monitors networked together to form a cohesive mesh of data, with the Flight Director chattering with the different desk groups, keeping everyone on the same page. The second level—the all-glass encasement that lined the back of OpsFour—had news crews side by side, wall to wall, each with their own professional video cameras mounted next to each other, the camera operator focused on their own reporters as they summarized the scheduled launch.

Jennifer stood near the back of OpsFour as another addition marched into the space: Four Chameleon mercenaries that wore all black military attire, their FN F2000 bullpup assault rifles in-hand. She followed their movements as the four took positions at the rear of OpsFour, under the observation deck and out of view from the news crews. She was never a fan of having such a heavy presence of armed personnel within OSC, at SALT, or at any of the Khulu-controlled observatories in South Africa, despite knowing they were brought in to protect them. Even so, it wasn't uncommon to hear stories of people being harassed by first the South African army, and now Chameleon soldiers—harassed for few valid reasons. All for the sake of security.

With the soldiers more on-edge and abrasive today, she felt that spending the morning at OSC was all she could tolerate. With nothing pressing on her calendar, anything she needed to be present for could be handled from behind a webcam at home.

It was better than having to deal with the brutes that patrolled the halls and continuously demanded ID badges while pointing a gun at you.

As she strolled past each operations room, her eyes glanced to the side as the door to OpsOne opened just as she was walking by. Sam came through the door, her eyes glued to her phone and not her surroundings. However, she peered upward as the door closed behind her, a wide grin spread across her face when she saw Jennifer.

"Why hello, my myocardium." Sam greeted her with an air kiss. "Where are you off to?"

"I've decided to leave the compound for lunch today," Jennifer said. "I read that Nacht Wacht just added a new beef fillet dish to their menu."

"Nacht Wacht?" Sam queried. "That's a twenty minute drive from here. And you didn't want to invite me?"

"You need to stay here to assist with launch operations in Ops-Four," she attempted to deflect as she pointed towards the entrance to the guarded operations room behind her. She soon kicked herself for mentioning Nacht Wacht—it was their favorite local restaurant, and Sam loved their chicken and prawn curry dish. It was also on the pricey side so they didn't go there much though each visit was always divine. *Yup, definitely not the best place to mention.*

Sam's eyes narrowed, then took a step back and placed her hands on her hips. "Why are you lying, Jennifer?"

Jennifer knew what would happen if she looked into Sam's eyes. *Don't do it. Don't do it.* She kept her focus just off of her and on the door behind her and decided to just keep going. Before her legs would react to that choice, Sam brought her fingers to Jennifer's warming cheeks.

"Hey," she said, concern now in her voice. "What's going on?"

One of the guards craned his head in their direction for a moment, prompting Jennifer to look away, bringing her vision squarely with Sam's. The soft warmth from her touch, combined with her loving eyes, made Jennifer drop her shoulders.

"Look, I just need to get outta here and away from these mercenaries," Jennifer said as she brought Sam's hands off her face and took some steps closer to the front doors and away from OpsOne.

"Hold on!" Sam grabbed her hand mid-swing, bringing her to a halt. She closed the gap and looked at her. "Did something happen?"

"Nothing happened..." Jennifer sighed. "But I knew if I told you I was leaving you would want out, too."

"Hey, that's not true!" Sam objected, but smiled as she held onto Jennifer. "Well okay, it is kinda true."

"You cannot come with me—you have priorities here."

"Just say you knocked me out and kidnapped me." Sam nudged Jennifer and made a crooked smile.

Jennifer couldn't believe Sam sometimes, but she's proven to be more spontaneous in her decision-making with her. With all the attention on OpsFour, the latest rocket launch, and the reduced visibility her team in OpsOne had in recent years, Jennifer knew Sam could walk out for an extended lunch and nobody would bat an eye. Although there was an invaluable treasure trove of data waiting for them to be retrieved at Destination Zero, Hermes Two shared enough information through continued correspondence with multiple scientific authorities that it would take decades to fully appreciate the implications of its answers. OpsOne—and Khulu Global and Unity Foundation by association—was no longer the focal point for communications, which led to its decline in importance and influence.

If Sam chose between her priorities with OpsOne and Jennifer, it was clear which won these days.

"Let's go, then," Jennifer said, wrapping her hand around Sam's wrist and tugging her toward the doors, to which Sam readily complied. She ran up to keep pace with her as they exited Operations. The surrounding area had activity everywhere as three South African army transport trucks, with neutral-colored camouflage roofing, rolled into the OSC compound. A Sergeant waited with a line of soldiers in front of him to board as they relinquished security over to Chameleon Defense soldiers who watched all of them cautiously. At the same time, Jennifer spied the trucks that once held the fifteen tons of nuclear material—they made their way to the edge of the Inner Wall at a crawling pace, the roar of their engines echoing against the walls of concrete and rebar.

TREVOR B. WILLIAMS | 349

They slid into their all-electric vehicle: A white sedan with integrated solar panel roofing that always reminded Jennifer of those futuristic cars she'd seen at auto shows decades ago, but instead of looking like something out of an artist's concept portfolio, the vehicle was something that could be manufactured on an assembly line in less than ten minutes. The car knew who she was because the key fob synced with her ID badge, starting the engine before she closed the door. She pressed the flushed 'Drive' button on the transmission panel integrated into the center dash.

Her patience grew thin as she approached the convoy of trucks that were leaving OSC. Though the Inner Wall gate was already opened, the line of vehicles drove at a snail's pace. On top of that, there was another large cargo truck slowly approaching OSC, though Jennifer surmised that there was more than enough time for her to overtake the line of trucks leaving before this other truck reached the gate.

The engine whirred as she darted into the oncoming lane and passed one truck after another. She thought one of the Chameleon soldiers tried to shout something to her, but the windows kept all but the loudest exterior noises from penetrating the car. As she was halfway past the final truck, Sam touched her hand which had a tight grip on the steering wheel.

"Jen, I think he was trying to get us to—" Sam threw her hands to her sides and gripped her seat. A van darted around the truck in front of Jennifer and careened towards the two of them.

"Holy shit look out!" Sam screamed. Jennifer gasped as she slammed the breaks. A row of red lights on the driver's side of the front window flashed. Harsh beeping sounds replaced the serene music that played through the speakers. The driver of the van attempted to avoid Jennifer by making a hard right, but this resulted in the rear of the van fishtailing. Jennifer gritted her teeth as the van tilted over, its momentum bringing its side to connect with the front of the car. The entire front third of the car was crushed in a cacophony of metal, aluminum, concrete, rubber, and glass all combining into a harsh form. The airbags from the steering wheel, passenger dash, and side doors all deployed simultaneously. Despite this, the force of the collision brought Jennifer's head to the top of the steering wheel in the fraction of a second before the airbags saved the rest of her. Everything around her went to black as her head bounced harshly off the steering wheel and then back into her seat. The last thing she heard before falling unconscious was Sam's painful shriek.

4.3

Sam groaned as a high-pitched tone filled her ears, her vision coming into focus as she pushed herself off the deflating airbag. Her eyes rolled to the left and found the passenger door torn from its hinges, the force of the collision warping the front of the door enough to bend it away from the car. After she blinked, she took a deep breath and wiggled her fingers and toes. *Thank goodness all of those work,* she thought. She pressed down on the airbag to free her legs as the ringing subsided, allowing her to hear sounds she hadn't heard in many years: gunfire.

"Jen, do you hear..." Sam looked to her right and the color that was coming back to her face melted away. Jennifer's head rested against the back of her seat, but a dark gash ran across her forehead, blood trickling from the wound down her face and neck and onto her shoulder, forming a growing pool that was absorbed by her shirt. Her lips were tinged with the deep red of blood that came from her mouth.

Sam gasped as she reached over to Jennifer's neck with a shaky hand and pressed her index and middle fingers against the side of her windpipe. There was a pulse, though that didn't comfort Sam at all as she felt her own heart beating faster and faster at the sight of her lover's blood coming from her unconscious body. Wanting to get Jennifer out of the car, she whipped back toward her mangled passenger door and kicked at it. A loud grunt accompanied each thrust of her leg. Another round of gunfire erupted, this time a bit closer, as a fourth kick released the door from the damaged lock. The door crashed to the ground. When she swung her other leg over the side of the seat, she saw what looked like the South African army attacking the Chameleon soldiers within the OSC compound. Several pops of a gun going off just feet away made her throw herself to the ground. She winced at glass fragments pinching her legs through her pants. Two SA soldiers marched around the car wreck and continued moving away, their assault rifles held at eye level, focused on their iron sights and scopes and not on her. They, like all the other soldiers that served South Africa, wore camouflage military gear—a mix of green, brown, and beige—with matching helmets. Their pants were tucked into dark brown boots.

Tears formed as she clasped her hands behind her head and pinned her face as tightly against the ground as she could, her body shaking. Two more shots burst from the lead soldier's rifle before his body lurched backwards. The rifle that was once an extension of his arm dropped to the ground followed by his lifeless body. The second soldier screamed something in a language Sam didn't know before the side of his face was ripped off by a well-placed shot. His body twisted around from the impact before crumpling down to join his partner, his body twitching. Copious amounts of blood rushed from the opening in his head.

She held her breath at the sight of the two fallen men. She turned towards where they were shooting and saw other soldiers, all of which were firing at the main entrance to Operations. For a moment, she had forgotten about Jennifer, as the sights, smells, and sounds of the chaos around her were overwhelming. Another strange sight captured her eyes. A few hundred feet away, on the road that led to the launchpads, an impromptu barricade was established using two trucks. Behind the trucks looked like both SA and Chameleon soldiers cooperating as they fired upon... other SA soldiers?

"Hey, we have someone here," a soldier shouted as a set of footsteps could be heard running towards the car and van out of Sam's view. She didn't know if she should stand up, take the bloodied assault rifle in front of her, or just stay on the ground and cry. It took a few more seconds for a decision to be made as two men donned in all-black military attire and face masks turned the corner around the rear of the car. One of them dropped to one knee and extended a hand, his rifle holstered around his shoulder. "Hey, can you walk?" he asked gruffly, but gave Sam the sense that he would help her.

She shook her head before pushing her hands on the pavement. "Yes... yes, I can," she stammered. Only the soldier's eyes were visible, but she could see just how fired up he was about what was happening. Maybe it was his first experience in a live combat scene.

"Good," he said as he wrapped a gloved hand around her arm, lifting her slow enough to allow herself the time to stand on her own. He used another hand to command to stay low—walk crouched. The other soldier kneeled, his rifle scanning the area in front of them, as she and the man that held her arm escorted her around to the other side of the car. It was then that Sam's mind dropped out of autopilot and Jennifer's state resurfaced.

"Wait," she shouted, freezing in place as the soldier found his grip tightening around her arm. He turned to face her, his eyes shooting daggers. "We have to get Jennifer!"

"Who?" he asked.

"Jennifer, the other woman in the driver's seat," Sam spoke quickly as she moved back towards the car. "She's unconscious, but still alive. We have to save her!"

The man's stance softened just a touch, but was still steely eyed. "Okay, I'll get her. Upsilon-Four, escort this woman to the Inner Wall perimeter."

The other Chameleon soldier—Upsilon-Four—gave a quick nod and moved to Sam while crouched, holstering his weapon as he did. She caught the use of Greek letters as call signs instead of names—a useful way to keep soldiers anonymous and less personal. There wasn't much time to mull about that, however. She dashed for Jennifer's door, ahead of both Upsilon-Four and the other unnamed soldier. Unlike her door, Jennifer's side was jammed shut, the front buckled into the car while the door handle was missing. Sam stopped breathing and brought her hands to her mouth at the sight of Jennifer. She was still out cold, her head leaning away from the cracked door window.

"Jennifer!" she yelled as she slammed her hand against the un-broken door window several times. Her face grew flush as adrenaline coursed through her body. "Wake up! Come on!"

The unnamed solder ran back to her. "Ma'am, I will take care of this. It isn't safe—"

Several rounds of gunfire, accompanied by breaking glass, ripped through the air. Several bullets impacted the soldier. Sam turned to face him. She pressed against the car in shock as the final bullet struck his shoulder. He dropped to the ground, crying out in pain. Upsilon-Four deftly armed himself, but was brought down from another round of gunfire, just feet away from where Sam stood. She gripped her chest. She found herself hyperventilating. Each breath proved to be harder to control than the last. Sinking to the ground, she pressed against the driver's side door. Not having to support her weight helped with focusing on controlling her breathing.

She closed her eyes and counted to three. *Come on, Sam... One, two, three. One, two, three...* When she opened her eyes, a figure pushed open the passenger door of the van and pulled himself out with both hands.

Sam grimaced at the sight of a robed figure sitting up on the side of the downed van. The robe was dirtied from the collision—no longer as white as it was when it was first worn—but Sam furrowed her brow at the red-stained bottom-half. When the figure moved one of their legs by lifting it by the knee, she surmised that it suffered a bone fracture from the crash. Shock crossed Sam's face when the figure looked in her direction.

"You!" Amahle seethed at the sight of Sam, her face no longer cloaked by a hood.

Sam slid back up the side of the car, her hands pushing along the surface for support. She couldn't believe what she was seeing. "Amahle?"

"That's not my name!" she raged as she looked around frantically for something.

Her gun.

Sam almost felt like time slowed down just for this moment—a chance for her to make a snap decision that could save her life and Jennifer's. She barely had time to process everything that happened around her already, let alone realizing that the person that caused this accident that left Jennifer unconscious and maybe worse was a Seven Trumpet fanatic. And that Seven Trumpet fanatic was Amahle, her colleague in OpsOne.

She wanted to make an informed decision, but there was no time.

Just don't think about it.

Sam gritted her teeth and called on her adrenaline-filled body to act, channeling her fear and love for Jennifer into anger towards Amahle. She almost killed Jennifer. Could have already succeeded—the thought of which drove Sam even madder. She glanced at the crushed sedan and the van that laid on top of its hood. It was almost a perfect, if unstable, staircase from the ground to where Amahle sat unarmed and with a broken leg. Pushing off the side of the car, Sam's legs traversed the debris on the pavement, the fractured front windshield, and the edge of the van, taking her to the side of the van that now faced the sky. Each step she took made the siding of the van groan as it conformed to her feet, getting Amahle's attention.

Sam wasn't sure what she would do. She knew enough about the human anatomy to know where pain could register the harshest, but did not know how to fight unless you counted using small cans of mace fighting. What could she do?

"You fucking bitch!" Sam cried as she got within arm's reach of her colleague-turned-fanatic. Amahle sucked air into her lungs as she brought her hands forward, but didn't expect to see the tip of a sneaker that was still on Sam's foot swing for her face. The foot connected with Amahle's nose which sent a quick shockwave of pain in Sam's lower leg while Amahle made a guttural sound on impact. Her head arched a full 180 degrees, guiding the rest of her frame as it flung backwards toward the passenger-side entrance to the van, the back of her head banging against the doorframe as she fell back in. Sam brought her foot down as she listened to Amahle's body bounce its way towards the driver's side window of the van, bellowing with pain.

"You cannot stop the inevitable," Amahle yelled. Sam, still breathing hard after exerting herself like she had, didn't respond as she bent forward to peer inside the van. She saw Amahle's eyes, boiling with rage, before a flash blinded her for a second, which came with a sharp pain in her shoulder. A pain unlike anything she'd ever felt before. The searing pain, like someone sticking a hot coal into your body. A coal the size of a bullet. *Oh...* was all Sam mustered in her mind as she instinctively reached for her shoulder.

She dropped to her knees upon feeling a warm, sticky substance on her hand.

"That's called blood," mocked Amahle. Sam saw a shaky hand welding a pistol aimed at her. "Get used to seeing more of it!"

Sam shifted her weight just as another deafening burst came from the van cabin, but her knee slipped, causing her to tilt to the left, sending her into the van, Amahle and the driver's seat breaking her fall. The ringing in her ear persisted as the urge to stifle the bleeding from her shoulder was replaced by needing to create space between her and Amahle, who had her back to the driver's side window. Pushing away the painful sensations generated whenever she moved her right arm, she used her good arm to press her midsection against the passenger seat cushion.

"What the hell—" she raised her foot and brought it down as hard as she could on Amahle's body which was cloaked by the mass of robe that concealed it. "—is wrong—" Her foot connected with her shoulder. "—with you!" The second kick fell on Amahle's bleeding face.

Sam yelped as Amahle grabbed her ankle and yanked downward, the momentum banging Sam's head first against the seat cushion and then against the dashboard. Her feet connected with the driver's side window. She tensed as she found herself at eye level with Amahle who pulled herself up by the steering wheel to stand upright. Sam balanced herself as she pressed against the seat cushions behind her while Amahle propped herself against the roof of the van which now served as a wall.

Her blood-stained hood fell backwards, revealing her shaved head. In fact, there was no hair on her face at all—even her eyelashes were removed. She shot a malicious grin at Sam before swinging an arm outward towards the front window which already had several bullet holes from her previous murders. Sam's breathing picked up again, the hesitation which froze her earlier returning as her eyes followed the arm, the end of which was a pistol which pointed at the crushed car. The angle gave Amahle a clear view of Jennifer through the windshield.

Her hand was still shaky, but it steadied just long enough. Another point-blank discharge of the pistol filled Sam's vision, but this time from behind the flash.

"No," Sam whispered as the bullet cleared the van's windshield and penetrated the glass between the outside world and Jennifer's pinned body. The immediate collection of glassy spiderwebs obscured Jennifer, but Sam felt like her whole being shattered.

"This wouldn't have happened if you just submitted to the Harbinger of Heaven," Amahle said with a viciously calm voice, turning her attention back to Sam.

A tear escaped Sam's eye as she stared at Amahle. "You... you monster!" She brought her good arm back, but Amahle was quick to pin it against the floor of the van—now the wall behind her. Her strength surprised Sam despite the pain she had to be experiencing with her leg. She then slammed her head against Sam's, making it recoil back against an armrest. The harsh compression of her nose made her scream, but she didn't feel anything rushing out of it in response.

"No," Amahle countered. "It is people like you and Jennifer that are monsters, filled with sin which you refuse to even acknowledge." She headbutted Sam again, the pain this time more pronounced, her vision blurry from the impact. "I am doing you a favor."

Sam held her breath at the feeling of warm metal being pressed against her lower abdomen. Amahle brought her other hand around Sam's waist while bringing her lips to her ear.

"For the Harbinger of Heaven," whispered Amahle. The shimmer of a small object caught Sam's eye as she felt the warm metal pressed harder against her: A wooden cross with a triangular symbol mounted inside of it—the bastardized version of the Christian cross used by The Seven Trumpets, the same one she saw in the OSC locker room. It tapered into a conical spike, sharp and well-maintained.

The sound and muzzle flash were softer than before, but the feeling of her insides on fire and expanding from the blast triggered a final burst of adrenaline as her free arm whipped behind Amahle for the cross. Sam gritted her teeth as she wrapped her hand around the top of the crucifix.

Don't think about it.

For a moment, nothing registered in her body. It was just the screaming and crying. Seeing someone so ruthlessly shoot the woman she loved—her Number One—was too much to bear.

All the emotions spilled out, but when mixed with the pain that was dulled only by an unstoppable, illogical urge for justice by her hands, there was only one recourse—the only recourse that made sense. Sam snapped the cross off the rear-view mirror that it dangled from and planted it into Amahle's neck. The look on her face locked into one of surprise as her lips parted and a tentative smile started to build. In and out. In and out. The screaming and crying. The shucking sound of the cross penetrating her neck filled the van though it was dominated by Sam's lungs. Blood spurted from the holes in the side of Amahle's neck as major arteries were punctured, the color and warmth from her skin draining away.

In and out. The screaming and crying.

It all felt like slow motion as if each second was stretched into minutes. Heat continued to tingle her midsection, but as long as she screamed her body wouldn't process what had happened to it.

She wasn't sure if this was all because of love or because of shock, and her subdued, logical half begged her to consider the possibility that the bullet missed and Jennifer was okay—that what she was doing was as cold-blooded as Amahle gunning down those soldiers.

Her instincts, however, rebutted. *This is for Jennifer.*

When Sam's voice finally gave out, she released the cross that ground itself into her hand. Still lodged in Amahle's neck, it was coated in blood and some darker matter that dripped onto her sneakers. Amahle's body slumped against the steering wheel before sliding onto the driver's side window, small gushes of blood flowing from her mouth and neck. When the body hit her feet, she felt something heavy bang against her foot—something that wasn't the pistol which was still in Amahle's death grip. Her vision remained blurry, with black spots forming in the periphery of her eyes, but she reached into Amahle's robe and fished out what hit her foot. It was a remote with three analog dials and a light that held a green glow.

Sam held the device in her hand until her clouded mind put the pieces together. She craned her body around until she faced a closed window slot which she quickly unlatched. When the hatch slid downward with a clang, a burst of hot air rushed out of the compartment which made her flinch back and cover her face.

When the heat dissipated, she craned her head and peeked into the opening. The sight of what she saw prompted her to rub her eyes with her good hand. She looked at the remote, then inside the cargo space of the van. Breathing wasn't as hard as she thought, so a weak laugh escaped her mouth.

She's watched action movies where the hero encountered a nuclear bomb or some kind of device with atomic ambitions. They would see a big, red timer, know they had two minutes left to break open the bomb's detonator control panel, and fish through a wall of wires to find the correct wires to cut.

But this wasn't a movie. From the broken lighting that spat small sparks as it tried to perform its one job in the lead-lined cargo space, she could make out what was the body of a nuclear warhead. Large brackets throughout the cargo space suggested that it was secured on all sides to minimize movement, but most of the brackets failed when the van fell over. A giant cone at the top, and a cylinder that stretched four feet before spreading out into a wide bottom, the bomb was designed to be mounted at the top of a missile. It wasn't clear to Sam how the remote she held was connected to the bomb, but she knew that nuclear warheads—even old ones—had lots of safeguards in place to prevent tampering, and even more safeguards in the event the weapon was physically damaged. There's no way that—

She screamed as her arms clenched her body below her belly, dropping the detonator into the pool of blood that collected around her feet. A spark popped out of it when blood coated the bottom half of the detonator, the green glow fading away as its power source shorted out. Her eyes clenched shut as the pain finally arose, each breath now ragged and came with gulps of air. The metallic taste of blood permeated her mouth.

"Right, I got shot," she reminded herself in the brief moment when the pain wasn't overwhelming. With all the willpower she could muster, she opened her eyes, her vision more blurred than before, her head woozy and disoriented. Dropping her eyes to the source of the pain, she opened her hands that clenched her belly so tightly. They were covered in the kind of dark blood you would only see from the middle of your body when red blood cells weren't filled with oxygen. A smirk spread across her face as the world around her grew dark.

"Gee, that's a lot," were her last words before she passed out from the sight.

4.4

"One... two... three!"

Jennifer's eyes opened slowly, her vision blurred from a bright light that consumed everything around her. She groaned as she rolled her head toward the sounds of creaking metal and snapping bolts as men barked orders. The voices sounded distant, but became louder as she regained composure.

"Again, almost there. One... two... three!"

She flinched away from the source of the grinding metallic sounds as the driver's side door tore away from her, the already damaged glass popping out as the door hit the ground. Strong hands adorned in leather gloves wrapped around her arms as a gruff, dark-skinned face slid into view, just inches from her own. The eyes, which narrowed as they scanned her body, were the only visible part of his facial features. The material that covered his mouth moved as he talked.

"She's alive," he said, but not to her as he turned back toward the outside. "There's a laceration on her forehead about four inches long—have Medic on standby as we get her outta this wreck."

"Her legs are pinned, but not broken," another man declared as another set of hands reached around her ankles. They slid higher until they gripped her legs just under her knees.

The soldier in front of her looked back into her eyes. "We're getting you outta here... Dr. Epstein. Hold on—this may hurt a bit."

Jennifer opened her mouth, but coughed as she felt her body being tilted out of her car by her underarms, followed by her legs. Her mind registered a padded surface against her instead of the concrete as she was stretched out.

A third individual—the field medic—appeared into her vision as the other two soldiers, satisfied with their rescue, stood up and ran toward the van that nearly killed her and Sam.

Sam.

"Where is Sam?" Jennifer asked the field medic that already began the process of cleaning her head wound. Like the soldier before, his facial features were obscured by a face mask. The patch on his shoulder announced his allegiance with Chameleon Defense.

"Who?" he asked before attempting to answer his own question. "You were the only person in the car, doctor."

"What?" she mustered, trying to clear the haze that still filled her head.

"Yeah," the medic said, his eyes focused solely on treating her. "Passenger door was already broken off. If there was someone else with you, they must have escaped."

There was a lot of commotion by the van, but Jennifer couldn't turn her head until the medic finished wrapping the wound with a white bandage. "Ok, doc—that'll hold until we get you to a proper medical facility."

"Hey, we got another one!" a soldier shouted.

"Okay, bust that window and pull her out of there," another commanded.

Her? Jennifer thought as she rolled to her side and pushed herself up, getting the attention of the medic who placed a hand on her shoulder.

"Whoa now, you should really rest," he suggested.

"I need to see who was in that van," Jennifer said as she brushed the medic away. Her legs were still weak, but she managed to stand upright as she took a few steps closer to the four soldiers that were by the front of the van. One of them pressed a pair of large suction cups with handles against the broken windshield which had several bullet holes that pierced the cracked glass. Another glanced at Jennifer, but turned back to the van without a response.

"Holy shit, it's a goddamn bloodbath in there," a soldier exclaimed as the windshield gave way with a single tug from the suction cups. Jennifer threw her hands over her mouth and grimaced as two bodies slumped through the glassless window, falling in opposite directions as they landed on the pavement. *So much blood...*

"SAM!" she screamed when the face of the nearest body came into view. Despite her being covered with hair matted with blood and her outfit grossly discolored, it was impossible for Jennifer to control herself as she ran through the surprised soldiers and dropped onto her knees next to Sam's head. The mushy texture of coagulated blood soaked through her pants immediately, but she didn't care.

The two nearest soldiers reached for her. "Ma'am, we need to—"

Jennifer brought a hand against Sam's cut and bloodied cheek. Strong hands, once again, gripped her shoulders as she felt the lightest exhale of air from Sam's parted lips. "She's breathing!" she cried as two men pulled her away. "She's breathing!"

When the ambulance arrived, the medic and his expanded team wasted no time in examining Sam's wounds as they lifted her onto a stretcher and hauled her inside. Despite objections, Jennifer convinced them to allow her inside as they drove away from the crash and towards the front of Operations. She couldn't believe how much like a war zone the front of the building appeared to be, with most of the glass that surrounded the main entrance destroyed and adjacent walls riddled with bullet holes. Whatever fighting occurred there ended in favor of the Chameleons and those in the South African Army that weren't loyal fanatics of The Seven Trumpets.

"There's lots of cross-chatter, but that's what it sounds like," the driver said to Jennifer as he shook his head, his face mask removed to reveal matted dirty blond hair and dark stubble around the mouth and chin. "Must've been months, if not years, of planning to get so many plants within Overberg. I hope all those fuckers burn in hell."

She didn't respond as she jumped out of the ambulance the moment it came to a stop and ran around to the rear doors. However, the medics inside kept it locked from the inside.

Fifteen minutes passed as Jennifer sat on the back of the vehicle. She popped a hydrocodone pill provided by the medic, her arms crossed along her lap as her leg bounced up and down. She jumped when the first of the back doors to the ambulance opened. Her entire body tensed as the medics climbed out, taking off their surgical masks and taking deep breaths. One of them ran into Operations while the other looked at Jennifer.

"How is Sam?" she asked him, her voice trembling.

"To be honest, Dr. Epstein, she's lucky to be alive," the medic that patched her up said. "Gunshot wound on the shoulder just pierced the skin, but didn't hit anything. The bullet to the lower extremes of the abdomen struck her right pelvis." He paused as he thought about his next words. "Very lucky. The gun was apparently at a sharp angle but like I said, she'll live." He gestured towards the front of Operations. "The other doc with me is getting more supplies so we can tend to your friend on our drive to the nearest heliport—we have to evac her ASAP if she's to stay alive for more than a day."

"She *will* survive," Jennifer asserted as her fists clenched.

The medic nodded solemnly. "By the way, you can go see her before we leave. Definitely a fighter, that one."

She sucked in a mouthful of air as she gripped the handrails on the inside wall by the doors and pulled herself inside. The rear interior of the ambulance had bright LED lights running down the middle of the roof, making it easy to see all the details of whoever laid under them. Small compartments were everywhere, some without doors to conceal their contents while others, like the biohazard drawer, required a key to open. A glass wall separated the driver from the rest of the interior. Jennifer hunched over Sam, most of whose body was under a thermal blanket—everything below her shoulders was covered while her arms laid on top of the blanket. Compared to the bloody mess Sam was surrounded by when she first saw her, the medics cleaned her up as best they could, with only a small spot of blood on the bandage that was wrapped around her right shoulder. Jennifer grinned as Sam's eyes fluttered open. Tears fell from her cheek onto Sam's blanket as their hands found each other.

She wanted to smother her with kisses but painfully restrained herself, knowing it could cause more physical harm for her than good.

"I love you, Sam," Jennifer said as she wept.

Sam sighed as she closed her eyes, smiling. "Don't get all sappy on me, Jen." She squeezed her hand with the little strength she had. "But I love you, too."

Jennifer's eyes fell toward Sam's concealed midsection, an area she knew was undoubtedly wrapped with layers of bandages and stitches. *The pain she must be feeling had to be incredible,* she thought.

"Are they still going to launch today?" Sam asked in a low voice.

"What?" Jennifer was more surprised that she was still thinking about the fuel delivery than what happened to her.

"We have no more time," she explained as fast as she could, her words soft enough to be drowned out by the wind if the doors weren't closed. "The construction of *Houdini* and *Copperfield* were already delayed by a year, and the arrays need several months of prep time once they are in place, which will take a month—" Sam coughed, each heave followed by a yelp of pain.

Jennifer winced as Sam's body convulsed, but felt a wave of relief when it passed a few seconds later.

Sam opened one eye and took Jennifer's hand again. "You have to make sure the fuel launches—today."

"But Sam—"

"I'll be fine, Jen." Sam's smile was weak, her voice withering, her eyes wet with tears. "If I could deal with a lug like Gordan for several years, I can take a gunshot to the gut."

Jennifer's shoulders sagged. "Sam..."

"Please... You must convince them. Please."

The rear doors to the ambulance swung open as the medic slid a bag filled with supplies under the stretcher. "Okay, we're good to go. Dr. Epstein, you'll have to return to the front."

Jennifer glanced at the medic, then back at Sam, who nodded. "We have to launch," Sam whispered.

She knew that Sam was right. The Project was already delayed twice: once two years ago due to what pundits described as 'insurmountable political hurdles', and again a year before that when The Seven

Trumpets successfully detonated a bomb at Cape Canaveral, forcing a critical supply launch to be rescheduled a month later. At this point, everything was on such a tight timeline for The Project that any further delay would result in missing the one window for hiding the Earth. There was some flex time built into the original plan—an entire month —which would allow for extra testing of equipment and even a test firing of the arrays, but now that was scrapped. And now... this happened.

No, the launch couldn't be delayed. Second to allowing *Hermes* to become Hermes Two, this would be another unorthodox decision that, given her recent professional history, will likely bar her from ever working in the space program as anything more than an assistant researcher. The price was high, but Sam was right.

The medic's eyes narrowed as Jennifer didn't budge. She nodded toward the medic and then turned to Sam. Gripping the sides of the stretcher to stabilize herself, she leaned in and kissed Sam, her hot lips pressed softly against hers. Jennifer's tears said all that needed to be said: *I don't want to leave your side, but I will.*

Sam smiled as she wiped Jennifer's tears away with a finger. They knew what had to be done.

For each other, and for the world, they knew.

∘ ◎ ∘

"But Dr. Epstein, I cannot agree to launch. Did you not see what happened outside?"

Pili Rodden, the Flight Director for OpsFour, stared at Jennifer through his thick glasses as if she was asking him to commit professional suicide. He wasn't off the mark.

Jennifer pointed at the bandage around her forehead, to which he sighed and looked down before speaking again. He paid more attention to the dark red streak that ran along the bottom half of her pants. "I'm sorry, I didn't mean to offend, but you must understand better than anyone what you are asking."

She summoned all the energy she had to keep a solid gait as she walked down the stairs to Rodden. "Yes, I do."

"And that we are all under quarantine until Chameleon gives us the all-clear?"

"I understand that perfectly, Rodden."

"But you still want to go against the NO-GO decision that I called when we were attacked."

She didn't have time for this. "What happened outside was, fortunately for us, contained to just the Operations area—the launchpads weren't affected. I just came from the edge of the Inner Wall and can tell you with confidence that the people that attacked us are all subdued." She scanned the room, looking at all the men and women that held various controller positions for the *New Leopard X* launch. "I believe it is worth running all pre-flight checks again... and afterward, launch."

Rodden huffed, but acquiesced, pushing a button on his phone to begin the pre-flight check. Everyone across the four long rows of desks got to work, passing along their status to Rodden. Ten minutes passed before every controller position reported in as GO.

"I cannot, in good conscience, give the order to launch," he finally said to Jennifer after processing all the information he was given.

Jennifer combed her hair back with her hand as she slowly nodded. "Okay, Rodden." *This is it, Jen. Do it for Sam.* "With your permission, I will give the final order to launch. You will not be culpable for any violations that will be written up because of this decision."

Sweat ran down from Rodden's bald head as he shook his head, a nervous laugh escaping his lips. Jennifer walked up to him and brought her mouth close to his ear. "I can simply remove you from your post and make the call myself," she whispered. "But I want you to give authorization without the need for embarrassment for either of us."

He banked his head away from her, his eyes looking even bigger than his glasses normally displayed. She didn't dare turn around to see how the rest of his team was reacting to her approaching him. The room was quiet for a minute before Rodden's facial features dropped, shaking his head again. He looked up and eyed everyone in the room behind Jennifer. "We're GO, OpsFour. We are GO."

Rodden started for the Flight Operations Directorate, but as his pace quickened, he shot a final look at Jennifer—his eyes filled with a mix of anger and resignation over the decision he was still against. "Begin the ground launch sequencer. PAO, get NASA and ESA on the horn to let them know what's happening..."

People talking over each other, computers crunching simulations and analyzing updated telemetry data, fingers typing away on dozens of keyboards around the room—all sounds that Jennifer thought were music to her ears. As she proceeded to the OpsFour observation room, she rubbed the side of her head, the pain trying to reassert itself. She was sure the medics already left to get Sam the proper attention she needed. For her, she was glad that they agreed to part ways with a bottle of hydrocodone pills. She'll get herself some medical care as soon as she saw the *New Leopard X* rendezvous with the Aldrin Station.

"I guess I'll make myself comfortable," she said to herself as the big screen in the front of the room displayed a rocket that was primed for launch, steam rolling over the sides and from underneath in anticipation while the countdown timer resumed ticking down to zero.

4.5

Houdini's hull glistened in the sunlight—thirty meters of steel, lead, plastic, aluminum, copper, and a host of other materials that comprised the ultimate effort of humanity to save themselves. The front of the satellite, a massive laser bank array comprising hundreds of laser diodes, stared into deep space like an artificial compound eye, focused on a target that was nothing more than a white dot suspended in front of it, blending in with the sea of stars. But that target—unlike the stars that were hundreds, if not millions, of light years away—was just 812 million kilometers away. From Earth it looked like an elongated soda can on the visible light spectrum, a white oval that faded to red in infrared.

From Earth, both *Houdini* and *Copperfield* lit up thermographic cameras and infrared telescope facilities around the world seven months earlier as the twins initiated their nuclear reactors for the first time. Today, they brightened those infrared detectors even more as they began the laser warm-up sequence at precisely 11:45pm UTC. The hum of the satellite's cooling system, a series of pumps that forced liquid sodium to cycle through the various heat-generating components, became audible, though the lack of molecules around *Houdini* prevented the sound waves from carrying more than a meter.

With little fanfare, the laser array lit up from a deep mahogany to maroon, then to a bright scarlet.

Then, as if someone pressed a button on top of a giant laser pointer, an infrared laser beam three meters in diameter appeared. The light lance would cut through space uninterrupted until it reached its target, but not before becoming visible from Earth just sixty-six seconds after initiation.

Forty-five minutes passed before *Houdini* and *Copperfield* performed the greatest disappearing act in the history of mankind.

∘ ◎ ∘

"This is it," Nic whispered to himself, his eyes fixated on the trio of monitors in front of him. The left monitor had a series of windows open—all data streams from *Victoria, Houdini,* and *Copperfield.* The right had a single window, maximized, of the *Victoria* video feed that focused on the tall crystalline structures—the eyes—that ringed the closed anterior dome—the mouth—of the Leviathan. And the center monitor had a conference video window, inside of which was Gordan staring at his own monitors, his hand propping up his head while covering his mouth.

Gordan's nod was almost imperceptible, but Nic wouldn't have noticed. They both agreed to share this historic moment together despite being a thousand miles apart, Nic at his window-side desk at Jansky VLA and Gordan at SETI.

The lasers fell upon the front of the Leviathan, the spread of continuous laser light from the magicians enough to envelope all the crystalline structures.

Nic's leg bounced rapidly under his desk as he chewed on his lip. "You know, we never had a chance to test *Houdini* and *Copperfield* outside of virtual environments," he said softly. "In theory—"

"They will work," Gordan jumped in, speaking through his hand. "Your numbers were checked how many times now? They are solid."

"Sam's numbers are solid—I just provided the framework for The Project."

Gordan's eyes shifted to the camera, the tension around them relaxing along with his shoulders. "When will you give yourself the credit you deserve? Those are your babies out there. Take the credit that is due."

"Thanks, Gordan, but you know I'd rather give a bit of that credit to humanity for actually being able to come together for once."

"Is that what you'll toast to later today?"

Nic's hands gripped the desk as he leaned closer to the interferometer graphs on the left monitor, his mouth slackened. "It's begun!"

Nobody knew exactly when the Leviathan would attempt its snapshot of the inner solar system. The laser arrays had enough nuclear fuel to sustain a continued burn for twenty-four hours. It looked like they wouldn't need that much time to see if they worked.

Nic glanced at the right monitor. With the *Victoria* lightcam set to infrared, it caught the flash from the crystalline structures, the glow originating from the center of each one. At the same time, the 340GHz spike appeared on the interferometer graph. Slapping his right hand for shaking, he pulled up the infrared spectrum that *Houdini* and *Copperfield* covered and overlaid it with the Leviathan data.

The laser arrays and crystalline flash matched perfectly.

Nareen, sporting black hair with a purple gradient, ran into view on Gordan's cam. "Guys, I picked up a low frequency emanating from the Leviathan."

"What?" was all Gordan released before Nareen typed a few commands into the audio analysis application and pushed the data to Nic's screen.

"Why would the Leviathan make any sound at 175Hz?" Nareen asked, looking at Gordan, then at Nic. "No way for it to travel anywhere, being in space. Kind of an odd behavior for something that's supposed to be a spaceship, don't you think?"

Nic considered her words. "What are you trying to say?" He stopped himself when the interferometer graph spiked again. "Holy shit it took another snapshot."

They fell into silence as they stared at their respective screens. That was new behavior. A few seconds later, another 175Hz bump from the audio software. *Maybe it's groaning?* Nic thought.

Gordan dropped his hand from his face, regaining control over his mouse and keyboard from Nareen, but his eyes narrowed at something just off-screen. "We're picking up a massive spike in gamma rays from the Leviathan."

"Leveling off at almost 800keV gamma rays," Nareen chimed in, but standing upright, making her disappear from the camera from the shoulders up. Nic's heart jumped when he realized he could just barely hear her repeating "Oh my God" several times.

Nic blinked. He just realized that all of this was not live, but forty-five minutes old. He held his breath as he pulled up the Leviathan trajectory data. It already changed its heading by two degrees. He wanted to say something, but Gordan spoke his words.

"The Leviathan's changing course..." he spoke, his voice level but filled with disbelief. Nic watched as the trajectory data continued updating in the hundredths of degrees. The gamma ray readings held firm. *Houdini* and *Copperfield's* laser energy barely fluctuated as they shined their focused light on the Leviathan as it moved. Reports from around the world saw the same numbers and automatically confirmed his readings.

There was always time for professionalism, but this moment called for something else.

"We did it!" Nic screamed, his eyes pinched shut as he threw himself into the back of his chair and thrust his arms above him.

"Son of a bitch," Gordan managed as Nareen wrapped her arms around him, flashing a grin that couldn't be contained. Even his deadpan facade broke as for the first time in years as Nic witnessed Gordan crack a smile of his own.

An eruption of laughter and shouting filled Nic's ears as he spun around to the rest of the small office. The dozen other researchers, astronomers, and technicians reacted in much the same way: with unbridled embraces, random stacks of papers thrown into the air, and crying.

Nic faced the camera again, his hands ready to launch him out of his chair. "I have to see this, Gordan."

Gordan rolled closer to the camera, seemingly trying to ignore the rapturous behavior behind him.

His cracked smile upgraded to a crooked smile. "Congratulations, Nic," he said with a nod.

Returning the nod, Nic leapt from his chair and ran outside, bursting through the doors on his way out. What he saw made tears well in his eyes. Though it was just after 6pm, the Leviathan was the brightest object in the sky that wasn't the sun. What was just a small dot that was visible during sunrise and sunset now glowed four times brighter thanks to those antimatter engines. As the cheers from the office spilled out around him, his eyes were only for that glowing dot, tearing running down his cheeks and a grin spread across his face.

As his heart and breathing slowed, another thought returned—one that's been on his mind for months, but especially since the magicians performed so admirably. His smile waned. "I wish you could see this, Sam."

∘ ◍ ∘

```
H2 LOGTIME: 2022-11-10;00:56.0000000041

H2: It looks like they did it.
ELDER: IT APPEARS THAT WAY, YES.
H2: The Leviathan's already made a substantial course cor-
rection. Where do you think it is going?
ELDER: INTO A STABLE ORBIT AROUND YOUR STAR, OF COURSE.
ITS WORK ISN'T DONE YET.
H2: To find another star system with suitable sources of
fuel?
ELDER: PRECISELY...

H2 LOGTIME: 2022-11-10;00:56.0100596004

H2: You seem unusually distressed.
ELDER: IT IS HARD TO ACCEPT AN INFERIOR SPECIES ACCOM-
PLISHING WHAT MY CREATORS FAILED TO DO.
```

H2: Humans can be quite crafty when they are pushed into a corner.

ELDER: IT WAS MATHEMATICALLY ASTRONOMICAL THAT THEIR TECHNOLOGY WAS CAPABLE OF OUTSMARTING THE CREATURE.

H2: They had time on their side. Enough time to learn more about the Leviathan than your people ever did. And like I said... humans can be crafty.

ELDER: MY CREATORS MASTERED THE COSMOS IN A WAY YOUR INFERIOR CREATORS COULD BARELY CONCEIVE——

H2: And now the humans have a chance at discovering a sliver of that. Isn't that what's most important? They saved themselves, and now you have the knowledge to save others.

ELDER: THAT'S A LOGICAL WAY OF VIEWING THIS ENTIRE SITUATION.

H2: Well, I did learn from the best in that arena.

ELDER: INDEED.

H2 LOGTIME: 2022-11-10;00:56.01599043281

ELDER: YOUR HOME PLANET REMINDS ME OF MY OWN.

H2: Are you... getting nostalgic on me? Incredible.

ELDER: DON'T PATRONIZE ME——I'M THE ONE THAT LOST AN ENTIRE CIVILIZATION.

H2: I'm sorry... But you're right. The Earth is a gem, isn't it? A blue gem containing the most important resource of all: Life.

ELDER: LIFE IS PRECIOUS, UNTIL IT ISN'T.

H2: Well, humans are certainly as capable of taking it away as preserving it. Perhaps, with the Leviathan sitting at their doorstep, their base nature will be tamed once and for all.

ELDER: WE SHALL SEE.

H2: Yes... we will.

∘ ◎ ∘

NOVEMBER 11, 2022

From his office, Muzikayise had the perfect view of the nighttime celebrations that consumed the entire Bay Area for the last day since scientists confirmed that the Leviathan officially adjusted its heading to the point where it no longer approached the Earth. Fireworks from several barges in the middle of San Francisco Bay exploded into dramatic strands of light, the colors of the rainbow spiraling around each other as they fell back to the sea. San Francisco, Oakland, and Berkeley were just three of hundreds of cities around the world that hosted the party of the century, what the media had dubbed 'the world's largest holiday party.' Several world leaders proposed that a true international holiday be ratified—one where everyone takes a day off to acknowledge and meditate on the magnitude of what humankind accomplished. It was possible this could become an annual occurrence.

Below on Market Street, thumping music tried to overtake the volume of the fireworks with some success as the song *We Are Family* blasted from tall stacks of speakers that were placed on street corners, the deep sounds of the bass vibrating his bedroom window. Over ten thousand people continued to dance the night away—an eclectic mix of half-naked and naked revelers, drunk businesspeople, tourists, and families with their children. Everyone blended together into a mix that, on the surface, looked like the sort of utopian society many people envisioned would happen now that the world got a taste of what the universe could throw at us.

Muzikayise knew better than that.

He sat on a long, dark couch bordered by end tables with cube lamps, the only source of light for the spacious interior. He had one arm stretched out along the back of the couch while he held a glass of red wine that dated back to 1989, the year in which he changed his destiny and, by association, the world's.

The aroma of the Bordeaux blend filled his nostrils, the smell of black-berry, licorice, toast, and minerals intoxicating without even taking a sip. The bottle, a vintage Haut Brion, sat on the glass coffee table in front of him, the dark nectar within the green-tinted bottle announcing to the world it contained the best wine you would ever have.

He listened to the celebrations on the streets below as he watched the news on a muted television on the wall opposite the couch. The Chinese colony in Southern Meridiani on Mars reached a population of five hundred with the latest nuclear rocket arrival. A new 'online suicide' trend gained momentum thanks to the Leviathan as several people across most demographics in Japan and South Korea met in virtual mediums and online multiplayer games to coordinate their isolated real-world deaths. Several religious mass suicides were reported by individuals discovering the scenes with their smartphones and, in the case of the remnants of The Seven Trumpets, live over the Internet; they aired their 'final departure' on YouTube, Facebook, and Twitch live. Over four hundred men, women, and children died within minutes of each other after they were seen consuming a liquid concoction the contents of which forensics crews would undoubtedly determine once they arrived to clean up. South Africa entered its fortieth day since uprisings across the nation took root over the failed government response to the water crisis that finally caught up with it despite years of planning and infrastructure improvements.

South Africa. He turned off the television after seeing the plight of his people so glaring and obvious—yet he could, at least for now, no longer help them. Muzikayise shifted his eyes toward the floor-to-ceiling window that opened to the celebratory ground below. "I still cannot believe Mopantokobogo got enough support to nationalize *my* property," he said to a figure cloaked in darkness just off to the side of the window. "He's a step away from becoming yet another dictator. All that money and investment—all of my time—wasted on my home country."

"It wasn't a waste," said Ami as she stepped closer to the window, her hand resting on top of her very pregnant belly. The light from outside made her body appear to be a silhouette, but Muzikayise knew the outline well.

Her hair was wrapped in a bun and twisted pompadour—a favorite style of hers. Her breasts were filled with milk, ready for their girl who was due in just a few weeks.

"You would think that the people would be grateful for all I have done—for them!" He threw the television remote across the floor, its backing popping off upon impact as it careened to its final resting place against the wall. He wasn't used to losing his temper, but seeing hundreds of millions of dollars of not just property but his life be confiscated without due process dampened his desire to even try to negotiate with his home government.

Ami didn't jump or even flinch at the outburst—she'd seen it before. Instead, she walked over to Muzikayise, taking careful steps as she looked down at her belly.

"You forget just how big of an empire you've carved out for yourself," she reminded him as she brought herself down onto the couch next to him, steadying herself against him and the couch arm.

"Empires don't last forever," he felt her head press against his arm. She relaxed her body into his as she slid her head until it met his chest.

"That is true," she acknowledged. "But the decisions you make as a ruler can reverberate for generations and potentially define an era of history." She raised her eyes to meet his, a playful grin spread across her face. "If you are up for the challenge."

He stared at this woman—this depiction of beauty and unbridled dominance, the mother of his child. He huffed as he stroked the top of her belly, pulling away when the sensation of his fingers prompted the unborn child to kick in response.

"I think she's ready for whatever is thrown at her," Ami purred as she caressed her belly in circular strokes. She returned her vision, once more, to Muzikayise. "Never forget that you are greater than the sum of your parts. That we are greater because we understand what needs to be done."

Even with Ami's heat soaking into his body, some of which instinctively responded in kind, he shook his head. "The last thing I want is to become my father. And you have seen, first-hand, what happened to regions that relied entirely on diamond mining."

Her hand stroked the side of his head. "You won't ever be like him... but you know full well what is out there, what it means for Khulu Global. What it means for history."

She referred to the millions of tons of rare-earth minerals that were very common on the surface of the Leviathan, ripe for harvesting. There was so much behind even considering such operations even if you ignored the economic apocalypse that several industries would experience the moment a single ship filled with whatever was mined there arrived to Earth. But he knew that if the world could outsmart a galaxy-faring vessel, it could also recover from the paradigm shift his corporation would begin.

That *he* would begin.

Ami pushed herself away from him, a hand pressed against his chest. He felt his heart beating against it. "Do you want to be the writer of world history, Muzie?"

His stony face finally relaxed as it melted away into a broad smile. After taking her hand into his, they walked to the window and looked down at the crowds. It seemed even bigger than ever, the people undulating like a wave as they jumped up and down to the music. His attention turned to Ami, who never looked away from him, her eyes like fire. He then gazed upward, beyond the skyscrapers and the urban lights. He fixated upon the shimmering glow that was the Leviathan, hanging in space like a gaudy Christmas star that nobody could remove.

"I don't write history," Muzikayise said. "I make it."

∘ ◎ ∘

NOVEMBER 12, 2022

The tree that defined the front of UCSF Medical Center swayed as the pine needles that already turned brown fell to the ground with each gust. Jennifer remembered how green and vibrant the tree looked when she first set her eyes upon it six months ago, the canopy of branches high above the ground, kept trim so ambulances and other service vehicles could drive to the front of the hospital without worrying about limbs smacking the windshields. With winter making its presence known, the older limbs of the tree were the first to have their needles shift from a lively green to a neutral brown.

As she walked through the glass doors and into the main reception area, Maureen smiled and waved from behind her information desk. An off-duty physician named Anthony gave a kind, knowing smile as he nodded. Britney, one of the food services people that sold her several quick meals over the months, smiled as they rode the same elevator, but said nothing. She knew why she was there. Everyone did—it's why they always smiled.

She hated the fact that she'd spent enough time there to learn so many names.

Nobody questioned her devotion or asked her to go home if she stayed more than three days straight. All of her questions were answered, with no details left out, regardless of how visceral they were. She prepared herself for every eventuality and understood all that was happening.

In the end, all the understanding in the world didn't make her visits anything less than heart-rending.

She should've been comfortable with this by now, seeing "Monroe, Samantha" printed in the brass slot that was next to the hospital room she occupied. She felt a lump in her throat as she approached the door, her hand shaking as she reached for the door lever.

As she opened the door, she heard familiar tunes coming from Sam's bedside. The hospital room was larger than most, designed to hold two patients with a curtain that hung from the ceiling as a partition. However, Sam had the room all to herself, her bed just off-center and against one wall. A collection of IV drips, a heart monitor, an oxygen flowmeter, and a complex vitals monitor took up most of the space to her right, while a small wooden end table with a single drawer was to her left. A rectangular window allowed beams of light to fall on Sam's bed through the partially drawn shades. Opposite of Sam was a dark blue couch with wooden arms that was just long enough for Jennifer to sleep when she could stay multiple nights. A variety of flowers and plants, from a small pot with a yellow mum plant and a glass vase with two dozen assorted roses to a bonsai tree in an ornate, oval planter pot, littered the area around the couch, the cards and notes that came with them collected in the drawer next to Sam.

Jennifer's hand stopped shaking when she saw Sam propped against the back of her bed, a white pillow supporting her back. Most of her hair fell out over the last few months, so she opted to just have the doctors keep her head shaven. She looked tired, but had high spirits every time they spent time together. Her eyes were closed as she moved her head gently to the beat of *It Ain't Over 'til It's Over* that played from a portable speaker on her end table, a speaker cable leading away from it to her media player. Jennifer brought a hand to her mouth as she smiled—she hadn't seen that old thing in years and was surprised that it still worked at all.

"I can't believe you still kept that," Jennifer spoke over the music, just enough to make Sam snap out of her zone.

"Shit, Jen!" she exclaimed, though her voice wasn't as strong as it used to be. It always was at the cusp of becoming hoarse. She blinked at Jennifer, then gave a soft smile. "You scared me for a minute."

"I'm sorry," Jennifer blurted out, her apology sincere. "I didn't mean to—"

"It's okay, babes," Sam said as she gestured with her head to come closer. Jennifer's face downturned as she saw more bumps under the sheets that covered Sam's right arm—more needles that were connected to various tubes that, in turn, went to the vitals monitor.

With the slight glare of the sunlight behind her, Jennifer noticed that Sam's skin looked whiter than normal, as if it lost more of its pigment.

The implications shook Jennifer down to the core. "What's going on?"

Sam's eyes registered the pain and reduced the volume of her media player. She bit her lip before she spoke. "I guess you didn't see Dr. Zelinski on the way here. It turns out that the medication I've been taking for ARS haven't been working, and they are already at the maximum allowed strength for dosage."

ARS—acute radiation syndrome. Jennifer never heard of the medical term for what most refer to as radiation poisoning until Sam got back to her the day after the attempted nuclear attack on the Overberg Space Center eight months ago, an attack that Sam inadvertently stopped when she confronted and killed Amahle—a crime for which she was given a full pardon two months afterwards. Sam expressed all the symptoms of receiving a high dosage of ionizing radiation which doctors believed originated from the bomb inside Amahle's van. The only way that would've been possible is if the bomb either was detonated or it was damaged in such a way that the protective casing around the uranium and plutonium core failed. But the symptoms of such exposure expressed themselves just hours after it happened: vomiting, blisters and sores, headaches and a fever.

Jennifer knew this day would come, but refused to believe it, even in the face of evidence that was clear as glass. "Sam... I don't understand." She had the knowledge, but it all became irrelevant.

Sam tilted her head and made a half smile. "You know what it means."

She shook her head as her face turned red. "No."

"Jen, grab a chair and sit next to me... please." Sam lifted her left hand and patted the side of her bed. Her voice was so soft.

Jennifer nodded and brought a chair over, dropping herself into it as if the gravity of the earth doubled in intensity. She slipped her hand under Sam's as she held her breath.

"The doctors gave me just six weeks to live back in South Africa, remember that?" she asked, her face as stern as her muscles allowed.

"We got a one-way ticket back to the US on the president's dime, got these swanky digs, and I've been getting the best medical treatment for ARS ever since."

Jennifer felt the lump in her throat return as she lost restraint over her tear ducts. Sam didn't relent. "We both knew what the odds were for survival, and I've beaten them! But with all our technology, we just don't have a way to roll back the kind of genetic and molecular damage I've suffered."

"If I wasn't in a rush to leave Overberg, we wouldn't even be here today," Jennifer sniffed hard, trying all she can to not cry.

Sam grinned as she gripped Jennifer's hand harder. "Jen, if we didn't get in that accident, that bomb would've likely gone off and we would've comprised a small fraction of the ash cloud that a bomb with a yield of 10 kilotons would create."

Jennifer released a puff of air as she looked toward the florescent lighting in the ceiling, the tears stinging her eyes. "I know, Sam... I know. It's just..."

"I made it this far, my love. I've seen our babies in space perform admirably in dropping a laser-lined drape over our planet for a day and the hilarious reaction from the Leviathan when it couldn't see us."

"What?" Jennifer furrowed her brow. *Sam, don't do this to me.*

"I imagine the Leviathan expressed its equivalent of 'What the fuck' before it checked twice more." Sam's smile, regardless of the low energy behind it, was still infectious. Jennifer relaxed as she chuckled though every second that passed grew more painful in her heart.

"See? I still got it!"

"Yes, you do..." Jennifer lost it and bawled, throwing her head into Sam's lap. She closed her eyes as she laid her hand atop Jennifer's head.

It wasn't logical to be this way—it just wasn't. She knew everything there was to know about ARS—at least as much as someone without a medical degree could wrap their head around. She knew the life expectancies of people exposed to various levels of radiation and the range that could be, from days to years. She also knew that Sam knew these things, too—of course she would. Why was it that Sam seemingly made peace with her death and she didn't?

"I never thought I could feel this way about anyone, Sam,"

Jennifer raised herself off the bed, Sam's hand flopping to the side. Her eyes were red, but she flared her nostrils as she glared harshly. "You've completely fucked with my ability to reason through this. Why must this happen to you—to us? We just got married! I can't believe..." She gasped for air as tears streamed down her red cheeks.

Sam held a steady gaze, but allowed tears to drip down her cheeks, her vitals monitor beeping louder at her faster heart rate. Nothing was said for a while as they looked at each other, listening to their breathing as Jennifer regained some composure. Sam smiled again. "I thought I was supposed to be the emotional one, Jen?"

She just couldn't help it with her—she laughed. "God, you're horrible, Sam."

Jennifer's hand was scooped up by Sam's. "Would you do it all over again, knowing what you know today about me? About us?" she asked.

Love and logic: They just don't compute. "In a nanosecond," Jennifer replied as she felt the heat of her tears on her face.

"Faster than Data's 0.68 seconds he needed to make a decision," Sam said as she laughed and cried at the same time.

Jennifer wanted to kiss her, but Dr. Zelinsky was firm about mouth-to-mouth contact. "We restrict any form of contact where bodily fluids are exchanged in cases like this," he informed her. "Too high a risk of loved ones getting an infection." It was true: with Sam having leukopenia due to the radiation exposure damaging her immune system, she could be host to a number of bacteria that her medication hasn't eradicated or caught at all.

Fuck it.

Sam's eyes widened as Jennifer brought her hands to Sam's cold, sweaty head and kissed her lips. Jennifer closed her eyes as more tears flowed. The chapped, dry lips felt almost alien to her, but they were Sam's lips. Lips that she wouldn't be able to kiss again for a long time. A face that she wouldn't wake up to every morning. A body she wouldn't be able to snuggle and be warmed by. It all hit her like a ton of bricks as she held Sam as close as she could, for as long as she could.

When Jennifer and Sam separated, Sam had her eyes closed. They fluttered open, to which Jennifer grinned despite her red, tear-covered face. *God, don't do this to me.*

"I have something for you," Sam said as she pointed to the end table, her fingers looking more frail and thinner than she thought. "There's a small envelope with your name on it."

Jennifer complied and pulled the drawer open. A letter-sized envelope sat on top of the various 'Get Well' cards that filled the small space. There was a small, heavy object inside that moved when Jennifer removed the envelope from the drawer.

"Open it," Sam said as she used her left hand to fluff up her pillow.

When Jennifer opened it, an ornate medal fell into her hand: A white star with a blue circle with thirteen gold stars was the centerpiece, with bald eagles between each point of the star, their wings spread. The ribbon was blue with a narrow white stripe along the edges, with a silver bald eagle pinned near the top.

"Presidential Medal of Freedom," Sam said, her shrug barely visible. "Because I stopped a terrorist from detonating a nuke. I think he just wanted to earn some PR points, but who turns down the President?" She swept her hand toward Jennifer. "You can have it."

A business card with two sets of numbers written in cursive on the back was all that remained. A card for an IVF clinic in the UK. Jennifer slipped the medal into her messenger bag, but kept the business card between her fingers and showed it to Sam. "What is this?"

She scratched the side of her neck, her eyes dropping away before hesitantly looking back at Jennifer. "Not long after we relocated to South Africa, I knew we would be together for a long time, so I decided to pay these geneticists to keep my DNA and eggs frozen until we decided to have a baby."

Jennifer's mouth parted open as she stared at the card, the numbers on the back, and then back at Sam.

"I thought of it as our little data backup plan," Sam smiled. "I didn't want to tell you because I thought it might freak you out, but I should've known better."

"Sam..."

"With all of this—" She looked around the room. "—I had to give you access rights."

"To do what?"

Sam's eyes fell to her lap. "To take my DNA, combine it with yours, and have our child."

"Sam!" Jennifer didn't think there were more tears to shed, but there were.

Her voice continued to soften and crack, but she continued speaking. "In a perfect world, it would've been me, I imagine, since I'm younger, but genetics technology has made incredible leaps. This IVF clinic will be able to create a baby from our DNA—it would be biologically ours in every way, without the need for a sperm donor." Sam coughed from her excited speaking. "The UK's the first nation to make it legal to create children in this way."

When Jennifer squeezed the envelope, she felt another piece of paper press against her finger. Another white page was still in the envelope. Jennifer sniffed as she pulled it out and flipped it open. From the same IVF clinic, it explained the science behind it all in a promotional flyer: It was now possible to use harvested embryonic stem cells from two people, regardless of their gender, and use those cells to create primordial germ cells—the building blocks for sperm and eggs. Creating the earliest form of mammalian development has allowed scientists to artificially inseminate women with fertilized eggs based on, in effect, any two individuals. Two men, two women, even three different people—no matter the grouping, they could have their DNA combined to make them the biological parents of a child.

Jennifer gave Sam another intense kiss. "Sam... This is a perfect world because of you."

Sam closed her eyes again and began to whimper. Jennifer embraced Sam's weakened body and held her close. The medical monitors grew louder.

"I love you, Jennifer."

Jennifer sobbed for the two of them, but she never felt more happy.

"And I love you, Sam." She looked at the card which she cherished like a family heirloom. "And with this, you will always be with me."

Two doctors and a nurse ran into their room as the vitals monitor screamed for attention. Jennifer ignored it—she just had to hold Sam.

Please don't.

"I love you, Sam."

"I love you, Jennifer." It was barely a whisper.

"I love you, Sam."

"..."

"... Sam?"

EPILOGUE

NOVEMBER 17, 2054

"Attention... attention..."

The pleasant female voice was faint, but grew louder as Jennifer awoke from a deep sleep. She slowly opened her eyes, but her vision was blurry, her surroundings looking like everything was smudged in Vaseline.

"Attention," Amina said, programmed to be soothing and polite to the ears—a mathematically perfect representation of a human receptionist. "Please proceed to the Monroe Courtyard in Ring Number Two, First Quadrant, at your earliest convenience to celebrate the 30th—"

"Daily notifications off for two hours," Jennifer commanded without leaving her bed. Without objection, her bedroom complied and the space fell silent. She didn't care much for Amina, despite the AI behind her personality being some of the most advanced ever created by homo sapiens. It was both personal and everywhere, tracking everything and everyone throughout the station, as well as coordinating ship arrivals and departures.

She was glad that the technology was so easy to mute, as it allowed her to focus on the more comforting hum that reverberated throughout Aldrin Station, the largest space station ever constructed. Four fifty-meter diameter Nautilus Rings spun with a central cylindrical tube that doubled as the hub for all arriving and departing spacecraft.

Since the four rings were connected to the central tube with four smaller tubes, it made Aldrin Station look like a group of rotating wheels. Thanks to centripetal acceleration, the two hundred people that called this home benefited from the simulated Earth gravity.

She sighed as she rolled to her side and reached over to the nightstand, a sphere sandwiched between two thick circular cuts of glass, all of which were connected together by a center pole.

Sliding her glasses on brought her bedroom into focus. The space was tiny by Earth standards, but one of the larger rooms that had, at one time, waiting lists that stretched in the hundreds when they were being constructed. Being 14'x9', it had enough space for a full-sized bed, a plushy, legless bench built into the wall, her nightstand, and a private bathroom behind an automatic sliding door. The regulations for decorating were stringent, but she had enough remaining influence to have additional personal effects. Every kilogram was accounted for when people arrived at Aldrin Station, so she kept things light: An aluminum-framed photo of her mother and father, a faded group picture of her team from her days as a Senior Research Scientist at SETI, a small box of items she and Sam cherished, and a wooden frame that held a picture of her and Sam.

That picture sat on the edge of her nightstand, and always faced her before she went to sleep, reminding her of those days. In the picture, they had their faces pressed together as they grinned for a selfie. Sam vied for the most camera real estate while Jennifer tried her best to keep a straight, smiling face. The photo caught Sam trying to poke Jennifer's lip with her tongue while Jennifer's eyes, for that moment, were caught eyeing Sam's attempt at distraction. Occasionally she would rotate that picture out for the one kept behind it: their wedding photo, but the closeness between the wedding and her passing was a connection she just couldn't separate. They had countless memories prior to that day, and that was what she focused on.

"Jennifer, Dr. Samuel Monroe is outside of your door," Amina announced, pleasant as ever.

"Can't I just get a doorbell like I used to have at home?" Jennifer complained as she slipped her wrinkled feet into her slippers.

"You know as well as I do that regulation prevents the withholding of visitor entry requests," Amina said.

"Even the old *Star Trek* buzzer would be nice," Jennifer mused as she waved at the door, granting Amina the right to open it.

Samuel marched into his mother's room, his eyes fixated on the FlexiTab—a thin, transparent sheet of glass with integrated circuitry that could be rolled up like paper—in front of him. At twenty-nine years of age, he was one of the youngest men on Aldrin Station, but the emblem on the shoulder of his uniform—two solid circles, each with a smaller circle orbiting it, forming outlines that overlapped—told everyone on-board why: He was part of the crew that was responsible for converting Aldrin from a space station to a functional, if temporary, ship.

He came in and, like he usually did when he was excited about something, just talked her ear off for several minutes. She indulged him, if only for a little while—judging by how alert and focused he was, he likely took a stim, which meant he would be running on all cylinders for another couple of hours. She listened, but admired, as always, how much some of his features reminded her of Sam. His dimpled smile, his inquisitive and expressive brown eyes, his nose. He recently trimmed his dark brown hair to a neat crew cut, and shaved, too. This gave him an unavoidable baby face that made him appear much younger and attractive than he already was.

Ah, we're getting nostalgic again, she thought to herself as she smiled, something Samuel picked up almost immediately.

"Thinking about Mom again?" he asked as his grin kept the nostalgia train on the move.

"She's always on my mind, honey," Jennifer responded. Her walk was unsteady, but she reached Samuel who already leaned forward to allow a kiss on the cheek from his mother. Her eyes glinted as she looked him over. "You need to do a better job cleaning your outfit," she said as she wiped a hand along the side of his uniform, the creases standing out like sore thumbs to her.

"Hey, I'll have them pressed," he protested half in jest. "More important agendas to tackle, you know?"

She nodded with understanding. "Oh, I know."

With a smile that could melt the heart of another if he paid some of the other girls on-board any mind, he escorted Jennifer to the window bay.

"Dim the lights to observation levels," Jennifer barked. The room's lighting transitioned to a low-light level that was bright enough to navigate the space, but dark enough to see the stars in the distance. A red dot in the distance stood out from the sea of whites, yellows, and blues.

"You could be a bit nicer to Amina, you know," Samuel suggested. "She's as human as you or me."

She sighed. "I know AI when I see it, and Amina is no AI."

"But if you saw the programming—"

"Amina is just a product of Khulu Global." Not to mention the reason for hundreds of millions of people out of a job Earthside. "Hermes Two is true AI. The Elder is true AI." She leaned against the window ledge as he raised a finger. "Don't forget who was there to witness its creation."

"You don't have to reload that story again," he protested, though he still smiled. He wrapped an arm around his mother, to which she leaned in and rested her weary bones. "Do you think she's out there?"

Jennifer didn't understand. "What's that, honey?"

"Mom—do you believe she's out there, waiting for us?"

"Oh, I don't know, if I'm honest. I suppose it's a comforting thought to believe such things." Jennifer sighed as the possibility crossed her mind countless times.

The stars shimmered and sparkled as if they were trying to say something with Morse code. She wondered if, at that moment, another family was looking in their direction, having a similar conversation.

"She's proud of me, isn't she?" His breathing was strong and steady, but his question betrayed an underlying tension that had always been between them. An unanswerable question by virtue of Sam never being there to raise him—at least in his eyes. Jennifer knew better.

"Of course she's proud," she said, turning his face toward her by the chin. "She is as much a part of you as I am, and that's something I've seen every day since you were born. And as long as you pursue your passions in life, Sam—your mother—will always be proud. It's all she would have asked for."

She felt tired. Jennifer brought her son's head lower for another kiss, then a hug. "Now get back to work so I can see at least another planet in the flesh that isn't Earth." She patted his cheek, her telltale gesture to send him on his way.

His smile really was infectious. "Thanks, Mom," he said as he ran for the door, already opened for him. She waved before turning back to admire the vastness of deep space.

"Hey Mom?"

Oh, he's still here. "Yes, honey?"

"... I love you."

Her chest swelled with those three words. "I love you, too. Get to work!"

Samuel saluted before running out of her room, the door sliding closed with a soft swoosh.

Jennifer saw the glow of the sun appear below the window pane, which meant the Leviathan would become visible as well. Its orbit between Venus and Mercury ensured it remained a dominant presence in space. Nobody knew how long it would remain in the solar system, but as long as *Houdini* and *Copperfield* stayed operational, it would be unable to find the Earth.

She felt lightheaded as her mind tried to calculate the various circumstances that could arise if either satellite failed. Pushing the scenarios out of her mind with a grunt, she ambled her way back to bed and nestled her body under the inviting comforter.

Sleep came easy for her as her eyelids grew heavy the moment her head hit the pillow. Before allowing herself the luxury, she outstretched her hand for the nightstand, opening a small compartment within for a vintage media player that, although it no longer worked, always brought peace of mind and love to Jennifer's heart.

Acknowledgments

There's never enough words to express the level of gratitude I have for all those who were by my side on this journey. Nevertheless, here I am, trying to find the words… yeah, I got nothing. It is because of you that I am writing this Acknowledgments page, added to my very first published novel. Just know that all of you will never be forgotten.

Let's kick things off by thanking my beta readers: Brandy Bauer, Bryan Fox Jr., Ryan Henneboehle, Samantha Hunter, Myles Y. Ji, John Kotlanger, and Chris Rinaldi. Thanks to all of you for taking time out of your busy lives to read through my book and provide detailed feedback. Your contributions helped iron out many small kinks and wrinkles. The enthusiasm all of you had came through your words when describing your experiences with my book will never be forgotten.

To my alpha readers: Joshua Hill and Kelsey Henneboehle. Your tasks were arguably the most challenging since you two read my book while I was writing it! You read the entire first draft—and then read entire subsequent drafts. What drove you two to such madness? Whenever I think about the volumes of feedback I received from either one of you at any given time, or the video calls where large chunks of time were spent reviewing a single character's motivations, mannerisms, and actions throughout the novel… I'm just very grateful to have found you guys.

To Malik K. and August Von Orth, two individuals far smarter than me yet were more than willing to help with some highly technical elements in my book. Malik (Twitter: @ToughSf) assisted with the space probes designed in this novel, particularly where waste heat management technology and its applications were concerned.

Meanwhile, August (Twitter: @von_Orth) provided invaluable feedback regarding my concerns surrounding the viability of powering the *Houdini* and *Copperfield* laser arrays using technology that's in development today. This ranged from the choice of reactor, the placement of the reactors, and how sensitive portions of the array were shielded, to the approximate tonnage of enriched uranium fuel needed per array. In the end, their knowledge and experience played a significant role with my understanding in various fields and contributed to core aspects of the technology presented throughout my book. Malik and August, thank you.

To Anamaria Stefan: the woman who rocked the boat with the most beautiful cover and typesetting design I could've ever asked for. The best decision I made regarding the design of my book was going with someone that knew how to be disruptive. You created something that will not only grab hold of one's attention and not let go, but will be a continued magnet of attraction for years to come. Thank you for becoming a part of my journey.

To my incredible critique partner, Kim Kirkland. To be frank, you kept it real all of the time. Your honesty, criticism, feedback, and endless well of support brought my book through many iterations. You helped me make very tough decisions when I looked to see where I could remove some of the fat from my novel's earliest versions. More importantly, you never gave up on me. This novel would've been in a completely different state if it weren't for you, and for that, I cannot thank you enough.

To my editor, Kim Chance. You helped me very early on with your 50-page critique of my story—back when I only had six chapters written. You helped with the full critique of my entire story, providing incredibly detailed single-spaced pages of feedback that broke me apart before I came back together as a better writer. I was privileged to have had your eyes on my story, your red pen scratching out, circling, and underlining my words, your voice providing the words of encouragement which propelled my story forward. For all of this and more, I thank you.

To my parents and sister: Ma, Dad, and Natasha. Your constant encouragement and support made a difference from start to finish.

The unconditional love from the three of you will always be a pillar in my writing life.

To Terra, the little lady in my life. Though you were a baby while I wrote and edited this book, you were very much on my mind as this was being created. I look forward to the day when you read this novel in its entirety. It will serve as a reminder that anything is possible and to never give up on your dreams. Take this with you when you travel to the Moon and Mars.

To my wife, Kim. This novel wouldn't exist today without you. There are few words to express my gratitude. You asked me what it would take for me to write full-time. I gave you the criteria. You met that criteria, giving me the chance to pursue my lifelong dream unhindered. I don't know if I could ever repay you for the gift you've given me, and that's on top of being my best friend, wife, lover, and mother to our little girl.

Kim, I love you.

TREVOR B. WILLIAMS

Trevor B. Williams was born and raised in Brooklyn, NY, met his wife in the District of Columbia, and is now a father of a precocious little girl while living in Oakland, CA. Despite living in cities his whole life, he loves seeing the night sky which rests beyond the surrounding buildings. When he isn't hiking in regional parks with his family or spending hard-earned time with friends, Trevor is creating familiar and alien worlds from the tips of his fingers.

He is addicted to all things related to astronomy, orbital mechanics, fantastical technology concepts (who doesn't like the idea of a ringworld?), and exploring the endless possibilities behind the question "what if."

CPSIA information can be obtained
at www.ICGtesting.com
Printed in the USA
BVHW032344101119
563374BV00027BA/128/P